CW01645818

John McKay served in the Royal A
pursuing a career in the Fire and Res
Lancashire, with his wife, Dawn, and has two daughters and two granddaughters.

With a huge interest in all things World Wars One and Two, John took up writing a few years ago, embarking on an ambition he had held since childhood. This has led to an interest in the Russian/Arctic Convoys of World War Two and him completing the wartime memoir of a veteran of those voyages, Charlie Erswell (*Surviving the Arctic Convoys, The Wartime Memoir of Leading Seaman Charlie Erswell*, Pen & Sword, 2021). He has also written an in-depth account of PQ18, one of the most significant seaborne operations of the whole war (*Arctic Convoy PQ18, 25 Days That Changed The Course of the War*, Pen & Sword, 2023).

John's novel, *Hell and High Water*, won the inaugural Aspects of History Historical Fiction Award and was published by Sharpe Books. His *Manner of Men* series pays homage to Britain's airborne forces of World War Two. Books in the series have been endorsed by renowned historians and authors, Damien Lewis and Saul David.

Also by John McKay

Historical Fiction
Hell and High Water
Operation Codicil
Target Arnhem
In For The Kill
The Sun Will Always Shine
The Absolution of Otto Finkel

Non-Fiction
Surviving the Arctic Convoys - The Wartime Memoir of Leading Seaman Charlie Erswell
Arctic Convoy PQ18 - 25 Days That Changed the Course of the War

Contemporary Fiction
Mosquitoes

CODENAME GREYMAN

John McKay

Copyright © John McKay 2019

The right of John McKay to be identified as the author of this work has been asserted by him in accordance with the Copyright, Designs and Patents Act, 1988.

This edition published in 2026 by Jelso Publications.

All rights reserved.

No reproduction, copy or transmission of this publication may be made without written permission.
No paragraph of this publication may be reproduced, copied or transmitted save with the written permission of the publisher,
or in accordance with the provisions of the Copyright Act 1956 (as amended).

Any person who commits any unauthorised act in relation to this publication may be liable to criminal prosecution and civil claims for damages.

This is a work of fiction. Names, characters, businesses, places, events and incidents are either the products of the author's imagination or used in a fictitious manner. Any resemblance to actual persons, living or dead,
or actual events is purely coincidental.

ISBN: 978-1-9193378-4-5

Cover by The Book Khaleesi

Opening quote from *Special Operations Executive Manual: How to be an Agent in Occupied Europe*, William Collins, 2014 (National Archives)

For my sister, Barbara Ashton

Subversion, properly applied, is one of the most potent weapons one can use. It is the fourth arm in modern warfare.

Opening address to new SOE Agents, 1943.

Prologue

Lyon, France - October 1943

Francois Aubuchon, codename “Grey Man”, knocked firmly on the front door of the ground floor apartment.

He was bitterly cold and soaked to the skin. The rain that had started as a fine spray earlier in the evening had turned into a downpour that would have kept everyone off the streets even if a curfew was not in force. With the collar of his overcoat turned up to protect his neck, and his hat pulled down low, he had cut a hunched figure as he hastily walked the dark streets.

He was angry beyond words. Monique’s stupidity could have serious repercussions on him and many others in the circuits he controlled. He found this selfishness completely unforgivable. He would need to relocate yet again. Baker Street may even order his return to London.

Above the noise of the rain bouncing off parked vehicles he could hear shuffling behind the door. The sound of someone moving awkwardly, as though aged or injured. He pulled the pistol from the deep pocket of his overcoat and moved his left hand to his face to twiddle the edge of his moustache, something he was aware he did when the adrenalin was kicking in; an automatic response, a nervous tic.

Maybe this was a trap, he thought. He glanced to his left and then looked right, but saw no-one. He was too long in the game now, he realised. He would have known if he had been followed by the Milice or Gestapo. He would have sensed it. But it did not stop him from feeling a sudden bout of anxiety, an unease that was becoming familiar to him the longer he stayed in the field.

From behind the door he heard a voice, hushed and nervous. A familiar female voice. ‘Who is it?’

‘Who do you think it is?’ he replied irritably. ‘It’s me. Francois. Open the bloody door and let me in before somebody sees me.’

There followed the sound of a key turning in the lock and a key-chain being removed. The door opened and Monique stood before him.

She looked harassed; more so than usual. Her long, dark hair hung unkempt and dishevelled over her stooped shoulders. She had painful looking marks on her face; scratches to her forehead and a redness to her left cheek which appeared to have been very recently struck. Her right eye was also starting to blacken. Francois had found her very attractive when they had first met, her pale green eyes being possibly the prettiest he had seen on any woman. Prettier even than Jenny's. Monique had had an air of confidence about her back then. A self-assurance that had gradually faded away over the last few months. He knew that he, himself, was partly to blame for that attribute in her diminishing.

Quickly he brushed past her. Once inside he turned, pulled her to one side, and closed the door.

'Where is he?' he asked firmly. The rainwater dripped from his coat to form a small puddle at his feet, on the hard wooden floor. He looked over her shoulder and noticed a black raincoat and SS officer's cap hanging on the coat stand.

'I didn't know what to do,' she said, ignoring his question, tears flowing freely down her face. 'I'm sorry, Francois. I really didn't know what to do. I'm so sorry. What's going to happen? I've never done anything like this before. I couldn't do it anymore. He told me she was dead. Is it true, Francois? Please tell me it isn't true…'

'Shut up for a second, will you,' he replied. 'I can't think with you blubbering like this. Now, again, where is he?'

She nodded towards a half open door to her left which led to the living room. Through it he could see a fire burning brightly. A half knitted sweater lay bundled in a heap on a high-backed chair to its right, the ball of wool somewhere on the floor out of sight.

He left her in the hallway and entered the room.

'Jesus Christ,' he said, when he saw the corpse lying on the floor. The eyes as cold in death as they had been in life.

'Come here,' he called to Monique. 'Get your backside in here, right now.'

Timidly she moved towards him but stopped at the doorway, unwilling or unable to advance any further.

'I can't,' she said, her voice giving way to sobs. 'I can't.'

She stepped back against the wall, to the side of the doorway, and slid down until she was hunched in a ball, her legs drawn up against her chest. She wrapped her arms around them and put her forehead onto her knees.

'You're just like him,' she sobbed. 'You're all the same. You use people for your own ends and don't care for the consequences, what it does to them.'

'Okay,' said Francois, exiting the living room and sitting down beside her. 'Tell me what happened. Everything. Miss nothing out. And when you've finished, you'd better pack a bag.'

***

An hour earlier

The rain was getting heavier. Monique was thankful she was not out in it. She had closed the shop early and gone home, business not being so good these days. It seemed the Occupation made everyone nervous about spending their money.

She was glad of the warm fire that she had at first struggled to get going, and had settled for the evening to continue with the pullover she was knitting. Soft music played on the radio as she moved the needles deftly in her petite hands. Knitting relaxed her. The rhythm of it was hypnotic. It allowed her thoughts and worries to be evicted from her mind, made them go away for a short period. She was yet to make up her mind whether to add this garment to the shop's stock or give it as a gift to someone who may be in need of it. She would decide once it was finished.

After a while she looked up and saw the rain lashing against the window, coming at it in waves as though an ocean was trying to break through into the apartment.

She wondered if this bad weather would make him think twice about making the journey and he would stay away. At least she hoped so.

She was sick of the whole situation. But she knew she had no choice in the matter. She never did. Doing this man's bidding was the only way in which she would ever get to see her sister again. She would do anything for that. She would do anything for Catherine. She could not abandon nor condemn her, no matter how much her younger sister's misadventures had dragged her into this whole sorry situation.

She always knew things would go awry one day. Catherine had been playing a very dangerous game, right up to the point of her inevitable capture. Monique had warned her often enough that she was sailing too close to the wind and it would all end in tears.

And that arrogant Jean-Luc to whom Catherine had devoted herself. That man who treated her with such utter disrespect despite her loving him so madly. She had always known it would lead to her downfall, what with him being a Jew and all the trouble that alone would bring. She had been convinced of it. She had advised her many times to walk away from it all before the authorities found out. But Catherine never wanted to listen. She never had. Even as a child she always ignored the advice of those who knew better.

And now, through absolutely no fault of her own, Monique herself had become mixed up in the whole thing.

After a while, there was a knock at the door. The knock she had been dreading all day. A hard rapping sound, as though he was using the butt of his pistol instead of the knocker attached to the middle of the door. Why he would do this she had no idea. She assumed he did it as another way of showing his strength and superiority over her.

Putting the knitting to one side, she stood up, adjusted her dress and went to the mirror above the fireplace. Did she look presentable? Not quite, she thought. But then she was past caring. He would have to take her as she was.

She could hear his impatient voice calling from outside.

'Come on. Come on. Open the fucking door. It's pissing down out here.'

Not wanting to be the brunt of his wrath she unlocked the door and opened it.

Gerhard Keller was not quite six feet but the cap he wore made him appear taller. He would have been quite a good looking man had it not been for the malevolence in his eyes that made him uglier than anyone else she had ever clapped eyes on in her entire life. He had strong features; piercing blue eyes and dark, almost black hair, the fringe of which hung loosely over his left eye. Physically, he was nothing special, but he was much stronger than she was, her being only a petite five feet two inches. On the occasions he forced himself upon her, he always won easily. She was convinced he liked it better that way; the times she put up a fight. He liked to dominate her. To control her. To show her he could do whatever he wanted to her and there was not a thing she could do about it.

She cursed Francois for putting her in this position, but ultimately knew she had no choice. By working for Francois and the Resistance, she was, in her own way, controlling Keller and not the other way around. Either way, she was repulsed at what she had been doing and always would be, no matter how long the war lasted, no matter how long she lived.

She was never too sure if the information she gained was of any use to the Resistance. It all seemed like a waste of time to her. In fact she was not sure if both sides were playing her, each giving false information to pass on to the other side. All she was certain of was that she was sick of the whole thing.

Keller walked in. Without looking at her he took off his black overcoat and shook it, letting the rainwater spray over the floor and walls. He hung it on a coat stand to the left of the doorway and placed his hat over it. He was always impeccably dressed; his uniform neat and sharp, his boots highly polished. Running his fingers through his hair he walked to the lounge and sat on a chair to the left of the fireplace, facing the one Monique had just vacated.

Gingerly she sat down again, picking up the knitting and resting it upon her lap. Keller took a cigarette case from the inside pocket of his jacket and took out a cigarette. Without asking permission, or offering one to Monique, he put it into his mouth and lit it from a silver lighter he took from his trouser pocket.

She hated it when he did this. Not saying anything. It always led to bad news followed by him dragging her to the bedroom and having his way with her, leaving her disgusted at herself for allowing him to do it.

After a while he said, ‘So how’s your day been?’

She looked up.

‘Fine,’ she replied. ‘I shut the shop early. The…’

He raised his hand as though already bored with the small talk.

She let him smoke his cigarette for a little while longer before attempting to speak again.

‘Have you any news?’ she asked.

‘About what?’

She could sense him sniggering at her.

‘About Catherine.’

He continued to enjoy his cigarette for a while longer, blowing smoke into the middle of the room where it hung like mist in the stifled atmosphere.

‘As I’ve told you many times, Monique, you really have no need to worry about your sister.’

‘Have you heard anything?’ she pressed. ‘I can’t go on like this for much longer.’

She could feel tears start to form in her eyes. When she looked over at him, she could see that he was enjoying the exchange. He fed off her helplessness like a ghoul. She could see his self-assurance grow the more hers drained away.

‘Listen, Monique,’ he said, crushing the half finished cigarette into an ashtray he’d placed on the chair arm. ‘Things are going to change around here. I can protect you no longer. Do you understand me?’

‘What do you mean?’

‘My superiors want to question you a little more. The information you provided was worthless. Last night was a total waste of our time and resources. You made me look a fool. They feel you probably know more than you’re letting on. Quite frankly, I’m inclined to agree with them. Your sister was a member of the Resistance. For you to tell us you knew nothing of this is quite simply unbelievable. In fact I’m sure you’re actually working for those terrorist scum right now. The information you claim to be real was utter garbage.’

‘I just did as you told me. You can’t blame me if I’ve been lied to.’ Monique paused, placing the knitting onto the small table to her side. ‘What do you mean *was* a member of the Resistance? What do you mean by that?’

'Come now,' replied Keller, taking another cigarette from his case and putting it between his lips. 'Even you can't be this stupid. Do you think someone like that is just kept safe and well in a room in the Terminus? Do you think she's been sitting there, with room service bringing her cake and wine when she rings her little bell? She's gone Monique. She's been gone for quite a while now.'

Monique could not believe her ears. What was this animal telling her? That her sister was dead? That he'd been lying to her all along and making her sleep with him under the false promise he could help her? Had it all been an evil lie?

And what of Francois? Had he been lying to her too? Had he made her sleep with this animal in order to gain information when he also knew there was no hope for Catherine?

She felt sick. And despite the heat from the fire burning in the hearth beside her, she felt cold too. As cold as ice.

'Where is she?' she muttered. 'Where's my sister?'

Keller began to laugh. A deep humourless laugh. 'Your sister hasn't been around for some considerable time, you fool. She was shipped out to Drancy the very day she gave her friends up. We knew she'd told us all she knew. It was pointless questioning her further. So Barbie had her on a train that evening, after we returned from St Etienne. And another thing, tell me all you know of the "Grey Man". Is it him you've been working for?'

Monique felt as though she was about to vomit. She could not speak. All the oxygen seemed to have evacuated her body. She struggled to breathe, gasping as though someone was choking her. For months this man had led her to believe her sister was still alive and he could help with getting her released. She had willingly given herself to him for that reason. She felt repulsed each time it happened, but consoled herself with the understanding it would lead to Catherine's freedom.

'Do you think we don't know what you've been doing?' said Keller calmly. 'Do you think we're so stupid we don't realise you work for them also? This "Grey Man" as he calls himself.'

Monique found her voice.

'I don't know what you mean.'

'Don't treat me as though I'm an imbecile, you stupid bitch,' he said venomously, rising from the chair. 'You're as much a part of those Resistance scum as your sister ever was. You've been sleeping with me to see what information you can gain. To pass on to them, you disgusting whore. It's time for you to come with me. This charade must end.'

Monique rose from the chair to face him. All the anger and frustration that had been stored up inside her suddenly came to the surface. She couldn't help herself. Her body seemed to have a will of its own and she launched herself at him with all the fury and rage of a cornered tiger. He pulled a Luger from his pocket, and as she approached him, her arms outstretched to claw at his face, he struck her across her left cheek with it, forcing her to her knees.

'You dare to attack me?' he yelled. 'You dare to raise your hands to me! I should kill you for this.'

He struck her again. This time with the back of his left hand, knocking her down so she lay prone across the floor. He kicked her in the ribs as she lay there, so hard that she screamed in pain. The adrenalin that had appeared so suddenly, just as soon vanished, leaving her frightened and in agony. As he kicked her again, she began to fear he was going to kill her.

She scrambled back towards the chair, her back to him, and heard him cock the pistol. She realised if she did not act quickly then he would likely put a bullet into the back of her head. She could hear him muttering to himself in German, the words making no sense to her. She grabbed the first thing that came to hand, the only thing within her reach, and forced herself to stand up. She gripped the knitting needles tightly in her right hand.

She turned to face him. He was struggling with the pistol, his face reddening and his anger rising; maddened at the fact that she had tried to attack him.

As he raised the pistol again, she lunged at him, thrusting the needles upwards with all the strength she could summon, ramming them as hard as she could into his face.

And then he was falling, backwards, onto the hard wooden floor. His body stiffened, his left shoulder knocking against the chair he had been sitting in only a few moments earlier, causing it to topple over on top of him with an almighty crash. The Luger spilled from his hand and slid across the floor.

It was suddenly quiet, almost peaceful. The rain lashing against the window, the fire flickering in the hearth and her own laboured breathing the only sounds to be heard.

She dared not look at him but forced herself to do so. Slowly she approached Keller and moved the chair from him, setting it aside.

He was clearly dead. His eyes stared vacantly towards the ceiling, an expression of shock upon his face. The knitting needle had entered his nose and was sticking almost comically from it. At least four inches of it was buried inside his head. It had been a one off, she realised, a total fluke.

She was numb. She did not know what to feel. Shock? Revulsion at what she had just done? She had never killed anyone in her life. Although the thought of it sickened her, she felt an immediate sense of relief. Keller had been about to kill her. Or at least seriously harm her and take her away to endure the same fate as her beloved Catherine. If nothing else, she had prevented that from happening.

She sat down in the chair. This piece of scum had been lying to her for months. She had given herself to him in the hope his influence would lead to the release of her sister, when all along he knew he could not help her. He had never any intention of doing so.

Her thoughts turned to Francois. Or whatever his real name was. The English agent who had persuaded her to carry on seeing Keller to garner whatever information she could. Had Keller known all along this was the case? Had both sides been using her for their own ends? Was it all a game to them?

As she sat there, with the rain lashing against the window and the adrenalin wearing off, she could not work out who had been using her the most.

She started to shake. Her whole body went into a spasm. The shock of what she had just done was starting to have a physical effect upon her. She needed help. If the Gestapo found out, then she would be killed immediately. No trial, no judge, no jury. Just a death sentence that would be carried out without hesitation.

Although she despised him, she knew there was only one person who could help her right now. There was only one man who could possibly get her out of this mess.

She moved to the hallway where the telephone was located and picked up the receiver. She opened the drawer of the stand and took out the notebook he had reluctantly written his number in a few days ago. He had told her only to use it in case of dire emergency. A matter of life and death. If this was not such a time then she did not know what was.

She dialled the number and waited. A minute later a familiar voice came on the line.

'Who's this?'

Upon hearing his voice she broke down.

'It's Monique,' she sobbed. 'I need your help.'

Part One

1940 - 1941

Chapter One

July 1940

Stephen Graham sat in the kitchen smoking a cigarette. From the window he could see the sea just under a mile away, the morning sun's rays reflecting back off the surface of the English Channel, the body of water separating Britain from Europe, which had proved to be the country's protector for many a century. Most recently it had been the barrier that had stopped the momentum of the German blitzkrieg from continuing on to England. Although he was grateful for that, and the fact so many soldiers had been rescued from the beaches of Dunkirk only five weeks ago, when he looked at the water he felt a colossal sadness, an immense grief he knew would stay with him until his dying day.

His eldest son, Jack, a lieutenant in the Royal Fusiliers, had been killed on the retreat to the French port. From what he had so far found out he had managed to make it onto a boat, but it had been sunk by a German plane, taking his young body down with it. He had been a mere twenty-three years old. Absolutely no age at all.

Stephen, himself, had served in the trenches during the Great War. The conflict that was supposed to have ended them all. A war to end all wars, they said. Yet here they were a little over twenty years after the armistice, with the same enemy achieving in a matter of weeks what they had failed to do in over four years of senseless slaughter. Although he had left France with no lasting physical scars, Stephen was under no illusion his own personal wounds had been purely psychological. His late wife, Margaret, had understood this. She had always been very supportive and patient with him whenever he had, what she described as, one of his "episodes". Thinking about her now, his grief felt all the more powerful. He held on to the small comfort that Jack would again be with his mother. At times he longed for the day when he would join them both.

But then he still had another son to worry about.

Of slightly above average height, with dark hair and blue eyes, twenty-one year old Frank Graham had turned into a fine looking young man. Due to his recent military training, he generated an air of confidence that he had lacked as a child, when he would follow his big brother around like a lapdog.

Stephen was thankful that due to training commitments, his youngest son had been spared the horrors of France. Frank had not been with the British Expeditionary Force that had been so swiftly defeated by the Germans. He also understood that the worry he had shared between his two sons would now be doubled for Frank. He let out a sigh. Whatever the future held, there were certain to be dark days ahead. Very dark days indeed.

There was a noise upstairs. Instinctively he looked to the ceiling. Getting to his feet he walked to the stove, picked up the copper kettle and filled it at the sink. Then he lit the stove with a taper and put the kettle on to boil.

Frank had managed to acquire seven days leave before he was to join his unit and had chosen to spend the time with his father. The death of his brother had hit Frank hard, as they had been very close; Frank had always looked up to Jack. He appreciated that his father had lost both his wife and son in a matter of only a few years and knew he would be desperately lonely.

Stephen smiled to himself. Frank had always been the thoughtful of the two, Jack being more impulsive and sometimes quite demanding when they were younger. Frank had become more outgoing whilst at university. This aspect of his character was beginning to show itself now he had reached adulthood.

After a couple of minutes Frank walked into the kitchen and sat down at the table. He was wearing a white vest, the braces attached to his trousers, hanging loosely to his sides.

'Morning, Dad,' he said cheerily. 'Anything planned today?'

'I thought we might take a stroll along the beach later, if you fancy it,' replied Stephen, pouring the boiling water into a teapot.

Frank yawned. 'Yeah. Sounds good to me. It looks a nice day. A bit of fresh air will be good.'

As he watched his youngest son sitting at the table, lighting a cigarette, Stephen wondered what would become of him. He was a highly intelligent young man who had recently acquired a degree from Oxford University in modern languages, majoring in French. From there he had gone straight to Officer Training School at Sandhurst, completing his training only a few days ago. It had seemed ironic that, as he was enjoying a pleasant day at his passing out parade, the whole of the venue seemed somewhat subdued. As though the failure of the British Expeditionary Force and the losses suffered were being felt by the whole place. Not only the officers in attendance, but by the very buildings themselves. The college emanated a sadness and a nervousness for what was to come.

Watching his young son marching proudly before him, Stephen had realised that whatever was to happen following the fall of France, his son Frank would play some part in that unknown future. He did not think he would be able to cope with losing both of his boys.

'Don't worry, Dad,' said Frank, looking over to his father and sensing his sadness. 'I'll be fine. I know how to look after myself.'

Stephen could not think of a response and so merely smiled at him as he handed him his tea.

It was easy to say those words, he thought. But it would not be as easy for Frank to keep the promise. He was reminded of when Jack had told him the very same thing just before he'd been shipped out to France.

***

Two hours later they were walking back from the beach. Joey, the black Labrador bounced on happily ahead of them. As they got closer to home Stephen noticed a black, official looking saloon car parked outside the house. A tall, bald-headed gentleman with a thick bushy moustache, in an army officer's uniform, stood at the door.

'You weren't expecting anyone, were you?'

'No,' replied Frank. 'I've no idea who he is.'

As they got closer they were able to get a better look at the man. He was well over six feet tall, his Colonel's uniform immaculately pressed. Although he at first appeared strong and confident, the way he fiddled with the cap in his hand gave them both the impression he was somewhat nervous about their meeting.

'Can I help you?' asked Stephen.

'Are you Mister Stephen Graham?' asked the man in a deep, strong voice.

'I am,' he replied. 'May I ask to whom I have the pleasure?'

'And you must be young Francis?' replied the officer. 'Or, should I say, Second Lieutenant Francis Graham?'

'That's correct, sir,' replied Frank, raising an eyebrow.

'Good day to you both,' said the officer stepping toward them, his hand outstretched. 'Major… I beg your pardon… Colonel Herbert Harding at your service. Can't get used to this new rank, you know. Doesn't seem to fit quite yet.'

Stephen took the man's hand and shook it. Although Harding was huge, he was still surprised at the strength in the handshake.

'Nice to meet you,' he said. 'What can we do for you, Colonel Harding? You wouldn't happen to be the same Harding as was my Jack's commanding officer, would you? "Double H"?'

'The very same. The very same,' he replied, now shaking Frank's hand.

'Please, come inside,' said Stephen. 'Let me get the kettle on and you can tell me the reason for your visit.'

Once inside and settled in the lounge, each with a cup of tea in their hands, Colonel Harding began to speak.

'I just wanted to visit you, Mr Graham and speak to you face to face about what happened out there. With your boy Jack, and such. I felt it only fair I came to see you. Somehow I don't think a letter or a telegram is quite enough. Too impersonal, don't you think?'

Stephen let out a weary sigh. 'You're quite right. It's not. Thank you for doing this. I understand you didn't have to. I'm very grateful.'

Frank sat silently watching and listening, not able to bring himself to speak. He was not sure he really wanted to hear all the details about his brother's passing. Although at the same time he felt he needed to find out what had taken place.

'You see,' continued Harding, 'It was all very chaotic over there, you know. Very chaotic. I understand that you served in the last war, Mr Graham, as did I. But you see, this was nothing like that. It was all so fast. The Germans had the momentum and I believe that's what carried them to the sea. It was shocking in its pace. It really was.

'At one point, your son, Jack, and a few others, got cut off from the rest of us as we were heading for Dunkirk. I'm not totally sure how it happened. A few days later, when we were on the beach, he turned up again. Appeared right out of the blue. He was on his own and it was quite by chance he happened to bump into us. He filled me in with what had happened to him and I had him write a report on the beach, there and then. Some of what he told me shocked me to the core. And it takes a lot to shock me, believe me.'

'So what happened to him?' asked Frank, suddenly intrigued. 'Before he found you.'

'It appears he and his corporal were witness to an atrocity,' continued Harding solemnly. 'He saw around twenty British POWs massacred by a group of SS soldiers. If you can call them soldiers. Lined up against a wall and machine-gunned to death. All of them. Murdered. Apparently Jack and his corporal were hiding in a building across from where it happened and saw the whole thing.'

Stephen was shocked. 'That's terrible.'

'Isn't it just,' replied Harding. 'But hardly surprising though, truth be told. Those bloody Nazis are capable of all sorts. I've seen it happen. One thing it's convinced me of, is that these people need to be stopped. Even if we have to stand alone to do it, they must be stopped. Anyway, I digress…'

Harding leaned forward. 'Does the name Otto Finkel mean anything to either of you?'

Frank sat up straight while Stephen contemplated the name.

'It kind of rings a bell,' he said thoughtfully.

'Yes. The name means something to me,' interjected Frank, confidently. 'One thing I'm very good with is names. My memory's excellent. Father, you know who that is, surely. It's the boy from the boat. St Malo. When I was a kid. That was his name. Otto Finkel. Where have you heard that name, Colonel Harding?'

'Apparently this Finkel character was the officer commanding the SS who shot the prisoners…'

'No way,' interrupted Frank sitting back in his chair. 'He was a pleasant young boy, from what I remember.'

'Well he's far from a pleasant, young boy now,' replied Harding, taking a sip from his tea. 'I have a sworn affidavit from your brother, God rest him. He names him as the perpetrator of the crime. This fellow had a really bad scar down the left side of his face, apparently.'

'Jesus…'

'I'm finding this difficult to take in,' said Stephen. 'I remember that day as though it was only yesterday. To think it was Jack who saved his life. And now he's a Nazi. Maybe it would've been better if Jack had let him drown…'

'When this war's over it's my belief there will be a reckoning,' continued Harding. 'And when that reckoning comes, people like this Finkel will be held to account. I truly believe that.'

'So what happened to Jack?' asked Frank. 'If he was alive on the beach, what happened to him?'

Stephen twisted awkwardly in his chair but remained silent. He was not sure if he wanted to hear the rest but at the same time felt he needed to know. It was also clear Harding was finding this part of the tale quite difficult to relate. He could not look at either of the two men as he spoke.

'We took our place in line on the East Mole and managed to get on board a fishing vessel, which was to take us out to where Royal Navy ships were waiting in deeper water,' he continued. 'We were some distance away when a Messerschmitt came at us and shot up the boat pretty badly. Jack was helping with the wounded when the plane came around again. We were pretty much sitting ducks out there. We tried to return fire but we were no match for the Jerry plane. It all but finished us off. Jack was hit in the second pass and although we tried to save him, he was too badly wounded. He died in the arms of his close friend, Dan Wilson.

'The boat was sinking and it was a miracle we were able to get to a nearby destroyer and get on board before it finally went under. Unfortunately Jack's body went down with the boat.'

Stephen turned his head away and wiped a tear from his eye.

'I'm sorry if I've upset you, Mister Graham. I just felt you deserved to know. Your boy was a fine and brave officer. You should be very proud of him. He showed exemplary leadership. All his men looked up to him. Those who made it out have been very much upset by what happened to him.'

'Thank you, Colonel Harding.'

'What happened to the corporal who was with him?' asked Frank. 'I think I'd like to meet him, if I may.'

'Unfortunately, we don't know,' replied Harding. 'He's either dead or captured. He didn't make it home. We really don't know.'

Stephen stood up.

'I think I need some air,' he said and left the room, leaving Harding alone with Frank.

'So, young man,' said Harding after a moment. 'I understand you've recently passed out of Sandhurst. And from what I understand, you did very well.'

'Yes, that's true, sir,' replied Frank. 'It's nice to know you've taken an interest in me. Jack spoke very highly of you in his letters.'

'Quite,' replied Harding, twiddling his moustache thoughtfully. 'Tell me. How's your French? I understand you studied the language at university.'

Frank was confused at the sudden change in subject.

'Erm, I think it's fine,' he replied. 'I'm pretty fluent and been told I speak it with a slight Parisian accent. I visited France a few times as a child and have been across there regularly during my time at university, to get to know the culture and practice speaking it.'

'That's good to know,' replied Harding thoughtfully.

Placing the cup and saucer on the table in front of him, Harding picked up his cap and stood up.

'I think I've taken enough of your time, young man. I'll leave you in peace now. I'll say goodbye to your father and be off.'

Frank stood up.

'It was a pleasure to meet you, Colonel Harding,' he said and shook his hand.

Frank watched as Harding walked from the room in search of his father and sat back into his chair. It had been good to finally put a face to a name. Jack had indeed spoken highly of Harding, who had been a major until very recently. He had also described him as something of an eccentric and often blustering character. Jack had initially feared, then respected, and ultimately loved this man.

Frank had expected to see a more extrovert character. He did not share the same impression of him as his brother had. But then, he mused, France and Dunkirk had just happened. Maybe it had affected Harding deeply. After all, he had witnessed his men being killed in front of him. That would probably change anybody.

After a short while he heard the sound of a car engine starting up and driving away. He wondered why Harding had taken such an interest in him. Frank had not been posted to the Fusiliers and was to join the Royal Artillery. So he did not understand why the man would look into his career with such interest. Maybe, he thought, it was because he wanted to show he cared and thought it a respectful thing to do seeing he had commanded his brother. Frank was not sure. It all seemed rather contrived.

Something told him he had not seen the last of Colonel Herbert "Double H" Harding. He wondered if the man would ultimately be a similar influence upon him, as he had been for his brother.

With a sigh, he grabbed a packet of cigarettes from the sideboard and went outside to join his father.

Chapter Two

Early October 1940

Frank sat at his desk and pulled another piece of paper through the typewriter drum. He straightened it, clipped it down and began to type. Another disposition report, to be completed in triplicate.

This was not his idea of effective soldiering and it bored him senseless.

He had joined his unit in Surrey just over two months ago and felt he was settling in to the routine of army life. He preferred to be outdoors, doing the more practical part of the job. Putting the gunners through their paces as they prepared for action. Sitting in an office doing paperwork was not really his thing, although he knew it had to be done.

The army needed to get organised again. The debacle of Dunkirk had given way to an all out assault in the skies, as the Luftwaffe attempted to destroy the Royal Air Force. If they succeeded it would open the country up to invasion. The Nazis knew without air support any invasion fleet would be doomed. And so, along with the whole population, Frank held his breath and prayed that those young men in their Spitfires and Hurricanes would do the country proud. It was a nervous time for everyone. The feeling of anxiety was prevalent all around, particularly in the faces of the men he now commanded, some of whom had endured the evacuation from France less than four months previously.

Frank felt that not only was he responsible for the training and discipline of those under his command, he was also accountable for their morale. He fully intended to try and be as upbeat as possible to stop the men from falling into despondency. He was under no illusion that as he was young, inexperienced and had not been with them in France, they did not consider him nearly competent enough to lead the battery. This lack of faith in him was something he was determined to overcome.

But he could not do that whilst he was stuck in an office doing paperwork somebody else could easily be doing. It had been Major Lowndes, his commanding officer, who had tasked him with the job, so he had no choice.

'Lieutenant Graham, a word please. My office.'

Frank looked up and saw the balding head of the very same Major Lowndes peering at him from around the doorway.

'Yes, sir,' he replied. 'Straight away.'

Frank did not particularly like his commanding officer. He found the man to be unnecessarily pompous and abrupt. Lowndes did not suffer fools gladly, but then Frank was no fool and resented his sometimes sneering and patronising attitude when in his company. He put this down to a jealousy of his youth. The man presumed that, as Frank was so much younger than he was, then he was in some way a lot less intelligent. This was so far from the truth Frank found it laughable.

He found out very fast that one thing Lowndes hated was being kept waiting by any of his subordinates. He was quite happy to dress them down in front of others, no matter their rank, not caring about any embarrassment it would cause to the unlucky soldier who felt his wrath.

As he entered the office, Lowndes told him to shut the door and to sit in the chair facing his desk.

'A quick word, Graham.' He held a piece of paper in his hand. Something seemed to be irritating him.

'Yes, sir,' replied Frank inquisitively.

'I've been given instructions to provide you with a rail warrant to London. I've no idea why. I'm just to inform you that you're to go to St Ermin's hotel on Caxton Street. Apparently that's in Westminster somewhere… You've got to be there on Friday morning at 0900 hours. Have you any idea what this is for? You haven't volunteered for something without passing it through me first have you?'

Frank was shocked.

'I truly have no idea what this is about, sir,' he replied. 'Do you know what I'm to go there for.'

'It doesn't say,' said Lowndes, looking at the letter in his hand. 'Are you sure you know nothing about this? This is all rather odd. The letter is signed by a Colonel at the War Office.'

'What's his name?' asked Frank. He had no clue as to what was going on. He certainly had not volunteered for anything. He was as bewildered as Major Lowndes appeared to be.

'Harding. You heard of him?'

'I believe I have, sir, yes' replied Frank. 'He was the commanding officer of my late brother. He came to visit my father and I a few weeks ago. I've no idea why he'd want to see me in London. He's in the Fusiliers after all.'

Lowndes frowned. 'It doesn't say that here. Just says "by order of the War Office" whatever that's supposed to mean. All very cloak and dagger, Graham. I'm not so sure I approve… But I suppose there's little I can do about it seeing that it's from the War Office and the Colonel outranks me. Just go down there, see what it's all about and then get back here as fast as you can. The unit can't have you away for too long. We've things to do. You've things to do! A battery to get into shape for one. Dismissed.'

Frank left the office and returned to his desk.

For the rest of the afternoon he could not concentrate on the paperwork, his typing so poor he had to restart the form three times before he got it right. It was early evening before he was content with what he had produced.

By the time he left the office it was getting dark. After a quick meal in the officers' mess, he headed to his room. He sat at his desk for a while and wrote a letter to his father before getting into bed. Although he was feeling very tired, he found it difficult to find sleep, questions running around his head concerning why "Double H" Harding had requested to see him, in an official capacity, in London in a couple of days' time. It did not make any kind of sense. Despite what Lowndes may believe, Frank had not asked for a transfer or volunteered for special duties.

Although he was not altogether one hundred percent content with his current posting, he had no desire to leave it just yet. He preferred instead to make the most of it and to see what the future may bring. He was not the type to give up.

Just when he thought he would never get any sleep he was awoken by the alarm clock ringing loudly at the side of the bed, telling him it was seven o'clock and it was time to get up.

***

St Ermin's Hotel lies just behind St James Park underground station on Caxton Street, off Broadway, in Westminster.

Frank had arrived in London the previous evening, staying in a much cheaper and less extravagant establishment than the one where he was to have the meeting. He had eaten a somewhat inadequate breakfast before heading out to walk the mile to the hotel.

As his train pulled into the station the day before he had seen fires burning in the east of the city. It had not been long after he checked in when the air raid sirens sounded. He spent the following six hours in a tube station waiting for the all clear and finally got to bed at two o'clock in the morning.

As he had sat on the station platform, squeezed next to a young family who seemed unperturbed by the whole thing, the sound of anti-aircraft guns, and bombs exploding nearby could be heard even though he was nearly fifty feet below ground. He was impressed and deeply moved by the way Londoners were coping with the bombing, which, by all accounts, had become a way of life. Having failed to destroy the Royal Air Force, the Germans were now concentrating their efforts on bombing the major cities, in an attempt, it seemed, to force the country into submission. But if the resilience of the people he had spent the evening with was anything to go by, then this effort was also doomed to failure.

Frank entered the hotel and found himself in a wide, open lobby with a large Victorian staircase facing him. A long reception desk was to the left. The staircase led to a mezzanine which was filled with people, both military and civilian. Some held documents and talked animatedly in hushed voices. More people moved between the groups bustling in and out of the hotel rooms. All appeared serious and determined, as though what they were doing was the most important thing in the world. A small group of military personnel sat on soft chairs and sofas to the right of the staircase, smoking cigarettes. None looked to be engaging with one another, which, to Frank, seemed quite odd.

There was a short line at the reception desk and so Frank joined it. He waited behind a Flying Officer of the RAF, who turned to him as he approached.

'Good morning,' said the RAF man with a smile. He had a clipped southern accent and pilot wings sewn onto his tunic. He looked around the same age as Frank, with blond hair and bright blue eyes. His nose was quite large for his face but not in an ugly way. This made him appear distinguished and confident. 'All a bit odd, don't you think?'

'Very much so,' replied Frank. 'Have you any idea what all this is about?'

'I'm not quite sure, to be honest with you. Just got told to report here this morning by my CO. He seemed quite keen I should come. I honestly think that I'd be more use in a Spitfire to tell you the truth.'

Frank thought the young pilot had a point.

'Frank Graham, Royal Artillery,' said Frank holding out his hand.

The pilot shook it.

'Francis Holbrook,' he said with a smile. 'Royal Air Force. Pleased to meet you.'

On reaching the front of the queue, Holbrook smiled to the woman behind the counter. 'Hello, I'm here to see a Colonel Harding. Could you please let him know I've arrived. The name's Holbrook, Flying Officer.'

'Yes,' she replied, ticking his name off a list. 'If you'd like to wait over there with the others he'll be down shortly.'

Holbrook walked away to join the group at the right of the staircase. Frank presumed they were all there for the same reason.

'Second Lieutenant Graham,' he said, when the receptionist raised her head from the list. 'I'm probably here for the same thing.'

She smiled at him and nodded. He turned away and joined the group.

It was clearly evident not a single person who had been asked to the hotel had any idea as to why they were there, the majority claiming they'd better things to do than be taken away from their duties.

After ten minutes of waiting, Frank noticed a familiar figure walking down the staircase, looking over towards them.

'Gentlemen,' said Colonel "Double H" Harding. 'If you'd like to follow me I'd be most grateful.'

Those smoking stubbed out their cigarettes and rose from their chairs. The group followed the colonel up the stairs to the second floor. Harding opened a door to what appeared to be a small conference room. Inside, chairs and desks were laid out in rows with paper and pencils on each of the desks.

'Can you please close the door,' said Harding when the last of them had entered the room. 'Please, gentlemen, take a seat.'

Frank seated himself in the second row and looked about him. There were fifteen of them in total, all wearing the uniforms of the armed services of both officer and junior ranks. A couple of naval officers, three RAF airmen, including Holbrook. The rest were made up of soldiers from various regiments and corps.

There was a door opposite which he presumed led to an adjoining room. After a few moments it opened and a middle-aged man wearing civilian clothing walked through. He was quite short, around five feet six inches in height, and wore wire-rimmed spectacles. His greying hair was parted in the middle and slicked back with oil. He held a clipboard in his hand.

'Good morning, gentlemen,' he said in a deep voice that seemed out of place for such a small man. 'Can I first thank you all for coming here today. I understand you must all be very busy and so we really appreciate you giving up your time. We wouldn't have taken you away from your duties had it not been important.'

He paused as he looked over his spectacles at the paper on the clipboard he was holding.

'You each have a pencil and paper in front of you,' he continued. 'Please bear with us. I'm going to say a series of sentences to you, in French, which I want you to translate and write down in English on the paper provided. Please be sure to put your name at the top of the paper.'

There was a murmuring in the room as, confused, the men looked around at each other.

'Please, gentlemen, just humour us,' said Harding, noticing the unease in the room. 'This won't take long.'

'Okay, lets begin. *Le chien fuit le fermier*,' said the civilian slowly and clearly. Then he repeated. '*Le chien fuit le fermier*.'

Although the man's French accent left a lot to be desired, Frank scribbled down the translation.

'*Ce café n'a pas bon goût*,' continued the man with the spectacles. '*Ce café n'a pas bon goût*.'

Again Frank wrote down the English translation. He was starting to believe this was all some kind of a joke. What on earth was the point to all this? Writing down banal French phrases that meant absolutely nothing at all. *The dog runs away from the farmer. This coffee does not taste good.* It was ridiculous.

He looked around the room and could see, from the almost vacant expressions on the faces of his temporary colleagues, that they were as bewildered about the whole thing as he was.

This went on for short while longer. One odd phrase after another. He could not understand if this was some kind of examination to test who would throw down their pencil first and walk out. A test of resilience and patience maybe.

Finally Colonel Harding spoke.

'Thank you, gentlemen. That's part one of the process over. If you'd like to return to the foyer there will be tea and coffee. Then we'll call you up one by one for the second part of the process.'

As they were leaving the room Harding spoke again.

'Mister Graham, would you be so kind as to stay behind.'

Frank stopped. 'Of course,' he replied.

When the last of them had left the room and the door was closed, the civilian spoke once more.

'If you'd like to take a seat, Mister Graham, we can begin.'

Frank sat down.

'Before we start, can I ask a question?' asked Frank. When neither man replied he continued. 'What's all this about? I've absolutely no idea what's going on. If I go back to my unit and tell my CO that I was dragged all the way to London to take a French grammar and vocab test, I don't think he'll be very pleased.'

'Let us worry about that,' replied Harding.

'Please forgive me,' said the civilian, taking off his spectacles. He pulled a chair from a nearby desk and sat on it, facing Frank. Colonel Harding did the same.

'You see, Lieutenant Graham, we need you to be quite discreet about all this,' he continued, placing the arm of his spectacles into his mouth. 'This is all rather hush-hush at the minute and we need you to keep all this to yourself. You mustn't tell a single soul about what you've been doing here today.'

'To be honest,' replied Frank. 'I don't think I'd like to admit what I've been doing here today.'

'Do you love your country, young man?' interjected Harding seriously.

'Of course I do,' he replied. 'I want to do something positive for the war effort. I don't see how taking a schoolboy French exam can achieve that.'

'I'll get to the point,' said the civilian. 'This may seem a bit odd to you, but it's absolutely necessary we get the right people. You must understand that.'

'The right people for what?' asked Frank. He was beginning to feel exasperated now. He was getting nowhere.

'When I visited you and your father recently,' said Harding, 'I noticed something in you that reminded me an awful lot of your brother. Despite what he may have thought, I had a lot of time for young Jack and it affected me greatly when he was killed. I wasn't lying when I told you he was a fine young officer. Resourceful, capable and didn't crack under pressure. He was a fine fellow. I'm hoping you're the same, young man. I'm sure there are many other people in the army, and the other armed services too for that matter, that are as equally talented as you. But then, Lieutenant Graham, you have one attribute that most do not.'

Frank looked at him blankly.

'You speak French,' said the civilian. 'Fluently.'

'Yes, you speak French,' continued Harding. 'And that stands you out above the others.'

'What exactly is going on here?' asked Frank. 'I haven't volunteered for anything.'

'Of course you haven't,' replied Harding. 'We know that. For what we have planned this isn't something we can put up on noticeboards in barrack rooms, asking you to write a memo to your commanding officer. This is all very new. Discretion is an absolute must.'

'We want to propose something to you,' said the civilian, taking the spectacles from his mouth. 'Do you want to do something to strike back at the Nazis? Back at the people who killed your brother? At those who are responsible for the killings of unarmed British Prisoners Of War, like that fellow Colonel Harding has told me of. This Otto Finkel… and people like him? To hit out at the regime that's currently dropping bombs on this very city, and others, each and every night?'

'Of course I do,' replied Frank. 'That's exactly what I want to do. Isn't that what everyone wants to do?'

'How's your French?' asked the civilian, who Frank now assumed to be somebody from the government. Probably from the War Ministry, he thought. 'Honestly, now. Do you think you could pass for a native?'

It was slowly dawning on Frank what this whole day had been about. They were testing him out for some form of special operations. Probably in France and probably highly dangerous, he guessed. For some unknown reason this appealed to him. It appealed to him greatly.

'To be honest, sir,' he replied. 'I think I probably could. I haven't been to France for a year or so but went a lot during my studies. I spent the summer of '37 with a family in Lyon. It was some kind of student exchange thing set up by the university. The family spoke no English at all but I got on famously nevertheless. Maybe with a bit of practice on my accent I could fool most people.'

'Bravo,' said Harding. 'Music to our ears, young man. Music to our ears.'

'We aren't promising anything,' continued the civilian. 'All we can offer is a chance to join us. We're forming a new unit, of which we're looking for suitable young men such as yourself… and young women, come to that. It'll be dangerous work. And, as I'm sure you've guessed by now, it'll be behind enemy lines… and in civilian attire. And you know what that means should you be captured. It'll require intensive training beforehand. Should you fail in any aspect during that training then you'd be returned to your unit.'

'So,' said Harding, leaning forward in his chair and looking directly into Frank's eyes. 'Would you be at all interested in this type of thing?'

'I think I may, sir,' replied Frank.

Harding suddenly sat back in his chair. 'Take some time to think about it, young man. I believe you have a two day pass. I suggest you use it and enjoy the city if you can. That's if this infernal bombing stops, which is highly unlikely. All the same, take some time. Go back to your unit and wait to hear from us.'

'And mention this to no-one,' said the civilian firmly. 'This is strictly top secret. Tell anyone who asks where you've been that you've been dealing with a family matter and leave your CO, Major Lowndes, isn't it?... Well leave this Lowndes fellow to us.'

Harding and the civilian stood up, signalling the end of the conversation.

Frank rose too and shook their hands.

'Like we say,' said Harding, 'we'll be in touch. It may be a while, but rest assured we'll contact you when we're ready. Now, a bit of advice if I may.'

'Certainly, sir,' replied Frank.

'Grow yourself a bloody moustache. You look about twelve years old.'

***

When Frank left the hotel a few minutes later, he decided to take a walk towards Parliament Square. As he wandered along Tothill Street he could smell burning in the air. On reaching Westminster Abbey he looked in the direction of the East End. Palls of smoke rose into the air where they met the barrage balloons, those odd looking contraptions that attempted to keep the German bombers at bay. It was clearly evident to Frank that they were not having the desired effect, because the city was burning despite the best efforts of the RAF, the London fire brigade and the War Ministry to protect it. The capital looked different, that much was true. Many windows were boarded up and others had black tape across them to prevent shattered glass from falling into the street. Blackout curtains could be seen in every window and sandbags seemed to be at the doorways of every important looking building he passed.

Yet the buses were still running, the shops and offices still open and nobody he passed seemed in any way fazed by it all. They just went about their lives as though this was the most normal thing in the world.

He took a pack of cigarettes from his tunic pocket and lit one from a book of matches he had picked up from the hotel earlier. He shook the match to extinguish it and threw it to the ground.

He did not know if anything would come of it all but he felt this was something he was born for. He could feel it in his blood. He hoped the call from “Double H” Harding and the mysterious civilian would come sooner rather than later. He did not think he could stand a day more typing up inventory reports for Major Lowndes.

Chapter Three

The bar was crowded. At first Frank struggled to find a seat.

He found the pub just off Leicester Square, not too far from the hotel where he was staying. It was filled to capacity, everyone trying to get a quick drink before the inevitable air raid that would cut their leisure time short.

After spending the rest of the day sightseeing and wandering around aimlessly, he returned to the hotel to freshen himself up before heading out in the early evening to get a drink. Knowing he would probably end up in an air raid shelter once more, the decision to return to his unit first thing in the morning made sense. He saw no reason to stay any longer than was absolutely necessary. He had many things to do back at base and was sure Lowndes would not be happy if he found out he had stayed away longer than he needed to.

The latest rumour was they were to be sent to North Africa. He wanted to make sure everyone and everything was prepared in the event this was the case.

Having paid for a rather flat looking beer at the bar he noticed a couple of vacant chairs in the corner, to the side of a table occupied by a group of soldiers. He walked over and sat down on one. The air was heavy with loud conversation and cigarette smoke. He instantly regretted his decision to stop here. He had thought getting out and joining in was a good idea, but now he was in the hubbub of the place, he realised what he really wanted was a little peace and quiet. He wold have the one drink and return to the hotel.

'You look as though you'd prefer to be somewhere else.'

At first, Frank did not realise the young woman standing to his left was speaking to him.

'What's that? Cat got your tongue?'

She wore the uniform of the First Aid Nursing Yeomanry, or FANYs as they were referred to. This organisation provided drivers, wireless operators and secretaries to the armed forces. She was quite petite, standing at around five feet three inches tall. Her auburn hair was tied in a bun at the back of her head and she wore minimal make up, which made her look naturally attractive because of it. Her spectacles made her green eyes look slightly larger than they actually were.

Frank was instantly attracted to her.

She was standing with another FANY and an RAF flight sergeant who were deep in conversation, probably unaware they were actually ignoring her This left her appearing alone although in their company.

'I'm sorry,' replied Frank. 'I didn't realise you were talking to me.'

'I was saying, you look quite lost,' she said, sipping at the half pint of stout she held in her hand. He watched as she wiped the froth from her upper lip with the back of her hand.

'Not really,' he replied awkwardly. 'I've just popped in for a quiet drink.'

She laughed and looked around. 'And you chose here to have a "quiet" drink?'

'Yes, it does look somewhat of a strange choice,' he smiled.

She held out her hand and he stood up to take it.

'Jennifer Crane,' she said. 'Pleased to meet you, Lieutenant?…'

'Second Lieutenant Graham,' he replied. 'Frank Graham.'

'Well nice to make your acquaintance, Second Lieutenant Graham,' she said, doing a mock curtsey.

'Please call me Frank,' he said. He was suddenly aware he had held onto her hand for longer than was appropriate and quickly let it go.

'So what drags you to the city, Frank?' she asked.

'Oh, you know… war stuff.' Indicating the vacant stool beside his own, he said, 'Would you like to sit down, Miss Crane?'

'War stuff,' she laughed, as they both sat down. 'There's plenty of that around at the moment. Do you want to elaborate? And it's Jenny, not "Miss Crane".'

'Not really,' he replied. 'Wouldn't want to bore you.'

He was aware the girl was merely making small talk, but he was conscious of what he had been told by Harding and the mysterious civilian earlier. He did not want to give anything away.

Now sitting beside her, he took the opportunity to study her more closely. She really was striking, and any thought of returning to the hotel after his drink vanished instantly. He might just stay out a while longer after all.

Jenny Crane told him she had joined the FANYs only a few months earlier and was enjoying her posting. She had been assigned to a rather eccentric army officer as his driver. Although the old man had his odd ways, he was really "quite sweet" as she put it.

'So are you able to stay for another drink?' asked Frank when he saw her glass was almost empty.

'I've maybe time for one more,' she replied. 'But I've to pick up the Colonel in an hour and take him home. I don't think another stout would be a good idea, though. I don't want to be light headed.'

'Hey, Jen,' said her friend, suddenly turning to her. She was hanging off the flight sergeant's arm as the man, clearly worse for wear, held on to her almost desperately. 'Charlie, just give me a minute,' she said pushing him away playfully.

'Yes,' said Jenny, turning to face her.

'Charlie and I here, we're going to make a move in a moment. Are you coming with us or?…'

'No. You go ahead,' interrupted Jenny. 'I'll see you on Friday.'

'Okay,' she said and turned back to Charlie who waved at them drunkenly as they headed for the door.

Frank watched as they left the building and laughed.

'Now there's a funny one.'

'Oh, Tina's quite flighty,' laughed Jenny. 'She's a love really. A bit too affectionate for her own good sometimes though, if you know what I mean. I fear poor Charlie may be left a tad disappointed to-night.'

They chatted for a while longer. Then Jenny got to her feet.

'It's been lovely talking with you, Frank,' she said. Then she paused. 'When did you say you were going back?'

'I'm not required to be back at base until tomorrow evening,' he replied and then he added, almost too hurriedly, 'We could meet for lunch tomorrow before I head back, if you're free. Or am I being too forward?'

'Not at all,' she replied smiling. And then she too paused. 'Where did you say your hotel was? I could give you a lift if you wish. I have the car outside.'

'I wouldn't want to trouble you,' he replied. 'It's not too far and I don't mind walking.'

'Nonsense. It's really no trouble. Come on. Let's go.'

She turned and walked towards the exit. Frank swallowed the remainder of his beer, placed the glass down on the table and hurriedly followed her.

'Really,' he repeated as he caught up with her. 'I don't wish to trouble you.'

'Think nothing of it,' she said, stopping at a black two door Austin staff car. It was parked a couple of feet from the kerbside. 'Come on, get in.'

Without waiting for a response Jenny got into the driver's seat and started the engine. She wound the window down and leaned her head out.

'Come on,' she said sharply. 'Get in. Chop, chop.'

'Very well,' he laughed. 'You win.'

Jenny pulled out into the traffic, instantly cutting across a bus that was going in the opposite direction. The bus driver sounded his horn and waved his fist angrily.

'Jesus!' exclaimed Frank, cringing into his seat.

Jenny laughed.

'Don't worry. I'm an excellent driver,' she said. She either did not care or was oblivious to the mayhem she had just caused.

She drove around the streets as if her life depended on it, taking corners without indicating and cutting across other vehicles, narrowly missing some as she impatiently went to overtake.

'You can slow down, if you like,' said Frank nervously. 'We're in no hurry after all…and I think you're going the wrong way.'

'Well how would I know what the right way is?' she asked with a giggle. 'You haven't told me where you're stopping yet.'

'I'm at the… good God,' he yelped as once more she cut in front of a bus as she took a hard right turn, forcing him to put his hand on the dashboard as his shoulder hit the door.

'So why did you say you were here?' she asked almost nonchalantly.

'On war business,' he replied. 'Nothing too important.'

'Oh, go on,' she pressed. 'You can tell me.'

'Okay,' he relented. 'I'm here to sort out the logistics for an exercise my unit's involved in.'

She did not respond and slowed the vehicle down.

A few moments later she pulled to the side of the road and turned the lights and engine off.

'Come on,' she said opening the door. 'There's a bit of a party going on here. It'll be fun.'

'I thought you were going to take me back to my hotel,' he said, bewildered at her strange behaviour.

She closed the door without answering and walked towards a flight of steps that led to a large three storey Victorian terraced house with a brown oak door. Frank could see lights on all the floors and the shadows of people moving around inside. As he had absolutely no idea where he was, he thought it best to follow her.

He caught up with her at the door. As he was about to speak, she said, 'It'll be fun, Frank. You need to relax. You look really nervous.'

'I am really nervous,' he replied. 'I've only just met you and you've nearly killed me more than once, the way you've just driven here. And I've ended up at a party I'm not too sure I'm actually invited to, or even want to go to.'

'Oh, nonsense,' she replied dismissively. 'There's nothing wrong with my driving and I'm sure you'll have fun.'

The door was opened by a young RAF officer sporting a handlebar moustache. He was holding a glass of white wine in his left hand.

'Ah,' he said, raucously. 'Here she is. My favourite FANY.'

'Hello, Charles,' said Jenny, brushing past him.

'And with your latest beau, I see?'. He was clearly drunk. 'And to whom do I owe the pleasure,' he said, turning to Frank as he followed Jenny into the hallway.

'Frank Graham, Royal Artillery.'

'I can see you're Royal Artillery, old chap,' he said. 'After all, it's written on your shoulder.'

Frank took an instant dislike to the man and ignored him as he walked on behind Jenny.

He was beginning to feel uncomfortable. He decided he would have one drink to be polite and then make his excuses and leave. He would somehow find his way back to the hotel and then depart in the morning as he initially planned. Jenny had annoyed him by bringing him here. The thought of having lunch with her the following day was now not such a nice idea as it had been earlier.

He followed her into a large room to the right where rows of glasses of wine were laid out. The room was filled with armed forces officers, important looking civilians and women dressed in both uniform and civilian clothing. Jenny handed him a glass of wine.

'What is this?' he asked. 'And who was that annoying fellow at the door.'

'Oh, don't worry about Charlie Benson,' she replied. 'He's just one of those smooth RAF types. Full of himself and all that. There's no harm in him really but he can be quite a bore sometimes. Don't take it personally. He's like that with everyone.'

Frank took a sip of the wine and winced. He wasn't much of a wine drinker and if he did have a glass of the stuff he preferred it to be red. This one tasted more of vinegar than anything else.

He placed the glass on a window sill. When he turned around he found Jenny was gone. He could not see her anywhere. He noticed one or two people looking curiously at him and so decided to leave the room. When he got to the hallway he still could not see her and so decided to leave. He was heading for the door when he heard a familiar voice.

'Ah, I'm glad you could make it, my boy.'

He turned around and saw the familiar figure of Colonel "Double H" Harding coming down the stairs. He was in full dress uniform and was holding a glass of what looked like whiskey in his hand. The light from the chandelier seemed to bounce off his bald head. He was clearly grinning, although his bushy moustache covered most of his mouth.

'I'm confused,' said Frank. Which was true. Things were getting more "Alice In Wonderland" by the second. He had met the White

Rabbit and Mad Hatter in Jenny, and now here was "Double H" Harding, looking very much like the Cheshire Cat.

'Don't worry about that,' replied Harding. 'If you'd like to come along with me then all will be explained.'

Frank would have preferred to ignore the man and make his way to the exit, but soon realised that as he had no idea where he was, it may be better to play along with him and try and find out just exactly what was going on.

He followed Harding into a large drawing room where a young couple stood in the corner talking quietly, almost conspiratorially to each other. On seeing them enter they nervously nodded a greeting and left the room, leaving Harding and Frank alone.

'What's going on?' asked Frank. 'Jenny…'

'Ah, Miss Crane,' interrupted Harding, stroking his chin with his free hand. 'A bit of a live wire, don't you think? She's a lovely girl really. Drives like a crazy person. Don't worry about her.'

'With respect, Colonel,' continued Frank. 'I'd really like to know what's going on. Has this been some sort of set up?… a test?'

'That's exactly what it was,' replied Harding. 'And I'm glad to tell you that you've passed with flying colours… you look annoyed.'

Frank frowned. 'That's because I am annoyed. To tell you the truth, sir. All this cloak and dagger stuff. Well, I'm not sure I like it.'

'We've got to be certain,' explained Harding. 'You'd be surprised at the amount of candidates that go blabbing to the first pretty girl that shows them any kind of attention. I'm glad to see you weren't tempted to do that. Jenny has told me you behaved impeccably.'

'That's as maybe. I'll really need think about this, Colonel Harding. Trust goes two ways in my opinion. Although you know you can trust me, I'm not too sure if the same thing can be reciprocated.'

Harding sighed. 'Okay, young man. I take your point. Listen. Go back to your unit and spend some time to think about it. We could really do with men like you and I'm convinced you'd do well. There'll be a selection process, but I can't see that being too much of a problem for a fellow like you. Now go and get yourself a drink and enjoy the rest of the evening.'

With that, Harding walked towards the door, silently declaring the conversation to be over.

'Sir,' said Frank.

Harding turned. 'Yes.'

'What happens now?'

'We'll be in touch in due course, young man. Count on it.'

And with that Harding left the room.

Frank stood alone for a few moments getting his thoughts together. He did not know what to make of any of it. The last twenty-four hours had been possibly the strangest he had experienced in a long time. He would do what Harding told him and go back to his unit and wait. He was not too sure if his initial interest in being involved with this scheme was likely to remain, particularly after the underhand way in which he had just been treated. He would make his ultimate decision if and when these people got in touch with him again. He would make his mind up when he had to, and not a moment before.

'Ah, there you are.'

He was disturbed from his thoughts by Jenny Crane, who walked into the room holding a glass of wine in her left hand and a half smoked cigarette in her right.

'I thought I'd lost you for a moment. I hope the Colonel didn't bore you too much.'

'No,' replied Frank. 'But he's given me plenty to think about.'

'Come on downstairs and I'll introduce you to a couple of people.'

'No thanks. I'd like to get off back to the hotel. I think I've had enough excitement for one day, thank you, Jenny. If that's your real name.'

Jenny appeared affronted. 'Of course it's my real name,' she replied. 'I tell you what. I'll put this glass down and I'll run you back to your hotel if you like. It's the least I could do.'

'It is,' said Frank. 'But I think I'll get a taxi, if it's all the same. I don't think my nerves could take another journey with you driving.'

'Whatever do you mean?'

Frank did not wait for a reply but brushed past her and headed for the stairs.

Once outside, he stopped at the bottom of the steps and took a deep breath. Beneath the glow of a streetlamp he took a cigarette from a pack and placed it into his mouth. Once he'd lit it he took a deep drag, letting the smoke stay in his lungs for a few moments before blowing it out. He looked over his shoulder and could see the shadows in the window and hear the laughter of people inside the house. He was not sure just how many of those in the building had been party to what was taking place with "Double H", Jenny Crane and the curious government people. But at that moment he did not really care. He knew he just wanted to be away from them all.

As he walked away in search of a taxi the sound of an air raid klaxon suddenly filled his ears. He let out a sigh. So much for a quick return to his hotel, now he'd need to find shelter. Who knew how long the bombing would last? At least those idiots at the little shindig behind him would now have to pack up and also seek refuge from the Nazi bombs.

He saw the sign for a tube station and headed for it. As he took the first steps down into the bowels of London, he heard the crump of high explosive bombs as the first of them landed on the dockyards and warehouses of the East End.

Chapter Four

Northern Libya - January 1941

'This bloody place… I hate it.'

Major Lowndes wiped the sweat from his neck with a handkerchief and then returned it to the pocket of his khaki shorts.

'Can you imagine what it'll be like in the summer?' replied Frank. 'This is quite mild.'

'It's more this infernal dust and sand that's irritating me,' explained Lowndes. 'That and the bloody mosquitoes.'

They had set up their command post under a hastily erected awning to shield their heads from the midday sun. Adjutants and runners sat at folding tables, field telephones and maps laid out in front of them. Frank placed the binoculars he was holding to his eyes. From their elevated position he could easily make out the advanced companies of the Australian forces as they prepared for what they hoped would be the final assault on the small Libyan port.

'I can't believe the Eyeties haven't surrendered yet. We have them surrounded. Surely it's just a matter of time before they raise the white flag,' said Frank.

'Are your boys ready?' asked Lowndes. 'Hopefully when the barrage gets started, that'll be enough for them. They're sitting ducks down there. It looks like we have all sides covered. Even the sea. The navy has a cruiser out there ready to go at them too.'

Frank had arrived in Africa with his unit six weeks previously. Before long they had been moved into the line to support the Australian 6th Division in their pursuit of the Italian 10th Army. They had seen much success over the last few weeks, culminating in encircling several Italian divisions at the small port town that now lay only two miles in front of him.

'Yes, sir, they're ready,' answered Frank confidently. 'You can rely on them. They haven't let us down yet.'

They turned to look at the row of QF25 pound howitzers. Bombardiers and gunners, some of them shirtless, sat resting on boxes of shells or lay in the sand, waiting for the order to start firing the guns. Frank felt proud of them all. He had put them through their drills relentlessly before the deployment and not one of them had let him down. They had all performed perfectly well so far. Now they waited patiently anticipating another hot and tiring afternoon.

On the table beside them the field telephone rang. Lowndes leaned over and picked it up.

'Hello… yes, sir… right away.'

Frank raised his eyebrows as Lowndes placed the receiver back onto the cradle.

'Stand your lads to, Graham. The bombardment starts in five minutes.'

***

Frank watched as the column of defeated Italian prisoners filed past. They looked a ragtag group of war-weary soldiers, their uniforms dishevelled, faces showing days of stubble growth and their hair long and matted. Many were covered in a thick layer of dust that Frank assumed was down to the severe bombardment that had been laid down on them before the infantry and tanks had moved in to complete the rout.

Armed sentries with bayoneted rifles walked alongside them. They kept a watchful eye, although they knew none were likely to attempt an escape. Cigarettes hung loosely from the guards' mouths as they sauntered along, seemingly without a care in the world, as though the victory they had just won was nothing to get too excited about.

The Italians had no fight left in them. Despite their exhaustion, some openly smiled as they walked past the watching British and Australian officers, knowing the war, for them at least, was over. The wounded were assisted by their comrades. As they trudged by, medical orderlies pulled one or two out of the column to administer assistance, some being sent on to the first aid trucks at the rear for onward transport to nearby field hospitals. Although they were the enemy, they were still men; they would be looked after.

After hearing the story from Colonel Harding about his brother's experiences in France with the Germans, Frank hoped the British army would treat their prisoners with more compassion and respect, acknowledging the rules of the Geneva Convention. He still could not get his head around the young German boy he once met on holiday all those years ago being the perpetrator of such an awful and heinous crime.

An hour later, whilst his troops hooked up the howitzers to the trucks ready for moving on, Major Lowndes approached him. Frank was leaning against a truck smoking a cigarette. Lowndes was holding a piece of paper in his right hand. He did not look one bit happy.

'Looks like one of us has friends in high places,' he said as he came nearer.

Frank threw the cigarette to the ground and crushed it beneath the heel of his boot. 'Sir?'

'Just received this signal from HQ,' said Lowndes shaking it above his head. Frank was reminded of the newsreel of Neville Chamberlain disembarking the plane at Heston after the Munich conference, and had to stop himself from smiling. He decided not to say anything and let Lowndes get it out of his system.

'It appears they want you back in England. Post haste!'

'I'm not sure what you mean,' replied Frank, raising his eyebrows.

'I mean what I said,' replied Lowndes contemptuously. 'They want you back as soon as you can get there. Christ knows how that's going to leave us. We've orders to move out towards Tobruk.'

He handed the signal to Frank.

It was true. The message was short and to the point. He had to leave his current post with immediate effect and head to London. The address to where he was to report was unfamiliar to him, Orchard Court, but the signature at the bottom he recognised. Colonel H. Harding.

He felt his heart skip a beat as he realised what this meant. They were finally calling him up for special operations. He had put the whole experience of the previous autumn to the back of his mind. After his unit had embarked to Africa, he assumed the idea had been shelved. Or, more likely, they had found better, more suitable people for the job. He had calmed down since the episode in London and the underhand way in which they had made the FANY girl test him. He now understood the reason why they had done it and accepted it was necessary in the whole scheme of things, but the experience had annoyed him at the time.

'I suppose I'd better get my things together then,' he said looking from the signal to Lowndes. He handed the paper back to him and turned away, leaving his superior standing alone, sighing to himself.

After he said his goodbyes to all those under his command, who seemed as perplexed as Lowndes had been, he managed to persuade an Australian supply truck driver to give him a lift to Sidi Barrani. From there he could get onward transportation back to an RAF airfield near Alexandria and hopefully a berth on a plane or ship back to England.

As he sat in the cab of the truck as it trundled along the coast road, the blue Mediterranean Sea to his left, he knew he would miss none of this. North Africa had given him no reason to rush back. Although he had been involved in many battles in his short time on the continent, he felt he had not contributed nearly as much as he wanted to. He understood that being an artillery officer would not be enough for him; it would not cut it. He needed something more. He hoped this new organisation, and Colonel "Double H" Harding ,would be able to provide the adventure he craved.

Chapter Five

Four Months Later - Scotland

Frank cast the line into the lake and waited patiently.

It had been some time since he last had the opportunity to fish and the setting could not be more perfect. As far as he could see, he was the only person for miles around. None of his colleagues had wished to come to such a remote place so early on a Sunday morning, preferring to get a couple of extra hours sleep in their dormitories. He had asked a few of them to join him, more out of courtesy than anything else, and was half pleased when they had all declined the offer.

One of the instructors had told him of this place, advising that the lake, which was fed from a small stream to his left, was alive with trout. In the distance a low morning mist hung over the hills of Druimindarroch, giving it an almost mystical appearance. He half expected Robert the Bruce to come charging down from them at any moment, followed by hordes of Celts, brandishing claymores. On the far side, just beyond his view, he knew the beaches of Loch Nan to be only a couple of miles away.

He had managed to borrow a motor car and set out early, hoping to have a few hours of solitude before returning to the house for dinner. With this being the last weekend of paramilitary training, he understood he would not get the chance to visit this place again, having been given orders to go to Ringway, near Manchester, for parachute training the following week. From there he would move on to the final phase of his training at a manor house somewhere in Hampshire.

As he watched the float bobbing softly on the water he was suddenly taken back to St Malo almost thirteen years ago. At the time he had been just eleven years old and hated fishing. He remembered the time very clearly, recalling how he had been frustrated in having to follow Jack who had an obsession with catching the ultimate fish. His elder brother had become more and more impatient during that holiday as his attempts at catching anything at all were met with constant disappointment. Frank knew his brother's frustration had indirectly led to the events that followed and undoubtedly affected the lives of all those involved.

That whole holiday had turned into something of a nightmare. The brothers, along with three other children they befriended, had stolen a small boat and rowed it out into a cove. They had been caught up in sudden bad weather whilst on the water. He remembered the way the boat rocked violently and the young German boy, Otto, had fallen into the sea after hitting his head against the metal oar housing. Jack had not hesitated, diving into the cold sea and rescuing him with the help of the hotel janitor, a simple man as Frank remembered, named Claude. Claude had been watching from the shore and had rushed to help when he saw them in trouble. Frank was still filled with sadness when he thought about it, as the man had drowned, his body being washed up on a beach the next day. Otto, however, had survived.

The irony of it all was not lost on Frank. Jack killed at Dunkirk, whereas Otto had gone on to become an SS officer and commit a serious war crime. An event so shocking that Frank found it hard to believe it could be the same person. He always remembered Otto Finkel with fondness and could not understand what had turned that gentle, young boy into a cold-blooded killer. Colonel Harding had shown him the report, written by his brother. There was no doubt in Frank's mind that it was true. Jack had witnessed it all.

One day Frank wanted to confront Finkel. In fact, he was determined to see the man brought to justice for what he had done.

There was a ripple across the lake's surface as the float suddenly dipped beneath the water. He began to reel it in, but soon realised the bait was still untouched. Whatever it was that had caused the disturbance had moved away. He reeled in, and cast out again.

His mind drifted back to just over a month ago when he first came to Arisaig. Arriving late on the Friday night he was collected from the train station and taken to the large house. The following morning around twenty of them, including officers from all three services, were gathered together in a meeting room. Among them he had been pleased to see a familiar face. Francis Holbrook, the RAF pilot he met briefly at St Ermin's the previous autumn. They had formed a good friendship whilst on the course. It was Holbrook's car Frank had borrowed to bring him to the lake.

The training had been both physically and mentally draining. From that very first day when the lead instructor, Captain Lewis, told them the four objectives of the Special Operations Executive, as the organisation had been named.

'The purpose of the organisation to which you and I belong is subversion,' he said, whilst striding confidently between the desks where they were all seated.

'The first objective is to damage the enemy's materiel to the maximum extent and also all his communications and means of production…

'The second is to strain the enemy's resources of manpower…

'The third is to undermine the morale of the enemy…

'And the fourth is to raise the morale of the population of the Occupied countries in order that they may give us vital assistance when the time comes.'

What followed was six weeks of intensive training to give the candidates the necessary skills to achieve these objectives. They spent hours sitting in a classroom as the group was taught how to pick locks, handle being interrogated, create alibis and decipher codes. Importantly, they also learned how to set up of Resistance cells.

This classroom work was combined with field training. This included unarmed combat, how to handle and break down a Sten Mk II sub-machine-gun, the use of explosives and various other practical exercises to test their aptitude and increase their skill set. Every thought had gone into the training, down to the very last minor detail that would assist them to both blend into the environment and help them achieve mission objectives. Frank was constantly tested on his fluency by officers of the Free French who were assisting with the agents' preparations. He was pleased to hear that his master of the language was near perfect.

It had been extremely hard work, but Frank had enjoyed every bit of it. He was in his element and had never felt so alive. This was something he was born for. Due to his enthusiasm, he had performed exceptionally well.

With the parachute training and the final touches to complete in Hampshire, he was itching to get over the Channel. It could not come soon enough for him. Although he had seen action in North Africa, that had been against the Italians. He wanted to get back at the Germans. After all, it was they who had killed Jack and carried out the Blitz on London and other British cities. His hatred for the Nazi regime was growing on a daily basis.

He felt another tug on the line and knew this time the fish had taken the bait. He pulled back on the rod, reeling in the line as he did so. He saw the trout break the surface as it struggled to wriggle free. For a second he thought he may lose it, but then he felt the line become taut again and knew he had it.

He put his left foot forward to brace himself against the throes of the fish, which was a significant size, and felt the ice cold water of the lake fall over the top of his boot soaking his foot.

'Shit,' he cursed, nearly dropping the rod. He stepped back onto dry land and continued to reel the fish in, dropping the tip of the rod almost to the surface before pulling back and winding in the line. Finally he managed to get the trout close to the keep net. After an almighty struggle, where the flapping trout splashed cold water into his face and over his shirt, he managed to bring the fish in.

He was undecided whether to take it back to the house and give it to the cooks, or to do what he normally did and let it go. He felt an uneasiness in killing it, which he knew to be odd. After all, it was only a fish. How could he feel ill at ease at taking the life of a Scottish trout when under his orders the gunners of his former battery had undoubtedly taken the lives of many Italian soldiers?

He sighed to himself and leaned over to the keep net.

***

'Did you catch anything, old boy?'

Frank had returned to Arisaig a few minutes earlier. After emptying the fishing tackle from the boot he had gone in search of Holbrook to return the car keys. He found him in the corner of the common room sitting in an armchair, reading a newspaper, that was probably a few days old, and smoking a pipe. A fire burned brightly in the hearth and a cup of tea was on a small table to his side. He was wearing a white cricket jumper that was clearly two sizes too big for him, the cuffs rolled back to compensate for the length.

Frank threw the keys in his direction and he caught them instinctively.

'No joy, I'm afraid. I don't think they were in the mood this morning.'

'Oh, never mind, old thing,' replied Holbrook in his clipped southern accent. 'Better luck next time, what.'

'Thanks for the use of the car,' said Frank, sitting down in a chair opposite.

'No trouble at all.'

Holbrook folded the paper and put it on the table to his side. He picked up the tea and took a sip. He looked around the room.

'You know, old boy, I think I'm going to miss all this.'

'Me too,' Frank replied. 'But then I just want to get started. I want to get over there and start doing some good. I don't feel I've done anything yet.'

'Nonsense. You've seen action in Africa. You've already done enough for the war effort. But I know what you mean. I can't wait to get at Jerry again. After what happened… Oh well, not to dwell, eh? I'm not the only person who's lost someone in this bloody mess.'

Holbrook had lost his mother in the German bombing of London a few months before and he had learned that his cousin, a corporal in the Royal Fusiliers, was a prisoner of war in Germany. He had more reason than most to hate the Nazis.

'It looks like they won't be needing me overseas for a while,' said Holbrook, puffing at his pipe and blowing smoke out into the room.

Frank took out a cigarette and lit it. 'Why's that?'

'Apparently they want me in London. They think I may be of more use in the planning of these things rather than actually going out there and doing them. I'm not sure if it's what I want, but if that's how they think I can help then I suppose I'll just go along with it and see where it takes me.'

'I suppose if you don't like it then you can always go back to the air force,' said Frank encouragingly. 'But I doubt you'll be anything but fantastic in whatever it is you do.'

'Thanks for the support, old boy,' replied Holbrook smiling at him. 'I suppose we all have our own individual talents.'

'Maybe,' said Frank. 'But the sooner I get over there the better.'

Chapter Six

August 1941

Frank had been summoned to the offices at Orchard Court, near Oxford Street, and was waiting in the foyer to be collected. He wore his artillery officer's uniform and carried the cap in his hand.

He had been in London for the last six weeks, after finishing his training at Beaulieu house in Hampshire. The city had changed dramatically since his last visit. Most notably, the Germans were not conducting air raids with the same frequency as then, although the threat from the sky was always there. Frank was pleased to see people continued to go about their business, trying to bring some normality to their lives, even if it meant having to bypass the areas of devastation the Nazi bombs had created.

It was clear the recent invasion of the Soviet Union by the Germans in late June meant they had now abandoned their plans to invade Britain. Frank felt this strategy was a huge mistake by the Nazis. They had opened up yet another front against one of the largest and most powerful countries in the world. They were stretching themselves thin. He believed it was only a matter of time before they were defeated. He was convinced of it.

The delay in getting over to France had been frustrating. Nobody had yet given him a satisfactory reason as to why he had been left to sit on his hands in Caxton Place for so long. He hoped that being summoned to SOE headquarters would be to receive the news that he was about to put into practice all he had trained for in Scotland, Manchester and Hampshire.

He thought back to the final coaching in Beaulieu. He had enjoyed this even more than the paramilitary training in Arisaig. He had learned many new skills including surveillance techniques and how to operate various communications equipment. He had also been briefed on the current status of the Nazi occupation of France.

France had been split into two zones. The north and west of the country was occupied and controlled by the Nazis. The unoccupied zone to the south and east was administered by a puppet French government in Vichy, headed by Marshal Petain, "the hero of Verdun". Other significant politicians supporting Petain included Maxime Weygand and the fascist Pierre Laval. This had split the country into those who were either pro-Vichy or pro-de Gaulle, the French general in exile who headed the Free French forces.

Frank learned the Resistance movement was gaining momentum but was split into various factions, many of which had communist inclinations. He understood the SOE would need to work in collaboration with these groups, to set up cells and circuits and gain their assistance and support for any future Allied invasion of Europe, no matter their ideological tendencies. It would be a huge undertaking for every agent sent over to France.

He was also under no illusion that just being there would be highly dangerous. If any agents were caught then they were certain to be tortured and killed by the Gestapo. Despite all this, he still desperately wanted to get out there. He would just have to be careful, and use his new skills to avoid being caught.

'Ah, Frank, my boy. Good to see you again.'

Frank turned to see a familiar face coming down the stairs.

'Good morning, Colonel,' he said, shaking Harding's hand firmly.

'Follow me, young man. There are a few people I'd like you to meet.'

Frank accompanied Harding up the stairs to a small office.

There were three people in the room. Sitting behind a small desk facing him was the man Frank recognised as the civilian he had met during the initial selection test at St Ermin's hotel. Sitting on a chair facing the civilian was someone he had not expected to see; someone he would not have been bothered to ever see again. Jenny Crane nodded meekly at him and smiled. The third person, a man dressed in the uniform of a French soldier, stood at an open window to the right, smoking a cigarette.

Harding closed the door and went to stand behind the desk with the civilian.

'Please, Mr Graham, take a seat,' said the civilian indicating a chair to the side of Jenny.

Frank did as he was told. He could feel Jenny looking at him but did not acknowledge her.

'Let me introduce you to everyone,' said the civilian again. 'My name is Henry Marriott and I currently run F Section, although I'm soon to move on to other things. Colonel Harding and young Jenny you already know. My colleague by the window is Sergeant Pierre Benoit, a member of the Free French forces.'

The man nodded at Frank who smiled back at him.

'Do you feel you're ready?' asked Harding. 'Ready to go over there and give them what for?'

Frank turned back to face him. 'I've been ready for quite some time, sir. In fact, I'm at a bit of a loss as to why I haven't been sent over yet.'

'That will probably be down to me,' said the soldier in French, stepping from the window and stubbing his cigarette out in an ashtray on Marriott's desk. 'You see, they've been waiting for me to return from operations in Africa.'

'And why's that?' Frank replied in the same language.

'English please, gentlemen,' said Harding. 'I'm not quite as proficient in the lingo as you two boys.'

Marriott spoke again. 'I understand that you're quite familiar with the Lyon area, Lieutenant Graham. Sergeant Benoit here is from that area and he may be able to assist in getting you set up there. Contacts and such.'

'You see, I have a contact that may prove very useful to you, Lieutenant,' said Benoit, this time in English.

'And can this contact be trusted?' asked Frank. He was suspicious as to why they had not simply passed on this information earlier. Was there any need for him to wait for Benoit to return from Africa?

'Oh, he can be trusted. One hundred per cent. You see, he is my father.'

So that was it, thought Frank. Benoit wanted to see if Frank was the one who could be trusted. He wanted to assess him before giving out information to a British agent that could cause a problem for his father. He had wanted to see if Frank was capable.

'I can assure you, Sergeant Benoit, that I'm an extremely professional and competent individual. You've no need to worry in regards to your father, should you decide to assist us. Why have you not gone through your own people with this? Don't the French have their own section.'

'I may be a soldier of the Free French,' replied Benoit firmly. 'But I'm no Gaullist. In fact, if they knew I was assisting F Section they may not be too happy with me.'

Frank could not quite get his head around the different French Resistance factions and how they opposed each other, whilst at the same time all hating the Pétainists at Vichy, and looking to achieve the same goal. Surely it would make sense to work together until the common enemy was defeated. It seemed to him they were already jostling for position with the war still yet to be won.

He turned to Marriott. 'Okay. When do I go in?'

'We'll take you to the airfield tomorrow evening. From there we'll fly you to an area outside of Lyon where you'll parachute in and make your way to the address Sergeant Benoit, here, will give you. There you'll make contact with his father. As proof of your credentials, Benoit will give you a letter of introduction. You'll set up a series of cells and circuits and arm and train them. You'll then cause as much trouble as you can. As you know, Lyon is currently in the unoccupied zone so movement should be relatively easy. With the odd exception, the gendarmerie are quite clearly collaborating with the Nazis and will arrest you and hand you over to them should you cock up in anyway, so don't rely on any support from them. It's our belief that it's just a matter of time before the Germans move to occupy the rest of the country, despite the fact they need every man they can spare on the Russian front. We need to make things as difficult for them as we possibly can.

'Choose your targets wisely and try to avoid doing anything that will cause reprisals on the population. They'll not thank you for it, believe me.'

'Good luck, young man,' said Harding. 'Do your brother proud.'

'We'll be in touch in the morning,' said Marriott. 'Sergeant Benoit will accompany you to the airfield and provide you with all the information you need. Before then, your time is your own. Good luck and godspeed.'

Frank said his goodbyes and left the room.

As he walked down the stairs he found he was smiling. Finally it was happening. All that he had trained for was about to be put into practice. Although he felt a slight nervousness about the whole thing, he also felt an excitement he had not felt in a very long time.

'Frank… Frank… Wait.'

He turned to see Jenny Crane rushing down the stairs towards him. He stopped.

'Yes, Jenny. What can I do for you?' He was no longer smiling.

'I was just thinking. Seeing you have a free evening, would you like to accompany me to dinner… you know, by way of an apology for last time… if you want to that is?'

Frank looked at her. His initial thought was to tell her he was not interested and that she had irritated him beyond words the last time they were together. But he held his tongue. Was that genuine remorse he was seeing in her eyes? Maybe she really was sorry for the way in which she had treated him the previous year.

'This isn't some kind of test again, is it? Because I really can't be…'

She held up her hand. 'No, no, no. I really am sorry for last time and just want to apologise to you. I'm a nice person, you know, honestly I am. Don't laugh at me.'

Frank had not realised he was smiling at her. 'I'm not laughing at you. I tell you what. If you can promise me you won't try and test me again and we don't speak of work or the war or anything else of any seriousness, then I'll agree.'

She smiled. 'Okay, I promise.'

'In that case pick me up from Caxton Place at seven this evening. But this time don't drive like you've forgotten how to.'

'Hey. I'm a good driver…'

Frank laughed and turned away. 'See you later.'

***

Frank took the cloth cap from his head and stuffed it into the inside pocket of his corduroy jacket.

The rumbling of the twin engined Armstrong Whitworth Whitley he had been cramped into for the last two hours made it hard for him to hear the information being given to him by the unknown man accompanying him on the flight. It must have been unimportant as the man, realising Frank could not hear him, simply sat back in his seat and kept his thoughts to himself.

Frank had been taken to the airfield in Suffolk that morning. There he was given papers, in the name of Francois Aubuchon, with the backstory he was a self-employed motorcar parts salesman from a town in Alsace, visiting garages in the Lyon region. He'd been rigged out in clothing common to people of the area, with care that all labels had either been taken out or were French. He was given a Type A Mark III transceiver radio set in a small suitcase with instructions to make contact with London every second day at 2115 hours precisely, commencing the day after his landing. This schedule, or "sked", as they were known, had to be adhered to. If it was broken in any way then London may assume he had been compromised and all subsequent communications may well be ignored. The codename "Grey Man" was to be used at the start and end of each transmission.

His English cigarettes had been taken from him and replaced with French cigarillos in a silver case, a good luck gift from "Double H" Harding. He understood the colonel gave gifts to all those under his command who were being sent over the Channel.

In his pocket was a Colt .38 automatic pistol with four spare clips of ammunition, a supply of Benzedrine tablets and, more worryingly, a cyanide capsule, which he had no intention of ever taking. He knew that to be caught with all this equipment would mean interrogation, torture and a probable firing squad. Despite this, he would not end his own life. That was something he could never do. If the Germans wanted him dead, then they would have to kill him themselves.

The aircraft had taken a circuitous route to get to the drop zone. To avoid enemy radar it flew low over the English Channel, using the light of the moon for guidance, before rising to 8,000 feet to cross into France just south of Le Havre, where flak was least likely to affect them. The aircraft had then reduced altitude down to 2,000 feet, flying a pre-set pattern to avoid known anti-aircraft areas, only rising to cross mountains.

Frank had not spoken to any of the aircrew. None of them seemed in the least bit interested in conversing with him. He knew the mission they were undertaking, to get him to Lyon, was extremely dangerous. He did not want to disturb them from their concentration.

They had no fighter escort. The danger of meeting a Luftwaffe patrol was an anxiety he put to the back of his mind. He knew a Whitworth Whitley would be no match for a Messerschmitt should they have the misfortune to come across one. He could do nothing about that and so decided there was no point in worrying about it. After all, the aircrew seemed unperturbed, as did the gentleman from the organisation who had decided to join him on the journey.

After another half hour the door to the cockpit opened and the co-pilot nodded to them.

'Okay,' shouted the accompanying agent, leaning so he could be heard. 'Better get the joe hole open. Looks like it's time.'

The "joe hole" was the aperture cut out of the floor of the fuselage to allow parachutists to drop from the aircraft. Frank had jumped many times from this type of aircraft whilst carrying out his training at Ringway. He remembered seeing one recruit whack his head on the edge as he had dropped out, knocking himself unconscious. It was as well that the static line had opened the parachute for him as the man had still been out cold when he had landed on the ground, breaking his left leg to add to his woes. After seeing this, Frank ensured he was perfectly straight and rigid whenever he disembarked the aircraft.

With the assistance of his colleague, Frank opened the aperture. There was a sudden rush of cold, night air. The noise inside the aircraft seemed to double in volume. He attached the clip to the static line above his shoulder. Between them, they made sure all the equipment was attached and the straps securely fastened.

'Two minutes,' he heard the co-pilot shout above the increased din.

His heartbeat quickened as the aircraft descended to 600 feet, the designated height for an agent drop. He'd done this before, but never over enemy territory. A sudden jolt of fear struck him. He had no idea what awaited him on the ground. There were no German troops in the area, as far as he knew, but the gendarmerie were largely loyal to the Nazis. He could only hope no one would spot his descent and report it to the police.In the cramped fuselage Frank stood up as straight as he could. He could feel his chaperone behind him. 'Okay, get ready. Nearly time,' he said, placing his hand on Frank's right shoulder. 'Good luck.'

Frank watched the red light to his left and waited for it to be replaced by the green one underneath. The signal to jump.

He took a breath and blew out hard.

The light turned to green. Without hesitation he stepped out into the void.

Part Two

1942 - 1943

Chapter Seven

July 1942 - Lyon, France

'Christian… Christian. Wake up. There's somebody at the door.'

Christian Piaget turned over in bed, putting his back to his wife, Adele.

She continued to shake him. 'Christian. Christian…'

'Okay, okay,' he snapped irritably. 'What's going on?'

'There's somebody at the door,' she repeated. 'Listen. Who can it be at this hour?'

Piaget lay still and listened. She was right. There was unmistakably a tapping at the front door.

He leaned over and switched on a bedside lamp. Through bleary, sleepy eyes, he picked up his wristwatch which he'd left next to it. It showed a quarter past one in the morning.

'What the hell? '

Adele sat up. 'Who can it be?'

'I won't know until I answer it, will I?' he said abruptly. 'Now go back to sleep. I'll sort it out. It's probably a problem at the factory. Why they can't just ring me, I don't know.'

He got out of bed and walked to the window. Pulling the curtain to the side, he looked out. He could just make out two shadowy figures at the front door, their heads bowed. From his vantage point he could not see clearly who they were.

'I'll go down and sort it out, Adele. Now, please, go back to sleep.'

Fumbling in the dark, Piaget pulled on the trousers he had left lying on the floor and drew the braces over his shoulders. Shutting the bedroom door behind him, he walked down the stairs to the hallway.

Sighing, he unlocked then opened the front door.

Without waiting for an invite, the two men stepped into the hallway, forcing him out of their way. They closed the door behind them.

It was only once they were inside that Piaget realised both wore ski masks. One held an automatic pistol which was pointed at his chest.

'Christian, who is it?' came a shout from upstairs.

'Tell your wife there's nothing to worry about,' said the man holding the pistol. 'Tell her it's a problem at work.' There was something about the man's voice that, despite the fact he was pointing a loaded weapon at him, was strangely calming.

Piaget complied with the request. 'It's fine, Adele. It's work. Go back to sleep.'

The man with the gun indicated for him to move to the kitchen. Once inside, his accomplice closed the door behind them.

'If you intend on robbing me then you're wasting your time. I don't have anything of value here. All the money's kept in the bank or at the factory.'

The man with the gun spoke again.

'We're not here to rob you, Monsieur Piaget. Nor are we here to harm you or your wife. Unless you give us reason to.'

'Then why are you here?' he replied. 'I'm confused.'

'We're here to ask for a favour of sorts. You see, we need your help.'

'Then why didn't you just make an appointment to see me at my office instead of turning up at my house at this time of night, waving guns in my face and scaring my wife half to death?'

The other man spoke but his voice was not nearly as soft. 'Sit down, Piaget.'

He turned his head and looked at the man. Although he wore a mask, he could see his eyes had a hostility he did not want to test. He did as he was bid and sat down at the kitchen table.

The man with the gun spoke again.

'Monsieur Piaget. We're aware you're under orders to produce machine parts for German military motor vehicles, and have been doing so for the past three months. In fact you've made a nice profit from it, have you not?'

'I have no choice. I don't want to do this … '

He held up his hand and Piaget stopped talking.

'We know you're under orders from the Nazis, via this traitorous government. But we're going to offer you a chance to redeem yourself somewhat. In a few nights' time we intend to cause an explosion at your factory. We'll target only those machines you use for the Nazi war industry. We want you to allow our people to go in after midnight to carry this out. You'll accommodate them any way they see fit. You'll ensure all your staff are nowhere near the premises on the night in question. I don't care what reason you give them, that's up to you.

'In the next day or so, you'll get a visit from one of our associates. He'll give his name as Francois Aubuchon, a car parts salesman. He'll visit you at your factory and you'll give him the necessary keys to get into the building. He'll then give you further instructions.'

'This is madness. I can't agree to this. If the gendarmerie find out I'll be arrested…'

'Don't concern yourself with them,' interrupted the man standing behind him.

'That's easy for you to say. It's not you who'll be in trouble with them. What happens if I refuse?'

The man with the gun shrugged his shoulders. 'Should you refuse, Piaget, then we'll simply get the Royal Air Force to flatten your factory. All of it. They'll completely destroy the place and everything and everyone inside. At least doing this our way we can help you save most of the equipment and nobody will get hurt. All we ask is for your co-operation as a patriotic Frenchman.'

'Won't it be obvious I've helped you? It's not just me I'm worried about. My wife…'

'I can organise a plane to fly over as we blow it,' explained the man at the table. 'Trust me, I have those connections and the authority to order it. We can make it look like an RAF attack, should we wish.'

Piaget was quiet for a few moments.

'I'll have to think about it…'

'Well do just that. Think about it. But don't take too much time doing so. Our associate will expect your answer when he visits you. Be mindful of what we've said tonight.'

The man standing behind Piaget spoke again. 'If you mention to anyone what's happened here tonight, or try to report us to the authorities or warn them of what's going to happen, then we'll return and kill both you and your wife and anyone else who happens to be here. If Aubuchon is arrested or comes to any harm when he visits you, then we'll make sure both you and your wife die painfully.'

'I trust there'll be no need for that,' said the man with the gun. 'My colleague here speaks the truth. Don't think we won't do it, for we will. And should we find the gendarmerie there on the night, then we know whose door to come knocking on.'

He rose from the table.

'Now go back to bed, Monsieur. We'll be in touch.'

Piaget watched as both men turned and left the room. He waited until he heard the front door close behind them before he stood up and slowly walked up the stairs to the bedroom.

'Who was it?' asked Adele sleepily as he pulled the blanket over his shoulders.

'Nothing to concern yourself with, dear,' he replied. She seemed to accept this, muttering something he didn't quite understand before rolling away from him. A moment later she had fallen back to sleep.

He was annoyed. He had not asked for any of this. He was a businessman. That was all he was. An owner of a machine parts factory. He was very proud of his achievements, his successes. He had worked very hard all of his life to build up the business. He employed over eighty staff and when those government people had visited him and ordered he move part of his production to assisting the Germans, he had had no choice. None whatsoever.

Piaget did not sleep for the remainder of the night. Thoughts of the dilemma he now faced, and his wife's loud snoring preventing any chance of peaceful slumber.

Chapter Eight

From the shelter of the trees Frank crawled to the edge of the embankment and looked down onto the railway track. The rail yard was a hundred yards to the right, where a large locomotive was being prepared by a party of railway workers, their blue boiler suits clearly seen in the spotlights from the buildings nearby.

It had been a balmy evening, giving way to an uncomfortably hot night, the midges and mosquitoes buzzing irritably in his face. He wore dark clothes to blend in with the shadows. Although he had asked the members of this circuit to do the same, two of them had turned up in bright coloured shirts. He made them wait out of sight, near to the path that led to the trees. Their job to watch over the bicycles and keep lookout for any gendarmes that may happen to be passing.

Another two, David and Lucien, were alongside him as he settled into a more comfortable position.

'Do you have the plastic explosive?' he asked.

'It's here,' replied Lucien, patting a knapsack at his side. 'Don't worry, Francois. Everything is as planned.'

'Is it? Those two idiots back there…'

David spoke. 'They mean well.'

'I know that,' responded Frank. 'But if they can't follow a basic instruction on what to wear… well, I just hope they aren't going to be a liability.'

Frank had been uneasy about this circuit for a while now. He was convinced some of them were doing it more out of a sense of adventure than a belief in what the Resistance movement was all about. The two he had left with the bicycles were no more than seventeen years old. He feared their age was a problem. He did not need boys. He needed men.

His mind drifted back to a year ago when he first arrived in France. He remembered that night very well. Dropping like a stone from the undercarriage of the Whitley Armstrong. The momentary fear that the parachute may not open, before the utter, instant relief when it did. He remembered the landing, how he hit the ground awkwardly, his right knee smacking into his stomach knocking the wind from him. He had lain in the field for almost five minutes trying to catch his breath, expecting all the time for someone to approach him, having heard or witnessed him arrive. A gendarme maybe, or an unfriendly farmer. He remembered the sudden change in noise levels. From the deafening roar of the twin engines of the RAF aircraft, to the tranquil silence of the Rhone countryside. A silence broken only by the occasional hoot of an owl or the bark of a dog some distance away.

After dusting himself down and hiding away his parachute, he walked the six miles to the edge of the city, where he found a safe spot, in a cemetery of all places, to get some sleep. He had woken bright and early and then made his way to the address given to him by Pierre Benoit.

He found Pierre's father, Claude, to be a very relaxed fellow. Once he gained the man's trust and confidence, aided by the letter Pierre had written, Claude arranged for him to stay at the garage he owned on the outskirts of the city until they could find him more permanent digs. He was introduced to Claude's workforce, the cousins Michel Trouvier and Pierre Buque and realised that, as Pierre Benoit had told him, these men would be very interested in doing their bit for the Resistance. Frank found it easy to recruit all of them and was pleased with himself that he had formed his first circuit so easily.

Michel had later introduced him to a friend of his, Catherine Lambert, a young woman who was also recruited to the circuit. Catherine proved very useful as a courier, passing messages and often acting as lookout on operations. He found her amiable, albeit a little nervous at times. She told him of her boyfriend, a Jewish writer by the name of Jean-Luc Descartes and of how he may be of use to the group. The man's name seemed oddly familiar to Frank but he didn't know the reason why.

Frank managed to arrange a supply drop to equip them. The garage proved to be a useful place to store weapons and explosives. He had recently taken them to the south, to the Vercors Massif, where he trained them in the use of those weapons and how to effectively use the plastic explosives they now owned. Michel and Pierre had been very enthusiastic and were keen to get involved in sabotage operations.

He also acquired a radio set for them and gave strict instructions to use it only should their circuit be compromised and they had no way of getting word to him. He taught them how to send the pre-determined warning message to London.

Frank had soon come to realise he could trust these people. Any endorsement for a recruit from Claude was a good enough reference for him.

Frank found that they also had very strong stomachs and had no problem in killing collaborators, including members of the gendarmerie.

The establishment of the circuit had led to the formation of others. Potential names passed by Claude had been followed up. After a period of surveillance, contact was made to the one whom Frank thought may be of most use. He had chosen a lawyer by the name of Clement Vallin. Vallin then recruited his own team, much as Claude Benoit had done, and suggested names of more potential circuit leaders.

And so the network had grown.

Frank now controlled six circuits. Through them he was able to establish assistance in other areas. People who were prepared to help the Resistance. They worked in train stations, factories and cafés, each of them unaware of the other's existence. A network of Resistance members, all under his guidance, who could not betray any of the others if caught, because none, other than Frank, knew who they all were. It was the perfect set-up.

To remain safe he needed to move around. He would stay in one place for no more than a week at a time, initially stopping in small hotels and apartments. He soon came to realise he needed a more permanent base and so rented an apartment in the Montchat area of the city.

Although it was relatively easy to move around the Unoccupied Zone, Frank was more than aware of how difficult it was to stay anonymous. He could not drop his guard at any time.

Over the past few months he had found there were three trains of thought within the populace. Those who thought collaboration was the only way to save France; those who did not want to cause any problems for themselves and so accepted things the way they were, with an almost reluctant indifference; and those who wanted to assist the Resistance in any way they could. Frank was convinced that in the main most wanted what was best for France, it was just that their views differed on how this was to be achieved.

What he also found was those members of the Resistance to whom he had made contact and recruited all had one thing in common. Each one of them hated the Nazis, the Vichy collaborators and anyone who actively assisted them. He had personally given the go-ahead for assassinations of known collaborators, but knew that probably a lot more killings and beatings had taken place of which he was unaware. He chose to turn a blind eye to this. After all, this was their country and he merely saw himself as an assistant to them, a co-ordinator of operations, a provider of training and weaponry.

SOE had moved their headquarters to offices in Baker Street. He had been recalled to England a few months back for a debriefing, being picked up in a Lysander and flown to an airfield north of London. At Baker Street he met the head of F section, Maurice Buckmaster, who had been very impressed with what Frank had so far achieved. Whist there ,he was made aware of the uneasy relationship F Section had with RF Section, the group run by the Free French. There seemed a lack of trust between the two sections he found bizarre.

He was also informed that de Gaulle was hoping to join all the different branches of the Resistance under one control, as they were currently operating in separate factions with differing political objectives. In fact, some of their political beliefs were poles apart: from the downright communist *Front National* to the more Gaullist *Combat*. In January de Gaulle had tasked Jean Moulin to achieve this, as he was respected by all Resistance leaders. Moulin was to head up the *Conseil National de la Resistance*, or CNR, a council of representatives made up of Resistance leaders, trade unionists and the heads of pre-war political parties. The idea was to unify them all under one leadership in order to co-ordinate operations against the

Nazis and Pétainists, and to prepare for the governance of post-war France. Frank knew this was very much a work in progress and Moulin had not yet achieved his aim.

In a bid to improve relations between F and RF sections, Buckmaster informed Frank that he was to help in any way he could, should any request be made for logistical assistance, as Moulin was currently operating in the Lyon area.

Whilst there, Frank caught up with Colonel Harding and spent a very enjoyable few days relaxing with Jenny Crane, before making a quick visit to see his father on the south coast. It was not long before he was itching to get back into the field, and was soon on French soil again, having been dropped off by Lysander. Altogether he had been away for just six days.

Frank turned his attention back to the locomotive. He could see that the distance between themselves and the rail workers, coupled with the darkness of the moonless night, would be sufficient cover for what they needed to do. He was confident they would not be seen

'The train's due to set off in fifteen minutes,' whispered David. 'We need to get a move on.'

'Come on, Lucien. Let's do this.' Frank pulled a pack of five time-pencils from his satchel and, clutching them tightly, moved out of the cover of the trees, followed closely by the young Frenchman.

He could hear David cock the Sten gun behind him. His job was to provide covering fire should anyone see them and raise the alarm. A quick burst from the machine-gun would be enough to scare off anyone who might want to stop what they were doing.

Once at the track they worked fast.

Lucien had prepared the plastic explosives beforehand and speedily packed the four blocks against the track whilst Frank worked on the timing pencils. He inserted the safety fuse into the spring snout and squeezed the copper tube which crushed an ampoule containing the corrosive liquid that would break down the steel wire. He removed the black safety strip and placed the timing pencil into the explosive blocks.

He tapped Lucien on the shoulder. 'Come on. We've got ten minutes before they blow.'

Quickly and quietly they headed back to the safety of the trees.

'Come on, David. Time to go.'

'Aren't we going to watch it happen?' asked Lucien. 'Don't you want to see it go up?'

'Not particularly,' replied Frank. 'What I want to do is get as far away as possible before anyone sees us.'

'Francois is right,' said David, standing up. He unclipped the magazine from the side of the Sten and put it in his rucksack. 'Let's get out of here.'

They found the two youngsters with the bicycles. They were smoking cigarettes and laughing. They did not see the saboteurs until they were almost on top of them.

'We could have been gendarmes,' Lucien angrily whispered at them. 'You've got to be more alert, you fools.'

Quickly the boys threw down their cigarettes and muttered apologies.

Frank chose to ignore them all and grabbed his bicycle.

He cycled away and did not look back. He was four hundred yards along the path when he heard the explosion. He turned his head and saw the sky beyond the tree line light up. By the glow from the explosion, he could make out the silhouettes of the others still sorting out their things where he had left them.

Lucien and David were both competent operators, he thought, but the two youngsters they had recruited needed to buck their ideas up, or they would have to go. It was as simple as that.

Chapter Nine

The following day Frank met with Clement Vallin in his office. The lawyer sat behind his desk, Frank facing him. It was quite a small room on the second floor of a four storey office block not far from the centre of the city.

Frank liked Vallin a lot. He'd been recommended as a possible circuit leader by Claude Benoit, and when Frank approached him, he was very receptive. Frank followed the man for days after the initial approach, observing him from a distance. Being told he could trust him was one thing. He had to know for himself.

Frank asked to meet him a second time in a small café in the city centre. He had no intention of making the appointment, instead watching from a distance as Vallin did what he had asked, sitting at an outside table, where he could be seen clearly. Frank had not come to watch Vallin. Instead he was there to see if the lawyer had been followed, if any undercover police were monitoring him. When he was confident this was not the case, he made his way to the man's office, where the full recruitment process had taken place.

To the casual observer, Vallin looked an insignificant man. He was quite short in stature with a receding hairline that he tried to cover by parting his hair to the side and combing it over the top of his balding head. He had a somewhat bulbous nose, marbled with broken capillaries that gave away his love of fine wines. He was always smartly dressed, as his profession dictated, and his shoes were as shiny as "Double H's" parade boots.

The man was also hyper-intelligent with contacts in the judiciary and the gendarmerie that proved invaluable. Frank never asked about Vallin's own contacts and sources of information, preferring not to know for security reasons, but he knew he could trust any information Vallin gave him. The Frenchman was always quick to remind him that not all officers of the gendarmerie were sympathetic to Pétain's regime.

'Some of my people are getting restless, Francois,' he said, taking a cheroot from a silver case and lighting it with a match. He offered the case to Frank.

Frank waved his hand. 'How so?'

'They want to do more.' Vallin slipped the case into a drawer.

'Tell them not to worry. Their time will come, trust me. There's no way the Germans can ever win this war. They're fighting on too many fronts. They simply don't have the resources to succeed on all of them. And with the Americans now involved, I believe it's only a matter of time before the Third Reich comes tumbling down.'

Vallin blew smoke into the room, coughing slightly as he did so.

Frank smiled. 'They'll kill you one day. You know that, don't you?'

Vallin looked at the thin cigar. 'These? Maybe. A man's got to die of something, my friend.'

'Very true. As you know, I take my direction from London. But that doesn't mean you can't do other things. You can run your circuit anyway you choose, Clement. You're not restricted just to operations that I give you. Far from it. This is your country, your war. All I ask is that you keep whatever you do… well, keep it subtle, if that makes sense. We don't want what we do to have repercussions on the general public. That's a sure way to lose any support we have. As long as what you do has no impact on the operations Baker Street orders, then I personally have no problem with it.'

'Noted. You do know that your French is very good, don't you?'

'Just "very good"?' I was hoping it was rather better than that.'

Vallin laughed. 'It is. You're one of us now, Francois.'

It was time to get to the point of his visit.

'Do you have anything for me, Clement? Anything I can use?'

Vallin tapped ash into a glass ashtray in front of him. 'My source has been very useful. There is maybe something that you need to know. I'm not sure how it can help you, but it's a bit of information you may need to be aware of.'

'Concerning?'

'The Jews.'

Frank shuffled uncomfortably. The harsh treatment of Jews by the Nazis was common knowledge and the Vichy regime's collaboration with their puppet-masters did not bode well for them.

'What about them?'

'I've word that the government in Vichy has been told to… how can I put this… gather them together.'

'Gather them together? For what purpose?'

Vallin leaned back in his chair. 'I'm sure you've heard the rumours. The reason they're giving is that they want to use them as labour in Germany and Poland. I'm pretty sure that's not the truth.'

'Is your source reliable?'

'He has been so far. Apparently the gendarmerie are preparing to round up those on the lists.'

'Lists? They made lists?'

Vallin let out a breath. 'Yes, they did. Pétain and those traitors in Vichy voluntarily adopted the Statute on Jews back in October '40. All Jews were made to register at their local police stations. The authorities know who they are and where they can find them. It's an embarrassment to us all, my friend. Frenchmen giving up French men, women and children to the Nazis. It breaks my heart. It honestly does.'

'Have you any idea when this is to take place?' asked Frank.

'No, but I'm led to believe it's imminent. They're to be rounded up and then shipped out to Drancy for onward emigration to work camps.'

Drancy was a suburb of northern Paris. Frank was aware of the place. An internment camp for Jews had been established there the previous August by the Nazis. He understood it was currently being run by the French police force and many Jews had been detained there.

'This can't be good,' said Frank. 'Maybe we need to create a few more "disruptions" over the next few weeks and months. Divert resources away from them doing this.'

Vallin scratched his head thoughtfully. 'I can't see that doing any harm. Although I can't see the Germans staying in the north forever. They'll come into the Unoccupied Zone at some point.'

They sat in silence for a while, each of them contemplating what had been discussed. Finally Frank spoke.

'The supplies you've requested will be dropped early next week,' he said. 'Probably Tuesday night but it'll be confirmed later this week.'

'Thank you.'

'We'll need as many men as you can get for the drop. I can gather some too. I'll be in touch regarding location and time, et cetera.'

***

Frank left Vallin's office twenty minutes later and returned to his apartment in Montchat. He needed to make contact with the cell leaders to get together as many men as they could for the airdrop. He also wanted to tell each of them about the information Vallin had given him of the impending round-up of Jews. He had no idea how many of his people this affected, but knew not to warn them would be the wrong thing to do.

As he sat on his sofa hours later, drinking a cup of very weak coffee, he realised that he may be spreading himself a bit too thin. His network was now very large. Keeping tabs on them all was proving difficult, as they were so vastly spread out around the city and beyond. He just couldn't give them the attention they required. He also had the added problem of making himself available to make the "sked" every two nights. On one occasion had missed it completely, which caused all kinds of suspicions from Baker Street. It had taken him a long time to gain their confidence again. Being in the Unoccupied Zone helped, as at least they knew it could not be the Germans who were subsequently transmitting to them. This made him realise that what he actually needed was another agent to assist him, a radio operator maybe, someone to carry some of the weight he was beginning to feel pressing down upon him. He decided he would put in a request for an assistant.

Making a transmission always made him feel vulnerable. He was not the fastest morse code operator and so tried to keep his messages short and to the point. He would start by writing down the message he wanted to send and once coded, burned it in the hearth, making sure it was completely destroyed. Then he would take the radio set from under the bed and place it on the small table in the bedroom. He ensured he had music playing lightly in the apartment, lest an over-curious neighbour hear him tapping at the key. Then, when the time was right, he would start his transmission, beginning and ending with the codename: “GREYMAN”.

After he made his transmission he waited patiently for the response. Luckily the FANY at the other end of the communication was used to his slow style and sent her messages at a rate he could decipher. If a transmission was too fast then Frank was in danger of losing it completely, but this had not happened in a long time as the girl taking the message at the receiving centre in Kent knew of his limitations as a signaller.

Once the “sked” was over, Frank tidied the radio set away before decoding the signal he received. It was short and simple, just as he liked them.

They had acknowledged his request for an assistant which would be forwarded to F Section. The message went on to say the airdrop would go ahead as planned, weather permitting, on the Tuesday night. He was to send exact co-ordinates on his next “sked”. They also advised him he was to collect a “package” the following evening. He was to go to the café at the Central train station at 1900 hours and order a coffee. He was to ask if they had “anything sweet, a small cake maybe” and a man by the name of “Paul” would make himself known to him.

Frank was used to this kind of thing but it always made him smile. The triviality of it. Something so innocent and insignificant if overheard, but a cue to those observing that he could be trusted. He wondered what exactly the “package” may be, but knew that whatever it was, it was just one more thing to add to his workload.

As he burned the decoded signal in the hearth, where it mixed with the ashes of the other papers he had destroyed earlier, he sighed to himself.

Why on earth had he volunteered for this?

Chapter Ten

The train station was quiet.

The day's commuters had already passed through and would be at home now, their work done for the day whilst they awaited the dawning of a new one. As Frank walked onto the concourse he could see the café to his right. A young waitress was wiping down one of the tables of which only two were occupied. At one sat three rail workers who were either on a break or getting a quick coffee before heading for home. At the other, furthest from the counter, sat two men, both in their late twenties. One wore a cap pulled down slightly over his eyes. A tuft of blond hair could be seen at the back of his head. Whilst he appeared slightly nervous, his companion sipped indifferently at a cup of coffee.

Frank opened the door and walked in. As he did so, the two men at the back of the café looked over to him. He had the desire to go straight over to them but needed to play the game as dictated by London. He approached the counter. The young waitress left the table she was cleaning and walked behind it. None of the rail workers paid any attention to him.

The waitress wiped her hands on her apron. 'Yes, Monsieur. What can I get for you?'

Almost robotically Frank replied, 'A coffee, please. And do you have anything sweet? A small cake maybe?'

'We have…'

'Francois, is that you?'

Frank turned his head to see the man without the hat had risen from his chair.

'Hello, Paul,' he replied. 'How are you?'

'I'm fine, I'm fine. Please, join us.'

Frank turned back to the waitress. 'On second thoughts, I'll just take the coffee, please.'

'Of course, Monsieur. I'll bring it over.'

Frank walked past the rail workers who were engaged in conversation, totally uninterested in the apparent chance meeting of these three friends. He sat down facing the two men, his back now to the counter.

'Hello, Paul. How have you been?'

'I'm well, my friend. It's so nice to bump into you like this…'

The contrived conversation went on a short while longer, all the time the man in the hat remaining silent. After the waitress had brought the coffee, Frank heard a sudden burst of laughter from the rail workers.

He lowered his voice. 'I take it our friend here knows no French.'

'That's correct, Francois.'

'Therefore am I to assume that the package referred to is, in fact, him?'

'Again you are correct. Is there somewhere we can go a little more private?'

'My apartment's safe,' he replied, pulling a pen from his pocket. He took the napkin from under his saucer and wrote the address on it. 'Meet me here in an hour. Once you've memorised the address, burn the napkin… oh, and you can pay for the coffee.'

Frank stood up and drained the last of the beverage before putting the cup down on the table.

'It was so nice to bump into you, Paul,' he said. 'We should get together again soon.'

They shook hands and Frank left.

This was all he needed right now, he thought, as he walked back to his apartment. The last thing he wanted was to babysit an RAF airman. But he also understood that this too was important work. The more experienced pilots they could help get back home the better. Not only did it boost Allied morale when a downed pilot made it safely to England, it also annoyed the Germans, which, in Frank's opinion, was not a bad thing.

An hour later, as if on cue, there was a light knock on the front door.

Frank opened it and ushered the two men inside, closing it quietly behind them.

'I take it you weren't followed?'

'Not that I could see,' replied Paul.

'Okay. Now please keep your voices down. These walls aren't the thickest.' Frank switched to English. 'Do you speak English, Paul?'

The Frenchman nodded.

'Now listen, the both of you. Keep your voices low, especially when we're talking in English. My neighbours tend to keep themselves to themselves but you never know who you can trust.'

Frank saw the airman's face light up as he heard his native tongue being spoken.

'Hi, I'm Flight Lieutenant James Pearson,' said the airman, holding out his hand. 'Pleased to meet you… Francois?…'

Frank shook his hand. 'Just Francois will do. And that's already too much information.'

'You know you speak remarkably good English for a Frenchman,' said Pearson in all sincerity. 'In fact you could probably pass for an Englishman.'

For the first time in a long while, Frank laughed.

'Maybe that's because I'm from Hampshire.'

'Oh, I feel such a fool,' replied Pearson, reddening.

'So what's your story?' asked Frank.

'Shot down over northern France a few weeks ago,' explained Pearson, sitting down on the sofa. 'Didn't even manage to get our payload off. Not sure what happened to the rest of the crew, they all baled out before me and I never saw them again. I landed in a field in the middle of nowhere and took shelter in a barn. Luckily for me the farmer found me the next morning and took pity on me. He and his wife gave me food and shelter and after a few days some guys took me away. I've been passed from pillar to post for the last few weeks, to be honest…'

'Well expect more of that before you get home,' interrupted Frank. 'You're still a long way from the Pyrenees. Then it'll take a good while to get you back from there.'

'I understand there's to be a supply drop next Tuesday,' said Paul, switching back to French.

'You're remarkably well informed.'

'In that drop there'll be papers and other things that'll help Pearson find it easier to get to Marseilles.'

'I'm not taking him to Marseilles,' interjected Frank. 'I've far too much to do here.'

'Can't you get one of your contacts to accompany him? He can make contact with our people in Marseilles who can get him the rest of the way to the hills.'

Frank was beginning to get irritated. 'In the meantime, what am I to do with him?'

'Put him up here. Hide him in a cupboard, if it makes life easier. Whatever you want.'

Frank ignored the sarcasm. 'Can't we arrange a Lysander pick up?'

'We've already asked,' explained Paul. 'Limited availability and too dangerous, they reckon… just for an RAF pilot, anyway.'

'Let me speak to them,' said Frank. 'There may be a way of speeding up the process.'

Pearson had been trying to follow the conversation but had no idea what they were saying. 'I hope I'm not being too much of a problem to you all.'

Frank realised they were being rude keeping him out of the discussion. 'Not at all, Pearson. Not at all. We're just discussing the best way to get you out of here and back to Blighty… Did anyone see you come into the building?'

'I don't think so,' replied Paul. 'Certainly nobody followed us.'

Frank moved to the window and pulled back the curtain slightly. 'If nobody saw you come in then nobody, apart from the three of us, know you're here. Would that be correct?'

'It would.'

Frank looked out into the street. It was still quite light but the sun was beginning to drop low in the sky. Apart from the usual traffic and a few people coming and going, he saw nothing to make him think anyone was watching the building.

'Okay, here's what's going to happen. Flight Lieutenant Pearson will remain here, in my apartment, until such time as we can move him on. When I'm not in the building he's not to make any noise. He's not to turn on taps, flush the toilet, or anything else that may alert anyone within this building that I've a lodger staying with me. I'll get on to F Section and see what I can do in regards to helping him get home.'

'In that case my job here is done,' replied Paul, relieved that his part in the process was now at an end. 'I'll head back, if it's all the same with you.'

Frank accompanied him to the door. He glanced along the hallway. When he was content that nobody was about, he turned to Paul.

'Okay, it's clear. Did you destroy the napkin?'

'Sorry, old fellow,' replied Paul, pulling it from his pocket. 'Quite forgot.'

Frank snatched it from his hand and shut the door behind him.

He went straight to the hearth. Taking a cigarette lighter from his pocket, he lit the napkin and threw it into the fireplace.

He was furious. It was little things like this that could cause big problems. Should Paul have been caught or compromised in any way, then having Frank's address in his pocket would take some explaining. It would undoubtedly cause the gendarmerie to come knocking at his door.

He went back to the window and looked out. He saw Paul cross the road and disappear out of view around a corner.

Although he had been feeling slightly isolated and somewhat alone recently, this had made him realise that, in fact, he preferred to work on his own.

He turned to look at the "package" his SOE colleague had just delivered to him. Paul's stupidity was not this guy's fault, he thought. He was just a pilot trying to get home.

'Fancy a brew?' he said.

Pearson smiled. 'I thought you'd never ask.'

Chapter Eleven

'There's somebody here to see you, Monsieur Piaget. I'm afraid he doesn't have an appointment but he is quite insistent. A Monsieur Aubuchon. He says you're expecting him, but I see nothing in the appointments book.'

Christian Piaget looked up from his desk. He had not managed to do anything constructive all day, knowing this meeting was to happen at some point. He was just glad the man had arrived early in the day. He could feel his heartbeat quickening, and sweat developing on his forehead and the back of his neck. He hoped his nervousness was not too noticeable.

His secretary frowned.

'Are you all right, Monsieur Piaget? You've gone quite pale.'

'I'm fine, Claudette, I'm fine. I'm just feeling a little light-headed, that's all. I fear it's the hot weather and lack of sleep.'

'Would you like me to send him away? Do you want me to get you a glass of water?'

'A glass of water would be nice, thank you.' He took a deep breath. 'Can you show the gentleman in, please. And can you see if he requires any refreshment.'

Claudette left the room and a few moments later, a young looking man walked in. He was of average height with dark hair slicked back with oil and a thin moustache above his top lip. He wore a blue pin-striped suit and carried a briefcase in his right hand. Although he looked young, the man had an air of authority and confidence about him that belied his years.

Piaget rose from the desk and put out his hand. 'Monsieur Aubuchon. Please, take a seat.'

Frank sat down facing Piaget. Once Claudette had brought in a glass of water and closed the door behind her, he spoke.

'Monsieur Piaget, I take it you know the reason why I'm here.'

‘I do, yes. I met with a couple of your colleagues the other night. They frightened me half to death, which was rather uncalled for, if you ask me.’

‘I make no apology for that. You need to appreciate the seriousness of the situation. Your company is currently producing materials that are assisting the Nazi war effort.’

‘Like I told your friends, I have no choice in the matter. As you well know.’

Frank smiled wryly. ‘We all have choices to make, Monsieur Piaget. And you have one to make right now. I trust you’ve given some thought to the matter.’

‘I don’t wish to argue with you, Aubuchon,’ said Piaget, wiping the sweat from his brow with a handkerchief, ‘but you’re wrong. I really don’t have a choice do I? If I say no then you threaten to flatten this whole place. That won’t only cause me financial ruin but will destroy the livelihoods of everyone who works here. If you do as you said you were going to do the other night… for I know it was you pointing that pistol at me, sir, I recognise your voice… then we may get away with saving something. All this puts so much pressure on me and my family. The gendarmerie will be convinced I had something to do with it. Especially if you only destroy those machines making parts for the Germans.’

‘There is a way around that,’ said Frank. ‘Believe me, we’re not unsympathetic to your plight, Monsieur. I can arrange an RAF plane to fly over the factory at the time the explosions occur. It will seem that they have bombed the place and not us. This should clear you of all suspicion. But it’s up to you whether they actually drop those bombs or not. If they do, as I have already said, they will raze your factory to the ground.’

‘Then, like I say, I really don't have a choice.’ Piaget put his head in hands. He was struggling to hold back tears. He did not want Aubuchon to see him in this weakened state. He did not want to give him the satisfaction.

He stood up.

‘Come with me, Aubuchon,’ he said. ‘I’ll give you a tour of the factory floor. I don’t want you to blow up the wrong machines. You’ll need to know which ones to target.’

'Sit down, Piaget,' said Frank, sternly. 'There's no need for that. You can draw me a plan of the shop floor and mark the machines concerned with an X. I will not walk around your shop floor for all your staff to see me.'

'But how can I be sure that you'll get the correct ones?' asked Piaget nervously.

'By making sure your plan is a good one. I see you've pen and paper on your desk. Off you go.'

With a sigh, Piaget proceeded to do what Frank had asked, all the time muttering and mumbling under his breath. Frank found the man's demeanour quite comical and had to suppress a smile as Piaget hastily scribbled away on the paper.

'You must be very careful where you place your explosives, Aubuchon. You can't damage the others. As I say, people's livelihoods depend on this work.'

'And people's lives depend on the defeat of the Nazis, Piaget,' responded Frank. 'Consider this your patriotic duty.'

Again Piaget muttered something under his breath.

'Here,' he said finally, thrusting the paper in front of him. 'Take it. Do what you will.'

Frank leaned over and took it from him. 'All I need now is a copy of your keys.'

'Fine,' snapped Piaget, opening up his desk draw. He took out a set of keys and slid them across the desk. 'These are a set of spares. The one with the blue tape on the end is for the side door. You're probably better using that one as it's not as well lit as other areas of the building and it's also closer to the machines in question.'

Frank picked up the keys. 'Thank you. In three nights' time you'll ensure that the building is empty of staff…'

'I can't do that,' interrupted Piaget. 'There's always a nightwatchman on duty throughout the night, when the final shift finishes at nine o'clock. If I tell him not to come then he'll know there's something going on.'

'No matter,' said Frank dismissively. 'We'll deal with him on the night.'

'What do you mean?'

'Don't worry, he'll come to no harm,' said Frank. 'After all, we're not here to harm patriotic Frenchmen.'

He stood up. 'Thank you for your time and assistance, Monsieur Piaget. It will not go unnoticed. Feel content that what you do, you do for France.'

'Forgive me if I don't stand up and shake your hand, Aubuchon. You can see yourself out.'

Frank turned to go and then stopped.

'Let me remind you, Piaget, that should any harm come to me as a result of you opening your mouth to the gendarmerie, then my colleagues are under instruction to… how can I put this… settle the matter. Am I clear?'

'Yes, you have been quite clear.'

'Good. In that case, I bid you good day.'

Frank left the room without looking back. As he closed the door he could hear Piaget muttering under his breath again and nearly laughed out loud. As he walked past Claudette he noticed she gave him a strange, quizzical look. He smiled and nodded to her in farewell.

Once outside he took out his cigarettes and placed one in his mouth. Taking out a lighter, he lit it and inhaled the smoke, taking it deep down into his lungs before exhaling, blowing it out into the clear morning air. He took the plan that Piaget had drawn from his pocket and stared at it for ten seconds before putting the flame of the lighter to its corner. He let it burn in his hand until the flame was close to touching his skin before dropping it to the ground. He watched until the paper was nothing but ash and then put his foot on it, to make sure it was completely destroyed.

As he was about to set off out of the grounds, he had a feeling he was being watched. When he looked back to the building he noticed Piaget observing him from his office window. He considered raising his hand in farewell but decided better of it. The man had not been too pleased with the situation Frank had put him in. He saw no further reason to antagonise the man. Instead, he merely adjusted the hat on his head, put his hand in his trouser pocket and walked away.

***

Although the sun was low in the sky it was still as bright as midday when Frank stepped into Claude Benoit's vehicle repair shop. The shutter doors were wide open and he could see a pair of grubby boots poking out from beneath a dark Citroen that was raised on wooden chocks. He could not make out who was working on the car but presumed it to be Pierre, as Michel was standing near a dirty workbench drinking from a chipped enamel mug. When he saw Frank he put down the mug and called over to his cousin.

'Pierre, we have a visitor.'

Frank raised his hand. 'As you were.' He could not get out of the habit of speaking to them as though he was their military commander. If it annoyed them, they never let it show.

'Is Claude in the office?'

Michel nodded.

Frank walked past him and headed up the metal steps. He enjoyed visiting this group. They had been the first circuit he had formed and their enthusiasm for what they did was infectious. Like some parents who secretly favour their firstborn, he felt a paternal responsibility and affection for Benoit's band of resistants, a feeling he did not share so much with the other groups he had nurtured.

He found Claude Benoit sitting behind a very untidy desk smoking a thin cheroot and pouring cognac into a grubby looking glass. Benoit was a chain smoker and the air was thick with foul smelling fumes. Frank would need to wash his clothes when he got back to his apartment later, otherwise the smell would linger in his nostrils for days.

'You really need to stop smoking those godawful things, Claude. One day they'll kill you.'

'Come on, Francois. You know they're my only vice.'

Frank looked to the bottle of cognac in Benoit's hand. His gaze did not go unnoticed and Benoit laughed loudly.

'I don't consider this a vice, my friend. This is a necessity. Would you like a glass?'

'Not for me, Claude. A little too early just yet.'

Benoit shrugged and placed the bottle in the drawer. 'So what drags you all the way out here? Have you a job for us?'

Frank sat down on an old, stained chair facing him. Padding poked through tears in the seat. The whole place was a tip. In Frank's opinion all the fittings needed replacing and the current furniture throwing onto a bonfire. Paperwork and vehicle keys littered the desk, spilling onto the floor, and filthy cups and plates that hadn't been washed for days littered the room. Benoit seemed completely indifferent to the whole mess.

'Not just yet. Although I may need your assistance next week on a couple of matters.'

'As you know, you can rely on us.'

'I certainly can, my friend. Have you seen Catherine recently?'

'Not since our little trip to the Vercors,' replied Benoit with a frown. 'She's not in any kind of trouble is she?'

'Not that I'm aware of. Is she still seeing that Jewish fellow?'

'I think he's the reason why we're seeing less of her than we used to,' he smiled. 'I think she may be in love with the man, truth be told. You sure I can't offer you a drink?'

'Quite sure. It's just that I've come across some information that she may wish to know. It directly affects her beau. It seems the gendarmerie has been instructed to round up all Jews. It looks like the Germans want to ship them out to work camps in Germany and other places.'

'Surely that can't be right,' replied Benoit. He drained his glass and then opened the desk drawer, took out the bottle and refilled his glass. 'How reliable is your source?'

'As reliable as you are, my friend. I trust his word one hundred percent. His information has never been wrong before. Let's face it, we're all aware of their treatment of the Jews elsewhere, so it's hardly unexpected that they'd get to the Jews of France at some point.'

'Come on, Francois. I know Vichy is filled with bastards, but I can't see Petain agreeing to this. Or even Laval come to that.'

'From what I understand it's very much a done deal, unfortunately. It appears the hero of Verdun may not be such a hero of France after all.'

Benoit sipped from the glass. 'It saddens me, Francois, that it's come to this. This makes it even more important that our work carries on and increases in tempo. We need to defeat these thugs. There's no place in a civilised world for a regime such as theirs.'

'I agree, Claude,' replied Frank. 'But we've got to bide our time and be thoughtful in how we respond. We need to ensure we never carry out any impulsive actions that may jeopardise our ability to operate. Or compromise us in any way. We must never let our hearts rule our heads.'

'That's easy for you to say. It's not your country that's affected.'

'Come, come, Benoit. Let's not get into a discussion about whose country has suffered the most. It's times like these that allies should stick together more than ever. With the Americans and Russians now in the war, the Germans can't carry on forever. It's only a matter of time before they're defeated.'

'But in the meantime we suffer,' said Benoit.

'Listen,' said Frank. 'I have to go. Can you pass on the information to Catherine at your earliest opportunity? It may be that she can persuade her friend to avoid any such round-up. It may also be beneficial if you can warn anyone else you may know that has influence in such matters.'

'I'll see what I can do,' replied Benoit sadly.

Frank rose from the chair. 'Thank you, Claude. I'll be in touch soon in regards to your assistance in the other matters I referred to. For the time being it's best you don't know what they are. Until then…'

Frank left the office and walked down the stairs. Pierre was now standing with Michel, holding an equally damaged and dirty looking mug of steaming liquid. He raised it as Frank passed. Frank nodded in acknowledgement then left the building.

As he walked the streets back to his apartment, where he hoped Pearson had been keeping himself quiet as he'd instructed, he wondered just why he had felt compelled to pass on Vallin's information about the upcoming round-up of Jews, to Catherine. There was something about her boyfriend's name he recognised; almost like déjà vu in a way. He knew he had heard the name before and what was more, if his memory was right, he also knew exactly where and when.

It was such a long time ago now, and in another part of the country. Almost like another world, another life. Surely the coincidence was too much. After all, there must be hundreds of Jean-Luc Descartes' in France. The man Catherine had attached herself to was surely a different person. He had to be. But then Frank prided himself on his impeccable memory. He never forgot a thing. If that memory was as sharp as usual right now, he knew that the Jean-Luc Descartes he had come across as a child in St Malo all those years ago, had been there on a visit from his home of Lyon. So although improbable, it was not impossible that it could be the same person.

And then another memory hit him. He remembered it as though it was only yesterday. A trip on a boat into a secluded cove, the water getting too choppy for the five young boys to handle. The German boy, Otto Finkel, that very same person he now knew to be an SS officer, a murderer of British prisoners of war, falling and ripping his face against the metal oar housing and going overboard into the sea. He remembered how his brother, Jack, had not hesitated and gone in after him.

And then another Claude came to his memory. The janitor from the hotel. How he had lost his life attempting to rescue them.

He shuddered at the memory and carried on walking, trying to erase it from his mind.

Chapter Twelve

The keys Piaget provided worked without problem. Cautiously, Frank opened the door to the factory. The lights had been left on, despite the workforce having left the building almost two hours earlier. Slowly and carefully, the three of them, all wearing black clothing and ski masks and carrying a satchel full of plastic explosives, slipped into the factory, closing the door quietly behind them. They had prepared the bombs beforehand. All that was needed was to attach the timers. Frank did not anticipate being in the building for very long.

In his right hand he firmly held his Colt .38. He had no intention of using it on the nightwatchman, merely carrying it to intimidate him should the man discover them.

They moved quickly, expertly placing the charges where they would do most damage. Frank had briefed his accomplices beforehand, using Piaget's plan, the details of which were stored in his head. Although he had promised the factory owner that he would leave alone those machines not involved in Nazi war production, he attached charges to three more units nevertheless. After all, he thought, this way it protected Piaget to a degree, whether he liked it or not. Not even the RAF could bomb with such precision as to take out specific targets within a building. It was for the man's own good.

Quickly and silently they moved, each of them knowing their jobs. He placed a pack onto one of the machines and attached the timing pencil. He was aware of his colleagues doing the same on nearby apparatus. He had trained them well, each of them expert in carrying out this type of operation. They worked efficiently. If they had any apprehensions they did not show it.

He himself did not suffer from nerves too badly. He often got butterflies in the lead up to an operation, like an actor about to go on stage, or a boxer entering a ring for a bout. But when the action started, all this evaporated and the adrenalin took over. He was able to remain sharp, focused and alert. So far, all the missions he had taken part in had gone to plan.

As he crouched at the base of the last machine he felt a tap on his shoulder. He turned to see Lucien looking down at him. He pointed to the door, indicating he had completed his part of the mission and was leaving the building.

Frank nodded and pushed the timing pencil into the plastic explosives he had taped to the metal structure. Quickly he snapped the tip and placed the roll of tape back into his knapsack. He stood up and followed Lucien and David from the building, closing the door behind him. He was about to lock it but decided not to bother. After all, it was about to be blown from its hinges anyway.

Five minutes later the three of them were sitting in David's car on the roadway three hundred yards from the factory.

'How long until the RAF plane comes over,' asked Lucien from the rear seat.

Frank, sitting in the passenger seat in the front, looked at his watch. In the dim light he struggled to see the time and had to move his wrist until there was just enough light to see. 'It would be due in fifteen minutes… that's if I'd requested it.'

Lucien frowned. 'What do you mean?'

Frank laughed. 'It would have taken some great timing wouldn't it? I suppose it's possible, but let's face it, what does it really matter? Piaget is hardly going to admit to being involved. It might make him think again before he agrees to do work for the Nazis. I'm not really concerned about how it looks, if I'm being perfectly honest.'

Lucien did not reply.

Frank's thoughts towards those who collaborated with the Germans were becoming more unfavourable by the day. This was war, and people had to stand up for what was right. In his opinion, those who assisted the enemy deserved every bad thing that came their way. Piaget had been more concerned about personal survival and that of his company and the profits he made, than doing the right thing for France. He had claimed he had no choice when the reality was that everybody had choices. The Germans were still nowhere near Lyon. What could they do to him? The only people Piaget had to fear were the collaborators in Vichy, and Frank was sure that the man could have come up with some kind of excuse to avoid having to produce the parts he had been tasked to make. Frank was convinced Piaget had done it purely for profit and for no other reason than that.

It was on those grounds that Frank had decided against putting in a request for the RAF to fly over. He wanted this to be a message not only to Piaget, but to every other factory owner in the area. Should they agree to assist the German war effort against France's allies, then they were likely to suffer the same retribution from those who had the courage to stand up to them.

'What about the nightwatchman?' asked David.

Frank had thought to leave the man to his fate, maybe as a warning to Piaget and others. Being the cause of the death of an innocent Frenchman would not sit right with all the circuits he was involved with. Although a certain amount of collateral damage was somehow justifiable in the whole scheme of things, they were not here to let an innocent man be killed just for doing his job.

'Leave him to me,' said Frank. He opened the car door and stepped out. Pulling the Colt from his pocket he stealthily moved to the front of the building. Once there he banged as loudly as he could on the door with the butt of the weapon. He pulled the ski mask over his face and waited. He could see a shadow inside the offices and a few moments later the door opened.

Standing before him was a middle aged man of average height with curly grey hair. He was wearing a blue boiler suit and carried a clipboard.

Frank brought up the gun and pointed it inches from his face.

'I suggest you go home. Right now,' he said calmly. 'And speak of this to no-one. We know where you live.'

The man dropped the clipboard to the floor. He opened his mouth but no reply came out.

'I wouldn't waste any time, if I were you,' continued Frank. 'Trust me, it's in your best interests to make yourself very scarce right now.'

He lowered the gun and stepped back. Then he turned and swiftly moved away, running back to the car. Once back inside the Fiat, David gunned the engine and they drove away. As they passed through the entry gate, Frank observed the nightwatchman hurriedly climbing onto a bicycle, desperate to get away from the factory as fast as he possibly could.

Lucien spoke. 'Dear God. What did you say to him?'

Frank pulled up the ski mask and grinned. 'Nothing much. A little friendly persuasion, that's all.'

'Well you must be one hell of a persuasive person.'

'You have no idea,' Frank muttered in English.

They did not wait to watch the explosions but heard them clearly as the car travelled back towards Lyon. Frank could see the flash of light in the wing mirror and smiled to himself. He loved this. He found he actually enjoyed the thrill of it. From the preparation to the successful execution of the plan. He even enjoyed the danger and the power he felt when he pulled out the gun and pointed it into the nightwatchman's face. He knew the man was innocent in all of this but felt no sympathy for him at all. He also felt none for Piaget and the fact that they'd just caused considerable damage to his property.

Was it Piaget's fault he was being made to aid the German war effort? Maybe not, but Frank knew there were many people in the country who were resisting in their own way, no matter how small or ineffective some of those actions were. He had seen the graffiti scrawled on buildings and monuments. The anti-Pétain and pro-de Gaulle comments. The "V for Victory" signs. The anti-German slogans and comic Hitler drawings. Although these things were only minor in comparison to blowing up factories and disrupting communications and rail networks, they still showed that France had some fight left. On the other hand, people like Piaget, and, by association, his employees, were doing nothing.

This lack of empathy slightly unnerved him. Frank was acutely aware at what this job was doing to him. Daily he made decisions that affected many people's lives and felt nothing when he made them. He knew the war had to be won. Whatever he had to do to achieve that victory, he was prepared to do. He had lost his brother in the conflict and had seen combat up close in North Africa. His hatred for the Nazis was greater now than it had ever been. Whenever he felt any lapse in this hatred, he would think about Jack and of the soldiers his brother had witnessed being murdered by the SS back in May 1940, and the intensity of his loathing would return once more.

'That seemed to go well,' said Lucien, who had watched the explosion through the rear window.

'It did,' replied Frank. He took a pack of cigarettes from his pocket and put one into his mouth. He slouched deeper into the seat and closed his eyes for a moment, letting the smoke swirl in his lungs before blowing it out. Smoking relaxed him.

Once finished, he threw the stub from the car window and drifted off to sleep.

***

Frank was exhausted and slept long into the next day, waking in the early afternoon. He got out of bed and walked into the living room. Pearson was lying on the sofa. Hearing the movement the airman sat up and rubbed his eyes.

'Everything okay?' asked Frank.

'A bit bored, to tell the truth,' yawned Pearson. 'Any word on when I'll be moving on?'

'All in good time.' Frank sat down in the chair opposite him. 'Be patient. I'm sure it won't be too long now.'

'Oh, okay... this was slid under the door earlier.'

Pearson handed a small brown envelope to him. There was nothing written on it but when Frank opened it up, he found a short note inside.

'How long ago was this?'

'About an hour. Anything important?'

Frank stood up and took his coat from the chair. 'I need to go out. I shouldn't be more than a couple of hours.'

He left the apartment, stuffing the note into his pocket. It was from Claude Benoit, asking him to come to the garage as soon as he could. Something had come up in regards to Catherine's boyfriend, Jean-Luc Descartes. The gendarmerie had come for him that morning but he had given them the slip and was now seeking help from Benoit and his small group.

Frank was curious to see if the man was his childhood acquaintance as he suspected, but was also worried it may be someone trying to infiltrate the circuit. It was very important the man was assessed properly. From what he remembered of Descartes as a child, he had been very quiet and somewhat aloof. Frank had found it very difficult to converse with him, irrespective of the language barrier at the time. He would be very interested in what the man was like, as compared to the boy. If, indeed, it was him.

When he arrived, he found Benoit waiting for him in his office. Frank sat down in the chair opposite.

'What's happened?'

'From what Catherine tells me, two gendarmes went to pick him up this morning,' replied Benoit, taking the bottle of cognac from his desk drawer along with two small glasses. He poured two shots and handed one to Frank who took a sip and placed the glass on the desk.

Benoit drank the cognac in one gulp and poured himself another, before putting the bottle back into the drawer and closing it. 'Anyway, it's like you said would happen. They came for him because he was Jewish. The bastards are rounding them up.'

'How did he get away?'

'He managed to persuade them to go away and check their records. Apparently he never registered himself as he was supposed to.'

'A wise move.'

'Undoubtedly, my friend. One of them was an old schoolfriend of his and they both managed to persuade the sergeant to go back to the station. Once they'd left, he made a run for it. He's at Catherine's sister's shop right now. She owns a clothing store in the centre of Lyon. Michel and Pierre have gone to pick him up. They're going to bring him back here.'

Frank was uneasy. 'The sooner they do the better. The police will know where to go looking if they know about his relationship with Catherine. We could do without this. Catherine's sister, can she be trusted?'

'I hope so. I'm not sure if she's even aware of Catherine's activities. But then she's kept him hidden there all afternoon without alerting the gendarmes.'

'What do you know of Descartes?'

'Catherine speaks very highly of him, Francois. He's a writer apparently. He's had some success with a couple of children's books. She thinks he should be recruited.'

'Does she now?' replied Frank thoughtfully. 'And who else can vouch for him? No, my friend, we should play this one very carefully. He could be a spy for all we know. Let's just speak to him and see how things work out. I'll observe. But I don't want him to see me.'

'As you wish.'

Frank felt it unnecessary to let Benoit know he may actually know Descartes. There was no real point to it. Even if it was the boy he had known in St Malo all those years ago, it was so far in the past that he would not be the same person now. He understood that time and events had changed his own personality since then, as it undoubtedly had changed that of the German, Otto Finkel. Finkel had been such a nice boy back then. But now he was a murdering Nazi SS officer. It seemed to Frank that war, and growing up, changed everyone, both for good and for bad.

***

Frank waited in the shadows as Pierre and Michel led Jean-Luc Descartes up the steps to where Claude Benoit waited in the office.

As he had suspected, the man was clearly the same Descartes he had known briefly when on holiday in Brittany in 1928. Although the boy was now a man, there was no mistaking him. He still wore his hair longer than most other men and his eyes had the same intensity. Despite the danger he was in, he somehow appeared indifferent to the events taking place around him. Frank was again taken back to the boat on the cove, when a young Descartes had sat alone, daring the others to get in beside him, but at the same time looking not to care one way or the other whether or not they took up that challenge.

Once they were inside the office he quietly moved up the steps and into the room, Pierre having left the door open for him. Descartes was sitting in the same chair Frank had vacated minutes ago, with his back to the door and facing Claude Benoit. He did not turn around, not having heard Frank enter. Pierre and Michel stood either side of him. Pierre nodded to Frank as he noticed him. Frank put his finger to his lips and Pierre nodded again, acknowledging his wish for Descartes to be unaware of his presence.

Benoit spoke. 'So tell me everything that happened to you. The whole story.'

Descartes looked at the people to his side and made a move to turn his head, somehow sensing the presence of another in the room.

'Face me, Descartes. Do not look around. Concentrate on me. Nothing else is of your concern.'

Descartes checked himself and turned back to face Benoit. It was clear to Frank that the man was agitated. It seemed he did not like being told what to do.

'The whole story,' continued Benoit. 'From beginning to end. Leave nothing out.'

Descartes adjusted himself in the chair. 'They came for me this morning. The police.'

'Why?'

'They say I'm Jewish.'

Benoit stared at him quizzically. 'Are you?'

'It's not important to me,' replied Descartes.

'It is to them. Are you?' repeated Benoit.

'Half. My mother was Jewish, my father Christian.'

'To them, that's Jewish. And you know it. Why did they not take you?'

As Frank watched the exchange he was confused at Descartes' attitude. He seemed antagonistic when he really should be trying to endear himself to them. Without their help, Descartes would be in very serious trouble. He had turned to them for assistance yet he seemed reluctant to accept it now the chance of it was being offered. He had been an enigma as a child and he was as much, if not more so, now he was an adult. He had an aura about him that Frank could not fathom.

'I knew one of the gendarmes,' explained Descartes. 'I was at school with him. He helped me to persuade the other one, Rodier he was called, to check their records again and that I would wait.'

'Yet he knew you to be Jewish. This friend of yours knew you were lying, yet he assisted you?'

'He did,' replied Descartes.

'His name?'

'Henri Cheyrou. I wasn't that friendly with him at school. In fact I had few male friends at school.'

Frank was not surprised at this confession. Descartes was an odd character and he genuinely wondered what Catherine saw in him. But then he was very good looking, in a bohemian kind of way. Clearly some women went for men like him.

As Benoit wrote something down on a scrap of paper, Descartes moved his head again, clearly aware of Frank's presence in the room and wanting to see who was observing him.

Benoit spoke again, forcing Descartes to face him once more. 'How do we know you're not a spy?'

'Excuse me?'

'How do we know you're not a spy?' repeated Benoit. 'It is a simple question.'

Descartes was clearly affronted. 'I suppose you'll have to take my word for it. I'm not sure I care for the inference.'

'I'll need more than your word,' said Benoit. It was clear to Frank that Benoit was testing the man. There was not a lot more Descartes could give to prove he was genuine. Was he looking for a reaction?

'What can I say to you?' said Descartes, exasperated. 'I don't know what to say. If you cannot or will not help me then let me walk out of here and I'll work my situation out for myself.'

'There's a warrant out for your arrest, Descartes,' said Benoit calmly. 'If what you say is true then you'll be picked up by the morning and on a train to Drancy before you know it.'

Descartes let out a sigh. 'So are you going to help me? All this cloak and dagger bullshit. Is it really necessary?'

Frank decided to speak. After all, Descartes knew he was in the room anyway.

'It is necessary, yes. Just answer the questions.'

Once more, Descartes went to move his head, to see who was speaking to him.

'Face forward,' ordered Frank. 'Do not turn around.'

Descartes sighed again. Frank realised that it was dawning on the man that his only way out of his predicament was to humour them and to answer the questions, without getting annoyed. They were his only hope of survival.

'Listen,' he said calmly. 'I just need your help. My friend Catherine, whom I know to be one of you, part of your little gang, has told me you can help me. Believe me, I'm on your side. I believe in what you do. But all I am is a simple writer of children's fiction, minding my own business in life. Just plodding through it. Do you think that I need all this? My life has been turned upside down in the space of a few hours and I'm really annoyed about it. Truly I am. If you don't want to believe me then that's up to you and fine by me. Just get me out of here. But if you can help me… and want to help me… then please cut out all this nonsense and let me know what you can do for me.'

Benoit looked into Descartes eyes and, after a short pause, spoke again.

'Descartes. Our mutual friend, Catherine, speaks very highly of you. I can't see it myself, but she does. We have to be certain you are what you say you are before we're willing to help you. Your name is on no Jewish register. But I suppose it's clear why not.'

Benoit looked over to Frank. It was evident he was looking for some sort of direction on where to go next. Whether they were to provide this man with the assistance he needed or to leave him to his fate. Frank could not be sure whether offering Descartes help was a good idea or not, but something told him he could not abandon the man. There was a bond between them that had been forged on that cove all those years ago that he felt he could not ignore. And so, with a certain amount of reluctance, he nodded his head at Benoit, giving his approval to assist the man in whatever way they could.

Having seen and heard enough, Frank opened the door and left the office. Descartes was really Benoit's problem. He would help out where he could, but essentially Benoit would have to sort out what to do with him. After all, he had his own lodger to worry about.

He needed to organise moving Pearson on. Having him in the apartment was starting to make him feel uneasy. He just wanted to be rid of the man. The sooner he was gone the better.

Turning up the collar of his greatcoat and pulling his cap down low over his forehead, he set off on the long walk back to the apartment in Montchat.

Chapter Thirteen

The train had arrived on time. Through the carriage window Frank observed people on the opposite platform waiting patiently for their trains. It seemed odd that here in the unoccupied zone, life seemed to continue as normal, as though the war was not actually taking place. It did not seem to affect them on a day to day basis.

People could still go about relatively freely. They did not go hungry and they did not have the indignity of seeing German troops walking their streets as their countrymen had to endure in the north.

Crossing into the occupied zone, should anyone wish to do so, was not easy. Some people with relatives there had not seen them for many months, unable to get the required passes to cross through the checkpoints. If visiting the occupied zone could be avoided then it was best for people to do just that.

There was an underlying feeling of inevitability in regards to the current state of affairs. The Germans would not stay away too long, of that most were convinced. The threat of an invasion from the Mediterranean would be enough for German troops to be sent south. Currently, as long as the Vichy regime collaborated with the Nazis, then they could have those troops in areas of operations where they were needed most in other theatres of war.

Frank saw the irony of the situation. Whereas the Resistance could operate relatively freely in the unoccupied zone in the absence of the Germans, that would change significantly should they send their armies south. But then taking Germans away from where they were required was ultimately what they needed to achieve if they were to shorten the war.

Across from him, pretending to read a French newspaper, sat Pearson. Frank had told him not to open his mouth, speak to no-one and remain as anonymous as possible. If anyone was to address him then he was to leave any response to Frank. Once on the train, he had advised the young RAF officer to sleep, or pretend to, and he would wake him once they got to Montpelier which was a three hour journey away. Frank was slightly affronted he was not doing as he had instructed.

Sensing Frank staring at him, Pearson folded the newspaper and placed it to his side. He rested his head against the window and closed his eyes.

Frank had received instructions to take him to a café just off the Place de Strasbourg not too far from the train station, where they would be met by someone who would take the airman off his hands. They were to sit at a window table and ask for the wine menu. The contact would make himself known from there. It was all rather simple and Frank was happy with that. Frank liked simple. It made errors less likely.

As the train trundled through the southern French countryside, Frank was able to reflect on the past couple of years. He had joined SOE as something of an adventure. He wanted to contribute to the war in a way where his efforts would have more of an effect than had he stayed in the Royal Artillery. Although he understood and respected the contribution made by his comrades in the regular forces, he wanted to do something more unique, something that would have a direct impact in how the war was won. "Double H" Harding had provided him with that opportunity, and despite the somewhat underhand way in which he had been recruited, he realised he had a lot to thank the eccentric colonel for. He was made for this role.

He looked across at the airman and saw he was now asleep. Whether he was pretending or not, he did not care. The slow chug of the train was having somewhat of a soporific effect on him also, and so he pulled his cap low over his eyes and decided he would try and get some sleep too. He was happy in how relaxed he felt in his role, how comfortable he was in travelling freely. His French was fluent and nobody was yet to query his accent. In fact, he felt more French than he did British at times.

He did not know how long he had been sleeping when he was suddenly awoken by a raised voice. To his horror he saw that it was a ticket inspector and he was talking to Pearson, who sat looking at him blankly with a very red face.

‘Your ticket, Monsieur,’ said the inspector sternly. ‘Please, show me your ticket.’

‘Ah, Monsieur,’ interrupted Frank. ‘Please. You must speak slowly. My cousin is stone deaf. You’ll need to speak slowly otherwise he can’t read your lips.’

The ticket inspector turned to Frank, who held out two tickets to him.

‘Apologies,’ said the inspector, instantly calmed. ‘I thought he was some kind of idiot. I’ve been talking to him for a couple of minutes.’

‘He’s no fool,’ replied Frank, feigning indignation. ‘He’s a very intelligent person. He’s just deaf, as I told you. That doesn’t make him stupid. It just makes him unable to hear or understand you, that’s all.’

‘I’m sorry,’ apologised the inspector. He punched holes in the tickets and handed them back. ‘I meant no offence.’

Frank took the tickets and placed them back into his pocket. He turned his head away, dismissing the inspector who then moved on to nearby passengers. He glared at Pearson who turned his head away in embarrassment. They had just come very close to being compromised. Although he felt annoyed at the airman, he knew it was his own fault. He should never have fallen asleep. He needed to be vigilant at all times, no matter how tired he was. The Benzedrine tablets he used to take had run out, and he had not asked for more from London. He did not believe they were good for him. When he had taken the last one, he decided he would not take any more. Maybe now he would re-think this decision. He could not let things slip again.

They arrived at Montpelier with no further incident and left the train. As they walked towards the exit, Pearson whispered to him. ‘I’m really sorry about that… the ticket inspector…’

‘Don’t worry about it,’ cut in Frank. ‘And please, not another word. We can’t allow ourselves to be overheard speaking English. We’re not in the clear just yet. Remain silent.’

Frank glanced to his side and saw Pearson had bowed his head sheepishly. He felt a little sorry for snapping at the man. After all, it was Frank’s own fault for falling sleeping and dropping his guard. He really needed to be more careful in future.

But then he had not asked for this "package". If anything, the man had got in his way. He knew he would only feel happy once Pearson was off his hands.

Frank was grateful that the walk to the café was short, as the mid morning heat was very uncomfortable. The venue for the handover had been chosen well. The café was nondescript, one of many such small businesses in the area. Once inside, they sat at a table by the window as they had been directed. It was fairly quiet, a little too early for the lunch-time trade with only three more customers in the building. Two of whom, an old man and woman, sat at a table close by, sipping at coffee cups and barely speaking to each other. Another man sat in the opposite corner, smoking a pipe whilst reading a newspaper, a cup of coffee on the table in front of him.

A young waitress approached and asked what they wanted.

Frank ordered a couple of sandwiches and asked if she had a wine list. She walked away to get it.

The man in the corner lowered his newspaper and approached them, sitting down on a chair to the side.

'You have a package for me?' he said quietly. Frank knew instantly that the man was English.

'He speaks no French. Keep him quiet and good luck.'

He did not want to wait around exchanging pleasantries. Once the introductions had been made he stood up and left the café, leaving the two men together at the table. Frank had decided he did not want to be there any longer than was absolutely necessary. As he exited onto the street he did not look back. As far as he was concerned, his part in Pearson's escape was over. He was now someone else's problem.

He took a handkerchief from the inside pocket of his jacket and wiped the sweat from his brow. The summer heat was really quiet oppressive. Although it had been very hot in Lyon recently, the closer to the Mediterranean he was, the more uncomfortable the heat became. Sometimes he longed for the inclement weather that was so common back in England and felt a sudden bout of homesickness.

Had he been in theatre too long? Did he need a break? He knew the answers to both those questions was a clear no. He simply enjoyed it too much. So, was he becoming addicted to the danger of it all? That was the question that worried him more than any other. He could not let that happen. If he got too accustomed to it, too reliant on it to fulfil his needs, then he was more liable to make mistakes. He needed to remain sharp and vigilant at all times. He could not get too comfortable.

He decided that as soon as he returned to Montchat, he would pay up the rest of his rent and find another apartment, somewhere on the opposite side of the city. He needed to make a few changes and that would be the first.

He took off his jacket, folded it over his arm and walked the short distance back to the train station for the return journey back to Lyon.

Part Three

1943

Chapter Fourteen

April 1943

Twenty-one year old Arnold Jeunier looked across the kitchen table at his mother and smiled.

Putting her knitting needles to one side, she held up the light blue pullover she had been working on. 'Here, Arnie. What do you think?'

'Very nice, Maman,' he replied, taking a sip of water from a glass he held in his right hand. 'It's just what I need.'

'I'll start one for Charles now I've finished this,' she said. 'What do you think, Emil?'

Arnold's father, reading a newspaper in an easy chair by the fire, merely grunted in response. The clothing of his son and nephew was of no interest to him whatsoever.

For some reason Arnold could not understand, his father had not taken to his nephew. The circumstances of him being shipped to Lyon from Paris over six months ago, with a young girl to whom there was absolutely no family connection, was still a mystery to them all. They had both been involved in some kind of trouble. Charles's mother had wanted them away from the danger they had found themselves caught up in. His uncle, Michel Mercier, a gendarme in the capital, had managed to acquire the relevant train tickets and documentation for them both to take the seven hour journey from Paris to Lyon.

As far as Arnold was concerned, the two of them had provided a welcome distraction from life on the farm, which he was finding more and more mundane and tedious the older he got. Both of the unexpected lodgers had been very well behaved, clearly appreciating the sanctuary the Jeunier household had provided.

Charles had developed an attachment to his older cousin, but Arnold did not mind. He found the boy good company. Charlotte on the other hand was extremely quiet and had a sadness about her that no matter how hard he tried to entertain her, he could not cheer her up. It was obvious to them all that she had gone through a recent trauma and been saved from a terrible fate by her friend, Charles. Arnold liked them both a lot.

His father, Emil, had remained as standoffish with Charles as he had been when he first arrived all that time ago. If it was because he didn't want them there, or thought the danger they brought had been transferred to his doorstep by their relatives in Paris, then he didn't say. After all, Emil had fought at Verdun, winning a medal for gallantry. He hated the Germans with a passion. He had taken in the youngsters out of a respect for their bravery, but that didn't mean he had to be happy about the situation.

The farm provided a safe haven for the two teenagers. It was far enough away from prying eyes for them not to be overly concerned about arousing suspicion. As long as they kept themselves discreet, then the chances of discovery were quite minimal.

It was clear to Arnold and his parents that Charlotte was Jewish. They knew what the consequences would be should they be found hiding her on the farm. As Charlotte was from Paris and not connected to the family in any way, the Jeunier smallholding, two hundred and forty miles from the capital, should be the last place the Gestapo would think of looking for her, if they were even aware of her existence. The two children had been told to keep themselves out of sight of the roadway, which passed the property over a small ridge half a kilometre from the farmhouse.

Times had changed significantly in the last few months. The Nazis had finally entered the unoccupied zone the previous November, only a couple of weeks after Charles and Charlotte had arrived. They had soon established themselves in most major towns and cities. They commanded the region with an iron fist, and it seemed that the worst of them was Klaus Barbie, who was in charge of the Lyon sector. His infamy was growing by the day. The Nazi seemed to be on a personal mission to rid the area of all forms of Resistance, his methods being nothing short of brutal. The newly formed Milice; French fascists who openly collaborated with their German masters, assisted him in rounding up any Jews or suspected Resistance members. Arnold's hatred for them was stronger than that for the German invader.

Arnold was aware that Charles helping a young Jewish girl in Paris was not the only thing his cousin was fleeing. According to what Charles's mother, Celeste, had told them, he had been involved in other things prior to this that had given his family reason to worry. When Arnold had asked the boy what he had done to cause his family such anxiety, Charles had merely stated, "stuff". The young boy had then become emotional, and so Arnold hadn't questioned him further.

Arnold knew it must have been something very serious for him having to flee to Lyon. He felt a little envious that his young cousin had done something practical against the Germans whereas he, as yet, had done nothing. He was aware of Resistance activity in the Lyon area and wanted to get involved somehow, but he knew how dangerous that could be. He in no way wanted to place his family in any danger and, due to his commitments on the farm, he could not devote his time to much else.

But then his days on the farm could be numbered anyway, and through no choice of his own. Ever since the autumn, when Petain had signed the "*Law of 4 September 1942 on the use and guidance of the workforce*", Arnold had known that being forced to move away from the farm may become a reality for him. This law acceded to the German demand to make all able-bodied men, between the ages of eighteen and fifty, be available to work wherever the authorities saw fit, including moving to factories in Germany. This agreement between the Nazis and the Vichy collaborators, although initially on a voluntary basis, had led to the movement of thousands of French workers to Germany, to free up their own people to join the German armed forces. In return, for every three French workers agreeing to go to work in German factories, the enemy had agreed to release one French prisoner of war. Whether this part of the bargain had been upheld by the Nazis, Arnold did not know, but in his eyes this was the same as actually fighting for Germany against the Allies, something he had vowed he would never do.

With the Germans having to fight on many fronts and ensuring that the lands they had invaded had enough manpower to administer their occupation, the requirement for more foreign workers to relieve their own citizens had led to yet another order, signed by Paval at Vichy. The STO order, or "*Service du Travail Obligatoire*", agreed just two months previously, made it compulsory for men aged between the ages of twenty-two and twenty four to go to work in Germany.

In effect, this gave those it affected three choices: they could either go to Germany as demanded, disappear, or join the Resistance. Many men would not adhere to the order and had vanished before the Germans and gendarmes could collect them. Arnold had heard that a lot had gone to the hills to the south of Lyon, the Vercors Massif, and others to the Vosges mountains further north. There they had formed bands of 'maquisards', groups of young men who were arming themselves and forming bands of active Resistance, under the command of ex-French army officers. His twenty-second birthday was due in a few days time and he was fully expecting to be made to comply with the STO order. He was already preparing himself to join the maquis in the Vercors.

Arnold was yet to tell his parents of his intentions. The only person who was aware of his plan was his young cousin, Charles.

'Why don't you try it on?' asked his mother breaking him from his thoughts. She passed the pullover across the table. 'See if it fits.'

Arnold placed his glass on the table and picked up the garment. He pulled it over his head.

'Hmm. I think the sleeves may be a little long,' said his mother.

'Don't worry, Maman. I can just turn the cuffs back. Look, it's fine.'

She smiled. 'Very well. If you're happy with it. I like it. It highlights the blueness of your eyes.'

'I'll go outside and see where Charles has got to,' he said. 'He's taking a long time to finish off.'

Arnold found his cousin sitting on a bench near the cowshed. A young blonde girl wearing a green dress was sitting with him.

'Hello, Charlotte,' he greeted her. 'How are you feeling now?'

'Hello, Arnold,' she replied sheepishly. 'A lot better, thank you.'

'That's good to hear,' he said, sitting next to her. She had complained of feeling unwell that morning.

'Have you decided when you're going?' asked Charles.

Arnold looked at his younger cousin and smiled. One thing he liked about him was his directness. The boy did not engage in small talk, always getting straight to the point.

'Not yet.' He paused for a few moments. 'We need to think about what to do with you two when I go. The authorities are sure to come and look for me at some point.'

Charles ran his hand through his dark hair.

'I've been thinking about that,' he said. 'Why don't you take us with you?'

'I can't do that,' replied Arnold. 'You're too young.'

'Too young for what? I'm not scared if that's what you're thinking.'

'I know that,' replied Arnold. 'I think you've proven how brave you are by getting Charlotte here. You're better off staying here to look after her.'

'I don't need looking after,' said Charlotte suddenly. 'I want to kill Germans. I want to kill lots of Germans.'

Arnold was taken aback by the venom in her voice.

'I can't take you,' he insisted. 'It'd be too dangerous. You might as well just get that thought out of your heads right now.'

'Think about it,' said Charles. 'If you run away then you put all of us in danger. As you say, the Gestapo or the Milice will come looking for you and they'll tear this place apart. What will your maman and papa tell them about who we are? What will they do to all of us if they find a Jewess here? I've had dealings with these people. I know what they're like.'

Arnold was about to press him to explain just what he meant, but when he saw the tears in his eyes he stalled.

'Believe me, Arnie, those people are evil. They're capable of the worst things you can imagine. You can't put us all in this danger. You should either do as they say and go to Germany, or take us with you if you're joining the maquis. There's no other option. And I know how poor your parents are, and the burden having to provide for an extra two people has put on them. If we join you, it's less mouths for them to feed.'

It was clear his young cousin was wise beyond his years. Arnold assumed this was from his experiences in Paris. What the boy said made sense, but he could't be held responsible for the welfare of a sixteen year old boy and a fifteen year old girl, particularly when one of them was not related to him.

But he did feel responsible. Charlotte was as French as he was. Due to nothing other than her race, the Germans wanted to ship her out to God knew where, to suffer a fate that would probably end with her death. The rumours of camps where Jews were worked to death were everywhere. Charles had remarked on more than one occasion about a round up of Jews in Paris not too long ago and he knew all the Jews in Lyon had suffered the same fate. Sent away on trains, never to be heard of again. The very thought of it made him shudder.

'Let me give it some thought,' he said after a while. 'I can't promise you anything, just let me think on it for a while.'

This seemed to appease them. They sat in silence for a while.

'Come on,' said Arnold. 'Let's go inside. Maman will be serving dinner shortly. Best not keep her waiting.'

***

It had been a few months since Frank was last in London. From what he remembered from his first visit in 1940, it had not changed in any significant way from the dark days of the Blitz. Wherever he wandered, there was evidence the country was very much still at war. Buildings lay in ruins or severely damaged, although a lot of the rubble had been cleared from the streets. The air raids were now less frequent and any sound of aircraft he would occasionally hear were mainly those of the RAF and United States Air Forces, heading out to bomb targets on the European mainland.

There was no doubt the tide of the European war was turning. In Frank's view the Germans had made a huge mistake by invading the Soviet Union. When the Americans had finally been dragged into the war, following the Japanese attack on Pearl Harbour, there was a sense abounding that an Allied victory would not be too far away. He was fully aware that if that was to happen, then there was still a huge amount of work to be carried out. Still a lot of fighting to be done.

He entered the doors of SOE headquarters on Baker Street and handed his cap and greatcoat to the young secretary who offered to take them. He wore the uniform of a captain of the Royal Artillery, his promotion confirmed on his arrival from France the previous week. He felt odd dressed this way after spending so much time in civilian clothes, but it seemed that most people he came across in England wore uniform of some sort or other.

Frank preferred to be in the field. He liked to be where the action was. Even though he knew these trips back to England were necessary, he felt his skills were much better put to use in France.

Despite the city remaining much as he remembered, Baker Street had changed a lot. It now seemed busier. There were more people crammed into the place and everyone seemed to be in a hurry, moving purposefully between the offices and corridors. He found it claustrophobic and hoped "Double H" Harding would not keep him too long. He had things to do back in Lyon. He had not wanted to leave when the summons back to England had been received. Things in France had moved on at a fast pace since the Germans had entered the unoccupied zone. More and more groups of maquis were forming as young Frenchmen defied the STO order, bands of them springing up everywhere. Frank did not doubt their enthusiasm but they would do more harm than good if they were not properly organised.

Another, more sinister, group of people had also appeared on the scene. The Milice, an official group of Frenchmen, headed by Laval, the president of Pétain's Vichy regime. Wearing blue uniforms with brown shirts and wide blue berets, they openly collaborated with the Nazis. Some of these men had fought with German forces, their ranks containing ex-convicts, fascists and others who thought being a member could advance them in some kind of personal way. They assisted the Nazis in rounding up Jews and Resistance members and willingly handed them over to the Germans with an enthusiasm that appalled him. They had been known to carry out summary executions of anyone to whom they took a dislike. Unsurprisingly, they were despised by the majority of the population. Frank was more than happy to sanction any action by any of his circuits when they asked for permission to take out any one of them. After all, they were nothing but traitors. One thing he would not sanction was the killing of Germans. The repercussions for actions of this nature were horrific. For every German killed by the Resistance, they would execute many times as many innocent French civilians in reprisal.

He entered the offices of F Section. Colonel Harding was in the corner talking to a young woman in the uniform of a FANY. It was someone he recognised immediately.

Despite how much she could annoy and frustrate him, he could not help but smile as he walked over to them both.

Becoming aware of someone approaching, Jenny Crane looked up.

'Oh, hello stranger,' she smiled. 'Nice to see you again. It's been a long time.'

'Hello, Jenny. You're looking well…'

'You don't look so bad yourself, Captain Graham. I'm free this evening if you'd like to catch up.'

'When you two lovebirds are quite finished,' interrupted Harding, 'Mister Graham and I have much to discuss.'

'Apologies, sir,' said Frank, as Harding turned around and walked into his office. Frank smiled wryly at Jenny and followed him in.

'Shut the door, young man,' said Harding once Frank was inside the room. 'And take a seat.'

Frank did as he was bid and sat down to face his commanding officer. Harding looked down at a manila folder lying on his desk.

'I've read your report and can see things are coming along swimmingly. I really must say that you're one of our most successful agents in France. I knew you'd do well. You've the same qualities and attributes as your brother.'

'Thank you for the endorsement, sir,' replied Frank. 'I try to do my best.'

Harding sat quietly for a moment, looking again to the folder. Frank took a packet of cigarettes from his tunic pocket.

'Do you mind, sir?'

'Not at all. Feel free.'

As Frank lit a cigarette from a book of matches, Harding looked up again.

'It seems our friends in RF Section feel we're treading on their toes somewhat.'

Frank blew out smoke and crossed his legs. 'How so?'

'It's all getting very political here,' explained Harding. 'There are so many different factions of the Resistance. Communists, anti-communists, Gaullists, anti-Gaullists, and different groups within each of them. It's all getting rather complicated.'

'I get the sense of it out in the field,' concurred Frank. 'It's all quite obvious. And quite ridiculous too, in my opinion.'

'They know the war will be won and they're already jostling for places in the political framework before that framework even exists. Get's in the way. Bloody frogs. Why can't they just let us deal with the Germans? Then they can argue what they want to do after the bloody country's liberated.'

'That would make much more sense.'

Harding nodded. 'You're damned right it would. Anyway, the French in RF Section seem to want to run the whole show over there. But they don't stand a chance of achieving that when all their groups are poles apart politically. They don't seem to want to work together. De Gaulle is getting rather cheesed off with them and wants them to pull together for the common goal of getting rid of the blasted Jerries.'

'How's he going to do that?'

'As I mentioned the last time you were here. He's given Moulin the task of uniting them all. He's to hold a meeting in the very near future with all the leaders and argue de Gaulle's case.'

'So where do I come into all this?' asked Frank. He leaned forward and flicked ash into an ashtray on the desk.

'The meeting's to take place in your area of operations. Lyon. I don't have the exact location or date yet, and I'm not even too sure they'll give it to us. I want you to keep an eye on it, be aware of it so to speak. Use whatever influence you have there to make sure it goes ahead okay. The unity of the French Resistance is vital if we're to effectively use them when the time comes.'

'I'll help in any way I can,' replied Frank. He was not altogether too sure how he could be of assistance. The French were fiercely independent. He did not feel sticking his nose into their affairs would be appreciated too much. He had his own cells to supervise. He knew that any loyalty from them would be lost if he interfered in what was essentially a French issue.

'These maquis,' said Harding. 'Are they going to be of any use, do you think?'

Frank did not hesitate in answering. 'Very much so. They're young, enthusiastic and they despise the Germans. With the right supplies, organisation and training, they could be a huge asset if they're handled correctly. There's one problem though. In my area, Barbie is very, very pro-active in seeking out anyone involved in any kind of Resistance. He hasn't been there long, but with the help of those Milice bastards he's starting to become effective. Rounding up Jews and sending them off to God knows where. People are disappearing and everyone's scared.'

'We're hearing stories about camps,' said Harding, solemnly. 'We've no idea what's going on in them. Whatever it is, it won't be good.'

'I'm aware of them too,' remarked Frank. 'The rumours can't be ignored. From what I've seen of how the Nazis operate, I wouldn't be surprised in the slightest if they're true.'

'Me neither. Remember the report your poor brother gave me at Dunkirk? About that Finkel fellow?'

'Exactly,' replied Frank. 'Exactly. Now there's a man I wouldn't mind bumping into again.'

'Okay. See if you can make contact with those maquis groups in your area. Liaise with their leaders and help out with getting them supplied and organised. I understand some are ex-French army. See what assistance you can give them. Let's make use of them. See what you can do. When do you fly back?'

'In three days. I've one or two things to sort out beforehand. My father's coming up to London tomorrow to spend some time with me before I head back.'

'Well until you do, enjoy yourself, young man. You deserve it.'

When Frank left Harding's office he stopped at Jenny Crane's desk.

'Hello Frank. Did the meeting go well?'

'Yes, very,' he replied. 'Are you still available this evening?'

She laughed. 'Well, I haven't had a better offer in the ten minutes you've been in there.'

'Okay. Write down your address and I'll pick you up at seven thirty.'

She tore a sheet of paper from a notepad on her desk and wrote an address on it.

'Don't be late,' she said, handing it to him. 'I don't like to be kept waiting.'

He put on his cap, nodded to her and left the building.

***

Frank smiled across the table. Jenny really was very good looking. She had clearly made an effort to look her best. She wore her hair down and had on a simple, yet pretty blue dress and nice jewellery that looked beyond the pay grade of a FANY.

The girl was an enigma to him. She pretended she did not care one way or the other, as far as he was concerned. He was sure she had probably had her fair share of lovers whilst he was in France. He was not certain of his feelings about that. In the end, what she did was up to her, he thought. After all, they were not a couple. What she did with her life was her own business. They had always flirted, but he had witnessed her flirting with lots of men and had never really considered her serious in any way when she had done it with him. He, himself, had been celibate the whole time he had been away, but that was nothing to do with Jenny Crane. Romantic relationships were the furthest thing from his mind right now. He simply did not have the time for it and wanted to avoid complicating matters. In fact, when he thought about it, he was very much inexperienced with the opposite sex.

But it had been Jenny who had asked him out and she had put a lot of effort into making herself look good for him.

She picked up her glass of whiskey and water. 'A penny for your thoughts.'

'Oh, nothing,' he replied. 'I've a lot on my mind at the moment. So much to think about and all that.'

'You seem restless.'

'I feel restless,' he admitted. 'There's so much to do. I really should be back over there.'

'You can't do this all by yourself, you know. It's not all down to you.'

'I know that,' he said softly. 'I suppose it's ever since I found out about Jack that I've been like this. I feel a massive urge to do my bit. There are so many people over there suffering, especially since the Nazis occupied the south. Things are getting worse.'

Jenny put down her glass. She reached across the table and took hold of Frank's hands.

'You can't let it get to you, Frank. You can only do what you can do. From what Harding's been saying, you're doing more than "your bit", as you put it. You've a couple of days before you go back. Your father is coming to see you tomorrow. Why don't you just forget about everything and enjoy what's left of your time here. France is going nowhere. Your circuits can live without you for a few more days.'

Frank smiled. 'Of course, you're right. You know, Jenny, you confuse me sometimes.'

'Only sometimes?' she laughed. 'I think I confuse myself all the time.'

'Yes. I really don't know what to make of you. I never know if you're being serious with me, if you like me, or are just playing with me.'

'We have one life, Frank. Only one. We're living in strange times and, let's face it, we don't ever really know if, when we wake up in the morning, this is going to be our last day or not. The Germans could drop a bomb on our heads at any time. And it's worse for you. You're in constant peril with what you do. If you were ever caught then you know what the consequences would be. Yet you still itch to get back to it.'

'Did I ever tell you about Otto Finkel?' Frank asked, suddenly changing the subject. He really did not want to dwell on the dangers of his job.

'The name rings a bell…'

'He's the German officer who's responsible for the murder of British prisoners of war on the retreat to Dunkirk. My brother witnessed the massacre before he was killed.'

'Oh yes. I think Harding has mentioned him.'

'You see,' explained Frank. 'It's him that spurs me on in a way. I knew the man. Briefly, as boys back in '28. We were on a family holiday in Brittany and he stayed in the same hotel with his parents. Jack and I befriended him. He was a really nice kid.'

'So what turned him into a murderer, do you think?'

'What has turned any of them into murderers?' Frank pulled his hands away and leaned back in his chair. 'It's something I can't quite get my head around, if I'm telling the truth. There's loads of them, just like him. And some French too. It seems that thugs have taken over Europe. Anyway, Otto Finkel had an accident on that holiday that scarred him. He ripped half his face off when he fell from a boat into the sea. It was Jack who saved his life. He jumped in after him and dragged him out.'

'Do you think that's what made him the way he is now?'

'Who knows? It's possible. The thing is, that despite what I'm doing in France, Finkel is always in my thoughts. I know he didn't kill Jack, but he would've done had Jack been captured with the rest of those poor lads he had shot. I'm convinced of it. And so, with Jack being killed a couple of days later, by the Germans, I can't help but think that Finkel is personally responsible for Jack's death. I want nothing more than to catch him and make him pay for his crimes. In fact, I'm desperate for it.'

'I understand,' said Jenny calmly. 'But bringing these people to justice will probably need to wait until the war is won, which I'm convinced it will be. Especially with people like you fighting it.'

Frank did not want to talk about the war anymore.

'You know what, Jenny? You're right. We really should be using what time we have to take a break and enjoy ourselves for a short while. Drink up. I suddenly feel the urge to take you dancing.'

'Bugger dancing,' said Jenny, draining her glass. 'I have a much better idea for how you can burn off your energy.'

Chapter Fifteen

One month later

Frank pulled the Sten Mark II sub-machine-gun tightly into his shoulder and aimed at the target fifty yards in front.

'The effective range of this weapon is around a hundred yards. But if you can get closer to your target then you're more likely to be successful. It weighs around seven pounds and is very easy and simple to handle, once you know what you're doing with it. Fire in short, quick bursts. That way it stops from rising up as you fire. Don't just keep your finger on the trigger as it's more controllable in semi-automatic. Control the weapon, don't let it control you.'

To prove his point he fired a short burst at the two clay pots that had been placed on a fallen tree trunk, shattering them both.

He unclipped the magazine and placed the weapon on the make-shift table to his right.

There were around thirty of them. All young men eager to learn how to fire the weapon, so they could start killing Germans. Their enthusiasm to learn how to handle the weapons he had had London drop a few days ago was infectious. The biggest problem he would have, was to keep them disciplined. But then, there were some ex-French army officers in their ranks to deal with that, men who had the maquis organised into camps dotted around the plateau.

They were a ragtag assortment of young men who had fled their homes to defy the STO order and formed into small groups in the hills and woods to the south of Lyon and Grenoble. They had no uniform other than the traditional berets that most wore, their clothes unkempt and in some cases, downright dirty. They lived rough, at first scavenging for food from nearby farms, making camp deep in the hills, away from prying eyes. Some of their firearms, rifles and guns were from other wars, long since fought. Outdated weapons that had seen better days. They had minimal ammunition which made them pretty much useless. When Frank made contact with them, he was able to swiftly organise an airdrop, and now they had much better equipment. British weapons, as yet unused, and plenty of ammunition to go with them.

This was the second time he had come to see this group since the delivery and their ranks had grown gradually over that time. There were a few new faces, each as eager as the others to learn what he could teach them.

Frank was surprised to see one or two youths in their ranks. Clearly these boys were not affected by the STO order just yet, so he wondered what they were actually doing there. They were much too young to be involved in anything like this.

'Okay,' he said, clipping in another magazine. 'Anyone want to try it out.'

Several hands were raised, including that of a young boy, no more than fifteen or sixteen years old. For a moment their eyes met, but Frank instead chose the man sitting next to him. The boy looked disappointed.

'You,' he said. 'Come here.'

The man stood up and walked over, wiping his hands on his blue corduroy trousers.

'What's your name?'

'Arnold, Arnold Jeunier.'

'Hello, Arnold, Arnold. Have you ever handled a weapon like this before?'

'No,' replied Arnold. 'I've fired a rifle on my father's farm once or twice. At foxes and that.'

Frank smiled at him. 'This isn't much different, Arnold.'

'Arnie. My friends call me Arnie.'

'Okay, Arnie,' said Frank, handing him the Sten. 'You need to cock the weapon to make it ready. Aim at that tree over there and then release the safety. Squeeze the trigger, don't jerk at it. Remember, control the weapon, don't let it control you.'

Arnie pulled the sub-machine-gun into his shoulder, as Frank had demonstrated. He took a breath and then let loose a quick burst, hitting the tree, sending splinters of bark into the air.

'Well done,' said Frank, patting him on the back. 'You're a natural.'

Arnie placed the weapon back onto the table and turned to the others, smiling brightly.

Frank turned to the group. 'Anyone else?'

Everyone held their hands in the air, the young boy waving this time, in his eagerness to be chosen. Arnie went to sit by him. It was clear they were together.

Frank looked along the line of men and was about to call over a young man wearing a dark waistcoat over a shirt that looked too big for him, when the young boy stepped forward and walked over.

'Please, sir,' he said politely. 'I'd like to have a go.'

Frank looked down at him. The boy looked no more than fifteen years old. Despite his youth, he had a determination in his eyes that seemed stronger than that of the others.

'And what's your name, lad?'

'Charles. But I've been known as Victor on occasion.'

'Victor? Why would you have two names?'asked Frank, raising his eyebrows.

'It's a long story.'

'Okaaay… That's not a local accent either. Where are you from, boy?'

Charles ignored the question. 'It's a long story,' he repeated. 'Can I have a go?'

Frank was slightly taken aback by the boy's confidence. The lad clearly had a tale to tell. Frank was sure that at some point Charles would reveal what had happened for him to have travelled some considerable distance to end up in the hills of the Vercors with a band of maquisards.

'Charles, Victor. Which is it? What do you want me to call you?'

'Charles is my real name. You can call me that?'

'All right, Charles. Now you've seen how it's done. Let's see if you're as good as your friend, Arnie.'

Charles picked up the weapon and held it confidently. He pointed it at the target and fired. He was not expecting the kickback. The weapon rose in his arms, the bullets hitting branches higher up the tree. He dropped the Sten onto the ground and stepped back.

The others, watching on, burst into laughter. He turned to them angrily.

'Oh, shut up, you lot,' he said. 'Let's see you do any better.'

Frank placed his hand on the boy's shoulder. 'Don't worry about it, Charles. You'll get the hang of it. You just need a little more practice, that's all.'

This seemed to placate him and he walked away to rejoin the group.

Frank bent down and picked up the gun from the ground. He took out the magazine and placed it back on the table.

He had spent the past couple of days with this group and was pleased at their attitude. He knew once he had them trained, then when the time came, he would be able to rely on them. Although they were amateurs as yet, he had no doubt he could whip them into shape very quickly if they listened to his instructions. Then they may well become an effective fighting force.

That night, whilst gathered around the campfire with five maquisards, Frank noticed the young boy, Charles, sitting on his own, whittling a small twig with a knife. There was a full moon and he was silhouetted slightly against the skyline. He looked lost and out of place.

Getting up, he strode over to the boy and sat down beside him.

'Charles, isn't it?'

The boy did not look away from the twig in his hand, continuing to work, as though Frank was not there.

'It is,' he replied.

'Tell me your story, Charles,' said Frank, laying on his back with his hands clamped behind his head.

'What do you want to know?'

'I'm curious to know why you're here. You're very young and your accent is not from around here. You sound Parisian.'

'Neither's yours,' said Charles, his eyes momentarily meeting with Frank's. Frank noticed a slight glint in the youth's eyes, as though he was amused at the attention he was being given.

'Well, that's because I'm English. Where are you from?'

'You're right. Paris.'

Frank pulled a packet of cigarettes from his pocket and lit one. 'So how has a young lad from Paris ended up here?'

Charles shifted awkwardly. It was clear he did not particularly want to discuss it.

'It's a very long story,' he said after a while. 'But here I am now. I came with my cousin, Arnie. He's not from Paris, though. He's from Lyon. I was sent there by my mother after I got into a spot of bother.'

Frank was intrigued. 'What kind of bother?'

'If it's all right with you, I'd rather not talk about it,' replied Charles, quietly.

'That's fine,' replied Frank. 'I'm just a little concerned that you're a bit young for all this. This isn't a safe place for someone as young as you.'

'With respect,' responded Charles, clearly affronted. 'You know absolutely nothing about me. Other than I'm not very good with guns just yet. But that'll come with practice, as you said. And when I get better, I'll be able to do my bit and keep up with the others. I'm much braver than I probably look.'

'I don't doubt it,' smiled Frank. 'I'm not questioning your bravery. I'm merely pointing out that this is a dangerous business we're involved in. The Germans…'

'I know all about the Germans and what they're capable of,' he interrupted sharply. 'That's the whole reason why I'm here!'

A group of maquisards standing a few feet away looked over. Arnold, Charles's cousin stepped forward.

Frank held up his hands defensively. 'Okay, okay. I didn't mean to upset you.'

'Is everything okay?' asked Arnold.

'It's fine,' said Charles. 'Nothing to worry about.'

Frank stood up. He did not want to make the young lad feel any more uncomfortable than he already had. Whatever his story, it could keep until a time he felt more at ease to talk about it. He also did not want to upset the rest of the group in any way.

He decided he would keep an eye on the young boy. It was clear he hated the Germans, but he did not need anyone whose emotions may interfere with any future operations. The boy could be dangerous to the group without realising it. He made a note to talk to Sacha, the group's leader. If he could send the boy back to where he came from, then it may be beneficial to them all. One less thing to worry about.

He would head back to Lyon in the morning. He had spent enough time with this group. They were now equipped and partly trained. Frank felt he could leave them to their own devices for the time being, the training to be completed by those with military experience. He had spoken to Sacha and advised him to keep themselves to themselves for now. He did not want them to run before they could walk. He knew the hardest thing would be to keep them in check, but in reality, he knew he had no control over them and they would probably do whatever they wanted. They were their own fighting force, with their own hierarchy. He did not fit anywhere within it, other than to offer advice and liaise with London to provide weapons and ammunition when required.

That night he did not sleep well. He never did when he slept under the stars. He always felt vulnerable and exposed, as though he could be discovered at any time. As dawn broke the next morning, he quietly gathered up his things and made his way down from the plateau. He had a good day's walk before he would get to the train station from where he could get back to the city. He was conscious that the German and Milice presence there would be high, as they were on the lookout for maquisards they knew to be operating in the area, or picking up men who were making their way to the plateau to join them.

He would need to be careful, but was confident he would be fine. He always seemed to be. He knew of other agents, men such as himself, who had let their guard down and been captured. He had heard stories of how they had been tortured and shot, or whisked away somewhere never to be seen again. Others, maybe the lucky ones, had been shipped out to the work camps in Poland and Germany.

He did not want to suffer the same fate as them.

Chapter Sixteen

Frank stood in the alleyway across from the four storey apartment building. Staying in the shadows he could watch without being seen. A German Opel truck was parked outside next to a black staff car. A few yards from it, under the pale glow of a streetlamp, two German officers stood smoking cigarettes, talking calmly to a Gestapo officer. They occasionally laughed, the events they were overseeing seemingly of little concern to any of them.

Frank could see lights being switched on as the heavily armed soldiers banged on the doors of each apartment, working through the building methodically and efficiently. He stepped further back into the shadows, pulling the pistol from his pocket. He needed to be ready for any eventuality. Should he be spotted, then he had no intention of being taken without a fight. Although he knew to stay was dangerous, he was compelled to hang around and witness it all. He had to see how this played out.

Frank had arrived too late to help Catherine. On returning to the apartment he rented in the fourth arrondissement he had found an envelope under the door. Only the heads of each circuit had been given his new address, with strict instructions never to reveal it to anyone and only to make contact in case of dire emergency. The note inside had clearly been written in a hurry, the handwriting hard to read in parts. It was from Benoit, briefly stating an operation they had carried out had gone awry and the circuit was compromised. Michel and Pierre were probably dead, and he and Jean-Luc Descartes were on the run, heading for St Etienne. Catherine, was returning to the apartment she shared with her sister to warn her. She was then to follow the two men on the morning train. He also added he had sent the emergency message to England informing them of the problem.

There was nothing in the note that explained exactly what had taken place to cause this.

Frank always feared that at some point something like this would happen. It was almost inevitable. He had been concerned Benoit knew too much about him, but as long as the Frenchman did not fall into the hands of the Gestapo then there was nothing to be worried about in regards to his own personal safety. As far as Catherine was concerned, she knew very little and had no idea where he lived.

He gripped the Colt firmly in his hand, nervously flicking the safety catch off and on as he watched.

It was obvious he had been only a minute or two late. Although he was annoyed he could do nothing to help, at the same time he felt relieved. Being late had probably saved him. Had he been caught in the apartment with the women, then he too would have been captured. It had nearly all gone so horribly wrong, he realised; it had all been down to pure luck that he had not been captured.

He had no control over the situation and it made him uncomfortable.

The Germans were in the building for only a short time. He watched on impotently as two young women were dragged roughly out of the front door; one blonde, he recognised as Catherine Lambert, the other dark haired, he assumed to be her sister, Monique. They were dragged to the three men smoking cigarettes near the streetlamp.

The Gestapo officer leaned forward menacingly and said something to Catherine. When she did not answer his question fast enough, he struck her hard across the face with the back of his hand, causing her to scream sharply and pull back, despite being held firmly by a rough looking soldier. Her sister sunk between the two guards holding her by the arms. Frank realised she had fainted.

Quickly, both women were hauled unceremoniously into the back of the truck, the guards dragging the semi-conscious Monique across the edge of the wagon. Frank saw one of them grab her breast as they pulled her inside, which seemed to rouse her momentarily. On seeing what was happening to her, she began screaming wildly until one hit her hard across the face and her body went limp again. As the truck pulled away, Frank caught a glimpse of the two sisters huddled together. They were cowering at the feet of the two rows of soldiers sitting either side of them.

Having observed this, the two uniformed officers and the Gestapo man casually threw their cigarettes to the ground, got in the staff car and were driven away by a guard who looked on indifferently, following the truck as it turned a corner. Frank was in no doubt they would be heading for Gestapo headquarters at the Hotel Terminus and a meeting with Haupsturmführer Klaus Barbie.

Swiftly he crossed the road and entered the building. The sisters' apartment was on the ground floor, the front door opening directly onto the street. He tried the handle and the door opened into a small hallway. The apartment was typical of much of the rented accommodation he had seen over his time in France. Old looking furniture filled the hallway and living room, threadbare rugs lay on wooden flooring that looked in need of a good polish. Cheap looking pictures of flowers decorated the walls and equally inexpensive ornaments and lamps were dotted about the plac,e in an attempt to make the place look homely and inviting. To Frank, it had quite the opposite effect.

He could hear movement on the stairwell above and realised he did not have the time he would need to search the place properly before he would be discovered. He cursed to himself. He could not take the chance of being challenged and the possibility the authorities would be called back. He abandoned the search and exited the building. Hurriedly he made his way along the boulevard back to his own apartment.

This whole thing was a mess. There were some in the circuit who knew him; Benoit and Catherine in particular. Although he could trust Benoit to hold out under interrogation, at least for a while, Catherine was a different matter altogether. Although she knew little, she knew of his existence. He had survived this long due to his ability to remain invisible, to remain in the shadows. If he was not careful then all that good work would come to an end. Frank was in no doubt of the danger he was in. As far as he was aware, the Germans had no idea he was operating in the area.

He was under no illusion that that was all about to change.

What had gone wrong to cause such a mess? What could they have possibly done to bring the Gestapo down upon them so swiftly? Frank had made sure the circuits he had established operated independently of each other and sometimes independently of him; carrying out operations he was not privy too. They were empowered to pick their own targets and carry out minor operations without having to consult their handlers. He presumed it was the execution of one of these missions that had led to this current situation.

He needed to get into their apartment again, when it was safe. He had to be certain Catherine had left nothing that could lead the Germans to him. The last thing he needed was the Gestapo breathing down his neck. He was aware of the reputation of the man heading up the hunt for the Resistance. Barbie was someone he had to avoid. According to all accounts, the man was ruthless and sadistic, taking great pleasure in personally interrogating and torturing suspects. Many of whom had not left the Hotel Terminus alive.

As he strode purposefully along, sticking to the shadows, he made the only decision he could. With Catherine and her sister now in the custody of the Gestapo, he would catch the morning train to St Etienne and try and locate Benoit and Descartes. If he was able to make contact with them, then he would inform them of Catherine's capture and advise them both to get as far away from Lyon as they possibly could.

***

Frank bought a newspaper from a vendor on the platform and boarded the train. He took a seat next to the window in the rear carriage. From there he could observe passengers getting on and off. The station was busy, full of mid-week commuters as they headed to work, their seemingly indifferent expressions belying the general feeling of unease at having foreign troops in the city.

The train was starting to fill. A middle-aged gentleman with a large grey moustache sat in the seat opposite and took a small paperback from his pocket. Across the aisle a mother tried to control two small boys, one of whom sat down obediently and proceeded to pick his nose. Frank smiled as he watched the child examine the contents on his finger before wiping it on the window to his left.

As far as he could see, the war had not disrupted the efficiency of the French passenger rail system too much. Trains still arrived and departed from platforms on time. The Nazi occupation was yet to disturb its efficiency.

It was clear the travelling public seemed much more subdued these days. Nobody wanted to converse with strangers, going about their business without acknowledging their fellow passengers, keeping themselves to themselves. The once buzzing sound of chatter on the platforms had disappeared, replaced by a more sombre atmosphere. Nobody wanted to draw attention to themselves. They just did not know who was listening. Frank understood it was the trust that had gone. Trust in their fellow Frenchmen had given way to scepticism and suspicion. The Germans had not just conquered the country, they had also crushed the spirit of a lot of its people. It was none so more apparent than on the platforms and train stations of each city.

Frank was stirred from his gloomy thoughts by a porter blowing his whistle just outside the carriage window, startling him slightly. The man opposite looked up from his book and smiled, mildly amused. Frank ignored him and casually looked out of the window. The porter was about to wave his flag when he suddenly stopped. Some people were hurriedly walking towards the train. Frank was troubled to see it was a group of six SS soldiers, including an officer. Alongside them was a Gestapo officer he recognised as the man outside Catherine's apartment building the previous evening. More worryingly, was the final person that made up this small group.

Catherine Lambert was with them, the Gestapo officer gripping her firmly by the arm, forcing her to move quickly.

She had been cleaned up and was wearing a smart two piece suit and matching hat. They entered the train a couple of carriages ahead and were soon out of his sight.

This could mean only one thing. Catherine had talked and was leading the Germans to her colleagues in St Etienne, and there was absolutely nothing at all that Frank could do to stop it. He had no way of warning Benoit and Descartes. It was too late for that.

Frank knew if she had told them of the members of her circuit, then he could assume she had also informed them of the existence of the "Grey man", a Special Operations Executive agent and handler of Resistance cells in the Lyon area. Had she told them of the spare radio parts she kept for him, or the location in the Vercors where she had carried out training, where a maquis group had now set up their base of operations? He had no way of knowing. He just hoped there could not have been enough time for her to tell them everything. After all, it was only a few hours ago when she had been arrested.

He felt a panic set in, an unease. He had only ever had a feeling such as this once before and recognised it immediately. It was a fear for his own personal safety. The first time had been out on that cove in St Malo when he was a child. He had been terrified that he and the other children in the boat would drown.

He took a deep breath. He had to think. What did this really mean? How much danger was he actually in?

Catherine knew very little about him. She only knew he was English, his codename was "Grey Man" and he had been going by the name of Francois. He was unsure if she was aware of the surname he had been using.

But then it did not really matter what Catherine knew. She was leading them to Claude Benoit and he knew everything about Frank. He knew his full identity, where he lived, and who the heads of two more circuits were. There was no doubt in Frank's mind that should Benoit fall into the hands of Klaus Barbie, it would not be to long before they were rounded up, himself included.

He would contact Baker Street and take direction from them. And he needed to do it as soon as possible. It was possible they may recall him back to England, or give him papers with a new identity. Maybe he could be saved.

But what of the others? What of the rest of the circuit and those others Benoit was aware of? What would become of them?

Frank considered getting off the train and going straight to Vallin to warn him. Maybe Vallin could get word to the others and they could head to the Vercors to join the maquis there. Frank knew to do this would mean death or incarceration for their families. The whole thing was a mess.

He took another deep breath. Now was not the time to panic. Now was not the time to make hasty decisions without knowing exactly what the Gestapo's hand was. He decided to stay on the train and follow them. He would see how the morning played out and then make his decision on what to do next.

With the hiss of air brakes and the shriek of the porter's whistle ringing in his ears, the train finally pulled out of the station and headed south, on the short journey to St Etienne.

***

An hour later Frank disembarked the train onto a busy platform where commuters mixed with gendarmes. He could see groups of Wehrmacht guards dotted around the station, including two standing with the ticket collectors at the entrance to the forecourt. He stopped and leaned against a pillar, taking a packet of cigarettes from his pocket and lighting one. He took his time, allowing other passengers to pass him as they headed towards the exit.

Then, in his peripheral vision, he noticed Catherine. She was no longer accompanied by the Germans. She walked past him, within yards. He was tempted to grab her and make a break for it, but then noticed the Gestapo officer and the other Germans following her, at a discreet distance.

Catherine passed the ticket inspector without incident and headed directly towards the station cafeteria which was located near the exit. Frank squinted his eyes slightly and was able to see through the windows and make out a couple of men inside. They were sitting near to the counter. He felt the hairs stick up on the back of his neck as he realised it was Benoit and Descartes.

He turned his attention back to the Germans who followed Catherine. Frank put his hand into the deep pocket of his overcoat and felt the cold metal of the Colt. It was loaded, a round in the chamber and the safety catch on. A suppressor was attached to the barrel. All he had to do was to pull it from the pocket, flick off the safety, and he was ready to go. But then to do this would be suicide. There were too many for him to be able to shoot his way out of the station. He felt completely useless.

Catherine entered the café and walked over to the two men. A few words were exchanged and then, without hesitation, Jean-Luc Descartes stood up, raced to the door and ran out. Before the Germans could react, he was sprinting to the exit, barging through commuters who shouted insults at him as he went by. By the time the Germans had chance to do anything, he was out of the station, no doubt running for his life.

Frank turned his attention back to the café.

The Gestapo officer and two SS guards rushed to the door and entered. They marched over to the table where Benoit was sitting, Catherine standing before him. By now, many people were aware of something alarming taking place and there was an increased urgency to leave the station, nobody wanting to get involved or to witness what was about to happen.

Frank watched on helplessly as the Gestapo officer spoke to Benoit, who sat without moving, merely shrugging at the German indifferently. Frank understood that Benoit had simply given up. He had accepted there was no way out for him.

Suddenly, without warning, Benoit pulled a pistol from his pocket, put it into his mouth and pulled the trigger. It was a second later before the sound of the gunshot hit Frank's ears. The shock of it made him jump. Catherine's screams could be heard clearly from where he was standing. She had not managed to get out of the way, Benoit's blood spraying into her face and that of the Gestapo officer, who casually took a handkerchief from his pocket and wiped it away. He issued an order to the guards and headed out of the café, leaving Benoit's body slumped in the chair, blood and brain matter splattered on the counter behind his head. Catherine was then dragged outside, doubled over and screaming. She began vomiting onto the ground.

Two of the SS guards ran towards the exit, to assist in the apprehension of Jean-Luc Descartes. Under orders, gendarmes and rail workers entered the café and, with instruction from another SS guard, removed Benoit's body to the back and out of Frank's sight.

Realising there was nothing he could do to help Descartes, he decided to return to Lyon. He had no idea how much Catherine would have told the Germans. He needed to warn as many people as he could before they continued questioning her and she revealed everything she knew, if she had not done so already.

He fingered the pistol in his pocket. He was itching to take it out and assassinate the Gestapo officer standing arrogantly a few yards away.

He resisted the temptation.

***

An SS officer and two guards sat with Catherine in the carriage as it headed back to Lyon. There were few other passengers.

At no point had Frank left the station. Instead he had followed the group onto the train, sitting only a few seats behind. Catherine was unaware of his presence and sat quietly, weeping. The German guards did not seem remotely interested in her and smoked cigarettes as they watched the French countryside roll by through the windows. Every once in a while the officer spoke, telling her to shut up, or to give her abuse.

The train arrived at Lyon and Frank stood up, as though to exit. The Germans were taking their time, none of them appearing in any hurry to get up, preferring to finish their cigarettes before carrying on with their journey.

As Frank walked by, he stopped and looked down at them.

The officer, who was sitting opposite Catherine, looked up. 'Can I help you?' he asked, curtly.

'Non, Monsieur,' he replied.

'Well go away then,' snapped the officer.

Upon hearing Frank's voice, Catherine, who had been staring out of the window through red tear-filled eyes, suddenly turned to look at him.

Frank made a point of not making eye contact as he replied.

'Apologies, Monsieur. I'll be on my way.' He put his hand to his hat. 'Messieurs, Mademoiselle.'

Just as he turned to walk away, his eyes met Catherine's, and for an instant, they held each other's gaze, which went unnoticed by the German soldiers. In that split second he conveyed to her that no matter what the Germans were about to do to her, no matter how much they tortured and beat her, and ultimately if they were to end her life, she had to remain stoic. The fight would continue.

As Frank walked away, he heard the officer mutter something to his colleagues followed by a short burst of laughter. The remark was probably at his expense.

But he did not care. He knew Catherine would talk. He knew she already had. Benoit was dead and Descartes was God knows where, because of her lack of fortitude. Frank did not blame her for it. She had always been weak, truth be told. He had known from the start that if she, or any of the others in the circuits he oversaw, were ever captured, they would break under interrogation. No matter how fiercely they resisted at first, they would tell the Gestapo everything they knew. They were only human, after all. Those at the Hotel Terminus were anything but.

From this point it was all about damage control. He had much to do, the first being to get back to Lyon and search Benoit's garage and Catherine's apartment.

Chapter Seventeen

Frank wasted no time.

After getting off the train, he headed straight to Benoit's garage. Upon entering the street where it was located his heart sank. Parked outside was a German Opel truck and two staff cars. German soldiers stood guard outside and gendarmes, Milice and more troops could be seen moving around inside. Frank turned around. There was nothing he could do about it now and so headed in the opposite direction, back to where he had seen Catherine and her sister arrested the night before.

Upon arrival, he was pleased to see no activity there. Whereas the Germans were all over the garage, for some reason there was nobody, as far as he could see, watching the place. He could not be sure if they had already been, but it made him suspicious. He was aware the place may be being watched but he felt he had to take the chance and go in. He was not sure if Catherine had managed to destroy any documents or the radio crystals she had been holding for him. He had to be sure there was nothing in her flat that could link her to anyone else.

Benoit had done the honourable thing. His friend was not a stupid man and had understood that he too would talk eventually. A man can stand only so much torture, so much punishment, before he started to speak. Benoit had been aware he knew too much. He had known the names of others in other circuits and that Frank was an SOE agent and where he lived. He had sacrificed himself for the good of the Resistance and his friend. In Frank's view, that made him a true hero.

Although it saddened him, Frank knew the best outcome from all this mess was for those affected by the previous night's events, Benoit, Catherine and the two mechanics, Pierre and Michel, to have been killed. Jean-Luc Descartes was on the run. Without help and no idea of where to go or who to contact, it would not be too long before he too was in the hands of the Gestapo, if he was not already.

Frank was not concerned about his childhood acquaintance. After all, the other members of his group were either captured or dead, and Descartes did not know anything other than what Benoit may have told him. Which, knowing Claude, would not have been much.

One thing that was for certain. If Catherine had not yet told them, Klaus Barbie and the Gestapo would soon become aware there was an English agent operating in the area who had control over several Resistance cells. Frank was very much in danger.

Frank waited in the same alleyway from where he had watched proceedings the night before and smoked a cigarette. He observed the comings and goings of the inhabitants of the area as they went about their daily business, all the time keeping his eyes firmly fixed on the door to the apartment. He kept lookout for anyone who may be watching the place and was pleased to see, as far as he could make out, he was the only person showing any interest in the building.

After twenty minutes he decided to make his move. He had to chance it. He crossed the road and tried the door handle. It was still unlocked.

He entered, closing the door quietly behind him. Quickly he moved from room to room, looking in drawers and cupboards for anything that may be of any importance or interest to the Gestapo. In the bedrooms he lifted the mattresses from the bed frames, looking underneath. He turned up carpet, looking for loose floorboards where she may have secreted anything, and checked the toilet cistern in the bathroom where he found a small pistol, one he had given her the previous year. He checked the magazine, made it safe, and then pocketed the weapon. He made sure that in every room he searched, he replaced everything exactly as he found it.

The last room was Monique's bedroom, where again, he came up blank. A suitcase lay open on the bed, clothes, shoes and underwear thrown in carelessly, as though she had been packing in a hurry. He had been in the apartment for half an hour and his searching had revealed nothing. If Catherine had been holding anything then she had either destroyed the evidence, or it had been taken the previous night.

He sat on the bed, took his cigarettes from his coat pocket and put one into his mouth. He was about to light it when he heard the front door creak. Someone was entering the apartment.

He pulled Catherine's pistol from his pocket. Slowly and as quietly as he could, he cocked the weapon and stood up. He had left the door to the bedroom slightly ajar and walked over to it. He looked through the crack between the door and the doorframe. A young woman he recognised as Catherine's sister, Monique, stood in the hallway.

He watched as she closed the front door, picked up a key that had been left on a small wooden table to the side, and locked it. She then moved to the sofa, sat down, put her head in her hands and wept. She turned her body, lay down and buried her face in a cushion, now sobbing uncontrollably.

Frank was confused.

Why had they let her go? They had held her for only a matter of a few hours. It made no sense. She was the sister of a known Resistance operative. She lived in the same apartment as that sister so would be aware of what she had been up to, even if she was not involved herself. For the Gestapo to release her, unscathed, did not make any sense to him. It was highly suspicious. They were clearly up to something.

He was about to approach her when she suddenly sat up and wiped her eyes. Frank stepped back into the bedroom.

He watched as she walked to the bathroom and then heard the sound of running water. She was filling the bath. She moved back to the living room and switched on a radio that sat atop an old sideboard. As the sound of classical music started to fill the air, she walked in the direction of the bedroom.

Frank turned away, his back to the wall behind the door. As she entered the room, he stepped out behind her. Quickly, he put his left arm around her neck, covering her mouth with his hand and pushed the pistol into her right cheek. He felt her body stiffen against his.

'Do not scream, Mademoiselle,' he whispered. 'I have no desire to harm you.'

He felt her start to tremble and go limp in his arms.

'Promise me you'll not scream and I'll release you,' he continued, and when she nodded her head, he took his hand from her mouth and put the gun to his side.

She moved away from him and sat on the bed.

'Please don't hurt me,' she said, between sobs. 'I can't take much more of this.'

'I won't hurt you as long as you do as I say.'

She looked up. 'Who are you? What are you doing here?'

'I'm a friend of Catherine's,' he replied calmly. 'You've nothing to fear from me'. He pocketed the pistol and sat down on the bed next to her.

'What do you people want from me? I can't take any more of this,' she repeated.

'Why have they let you go?' asked Frank. 'It makes no sense to me. What have you told them?'

She turned to look at him, suddenly defiant. 'Like I told those animals, I've no knowledge of anything Catherine was up to. I don't know a thing.'

'And they believed you? Because I most certainly don't. There's no way you could be living with her and not have an inkling of what she's been doing.'

'You people make me sick,' she snapped. 'You play with people's lives, as though it's all a game. And now look where it's led. Catherine's friends are dead and she's been arrested. God alone knows what they're doing to her.'

'They were my friends too,' whispered Frank. 'And don't for one second think this is all a game to us. Now, tell me exactly what happened last night.'

'Why should I? I don't even know you.'

'I could always take out the pistol again,' Frank replied, putting his hand to his pocket. 'But let's face it. Neither of us want that. If I don't know what happened then I won't be able to help you. Now, again, tell me what happened after they arrested you both last night.'

Monique seemed to accept this. 'They came late last night…'

'No,' interrupted Frank. 'Before then. Tell me everything.'

She was shaking now. 'Catherine came home in a terrible state. She was crying and I couldn't console her, no matter how much I tried. I couldn't get out of her what had happened. She was telling me to pack my things and that we had to leave straight away. Then she told me one of her group had been caught. She didn't know if he was alive or dead. And another had been badly wounded. The others were running to St Etienne and we were to meet them there this morning.'

She broke off for a short time, wiping the tears from her face with the back of her hand.

She continued. 'But before we could even pack our suitcases they came… the Germans, the Gestapo. It all happened so quickly. They took us to the Hotel Terminus and locked us in separate cells for a while. I was left there for a couple of hours before they came for me. They took me to a room and sat me at a table. There were three men in the room and I think there was a fourth watching from behind. I didn't see him, but the others kept looking over to him. I was too scared to turn around. I didn't want to look at him, I was just too nervous.

'They told me Catherine was in serious trouble and kept shouting at me, asking me what I knew about it. They said her friends had murdered a policeman and his son and had injured some German soldiers. They said if I didn't tell them what I knew then they'd have me shot or send me away to Drancy. They were horrible.'

Again she paused to collect her thoughts. Frank did not know what to think. It all seemed so odd.

'So why did they let you go?'

She shrugged. 'They must have realised I was innocent.'

Frank pulled the pistol from his pocket and pointed it at her. 'Now I know you're lying. Do you think I'm a fool? I've been in this business long enough to know the Gestapo don't just release people so quickly. To them anyone connected to anything like this is guilty of something. I think you'd better start telling me the truth.'

Monique burst into tears and began to shake.

'They said they'd kill me and Catherine if I didn't do as they said,' she whispered.

'And what was that exactly.'

She wiped her eyes with the back of her hand. 'The one who was in charge. His name was Keller. He was in charge when they came to take us. He was such a creep, he kept looking at my breasts the whole time. He made me want to vomit. He told me to come home and to wait. He said someone from the Resistance would probably make contact and I was to report to him when that happened…'

'Are you going to report this?'

'I don't know what to do. They have Catherine.'

'Catherine is of no concern to me now,' said Frank bluntly. 'Catherine has already betrayed her friends, one of whom is now dead because of her. Another is on the run, if he hasn't been caught already. Good men, the both of them. And now they're dead because she couldn't keep her mouth shut for a few hours. She only had to hang on until this morning and they may have got away.'

Monique made to say something but on seeing the cold stare from Frank, decided against it.

'As far as I see it, Monique, you're now left with a choice. And it's a simple one in my view. You see, the Nazis can never win this war. The British have kicked them out of Africa, the Allies are winning in Italy and the Russians have fought them back at Stalingrad and have them on the run. From what I understand, they're failing everywhere else too. It's only a matter of time before they're defeated.

'And what do you think will happen after that? Once the Nazis are gone? Everyone will start to look closely at those who helped them when they were here. Those who collaborated with them. The Milice, the gendarmerie, those traitors in Vichy and elsewhere, including people like you, should you do as this Keller asks. Do you think they'll care that you were worried about your sister? That won't come into it at all. They'll just see that you helped them, that you conspired against your own countrymen. That you were one of them.

'The choice you are left with, Monique, is, like a say, a very simple one. Instead of being shot or hanged as a traitor, you can make yourself a hero when all the fighting stops. Instead of working for them, you'll work for me. You'll give this Keller whatever he wants and more besides. I'll provide you with that information. You'll let him think you're doing as he says. But in reality, you'll be doing quite the opposite.'

'I can't do this…'

'You can do this and you will do this.'

'But Catherine…'

'If he thinks you're doing as he says, then, if he's to be trusted, Catherine will be as safe as she can be.'

'You say I have a choice, but I don't, do I? I have no choice at all.'

'No, you don't,' replied Frank with a smile. 'Not really. But like I say, this could make you a hero where the alternative is quite the opposite. Your sister did her best. I know it's easy for me to say she should have hung on longer, but we all know everyone talks eventually. Her threshold is just lower than most I've known so far.'

They were silent for a while, Monique considering her position.

'What happens now?' she asked.

Frank thought for a moment before replying. 'For the time-being you'll do nothing. Wait for this Keller to get in touch again. I'm guessing he won't leave it too long. Tell him nobody has been to see you yet. Let him wait awhile. I'll be in touch in the next few days and we'll take it from there.'

'I didn't want any of this,' sobbed Monique. 'I want to live in peace,'

Frank could feel his temper rising. 'We all do. Do you think any of us want this? I've lost a brother to this war. Fighting to defend your country. Now men I liked and respected are also dead. I'll not let their deaths be in vain. Nor Catherine's sacrifice, for that matter. Nobody wants this war, Monique, nobody. But we all have to do our bit, whether we want to or not. I even know of young boys, only just in their teens, who are doing their best to defeat the Nazis. Youngsters, and old men alike. We're all involved.'

He stood up and looked down at her, sitting crying on the edge of the bed. He felt no sympathy, only contempt.

'How do I get in touch with you?' she sniffled.

'You don't,' he replied. 'Do you think I'm going to give you my address after what you've just told me. You could give it straight to Keller and then that's the end of this. I don't trust you, Monique. Not yet anyway. I'll be in touch with you. Just do as I say and we'll take it from there.'

Frank turned from her and walked out of the room.

As he strolled along the streets, heading back towards his own apartment, he was conscious that Monique may already be being watched. Thankfully, he saw nothing to confirm this. After taking a circuitous route home, he finally arrived at his apartment.

Maybe the situation with Monique was the one silver lining to losing the garage cell. Although he would have given anything for none of the events of the past twenty-four hours to have taken place, he could not change them. They had happened and there was nothing he could do about it. Maybe having a way in to the Gestapo and what was happening at the Hotel Terminus could prove a positive thing. But then he did not yet know how reliable a double-agent Monique may be.

He had offered her the choice on a whim; on the spur of the moment. Did he really know what he was doing? Was he creating a new and dangerous problem? He could not yet answer that, but his judgement had proved good in the past. He was good at this job and he knew it. But he also knew his luck could not last forever. At some point he may make a mistake and any error in this line of business would inevitably prove fatal.

He was mentally exhausted. He knew that now. The toll of everything he had been doing was having an effect on him. He had not asked for more Benzedrine tablets after they had run out. He did not want to get hooked on the drug. He did not want to rely on it, like so many other agents had come to.

With a reluctance he felt ashamed of, as though it was somehow a failure, he realised he needed help. He could not carry on doing this without it.

Then he made a decision. He would ask Baker Street for assistance when he sent his next “sked”.

Chapter Eighteen

Four days later

Frank sat alone in a café reading a newspaper. A cup of cold coffee on the table in front of him. He had waited too long already, and knew he could not stay much longer without arousing suspicion from the staff.

From where he had positioned himself he could observe anyone entering the square. It was mid-morning and the heat of the early summer's day was beginning to make its presence felt. From the clear blue sky, he could tell that today was going to be a warm one.

The message had told him to expect someone a half hour ago. They would make themselves known to Frank, which gave him to assume whoever Baker Street had sent, they at least would recognise him, if not him them. This made him feel slightly uneasy. For the first time in a very long while, he was beginning to feel he was not in control. After what had happened to Benoit's group and the subsequent impulsive recruitment of Monique Lambert, he had the feeling things were beginning to slip away from him, and he did not like it one bit.

He was about to give up and move position to another establishment further along the square when he spotted her. He did not know whether to laugh or cry. She could not be more obvious to him, but, fortunately, nobody she passed gave her a second look. Maybe it was only his own heightened state of vigilance that alerted him to the fact that the woman he was watching walk towards the café clearly did not belong there.

She was wearing clothing much too heavy for the weather, a pale green skirt suit and a dark overcoat which made her look as though she was heading for a business meeting. In winter. The shoes she wore were completely out of sync with the rest of her attire, imitation leather, scuffed and with mud caked around the bottom. She carried a small suitcase, which she swapped from hand to hand as she struggled with the weight of it.

Frank stood up. He could not have her coming into the café and drawing attention to them both. He placed some centimes on the table and nodded to the waiter, who stood behind the counter polishing a glass. The man nodded back in acknowledgement and Frank left the café.

The woman did not notice him until he bumped into her, knocking the suitcase from her hands.

'Pardon, Mademoiselle,' he said, bending down to pick it up.

As he handed it to her, he looked into her eyes. The look of surprise and shock on her face was immediate.

'Frank, thank God. It's so good to see you,' she said in English.

'French,' he whispered, forcing a smile on his face for any observer who may be watching. 'For Christ's sake speak only French. And smile. Take that bloody stupid look off your face.'

For a second or two Jenny Crane looked at him blankly. Then, realising her mistake, smiled back at him.

Frank could not be mad for long. Seeing a familiar friendly face had instantly cheered him up. But he needed to get her off the streets.

'There's a bar around the corner. The one with a blue front. Give me a couple of minutes and then meet me there. I'll be sitting at a table outside. And please, remember that people may be watching.'

'I'm sorry,' she replied contritely. 'I'll be more careful. It was just such a shock to see you.'

'You knew you were meeting me. It shouldn't have been a shock.'

'I know. But it was.'

Frank walked away. When he looked back Jenny was taking a packet of cigarettes from her pocket.

Five minutes later, Frank was sitting at the table outside the bar he had mentioned. A waiter was about to take his order when Jenny arrived.

'Ahh,' he said. 'Here she is now.'

He stood up, pulling a chair back for her, which she sat on.

'Two black coffees will be fine,' he said to the waiter, who walked away to get the order.

When he was out of earshot Frank said, 'What happened to your shoes? They look a mess. Pop into the bathroom here and clean them as best you can.'

'It's a long story,' she replied. 'I'm shattered, to tell the truth. It's been a long night.'

They sat in silence for a while as the waiter returned with their drinks. Again they waited until he walked away before speaking again.

'Why have they sent you? You've never been in the field. It's getting more and more dangerous here.'

'I think "Double H" thought a friendly face may cheer you up. I'm fully trained, Frank. I speak the language and, let's face it, I won't be doing much other than making sure your "skeds" go out on time and doing any other odd job you may find for me. They've been worried about you for a while now. They think you may have taken on too much. Buckmaster wanted to pull you out, but Harding argued you're one of the best we have and you're needed here.'

'I'll be perfectly honest, it's really good to see you, Jenny. What cover story do you have?'

She smiled demurely. 'Why Francis, we are husband and wife. I'm Madame Claudette Aubuchon. We've been married for the past two years. How could you forget?'

'This'll mean a move from the apartment I'm in. The landlord thinks I'm a single salesman. I can't just conjure up a wife that nobody's aware of.'

'Yes,' she agreed. 'I'm sure it's something we can sort out without much problem.'

'We'll go and see Vallin after we've had this drink. He can find somewhere for you to stay until we can arrange more suitable accommodation.'

'See,' she replied, sipping at her coffee. 'I'm sure it'll all work out.'

***

Clement Vallin was able to find a room in a safe house for Jenny, not too far from where Frank was staying. Frank informed the landlord he would be leaving his apartment in the next few days and was quickly able to find alternative accommodation for the two of them. It would be a few days before this could happen and so they had to make do with the situation until then.

Vallin had been shocked to hear the news of Benoit's death. Frank told him how Benoit had sacrificed himself to save the others, but he did not mention anything regarding Monique. He decided that, for now, he would keep that information to himself. It was not that he did not trust Vallin. Far from it. It was more out of a sense of embarrassment that he was treating the woman so poorly, particularly when she was going through a very difficult time.

That evening, Frank visited Jenny at the room Vallin had provided for her, which was in a small hostel. He took the transmitter with him which was concealed in a small suitcase. Once it was safely stored away under the bed they settled to talk, Frank on a chair in the corner of the room, Jenny sitting on the bed across from him.

'I have a gift for you.' She pulled a small envelope from her pocket and handed it to him. Inside was a gold wedding ring.

'Put it on,' she said. 'Let's see how it looks.'

'This is all rather odd,' he replied as he slipped the ring onto his finger. 'What possessed Harding to come up with such a cover story?'

'Maybe he's a romantic at heart,' she giggled.

Frank looked at her suspiciously. This was something "Double H" Harding would not have thought up himself. Frank had a feeling Jenny may have had more of an influence on the whole thing than she was letting on. After all, as well as having himself wrapped around her little finger, Harding also clearly had a soft spot for her.

Having Jenny with him was a welcome release from the pressure he had been under recently. He somehow felt instantly relaxed in her presence. She was good company, that was for sure, even if a little irritating and annoying sometimes.

He was not sure if having her here was altogether a good idea. On occasion she had shown a somewhat mercurial nature, tending to act on impulse at times, without first thinking through the consequences of her actions. This was something she had to lose if she was to survive in France. She had not been in the field before and her French was not the best. It was passable, but anyone listening to her carefully would soon realise she was no native. She needed work on her accent. For this reason, Frank made sure they always spoke French, even when alone and nobody could possibly hear them.

'If I can be honest, I never expected them to send you. This is all rather a surprise.'

'I'm fully trained,' she replied. 'You've nothing to worry about concerning me.'

'I just thought they'd send a man…'

'So are you saying you think women can't do this type of work?'

'That's not what I'm saying,' said Frank defensively. 'Of course I believe a woman can do a good job in this line of work. I just never expected to see you out here. It's like you are my British life, detached from all this. It's as though my two worlds have collided and it feels strange. Nothing more than that.'

'Like I said, Frank. They were getting a little worried about you.'

'In what way?'

'Missing "skeds" for one. It's so important you transmit when you're supposed to. When you don't, then they have to assume you may have been compromised. It's only lucky that the girl who takes your messages in Dover knows your style, so when you do get round to it, they can determine it's actually you and not some German agent pretending to be you. It causes a lot of worry and work when you don't send your "sked" on time, you know.'

Frank knew what she was saying was right. He could think of no suitable response. It was true. Recently he had been inefficient in carrying out his scheduled transmissions and he understood this would cause some issues back in England.

'Well, now that you're here, you can help me out with that.'

'Exactly. Like I said, they're aware of the pressures you're under. Buckmaster wants you back and would have ordered you to return had it not been for Harding. He feels it's only a matter of time before something happens that they'll have no control over.'

'Let's hope that doesn't happen,' responded Frank. 'I've too much to do here. There are groups springing up all over the Vercors and the Vosges and other places. Young men not prepared to be shipped out under the STO order to do the German's work for them. They need help organising. They'll come in useful soon, I'm sure of it.

I've met some of them, Jenny. They're good people… young, courageous and willing to learn.'

Jenny leaned over to her jacket which was hanging over the arm of a chair and took out a packet of cigarettes. She put one in her mouth and lit it, blowing smoke into the room.

'I've more information for you,' she said after a while. 'The meeting they spoke of in Baker Street… Moulin and the CNR. It's about to happen. Here in Lyon.'

Frank sat up straighter. 'Have you any idea when exactly?'

'No, but it's imminent by all accounts. Moulin's on his way. RF Section don't give much away. In fact sometimes they're openly hostile towards us, despite us being on the same side. Harding thinks it's because they feel a little impotent about all this. The British calling the shots in their own affairs. They don't like it. Almost as much as they don't like the fact that the Germans are here. But we have to do what we can to accommodate them. I think F Section want to build a few bridges.'

'It won't be a bad thing,' replied Frank thoughtfully. 'To be honest I don't know if there's a lot we can actually do for them. I certainly won't be interfering in the French Resistance's internal affairs.'

He leaned over and took a cigarette from the pack Jenny had left on the bed. She took out a silver plated lighter and leaned towards him, lighting it for him.

He continued. 'The fact they've so many underground organisations, all opposing each other. It's ridiculous, quite frankly. But I suppose we'll do what we can to help them if they ask for it. But there's no guarantee they'll want to accept our help.'

'The offer itself may be enough for them to see our good intentions,' replied Jenny. 'As long as they know we're here if they need us. Or want to utilise us in any way.'

'What did Baker Street say?' went on Frank. 'How will contact be made?'

'They'll get in touch, should they need to,' replied Jenny. 'To be honest, I wouldn't worry too much about it until then.'

Frank mulled this over for a while and then understood she was quite right. He had enough on his mind without having to take into account the obstinacy of the various sections of the SOE. He had better things to do with his time.

'You have a point,' he replied finally. 'I've loads to do and this is a distraction, to be honest with you. Tomorrow afternoon, after I've shifted my stuff to the new place, I need to go and see someone. You'll need to entertain yourself for a while.'

'Can't I come with you?'

'No. The less people you come into contact with, the safer it'll be.'

'I think you'll find I can keep my mouth shut. I'm a trained agent, you know.'

'I know you are. You've already told me. It's not that I don't trust you, it's just that after what's happened over the last few days, it's better all round that the less you know, and the less others know, the better it is for everyone. You'll just have to trust me.' Jenny made to speak but Frank raised his hand. 'No argument. Whilst you're here with me, then you really need to follow my instructions. Otherwise I'll send you home. Don't think that I won't!'

'Fair enough,' said Jenny, stubbing out her cigarette in a glass ashtray on the cabinet to the side of the bed. She started to undo the buttons of her blouse. 'Anyway, enough of all this. Seeing we're kind of married, sort of… maybe not in the eyes of God, but certainly in the eyes of everyone else for the time being… why don't you take off those clothes and get yourself into this bed. It's far too big just for me.'

Chapter Nineteen

Frank pulled the tip of his cap low over his eyes and hunched his shoulders. It was late and curfew was getting nearer. He had checked the area around the apartment and, once convinced it was not being watched, stepped out of the shadows and headed across the road towards the building.

He knocked purposefully on the door and waited. A nervous voice called from inside.

'Hello.'

'It's me,' he snapped. 'Francois.'

He waited as Monique fumbled with the locks. He'd spotted heavy bars at the top and bottom on his last visit and now waited, as she struggled to slide them free. His impatience mounted with every second. Finally, the door swung open.

Without saying a word, he marched past her into the hallway, taking off his hat and placing it on the coat stand.

With reddened eyes she closed the door behind him. Ignoring him she walked to the kitchen. He had disturbed her preparing a meal. A small pan of potatoes bubbled on a stove, steam misting the window that overlooked a communal yard at the rear. She turned it off and sighed loudly.

'What do you want?' she said, walking past him to the living room and seating herself in a high-backed armchair in front of an unlit fireplace. To the side was a small table on which a half knitted sweater was bundled, a ball of wool and two knitting needles resting on top.

'I want a report,' he replied. 'I need to know what's happened to you since I was last here.'

She rubbed her eyes before responding.

'I hate you,' she snapped. 'I want you to know that. I want us to be perfectly clear on that. I don't want you here. I wanted no part in any of this and now look at me. My life is destroyed. I have you on one side and that evil bastard, Keller on the other.' She shivered.

'My God, he makes my skin crawl and it's all your fault. Yours and that prick, Jean-Luc's. I hope they've caught him and I hope he's dead.'

'Why is it Descartes' fault?'

'She loves him, that's why… Catherine… And he doesn't deserve her love. She should have left him months ago. She only stayed with the Resistance because of him. One of them they captured the other night talked. That's why the Gestapo came for us.' She burst into tears. 'Now my life is in ruins.'

'Stop feeling sorry for yourself,' Frank snapped. 'You're free. Your sister's the one in an SS prison, not you…'

'Keller has been round,' she interrupted, clearly not listening to him.

'When?'

'Twice in the last few days.' She wiped her tears with the back of her hand. 'He wanted to know if anyone had been to see me. Anyone who may be involved…'

'What did you tell him?'

She glared at him. 'Don't worry, I told him I hadn't seen anyone. You need to be careful. They're watching this place, I'm convinced of it.'

'There was nobody watching tonight,' replied Frank.

'How can you be sure?'

'I've been doing this thing long enough to be sure,' he replied dismissively. 'What happened with Keller?'

She seemed to shrink into herself, reluctant to speak.

Frank sat down in the chair facing her. 'Tell me,' he said softly. 'Tell me exactly what he said and did.'

She wiped away the tears from her cheeks again and used a handkerchief to blow her nose before continuing. 'He told me they're holding Catherine at the Terminus and that if I want him to help her, then I had to agree to certain things.'

'What things?'

Her voice lowered as she glowered at him. 'Use your imagination.'

She paused. At first Frank did not understand what she meant. She raised her eyebrows and then it dawned on him. Keller did not care about what Monique knew. This was a personal thing for him. After all, Frank realised, the woman was quite beautiful.

'Dear God,' he muttered, shocked at his own naivety. 'I never thought for one moment…'

'That's the trouble. You people don't think. All you care about is your stupid war and winning it. You don't care about how it affects those of us who want a peaceful life.'

'We all want a peaceful life. That's why we need to win it. And did you comply with his wishes?'

'Like I told you the other day, I'm left with no choice in any of this.'

Frank had not expected this. But then he knew his own involvement with Monique, his request for her to work for him, would have had no effect on Keller's demands.

'No you don't,' he replied after a moment. 'That's just the way things have fallen for you, Monique. Look. If you want to help Catherine and get one over on this piece of shit, Keller, then help us. He may have information that may be of use to us. If there's anything you can tell me about anything he said…'

'Oh, he loves to talk,' she replied. 'Especially about himself and how wonderful he is. How powerful he is.'

'Go on.'

'He hates the Resistance. He sees all of you as murderers and terrorists. He was bragging that there's going to be a big meeting soon and he's going to smash you all. He says there'll be no Resistance cells left in Lyon very soon and he and his friend, Barbie, will be big heroes.'

'What meeting? What did he know about it?'

'I don't know. He said they'd already made an arrest and it would all soon be over.'

Frank stood up. This news was totally unexpected. Could the meeting Keller was referring to be the CNR gathering? The one Moulin was organising? How could the Germans be aware of it? Who had they arrested that could give them such information?

He had to get word to London that the whole thing could be compromised. The meeting had to be cancelled or at least postponed.

He needed to see Vallin.

Vallin may possibly know something of this. If he didn't then he may be able to find out who had been arrested through his various contacts at the gendarmerie.

Frank moved to the door. He had to leave right away.

'What should I do?' Monique called after him.

He stopped and turned to look at her. 'Just carry on with what you've been doing. If Keller comes to see you, do what he says and try and gather any more information you can from him. Remember, you work for us now. When the final victory comes, you'll be suitably rewarded.'

He felt a flicker of pity for her. She really cut quite a pathetic figure and he was treating her abysmally. But it had to be done. Some things were more important than the virtue of one woman. Everyone had to make sacrifices. Christ knew, he'd made enough.

He paused.

'Have you got a pen and paper?'

'In the drawer on the telephone stand.'

Frank turned around and saw a black bakelite telephone on a small table in the hallway near to the front door. He pulled out a notepad from the drawer underneath and wrote a number on the last page.

'Look,' he said almost apologetically. 'I'll leave a contact number here. Only ring it in a complete emergency. I'll let people know what I've done. So should the Gestapo come knocking on my door, my friends will know on whose door they should knock in return, if you get my meaning.'

She looked at him indifferently.

'I know this is hard for you,' he said. 'But what you're doing will not be forgotten. Like I said before, we'll win this war. It may take a little time yet, but the Germans will be beaten and Keller and all his cronies will be gone, out of your life forever. Think on that and maybe this can be endurable for you.'

He turned around and left the apartment without waiting for a reply.

***

Vallin leaned back in his chair and exhaled the cigarette smoke into the air above his head.

'I can ask a couple of questions,' he stated, 'but I've got to be careful. If the wrong people get to hear of it, they'll want to know why I'm so interested in who the Gestapo have incarcerated in the Hotel Terminus.'

'It's really important,' urged Frank. 'I wouldn't ask if it wasn't. You know you can trust me when I say that.'

'I know,' responded Vallin. 'I'll ask around and let you know.'

'It needs to be done quickly,' said Frank. 'There's somebody in custody who knows a lot about a very important meeting that's about to take place and he's informed the Gestapo. Even I don't know when the meeting is to happen, or where. All I know is that it's imminent. I just need to know who it is so I can forward the name on to my people back home. They need to evaluate the importance of it. You see, this meeting has to take place at some point. The top brass won't stop it. But I need to ensure it can happen without any danger.'

'Have you told your people about the situation?'

'I only found out it may be compromised an hour ago. My next "sked" is due tomorrow. I'll tell them then. Whether RF Section trust the intelligence is another thing. They don't get on too well with F Section… I know, I know, it's all rather childish, especially when you think of the importance of everything.'

Vallin nodded. 'Fine. I'll see what I can find out and let you know if I hear anything.'

'Thank you, Clement.'

Frank left Vallin in his office to make enquiries and headed for home. This whole thing was turning into something bigger than he alone could handle. He needed to get word to London and he needed to do it as soon as possible. Whether RF Section took any notice of his misgivings about the upcoming gathering was up to them, but he could not stand idly by and let the situation play out without letting them know what he had learned. He had been ordered to assist Moulin in any way he could. If that meant stopping the meeting, then so be it.

It did not take long for Vallin to provide him with an answer. Two hours after returning home, the telephone rang.

'Does the name René Hardy mean anything to you?'

'No,' replied Frank.

'Hardy was picked up a few days ago. It looks like he's a small cog in a big wheel that's the Secret Army. From what I can gather he's been questioned by Barbie himself and for some reason, they've let him go. Whether they've got nothing on him or whether they've turned him I don't know.'

Frank frowned. 'Barbie isn't the kind of person to just let someone walk away. Especially when they're a known member of the Resistance. I have a bad feeling about this. Do you have any idea where I can find this Hardy?'

Vallin gave him an address. 'This is his last known residence. Whether you'll find him there I've no idea. The best thing he could do would be to get the hell out of Lyon. If he's still here then it speaks volumes as far as I'm concerned.'

Frank thanked him and hung up.

He decided that later that night, he would go in search of Hardy and find out just what the hell was going on.

There was a noise from the bedroom.

'Are you coming to bed or what?' called Jenny. 'It's getting cold in here.'

Chapter Twenty

21st June 1943

It did not take long for Frank to find the building that housed Hardy's apartment. It was a modest white-fronted five storey structure not far from the city centre. He was playing this by ear, as he had no idea what the man looked like.

As he approached the building, he suddenly had a very bad feeling about the whole thing. A sixth sense seemed to tell him something was not quite right. Turning up the collar of his jacket, he carried on walking, as though he had no interest in the place, until he got to the corner of the street. He stopped to light a cigarette and as he did so, he cautiously looked about the area.

They were not hard to spot. One of them stood in a doorway facing the building, a youngish man trying his best to look as though he had a reason to be there, but failing miserably. Further along the road stood another, leaning against a streetlamp. He occasionally cast furtive glances towards the building and then to his colleague. Frank also noticed a delivery van at the end of the road that looked out of place. The antenna on the roof gave away its more sinister purpose. Two rough looking men sat in the cab. Frank smirked to himself. They really were a bunch of amateurs.

It was clear Hardy was still of huge interest to the Gestapo. He had obviously been released for a reason. Frank moved across the road and positioned himself behind a tall fence that separated the road from an old derelict warehouse. From there he could not be seen from the road, people passing only a couple of feet away unaware of his presence. Through a gap in the fencing he could observe one of the German spies and also see the door to Hardy's apartment building. It was a good vantage point.

He could feel his heart pumping as the nerves and adrenaline started to make their presence felt. He put his hand in his pocket to feel the reassuring touch of the Colt.

Two hours passed. The sun hung low in the sky, casting long shadows across the deserted streets; people heading for home before the curfew came into force. The van had not moved and the one spy Frank could see fidgeted restlessly, moving from foot to foot, no doubt the hours of being stood in the same place playing havoc with his feet and knees. Frank empathised, his own feet had been aching for some time.

Finally, when the sun had completely set and the street lamps cast their dim halos in a poor attempt at illuminating the area, the door to the apartment building opened. Frank watched as the Gestapo agent moved back into the shadows, observing the shortish man who had exited as he slowly closed the door behind him.

Frank knew instantly that this must be René Hardy. The fellow could not be acting any more suspiciously had he tried. Pulling a cap low over his eyes and raising the collar of a quite grubby looking overcoat, Hardy set off along the street, walking hurriedly along, apparently unaware of anyone watching him.

The Gestapo agent followed him, sticking to the shadows on the opposite side of the road. As Frank watched Hardy turn the corner and out of sight, the van's lights were turned on and the driver gunned the engine, setting off in the opposite direction. The second man, the one that had not been in Frank's field of vision, joined his colleague and they both followed the Frenchman. Frank waited until the van had disappeared from his view and then stepped out from his hiding place. As long as he kept the Gestapo men in his sight, then they would lead him to Hardy and to his ultimate objective.

Did Hardy know the Germans were following him? This was a question Frank pondered as he followed the Gestapo agents from street to street, all the time keeping to the shadows. It was ironic, he felt, that the Germans following Hardy were completely unaware that they too were being shadowed. Was Hardy leading them somewhere knowingly or was he just too stupid to realise that the Germans had released him for this very purpose? Was he actually completely innocent in all this? Frank could not decide one way or the other.

He had a very bad feeling about the whole thing. Why was Hardy sneaking out at night? Where was he going, and to what end? He knew he could not approach the man. It was simply too dangerous. There was nothing he could do, but to follow and observe.

They reached a relatively affluent part of the city, and Frank saw the Germans come to a halt. To the right, the van he'd spotted outside Hardy's apartment reappeared, pulling up a short distance down the road from where the two Germans now stood.

Beyond them, Frank could just about make out Hardy entering the grounds of a large building which was surrounded by a tall wall. Purposefully, the Frenchman entered through a large iron gate, pausing briefly to look about him, before disappearing from view, to walk up the gravelled path that led to the front door. Frank could see lights in one of the rooms on the second floor and the shadows of two or three people within it.

One of the Germans approached the delivery van and knocked on the back door which opened after a couple of seconds, briefly emitting a soft glow out onto the street before the door was closed and the area was once again cloaked in darkness.

Frank waited for a few more minutes. Another man approached the building, looking from left to right before going through the gates, exactly as Hardy had done. Over the next quarter of an hour, more men arrived.

Frank felt a nervousness unlike any he had felt before. This was more than likely the CNR meeting Jean Moulin was chairing.

And it was all about to fall apart before it had even got started.

Frank had to do something, but he knew he could not just walk up to the building without having to pass the Gestapo. He had to try and warn them before more Germans arrived. He took the Colt from his pocket and checked the magazine before replacing it and cocking the weapon.

He raised it into the air and was about to pull the trigger when he suddenly heard the screeching of tyres behind him, forcing him to step back into the shadows and out of sight.

Four Opel trucks, filled with SS troops, sped along the roadway and screeched to a halt outside the gates, accompanied by two staff cars containing German officers and men in civilian clothes he presumed to be more Gestapo men.

Frank put the safety catch on the Colt and put it back into his pocket. There was activity in the second floor room as the occupants became aware of the commotion outside.

Quickly the soldiers entered the grounds. He heard angry shouts from the troops as they efficiently moved through the building, barking orders and dragging the Resistance leaders out into the street where they were lined them up against the wall outside the grounds. It was all over in less than five minutes.

There were eight of them in total. Frank had no idea who any of them were, not having met any before, but he presumed that Jean Moulin was among them. He could see René Hardy standing to the far left of the line, nervously fidgeting with his cap. Whereas the others all stood stoic and defiant, he looked petrified. As though he was about to wet himself.

Frank took the pistol from his pocket once more and readied it.

One of the German officers stepped forward and approached the group. Frank saw in the half-light that he was a youngish looking man, not much older than himself, with quite a handsome, determined face. The officer grinned, clearly pleased with the outcome of his night's work. He had broken up an important meeting and captured some very significant leaders of the Resistance. He approached one of the men, a shortish man wearing a fedora hat with a white scarf around his neck. The German officer, who Frank now presumed to be Klaus Barbie, spoke at the Frenchman. Unperturbed, the prisoner responded calmly. Frank could not hear what was being said between them, but whatever the man said to Barbie, the smile immediately left his face. Even from this distance, Frank could see the sudden redness of anger covering the Nazi's features.

Barbie raised his hand in a dismissive gesture and barked orders at the guards standing by, their machine-pistols trained on the group of prisoners. The response was immediate. The guards shouted commands, shoving the group toward the waiting trucks. Those who hesitated were dragged or kicked into compliance.

Suddenly one of the captives broke free, barging past a guard and sprinting down the road, heading in Frank's direction. It was as though he was purposefully coming straight towards him.

Two of the guards began firing, their bullets missing the fleeing prisoner, ricocheting harmlessly away. Barbie shouted something at them and they stopped shooting. He barked out another order and two of the SS guards set off after the escaping man.

It was only now that Frank realised the fleeing prisoner was René Hardy.

As Hardy passed the entry from where Frank had been watching the events unfold, he stepped out and raised the Colt, firing repeatedly at the Germans until the magazine was empty, forcing them to dive for cover behind walls and parked vehicles. Expertly he let the empty clip fall to the ground before putting in another and firing again.

Frank was aware that Barbie had witnessed this. The Nazi leader was standing at the rear of one of the trucks, watching what was taking place. Frank pointed the pistol in his direction, but knew he had no real chance of hitting him, being well out of effective range. Defiantly, he fired two more rounds.

Barbie did not flinch as the bullets ricocheted off the cobblestones to his left. He simply stepped out into the middle of the road, glaring at Frank.

Without waiting to see what would happen next, Frank turned around and ran in the direction Hardy had taken, sprinting away as fast as he could. He could hear the Germans regrouping and soon he heard the sound of boots on the cobblestones as they gave chase.

Ahead of him he could see Hardy vaulting over a short wall and hopping from garden to garden, desperately trying to get away. Frank kept up the pursuit and gained on him. He was clearly much fitter than the man he was chasing.

Behind, he heard shouts as the German commanders barked out orders. As he continued running, their voices became more distant until at last, they faded completely.

He found it hard to believe they had given up so easily.

Happy with his good fortune, he concentrated fully on catching up with Hardy who was now only thirty yards ahead of him. Hardy entered the back yard of a large three storey property and as Frank climbed the wall, he saw his prey open the gate at the opposite end and casually walk into the alleyway at the rear, that led on to the main street.

Frank realised Hardy did not know he was still being followed.

Quickly he lowered himself into the yard and crept to the gate Hardy had exited. Poking his head out of the side he was astonished to see the man standing in the shadows near the corner of the alley-way, pulling a pack of cigarettes from his pocket. He had his back to Frank, unaware of his presence.

Slowly Frank moved towards him. As Hardy struck a match and was about to put it to the cigarette, Frank placed the muzzle of the Colt against his neck.

Hardy froze, dropping both the cigarette and the lit match to the ground, the match burning out at his feet.

'You and I are going to have a little talk,' whispered Frank. 'I've a few questions I need to ask you.'

'Who are you?' said Hardy, shaking. 'Please don't shoot me.'

'Shut up and walk,' ordered Frank, grabbing the man by his collar and forcing him back up the alleyway. Halfway along, he found a gap between two large refuse containers and pushed him against a wall. From there they could not be seen from the roadway. The lights on the upper floors of the buildings that backed onto the al-leyway were all out. Frank was happy they were not being observed.

'Okay, René Hardy,' said Frank menacingly. 'I think you'd better tell me what just happened.'

'Who are you?' repeated Hardy.

'Who I am is of no concern to you. Just tell me what happened and give me a reason for me not to put a bullet into your skull right now.'

He spun Hardy around and forced the pistol against his cheek. 'Now, gct talking.'

'I don't know what you mean,' said Hardy, shaking with fear. 'Please don't kill me.'

'Tell me what I want to know and I may let you walk away.'

'I got word today there was to be a meeting at Doctor Dugoujon's property… some very important people. I was asked to attend.'

'Where did you get the information?'

'From my normal channels… Don't expect me to tell you what they are.'

'Why did the Gestapo let you go?' asked Frank, ignoring the comment.

Hardy shivered. 'They had nothing on me. They realised I was of no use to them…'

'The Gestapo don't just let people go,' interrupted Frank. 'You're either a traitor or you're very stupid, not to realise they would have you followed.'

'I assure you I'm no traitor,' replied Hardy, affronted. 'I'm a hero of France…'

'No real hero claims to be one' cut in Frank. The man was starting to annoy him. 'So how do you think this looks? You get pulled in by the Gestapo. They quiz you, and in the end, although you are involved in what they consider subversive activities, a few hours later they let you go. The following day you lead them to a meeting being attended by some very important figures in the Resistance. The Nazis raid the house and arrest them all. Then you escape. They hardly put in any effort to catch you…'

'What are you implying?'

Frank pressed the Colt into his face, forcing him to grimace in fear. 'I'm implying that you made an agreement with the Germans to save your own neck. You knowingly led them to that meeting and were allowed to escape. That's what I'm implying.'

'That's not the way it happened,' stammered Hardy. 'You have this all wrong.'

'Then tell me what really happened.'

'I'm telling you the truth, honestly. I would never do anything to jeopardise the Resistance. I'm a patriotic Frenchman. Please, let me go. I've to get away from here before the Gestapo pick me up again. If you've any sense then you'd better get out of the city too. Get out of Lyon. Out of France. Who knows what they're going to confess to.'

Frank was close to pulling the trigger. The Gestapo had clearly played him.

He stalled. He could not be sure if Hardy was complicit or whether he was just remarkably stupid. Frank lowered the weapon.

'Go on,' he said with a sigh. 'Get the hell out of here.'

Hardy could not believe it. 'You're letting me go?'

'Just piss off, will you. Before I change my mind.'

Hardy lingered for a brief moment. 'Who are you?' he repeated. 'You're not French… Are you an English agent?'

'You're very perceptive,' Frank replied.

'Are you the one they asked me about? This "Grey Man"? What does it mean?'

Frank ignored him and raised the gun. 'If you don't bugger off like I said, then I really will shoot you.'

Hardy did not need persuading any further. Without saying another word he turned around and headed for the roadway. A few seconds later he was out of sight. Frank put the Colt into his pocket and headed in the opposite direction. He had a message for Jenny to send back to Baker Street and it had to be done immediately.

So Hardy had confirmed Barbie knew of his existence. The code-name "Grey Man" would most certainly have been passed to him by Catherine, or another member of Benoit's circuit. Of that he was now sure. He was not overly displeased Barbie knew this. It may even make the "Butcher" realise he was being monitored and would one day have to answer for his crimes.

Frank thought of Otto Finkel and the similarity between him and Barbie. They were both the same. In fact, they were all the same, in his eyes. Each as bad as the other.

As he walked away, keeping to the shadows, an immense sense of doom crept over him. He had been given a mission, a very simple mission at that. And he had failed it miserably. The heads of the French Resistance were now in the custody of the Gestapo and there had been nothing he could have done to prevent it.

This was the lowest he had felt since he had ever set foot on French soil.

Chapter Twenty-one

A week later

Frank felt at home with these men. They had become a close knit group with an objective they all believed in. They had accepted the training he had offered with enthusiasm, each of them keen to learn how to use the weapons and explosives London had provided. It was difficult to keep them from heading off the massif and confronting the Germans head on. He, and their commanders, had stressed the necessity of selecting their targets carefully as they did not want to bring the might of the enemy down upon them in a battle they could never win. Their time would come, he told them. They had to listen to their leaders and take their instructions from them.

But he knew controlling them was not down to him. He had no authority over them. Now that Moulin and other heads of the Resistance had been taken by Klaus Barbie, there was somewhat of a power vacuum within the whole of the French Resistance. This situation seemed of little concern to the maquis. They did not seem to care who was in charge. They just wanted to fight and to kill Nazis.

After the incident with Moulin, Frank had thought it safer to spend time away from Lyon, to let the dust settle. He had persuaded Jenny to pack some things and they had travelled to the Vercors the following day, taking the radio with them. Living rough was not new to Jenny, having successfully passed the SOE course, but it was clear she did not like it. She was the kind of person who enjoyed the finer things in life. Frank had no sympathy. She would just have to grin and bear it like everyone else.

It was early evening and the sun hung low in the west. They sat with a small group of maquisards around a campfire. Mosquitoes and midges buzzed irritably about their heads. The young boy, Charles Mercier, who had travelled from Paris, sat with them.

The boy intrigued Frank. How could someone so young be so caught up in it all? He felt the safest place for him was back at home with his mother. When he broached the subject, the boy shrugged.

'Paris is no safer than here,' he said, drawing at the dirt between his legs with a stick. 'Not for me, anyway. I was nearly caught by the Germans at one point.'

Frank leaned back onto his elbows. 'What could you have possibly done to irritate the Germans so much?'

Charles laughed, but there was no mirth in his eyes. 'You'd be surprised, Francois. Although I think I irritated my grandmother a little more than them. I got myself involved in a small Resistance cell, running errands for them, leaving leaflets and tracts in public places, that sort of thing. The thing is, they got caught and the Nazis killed them all.' He said it all so matter-of-factly.

But then his eyes began to fill with tears. Frank sat up and placed his hand on the young boy's arm. 'Don't tell me if you don't want to.'

'It's okay. I'm fine,' replied Charles. Then he continued. 'I was nearly captured myself. I came very close to being, but I was able to get away. My uncle Michel is a gendarme and managed to get the necessary papers for Charlotte and I to cross into the unoccupied zone. This was just before the Germans came, you see. I stayed with my uncle until very recently. When my cousin got his orders to go to Germany he decided to come here instead and join the maquis. I couldn't stay behind. I didn't want to stay behind. So I came with him.'

He looked over at Arnold who nodded his head in acknowledgement.

'Who's Charlotte?' asked Frank.

'She's just a girl I know,' he replied nonchalantly. From the glint in the boy's eye, Frank assumed she meant more to him than the flippant remark warranted.

'How so?'

'She's Jewish,' he replied. 'She lived in the apartment block next to ours. When the Germans came for her parents she escaped out of the window. We gave her shelter in our place. Her parents were taken to the Velodrome and then on to Drancy. We heard they were shipped out somewhere a few months ago. God knows where they are now.'

'Where's Charlotte now?' asked Frank. 'Is she safe?'

'She wanted to come with me but when my uncle found out we were leaving to join the maquis he insisted she stayed on the farm with them. She's as safe as she possibly can be, I suppose.'

The light was beginning to fade casting long shadows over the ground around them.

Sacha Marchand, a man of around twenty-five years old, their leader and ex-sergeant in the French army, approached.

It was time.

'Come on. Let's get going,' he said.

The men around the campfire slowly got to their feet, picking up their rifles and machine-guns. Frank stood up with them. Although he had been tasked with organising and training the group, he knew he did not hold a place within its hierarchy. He was merely an advisor; an observer. The group saw him as a foreigner. An outsider who they were not prepared to take orders from.

Sacha seemed a good man with a level head. He was tall with handsome features and was able to keep the group disciplined. When he spoke, they listened and obeyed his commands without argument or complaint. What the man's story was, Frank had no idea. He only knew he had been involved in the fighting during the Battle for France and had been living on the plateau for a long time now. Maybe one day he would ask him, but the opportunity to have a private conversation with the man had not yet arisen.

Frank pulled the Colt from his pocket and took out the magazine. He had cleaned and oiled the pistol earlier, ensuring all the others had done the same with their weapons, stressing the importance of keeping them clean and in good condition. The last thing anyone needed was for their guns to jam during a firefight. Frank had spare ammunition and two Mills bombs in pouches hung around his waist. A Fairbairn-Sykes commando dagger was strapped to his waistband.

He had advised Sacha against the operation, telling him to bide his time and await a more opportune moment to hit the Germans. But after the capture of Moulin and the others the previous week, the maquis leadership wanted to strike back at the Nazis as soon as they possibly could. It was more for morale than anything else, Sacha had explained. Having the group sit around twiddling their thumbs whilst brave men were being tortured by Barbie and his cronies was not something the man was prepared to tolerate. He also needed to occupy his men as they were getting increasingly restless with all the inactivity. Frank knew to continue with his argument would do nothing more than irritate them further, and one or two looked like they would not think twice about sticking a knife into him if he continued on that course. In the end he thought it best to go along with them and try to deal with any issues as and when they arose.

As they were about to leave, Jenny approached him. 'Promise me you'll be careful.'

He smiled at her. 'Don't worry about me. I can take care of myself.'

'All the same,' she replied, 'be careful.'

She leaned up and kissed him on the mouth. He could smell the muskiness of her perfume and for a brief moment he had the urge to tell Sacha he was no longer going to accompany them. He had a much better idea on how to spend his evening.

***

A couple of hours later they were in position.

They were outside a small town to the east of Grenoble. Sacha had received word two men who had been heading to the Vercors to join them had been captured and were being detained in the police station there. He was aware of a small garrison of around twenty to thirty German soldiers in the town, who were there to support the gendarmerie and Milice.

The plan was simple. They were to enter the town in the dead of night and take the prisoners. They would kill anyone who tried to stop them, be they German, Milice traitors or members of the gendarmerie. Sacha did not care. All that was important was to get those patriots away from their captors and add them to the ranks of his own band of men.

Once he knew there was no talking Sacha out of it, Frank reluctantly gave him operational advice. He wanted to minimise the casualties on both sides, as the last thing these people needed was the might of the German army chasing them into the Vercors and crushing them before they had even got started.

A main road ran along the edge of the village, from north to south, near a small forested area. The road fed off to narrower streets containing residential buildings and a few small industrial premises. To the far south an inn stood silent and dark, its patrons long since gone home to the safety of their beds. At the opposite end stood a small chapel, its steeple pointing almost accusingly to the heavens. Sacha positioned four men in the woods, out of sight, at both entry points with orders to stop anyone coming in or out of the town whilst the breakout took place. They were to consider any vehicles as hostile and had permission to stop them by extreme force should they feel it necessary. Due to the late hour, and the village being so remote, Frank did not envisage any vehicle movements in the short time it should take to complete the mission.

The rest of the group would make their way to the police station. The army barracks was a two storey building next door, the entrances to both buildings faced onto the main road. Four men would enter the station and demand the release of the two men. Should they meet any resistance then they would take them by force. The rest of the group were to position themselves to cover the barracks to provide suppressing fire should the Germans be alerted to what was going on.

Frank was to be the first to enter the village, prior to the main mission starting, to deal with any sentries that may be patrolling the streets. He would give the signal for the mission to start once he confirmed the area was clear.

Frank lay behind a fallen tree on the embankment overlooking the village, a pair of binoculars at his eyes. There were lights on in both the police station and the barracks. Apart from that, there was not much activity in the nearby houses. All was quiet. If they were to carry out this mission, then tonight was as good a time as any to do it.

'Are you ready, Francois?' asked Sacha, patting him on the shoulder.

Frank nodded. 'There's a sentry out behind that shop on the left. He'll need dealing with. It looks like he's on his own but there may be more of them about. Be alert. Once it's done, I'll stand on that corner over there and wave. You can bring your men down then. Let's make this as quick and silent as we possibly can.'

Sacha grunted and touched Frank's arm again.

'Okay. Off you go.'

Frank stood up. Behind him Arnie, young Charles's cousin, followed him down the slope. He was to be Frank's lookout whilst he took care of the sentry. They made their way quietly along the tree line, out of sight of anyone who may be observing from the buildings, until they came to a point where it was darkest. Quickly, they crossed the road. Frank was aware Sacha would be following his every move through binoculars.

Slowly, using the shadows as cover, they moved closer to the police station. As they got nearer to the shop where Frank had seen the German soldier, they stopped.

Frank turned to Arnie and whispered. 'Keep your eyes out for any more sentries. Stay hidden. I'll be back in a couple of minutes.'

Without waiting for a reply he set off. He put his hand on the hilt of the Fairbarn-Sykes knife on his belt, a reassurance it was to hand should he need it. He had no intention of killing the man. He could not have on his conscience the reprisals from the Germans should one of their men be killed.

He took a deep breath. He had to control the nerves he was starting to feel. All was silent apart from the noise of his own heart pumping the blood around his body, which felt like the loudest sound he had ever heard.

Swiftly he glided along the roadway, until he was behind the shop where he had last seen the sentry. Stooping behind a parked car, he saw the man, standing under the dim glow of a street lamp, his machine pistol hanging by the straps behind his back. He was lighting a cigarette. The man looked completely bored. This was a quiet town with nothing much going on, far away from any front line.

Once the cigarette was lit, the man set off again, slowly moving along the roadway.

Frank crept along. Quickly and silently he gained on him. The adrenalin had now kicked in and he no longer felt any nerves, just a sense of needing to get the job done as quickly and efficiently as he could. He had a brief flashback to his SOE instructor in Scotland and was thankful for what he had taught him.

The sentry had no idea what hit him.

Coming up from behind, Frank wrapped his arm firmly around the man's neck, covering his mouth with his free hand. With an efficiency developed through months of training, he squeezed hard, resisting the struggles of the German soldier as he slowly slipped into unconsciousness. Frank gently guided his limp body to the ground.

Quickly Frank dragged the inert soldier into an alleyway. After checking he wasn't going to wake any time soon he took the man's MP40 machine-pistol and rejoined Arnie, who waited nervously where he had left him.

'Anything?' he whispered.

Arnie's face was white. He had witnessed it all and stood stock still, unaware Frank had spoken to him.

'Did you see anyone else?' whispered Frank, more forcefully.

'Erm, no… no.'

'Good,' Frank replied. 'Let's get this done, so we can all go back and get some sleep.'

Frank moved to the corner of the building he had indicated to Sacha and raised his arms. He could not see any of the maquisards but knew they would be watching him.

After only a few seconds he saw movement in the trees across the road. A few moments later, the group emerged and crossed the roadway. Sacha joined him.

'All clear?' he asked.

'There was just the one we saw earlier,' replied Frank. 'But there could be more further back in the village. Make this quick and try not to cause too much fuss.'

Frank's part in the mission was now over. With Arnie following him, he crossed the road to the tree line and made his way to the fallen tree he had used as an observation point earlier. Once he was in position, he took out his binoculars and looked down upon the group as they proceeded with the mission.

He watched on as around ten of them stealthily moved towards the police station. Once there, Sacha and three others, all holding their weapons at the ready, entered the building. The others positioned themselves to cover the doorways of both the police station and the barracks.

Frank waited nervously as the seconds ticked by.

What was happening in the police station he had no way of knowing. He hoped the gendarmes were complying with Sacha's demands to free the two men, and the telephones had been ripped from the walls to prevent them calling anyone once the maquisards left.

After what seemed an age, the door opened and Sacha exited the building. Behind him, the two prisoners emerged, followed by the other three maquisards who had gone in with him. The group crossed the road and entered the trees. Frank made his way to Sacha.

'Francois. You and Arnie, take our guests back to base camp. We'll follow shortly.'

Frank was puzzled. This was not part of the plan.

It was then he realised that no others from the group had moved from their positions covering the police station or barracks.

'This wasn't what we agreed,' said Frank realising what was about to happen. 'We've got what we came for. Let's just get out of here before anyone gets hurt.'

'I'm the leader here,' snapped Sacha. 'Not you. I decide when the mission is over. Now either send Arnie back and join us, or go with them. I don't really care one way or the other. But if you're to stay, then you'll follow my orders.'

Frank knew to argue with the man would be pointless. Once Sacha's mind was set there was no turning him. He had the support of every single man in the group. He thought for a moment. Maybe if he stayed, he may have more of an influence on how things turned out.

'Arnie. Do as Sacha says,' he urged. 'Take our two guests back to camp. I'm staying here. Give me your grenades.'

Arnie did not need convincing. After handing over the four Mills bombs he carried, he moved off with the two released prisoners. Seconds later they were out of sight.

Sacha had not waited for Frank to make his decision and was already halfway down the slope back to where his men waited for him. Sacha gave an order and a small group headed to the rear of the buildings, no doubt to cut off any escape route.

Frank took out the Colt and checked it, feeding a round into the chamber and slipping off the safety catch. He had not planned for this. It had not been discussed with him. He could tell, from the efficient way the maquisards were reacting, that each man knew the part they were to play in what was to happen next. They had clearly planned this without discussing it with him.

Frank watched as a young French fighter swiftly moved to a ground floor window at the barracks. A light was on inside. He squinted his eyes and could make out the shadows of a couple of men moving within the room. Smashing the window with the stock of a Sten gun, the maquisard threw in a hand grenade, followed by a second.

Even from where he was watching, Frank could hear the panicked screams of those inside, before a flash and a double explosion filled the night air as the grenades went off.

Moving rapidly, Sacha and his group kicked in the front door as the second group moved to the window, firing their rifles and machine-guns into the room. Once the door was open, Sacha went in, followed by the others.

And then Frank could hear the sound of gunfire at the rear of the building, as the more alert Germans tried to escape.

Slowly Frank moved down the slope towards where the firefight was taking place. Although it seemed to be going well, he knew the men they were attacking were all highly trained. If they were allowed to get themselves in any way organised, they could cause major problems for Sacha and his men. They had to finish this before that was allowed to happen.

Frank surveyed the area closely. Telegraph poles aligned the road with communications cables, leading to the barracks. Those lines had not been cut. If any officer within the building moved quickly enough, they could easily call for reinforcements. It would not take long before a much larger German force from Grenoble would be mobilised. Had Frank known they were to do this, he would have ensured the plan would have been prepared more carefully.

As he got to the tree line, he saw movement in a room on the top floor. A window was lifted open and two German soldiers with MP40 machine-pistols appeared, immediately opening fire on those below. Frank watched in horror as two fragmentation grenades were also dropped onto the maquisards, blowing shrapnel in all directions. He saw two men fall, one hitting the ground noiselessly whilst the other screamed in pain, clutching at his legs. He too was silenced, as he took a burst from the German's machine pistol in his chest, the blood from his wounds pouring out onto the roadway.

Those covering the building at the tree line now opened fire and the two German soldiers retreated back into the room.

Frank sprinted across the road and entered the building. He could hear footsteps on the stairway to his right and moved in that direction, passing the room where the initial fighting had taken place. He glanced in, and saw dead and dying German soldiers lying about the floor. He did not stop, and within seconds was at the bottom of the stairs. He could see a maquisard crouched at the top, his arm hanging loosely, covered in blood. To his right another was firing. The sound of gunfire could also be heard to the left.

Frank raced up the stairs, grabbing the wounded man and dragging him down a few steps.

'Get out of here,' he shouted into his ear. 'Get to the trees.'

He forced himself past and knelt beside the other who was firing down the corridor to the right. He recognised this man as Hugo, an enthusiastic maquisard, who Frank had found to be a fine young man. He cautiously peered around the edge of the wall. A dead maquisard and several German corpses littered the area, the carpet on which they lay stained red with blood. He looked to his left and watched as Sacha and another of the group fired their weapons into yet another room.

Frank could not see any Germans and tapped Hugo on the shoulder.

'Go and help Sacha. I'll clear these rooms out.'

Without waiting for a reply he stepped past him, taking a grenade from his pocket. He pulled the pin with his teeth. Fitted with a four second timer, he released the lever and counted to two before throwing it into the first room to his left. He crouched against the wall, placed his hands over his ears and waited for the blast, which came a moment later.

He jumped to his feet, the Colt at the ready, preparing to fire.

The room was empty.

Quickly, as the firefight raged on behind him, he moved from room to room, repeating the process. In some he found Germans who had already been killed, but as he got closer to the end of the corridor, those still alive tried to put up some resistance. He felt movement behind and turned. Hugo had joined him. Within a couple of minutes, having thrown all their grenades into the remaining rooms, the resistance in this part of the building stopped.

Frank entered the room at the far end of the corridor. A young German soldier lay dead, his body draped over a bed. Lying next to him, another sat on the floor clutching his leg, which had been half blown off by Frank's grenade. He held out his hand in surrender and moaned softly in pain.

Frank looked down at the soldier. He was no more than twenty years old. He would not be causing them any problems.

He took off his belt and knelt down. Quickly he wrapped it around the young German's thigh, strapping it as tightly as he could.

He turned to Hugo who was standing behind him. 'Here, get me something to tighten it. We need to make a tourniquet.'

Hugo ignored him. Instead he raised his weapon and fired a short blast into the wounded German's chest, knocking him back to the floor. Blood seeped from the corner of his mouth.

'For Christ's sake, Hugo!' shouted Frank in English. 'There was no need for that.'

Hugo ignored him and turned around, leaving the room to rejoin the fight at the other end of the building.

Frank sat next to the corpse and took a deep breath. These men were uncontrollable. He had to get them back to their hideout and try to speak to them. Such a disorganised attack had led to the deaths of some good men and the wounding of others. It had all been so unnecessary.

Slowly he got to his feet and left the room.

By now the shooting had stopped.

He met Sacha at the top of the stairs. He was smiling. Dust, smoke and the smell of cordite hung in the air.

And the stench of death.

'We got all of them, Francois. All of them.'

Frank looked him in the eye. 'So I see,' he replied. 'Now if you don't want the might of the German army bearing down upon you, you'd better get these lads organised and the hell out of here.'

Frank brushed past him and went down the stairs. Stepping outside he noticed some maquisards standing by the open door of the police station. Pushing them aside he entered the building.

What he saw shocked him to the core.

There had been three gendarmes on duty. One of them sat in a chair behind a desk. His head had been pulled back and his throat cut, blood covering the whole of his chest. His eyes, already starting to mist over, stared sightlessly to the ceiling. Two other policemen lay face down on the floor near to the cells. Puddles of blood filled the area around them. A further corpse, wearing a blue jacket, lay hunched inside a cell. His face showed the signs of a beating. He too had had his throat cut.

Frank sensed somebody behind him.

'Don't feel sorry for them,' said Sacha calmly. 'They were all traitors. Milice bastards.'

Frank did not hide his disgust. 'They're not all Milice. Those there are gendarmes. They were just doing their jobs. You knew nothing about them.'

'I know they helped the Germans round up Jews. I know they help them now, seeking out our countrymen to ship them out to Germany to work for them. This I know.'

Frank did not reply and left the building.

The wounded were now being assisted to the trees by their comrades whilst others, with petrol cans in their hands, set about pouring it throughout both the police station and the barracks. As Frank walked up the slope, away from the carnage, he heard a whooshing sound and felt the heat on his back and neck as the buildings were set alight.

He carried on up the hill and did not look back.

***

The following morning Frank set off to see Sacha. He found him sitting with a small group of men, eating bread. He had a mug of coffee in his hand.

'Ah, Francois,' he said as Frank approached. 'Join us. Have some coffee.'

Frank sat down on a rock opposite him. A maquisard named Troy, smoking a thin cheroot, handed him a mug. Frank took it and sipped at it. He welcomed the warmth.

'You don't seem impressed with our success last night.'

'How many men did you lose?' asked Frank, ignoring the remark.

Sacha's smile faded. 'We had three killed and another two wounded. Quite badly, in fact.'

'Not much of a success then, was it?' replied Frank. 'You lose five trained men and gain two untrained.'

'We wiped out their garrison. We killed over twenty Germans and four traitors…'

'They have plenty more men,' interrupted Frank. 'They have hundreds. Thousands. We don't. You can't afford to lose people like that, Sacha. Not if you want to survive. Not if you want to strike the Germans properly. So they lose twenty men. So what? To them that's nothing. And for what? You haven't damaged their infrastructure in any way. You've gained nothing strategically or militarily. You haven't inconvenienced them at all. And why didn't you tell me what you had planned?'

'You'd have argued against it.'

'You're damned right I would've argued against it. It was foolhardy at best. Expect repercussions for this Sacha. How many innocent civilians will they murder now, because of this? A lot more than the number of Germans you killed last night, that's for sure. You've got to listen to me, Sacha. You can't do anything like this again without consulting me or your bosses. I'm here to advise you. I'm highly trained and have a better picture of what's going on than you do. I don't want to take over. I'm not questioning your authority. I'm here to help you make a difference. But last night was the wrong way to go about it.'

Sacha sipped at his coffee and looked over to where Jenny was sitting with the two wounded men. She was trying her best to comfort them and assist with their wounds.

'She's no nurse,' said Frank noticing his gaze. 'She's not here for that.'

Sacha turned to look at Frank. 'Okay,' he said after a while. 'Maybe you're right. But I had to do something. These boys were getting restless. They needed this.'

'Just promise me that in future you'll speak to me first before you do something like this. I'm here to help. But I can't help you if you don't speak to me.'

'Okay,' said Sacha. 'I promise.'

'We can stay a little longer,' said Frank after a while. 'But soon we'll need to go back to Lyon. I've a couple of ideas I'd like to discuss with you. A couple of operations that'll keep you busy and hopefully have more of an impact than shooting a few Germans and burning their buildings down.'

Later, when he and Jenny were alone Frank told her of the previous night's events.

'Wow,' she said. 'Do you think Sacha will do as you say?'

'I bloody well hope so. Otherwise they won't last very long. Anyway, we'll need to get back to Lyon soon.'

'After what happened with Moulin and the CNR, things could be difficult for us, Frank. The Gestapo will be cracking down. This Barbie is a madman. He's made it his mission to catch every Resistance member in Eastern France. It'll only take one wrong word from someone and we could be compromised. I for one don't fancy a stay at Gestapo Headquarters.'

'Me neither,' he replied. 'But we need to get back. I need to see Vallin and there's one or two other things I need to take care of.'

'Whatever you say, Grey Man,' she replied with a smile. 'After all, you're the boss.'

'Am I?' smiled Frank. 'Now that's something you've never called me before.'

Chapter Twenty-two

For Monique, life could not get any worse. She had not eaten properly in weeks and it showed. When she caught sight of herself in the mirror, on the rare occasions she bathed, she disgusted herself. Her ribs could be seen clearly, in her now flat chest, and her arms and legs had become very thin and weak. Her face, drawn and skeletal, had lost all the radiance it once possessed and her hair hung loose and lifeless around her bony shoulders.

It was no wonder Keller had not come anywhere near her on his previous visit, which was the only blessing she could think of.

She had never felt as lonely in all her life. She had closed the shop two days ago and had no energy to go back, though she knew at some point she would have to. After all, she still had a living to make. There had been no word about her sister for a long time now, Keller avoiding the subject. Each time she brought it up he would shut her down with a curt wave of the hand or fob her off with a story she found hard to believe. She was beginning to think the man knew nothing, or alternatively, knew something he did not want yet to tell her.

It was early evening when there was a knock at the door. Her heart started to beat faster as she walked to the hallway to open it. Glancing down at her chest, she could almost see it pounding beneath her ribs. She took a deep breath and opened the door.

She was surprised to see it was not Keller, but Francois. Although she saw this as the lesser of the two evils, as he would not be wanting anything more than information from her, she still had no desire to see or speak to him.

She reluctantly moved aside as he walked past her, closing the door behind him.

She followed him into the lounge and sat near to the fireplace. She felt exhausted. It did not take a lot to tire her these days.

He sat down opposite her.

'You look like shit,' he said.

'I've had better compliments,' she retorted. 'You don't look so good yourself.'

It was true. Francois had aged since the last time she had seen him. Although she knew him to be quite young, lines had started to appear on his forehead and one or two grey hairs were showing at his temples. The man looked stressed.

He ignored her comment. 'Do you have anything for me?'

'Like what?'

'Anything from Keller?'

'Keller's a brute.' She snapped. She could feel tears beginning to form in her eyes, but fought them back. She did not want to give him the satisfaction of seeing her totally broken. 'He avoids telling me anything. All he wants is one thing. He won't tell me anything about what's happening with Catherine. Do you know anything?'

'I don't move in those circles,' replied Francois dismissively. 'I'm afraid Keller is the only one who can help you with that. Has he mentioned anything at all about Moulin?'

'Only to brag about what a great job they've done in catching them all,' she replied.

She paused before continuing. 'He did say something about them looking for someone else. Another from that night who got away. Those they've caught are not telling the Gestapo anything. Keller thinks it's probably because they don't know anything.'

'Did he say anything about this person… who he may be?'

'Nothing other than he calls himself the "Grey Man". Or something like that. They've put a price on his head. Anyone giving information leading to his capture will be suitably rewarded, apparently. That's what Keller said. Whatever that means.'

Monique noticed a slight change in Francois' demeanour. He shifted slightly in the chair, as though suddenly uncomfortable. This was only fleeting, and he instantly reverted to the same calm manner he always displayed.

'Is that so?' he replied thoughtfully. 'Where did Keller get that information from?'

'He didn't say and I was hardly going to ask him.'

'You need to keep Keller sweet,' said Francois. 'If he loses interest in you then you'll become no use to him. He'll get rid of you. And I don't mean he'll just stop coming to see you when I say that. I mean it literally. For your own safety you need to brighten yourself up a bit. You're a good looking girl, but you've let yourself go. He's a Nazi. He won't stand for it for much longer.'

'I feel sick all the time,' she replied, tears filling her eyes. 'I'm worried about my sister and I disgust myself for letting him do the things he's done to me. The man's a sadist.'

'They can't win this war, Monique. This situation is merely temporary for you. One day they'll be gone, Keller included. In the meantime you need to endure.'

'That's easy for you to say,' she replied. 'It's not you suffering.'

'We're all suffering,' he replied angrily. 'Suffering is not exclusive to just you, you know. At the moment you have your liberty and your life. There are thousands enduring a lot more than you are, believe me. But the Allies are doing something about this. They're arming the Resistance. People are fighting back. In many ways. In a way you are too. You may not feel it, but you are.

'I want you to tell Keller that the Resistance have made contact with you. Tell him this "Grey Man" they are seeking has been to see you, to recruit you because of your sister. Let him believe you have their confidence. There's going to be an airdrop south of here in two nights' time. At midnight. More weapons and supplies for the maquis, outside a small village south of Grenoble called Pariset. That's where the drop will take place. But you're to tell him that it'll happen somewhere completely different. Tell him the drop will happen at Montaud. Have you got that? Montaud. You see, things like this are going on all the time. It won't be long before your own suffering is over and you can go back to your normal life, selling dresses and all the other things you did before the war.'

This didn't make her feel any better. Francois may be right. Maybe this whole thing was just temporary, each person having to endure their own private hell as best they could. She also knew he was right about Keller losing interest in her. She could not let that happen. Catherine's life depended on it.

Francois stood up. 'It may be some time before I see you again. Things are getting very dangerous. I'll visit when I can and if it's safe to do so. I'm taking a real chance coming here tonight, to be honest with you. But I was conscious I'd not seen you for a while. I didn't want you to think I was leaving you to stew. Remain strong and get as much information from this creep as you possibly can. It all helps.'

Monique did not stand up to see him out. She did not have the energy nor the will. As she watched the Englishman leave, she realised just how much she despised the man. He had put her in an impossible situation, by forcing her to endure Keller and all that came with him. Although Francois had never abused her in a physical way, he had still tortured her. She hated both men equally. The pressure she was under was overpowering. This had been going on for months now and she was no closer to finding out what had happened to Catherine as she had been the night she was taken.

She had a sneaking feeling that both men knew. And neither of them were telling her, both using her for their own ends. But Francois had just told her that Keller was the only who could help her as far as Catherine was concerned.

When she heard the front door close behind him she got up and ran to the window. Pulling the curtain to the side she watched as he reached the end of the street and disappeared into the shadows, vanishing into the night just like the vampire he was.

She turned away, pulling the curtain closed and then walked to the telephone in the hallway.

She took the notebook from the drawer, picked up the receiver and dialled the number written on the front page. The number a different abuser had recently given her.

***

Frank returned to the apartment he shared with Jenny. He relayed the conversation he had just had with Monique.

'Things are getting too much for her,' he explained. 'She's at breaking point. I'm not sure if she's a useful asset anymore. She also tells me Keller knows of the Grey Man.'

'How could he know?' she asked.

'Probably Catherine. Or one of the others from Benoit's cell. Or maybe one of those captured at Dugoujon's house knew of me. They could've intercepted our messages. But if they'd done that, they'd have probably caught us by now. Hardy knew of me when I confronted him. They're well aware of my existence now, and what I've been doing.'

Jenny raised her eyebrows. 'This doesn't sound good,'

'It's not,' he replied. 'For the first time since I've been here, I'm starting to get nervous. We'll see how things go for the next day or so. It may be an idea to leave Lyon for good. We could join the maquis in the Vercors, maybe. We're probably more useful there now anyway. Leave the circuits here to Vallin.'

Jenny did not argue with him. She knew it probably made sense. The Milice and Gestapo were clamping down on all subversive activity and they were doing a good job of it. If Monique was as on edge as Frank suggested, then she could prove a major problem in the future.

'Okay,' she replied. 'I agree. I'll keep a bag packed for a quick getaway. Just tell me when and I'll be ready.'

'Good girl,' said Frank. He kissed her on the forehead. 'I'm so glad I have you here, Jen. You've been a godsend. But I can't have you in any unnecessary danger. Just be ready to go at a second's notice should it be required.'

***

Two nights later - outside Pariset, Vercors Massif

Frank lay in the undergrowth, his binoculars clamped firmly to his eyes. Sacha and one of his lieutenants, a short tough looking fellow by the name of Alain, were positioned closely to his left.

'Can you see anything?' whispered Sacha.

Frank scanned the clearing from left to right. 'No, my friend, not yet.'

'This could be a complete waste of time.'

'It won't be a waste of time,' Frank responded. 'Even if nothing happens, it won't have been a waste of time. How many did you send to Montaud?'

'Four of my best men,' replied Sacha calmly. 'Don't worry, they won't be seen. Nobody will know they're there.'

Frank continued to move the binoculars, sweeping the tree line, searching for movement of any kind. He took out a small flashlight and, using his body to shield the light, shone it on the watch on his wrist.

'It's twenty to,' he said. 'There's time yet.'

Sacha gripped his arm. 'I can hear something.'

Frank turned off the flashlight and put it back into his pocket. He listened carefully. He could just make out the sound of vehicles coming from the right, on the road beyond the clearing. He put the binoculars back to his eyes and adjusted the focus. Through the trees he could make out the shadow of a truck. It did not have its lights on.

There then followed another. And then another.

'This could be them.' Frank had not wanted this. He had hoped the whole thing would be a complete waste of time, as Sacha had suggested it would be.

They waited in silence for what seemed like an age, and then there was movement at the tree line a hundred yards opposite. It was a German soldier, the shape of his helmet unmistakeable.

Gradually more appeared, each stepping out into the clearing, weapons unslung and at the ready. The sound of an officer's voice broke the silence and five flashlights cut through the darkness, scanning for signs of the maquisards they had clearly been expecting to find. The frustration in the officer's voice was apparent, even from this distance.

They were too far away for the beams to reach them.

'Come on,' whispered Frank. 'Let's get the hell out of here before they find us.'

Slowly and silently they crept backwards, further into the trees away from the German troops. Shortly they reached the sunken road by which they had arrived and were soon away from danger.

'Are you happy now?' asked Sacha when they were clear.

'Not one bit,' replied Frank. 'But at least I know. It means I have to go back to Lyon tomorrow. Maybe the last time for a while.'

As they trudged silently back to their hideout, a wave of sadness settled over Frank. He knew he had placed Monique in an impossible position. But the sympathy didn't last. No one had made her betray them. No one had forced her hand. That choice had been hers alone. And now, she would face the consequences.

He felt a drop of water hit his face and looked up to the sky. Grey clouds were starting to appear in the east. It looked like a storm was brewing. He pulled up the collar of his jacket and hurried along. He hoped this wasn't an omen for what was to come.

***

Frank arrived back at the apartment the following evening. It was pouring with rain and as he walked into the kitchen, he took off his overcoat and put it over a chair. Jenny was sitting at the table, the radio in front of her.

'I'm about to send the "sked",' she remarked without looking at him. 'Is there anything you need me to pass on?'

'Tell them we're leaving here for good in a couple of days' time and won't be contactable for a while. Things are getting too hot right now.'

She looked up at him. 'What's happened?'

'We can't trust anyone anymore,' he replied taking a packet of cigarettes from his pocket. 'It's becoming too dangerous. We need to get you back to England too.'

She took her hand away from the Morse key. 'Do you really think that's necessary? I can still do a job for you, Frank…'

'I wouldn't say it if it wasn't necessary,' he interrupted, then lit the cigarette. He took a couple of puffs, inhaling the smoke deeply before blowing it out into the room. 'The Gestapo are aware of me and that we're operating in the area. They've probably got detector vans out there right now searching for our transmissions. It's just a matter of time before they find what they're looking for. Agents are being caught all over the country. We've been lucky for too long now and that luck can't last forever.'

'What's your plan?'

'I'm going to ask Baker Street if I can move my base of operations to the the Vercors. I think I can be more effective with them. There'll be an invasion and I can't be too far away when that happens. I want those boys to be in a good position to cause as many problems for the Germans as they can when it happens. Their bosses have ideas on how to do that and as long as they get the support they need they can probably do a lot of good. They need to be organised and I can help them with that. Lyon's become too dangerous for us.'

Jenny was clearly ruffled. 'You're starting to scare me now.'

'Good,' he replied. 'We need to be scared. Do you know what they'll do to us if they find us? They'll torture us and then they'll shoot us. They'll make us disappear, as though we never existed. We need to remain a step ahead of them.'

'Okay. When do we go?'

'I need to see Vallin. I'll go and speak to him in the morning and then we'll head off. Just make sure you have everything you need packed. In fact, do it now.'

'It seems that I'm one step ahead of you,' she smiled. 'Already done. I'm ready to go any time you say.'

'Good girl…'

Then the telephone rang.

They looked at each other. This was the first time it had ever rung in the whole time they had been located at this apartment. There were very few people who had the number, all with strict instructions to only ever call if it was an emergency.

Jenny shrugged. 'Maybe it's a wrong number.'

'Maybe,' replied Frank. He sat a little longer, letting the phone ring. He knew it was stupid, but to him it sounded as though the telephone itself was telling him just how urgent this call was. It sounded like an angry ring, the phone demanding to be answered.

He stood up and walked to the hallway.

He picked up the receiver and put it to his ear.

'Hello,' came a familiar female voice. 'Hello… Is anyone there?'

'What's the problem?' he asked.

Upon hearing his voice, Monique's voice changed. She was clearly upset and it took a while for her to compose herself.

'Please come, Francois. Something terrible's happened. I don't know what to do.'

'Calm down,' he replied. The tone in her voice made him nervous. 'Tell me slowly what's happened.'

'Please, just come. I beg you. It's Keller. I think he's dead.'

Frank took a few moments to let her words sink in. 'I'll be right over,' he replied.

He hung up the receiver and turned to Jenny. 'That bag we just spoke about. Check it. Make sure you have everything you need in it. Be ready for a quick move.'

'What's going on?' asked Jenny. 'You look like someone just walked over your grave.'

Frank took his overcoat from the back of the chair. 'Maybe they did. I'll be back as soon as I can.'

He put on the coat and headed for the door. As he got outside, the clouds looked even blacker than they had when he was last out. The wind howled, lashing the rain almost horizontally, where they then appeared to bounce from the ground. It was the worst weather he had known since arriving in Lyon nearly two years ago.

He pulled up the collar of his coat and pushed the hat firmly onto his head. If anybody was out in this, watching him, then he knew they would find it very difficult to follow him in this weather. Without looking around, he moved as fast as the wind would allow. He headed in the direction of Monique's apartment.

***

Frank got to the apartment and knocked firmly on the door. The rain showed no signs of let up. If anything, it was coming down stronger.

'Who is it?' came a nervous, whispered reply.

'Who do you think it is?' he replied irritably. 'It's me. Francois. Open the bloody door and let me in before somebody sees me.'

Frank had considered getting in touch with Vallin to ask him to arrange for someone to dispose of Keller's body, but decided against it. It was just too risky and he did not want to chance any more good men being caught. He did not believe for one second that Keller had kept his visits to Monique a secret. Barbie would never have sanctioned her release purely to let his colleague have his fun with her. They had used her to lead them to more Resistance members, but in the end the whole thing had backfired. For both sides.

Despite her recent duplicity, he could not leave Monique there. He had been tempted to end it there and then. To put a bullet into her brain. But when he saw her distraught, pathetic face, he understood her downfall was as much his fault as it was Keller's. He knew he could not do it. Whatever this war had turned him into, he was no murderer. One day the conflict would come to an end and he would have time to reflect on all of this. When that hour came, he had to be able to look at himself in the mirror and know that everything he had done would stand up to moral scrutiny.

But God knew she had become a problem. She had not been as useful to him as he thought she might have been. In the end she had become nothing more than a huge complication. From what had happened the previous night, it was clear she had given Keller information that she need not have. Whether she thought it would save her sister or not, she had been prepared to betray her countrymen. There was no forgiving her for that.

Shortly, Monique was ready to go, a hastily packed bag draped over her shoulder. Frank was in the lounge. She could not bring herself to go back into the room.

Frank had removed the knitting needles from Keller's face and moved the body to the side of the room, where he covered it with a rug. There was little else he could do.

'Where are you taking me?' she asked through the doorway.

'To a friend.'

'Can you trust him?'

He came out of the room and grabbed her roughly by the arms. He turned her to face him and leaned in close, their noses only inches apart.

'Can I trust him?' he snarled. 'Who I trust and who I don't is no concern of yours. I don't think you have a choice in what happens from here, do you?'

She was shaking now, the shock starting to kick in. 'I… I'm sorry…'

'Pull yourself together,' growled Frank. 'We're going to leave now and you'll do everything I tell you. If the Germans get hold of you, they'll kill you. You've just killed one of their officers. They'll hunt you down until they find you and then they'll kill you. But not before Barbie makes you suffer. If you want to get out of this alive then you've no choice but to trust me.'

'Thank you.'

'Don't thank me. These men I'm taking you to will have their own questions for you. In particular, why the Nazis showed up in Pariset. The only people who knew there was supposed to be a drop there, were you and I. And I know for certain it wasn't me who told them…'

'Catherine…' she interrupted. 'My sister…'

'Your sister is probably dead,' snapped Frank. 'She's probably been dead for months. If she's not already dead then she'll be being worked to death in the east.'

Monique started to sob.

'You know it's true,' he went on. 'You've probably known it all along if you're honest with yourself. Keller and Barbie let you go to get to me, and people like me. Keller's been stringing you along ever since and having some fun with you whilst he did it. That piece of shit in there deserved what you did to him. But why did you tell him of Pariset? I did that to test you, to test your loyalty to France, and you failed miserably.'

'My loyalty is to my sister,' she sniffled. 'My loyalty is to my family first and then everything else comes after that. I thought if I did this, then Keller would set Catherine free.'

'You're so naive, Monique,' he said quietly. 'You stupid, stupid woman. Now you've both sides in this whole mess gunning for you.'

'What can I do?'

'You can take your chances with your countrymen,' Frank replied. 'I understand I've put you under a lot of pressure. All I can do is deliver you to them and you can put yourself at their mercy. The Germans won't give you any. So, like I've already said, you have no choice. I'll ask my friend to get you out of the country. Maybe you'll be able to return when the war's over.'

He moved to the window and looked out. The rain was still teeming, sweeping across the roadway as though the sea itself was falling upon the city, flooding the gutters, the drains unable to cope with the amount of water coming down.

Fifty yards along the road Frank could see a truck. At first glance it looked as though it was merely parked there, empty. He frowned. He had not seen it when he arrived. When he looked more closely he thought he saw the silhouettes of two men sitting in the cab.

'Come on,' said Frank. 'Let's get moving. Out the back. Quickly. If we're lucky we may be able to get to my friend's without being seen. This weather will keep everyone off the streets, hopefully. Let's go.'

***

Thankfully, the rain had stopped, the storm moving south and away from Lyon.

Frank waited in the shadows of an alley, a street away from his own apartment. It was close to two o'clock in the morning. A German patrol had come close by on a couple of occasions as he made his way back from Vallin's apartment, but he had so far been able to avoid being seen. As he crept along the alley he saw movement ahead of him.

He stepped back into the shadows and knelt down, making himself as invisible as possible.

He needed time to think.

Clement Vallin had not been pleased to see him. When he had knocked on his door an hour and a half earlier, he and Monique looking like drowned rats, his friend nearly shut it back in their faces. Frank knew he was asking way too much of him, but after some persuasion, he agreed to take her. He told Frank he would use his contacts and network to try and get her out of the country, possibly to Switzerland.

Whether or not Vallin would use those resources to do this, being aware of her treachery, Frank was not sure. He only knew that he was now rid of her. She was one less thing for him to worry about. If they chose to take her to Switzerland or to throw her in the Rhone, that was up to them. She was their problem now.

With what had happened earlier, he knew that should he stay in the city it would not be too long before the net closed on him and Jenny. They had to get out and make their way to the relative safety of the Vercors. From there he could arrange for Jenny to get back to England. He knew she would argue against it but he would put his foot down. This whole area was too dangerous.

And now the Germans were here, in force, outside his apartment building.

He had known leaving his number with Monique had been a foolish thing to do and cursed himself for it. He had felt sorry for her at the time, a feeling of guilt to have put her in such an impossible position. Her phone line had clearly been monitored and he was surprised they had not come for him whilst he was at her apartment. Why she had not passed on his own number to Keller, he simply did not know. Maybe she wanted to have something in reserve that she could use later. Or maybe it was simply because her head was not in the right place.

Slowly he crept along the alleyway until he could see the building where he knew Jenny was waiting for him. He took off his hat and overcoat and placed them on the ground, first taking the Colt and spare clips from the pocket, along with the commando dagger. He needed to be as agile as possible.

As he got to the end of the alleyway he could see two trucks parked across the road at the corner, out of sight of the apartment. Both of them were full of troops. A group of German officers and Gestapo agents stood beside them, talking quietly.

The easiest thing for him to do would be to leave the area and abandon Jenny to her fate.

But he could never do that.

Swiftly he retraced his steps. When he knew he could not be seen, he ran through the streets until he was one away from the rear of the building. There were a few cars parked along the roadway and after trying the handles of a couple, the door to a black Citroen opened. He leaned under the steering column and felt around until he found the ignition cables, cutting them with the dagger and baring the wires. This done, he closed the door and moved quickly to the alley at the rear of the building.

He knew he had to act fast, but at the same time he had to be careful. As yet the Germans had no idea he was aware of their presence. If they thought him to be in the building then it was only a matter of time before they broke in.

He was about to run to the back door when, out of the corner of his eye, he saw movement to his left. Two German soldiers, roughly ten yards apart, were watching it. Each of them were crouched behind refuse containers and were holding MP40 machine-pistols at the ready.

Frank checked his pistol, chambering a round. He put it into his waistband and once again pulled out the dagger.

Stealthily he crept up behind the first one, his senses on high alert. The man was slightly behind his comrade, out of his line of sight. It was now that Frank realised he felt remarkably calm. Was he getting used to this? After the skirmish in the Vercors, was killing becoming easy for him? He put these thoughts to the back of his mind and concentrated on the task ahead.

In one quick movement, he grabbed the man's head and twisted it to the side with his left hand, thrusting the dagger deep into his neck, slicing through the man's trachea as he pulled the blade out. The only sound the soldier made was a small sigh as the air left his lungs for the very last time.

Slowly and carefully, he lowered the body to the ground, as quietly as he could.

But it was not quiet enough.

'Tomas?' whispered his colleague, turning his head to see what was happening.

When Frank thought about it later, he knew that it was a completely lucky shot. It was something he had never practiced before, acting purely on instinct.

Quickly he pulled the dagger from the dead German's neck and threw it with force at his comrade, the blade plunging deep into his throat. The soldier's hands raised towards the blade, his eyes bulging in surprise and agony. Then they dropped down and he fell to the ground, blood pouring from the wound and his mouth.

Swiftly, Frank moved over to him. The German was still alive, his legs thrashing, kicking out as he clung on desperately to life. There was a danger he would kick over a bin and create an unwelcome noise. Quickly, Frank grabbed the dagger, yanked it from his throat and plunged it deep into his heart. Frank moved aside as the man's body spasmed and then became still, all life extinct. He removed the dagger, wiped the blood on the dead man's tunic and replaced it in the scabbard in his pocket.

Frank removed the MP40 machine pistols from both soldiers and slung the straps over his shoulder. Grabbing as many magazines of ammunition as he could carry and taking two stick grenades from one of the dead men, he moved to the back door of the apartment.

He tried the handle, but it was locked. He banged on the door. A few moments later, as he was considering breaking it down, it opened. Jenny stood before him, her mouth agape.

'Frank? What the hell?… ' she stammered.

He pushed past her. 'Get your shoes on. Now! The Germans are outside. They'll be here in seconds.' He handed her one of the MP40s. 'I take it you know how to use this.'

She took it from him and looked at it blankly. 'Of course. What's going on?'

'I've just told you. The Germans are outside. They've come for us. Go and get the radio. Now.'

The initial shock suddenly left her and she reacted, slipping on her shoes before rushing to the bedroom to retrieve the radio. Frank moved to the window and shifted the curtain slightly. He could see troops getting into position outside. They were about to break the door down.

Jenny came into the room, carrying the small suitcase in her left hand, the MP40 strapped over her right shoulder, holding the pistol grip in the firing position.

'Out the back, now,' said Frank. 'They're here.'

There was a loud bang on the door and the sound of a German officer shouting for them to open up. He pulled the two grenades from his waistband and pulled the cords at the bases of the handles, throwing them both in the direction of the front door. He then turned and followed Jenny out the back.

He heard the front door give as the soldiers broke it down followed a second later by the blasts of two explosions as the grenades went off. Screams of agony followed. At the end of the yard he found Jenny waiting near the gate. She had the MP40 trained along the alleyway.

'It's clear,' she said as Frank arrived.

'Come on,' he said, grabbing the radio from her. 'Follow me.'

He led her down the alleyway, stepping over the two dead Germans as he did so.

'Frank?…' he heard Jenny say as she saw them, but he ignored her.

A second later the air was split with the sound of gunfire as German soldiers followed them outside. Dropping the radio, Frank turned and crouched onto one knee, firing the MP40 back in their direction. To his right, Jenny also fired blasts from her machine-pistol. More cries of agony followed as their bullets found their mark.

'Quickly,' said Frank. 'The car's just around the corner.'

'Car?…'

They sprinted into the roadway as bullets pinged and ricocheted around them. The Germans were starting to get organised. Frank knew that if they didn't hurry, it was inevitable that they would be caught. Or worse still, killed. They were running for their lives.

They reached the Citroen and Frank opened the door, flinging the radio into the back.

'Get in!' he shouted to Jenny. 'Let's get the hell out of here.'

Jenny did not answer. Instead she was firing the MP40 furiously. 'More ammo, Frank,' she shouted.

He turned to see a group of soldiers turning the corner, some diving for cover to avoid being hit by Jenny's bullets. Others, kneeling in the roadway, raised and fired their rifles and MP40s.

There was no more time. 'Get in', he repeated. 'Start the car.'

He knelt at the side of the Citroen and fired wildly in the direction of the Nazi troops, emptying a full magazine before expertly replacing it with another, and continuing to fire.

He heard the engine start and glanced to his right. Jenny was at the wheel and putting the car into gear. 'Come on!' she yelled above the roar of the engine.

Frank stopped shooting for a brief moment. One of the Germans was standing in the middle of the road, a Luger pistol in his hand, pointing it towards him. There was something very familiar about the man. For a second their eyes met. Then the German lowered his gun. Frank recognised him as the officer who had been in charge of the capture of the Resistance leaders a few weeks ago.

Haupsturmführer Klaus Barbie.

Frank fired one last burst before opening the rear door and jumping in. Jenny wasted no more time and set off, the door swinging wildly before its own momentum slammed it shut behind him. Using the butt of the pistol grip, Frank smashed the rear window and fired out. His bullets flew harmlessly around the soldiers as Jenny swerved the car from side to side to avoid the German gunfire. Despite her efforts some enemy bullets thwacked into the side of the car. They reached a junction and she turned into the corner, taking the car out of sight of the pursuing troops. Frank was thrown from one side of the car to the other, dropping the gun into the footwell.

As Jenny drove through the streets, he was reminded of that first time they had met, back in London, so long ago now. At the time he had been scared half to death by her indiscriminate and dangerous driving. Now he thanked God she was at the wheel. He doubted he could have handled the vehicle so skilfully.

He climbed into the front seat beside her.

'Bloody hell,' she laughed. 'That was close.'

Frank gaped at her. 'You're laughing. You're actually laughing.'

She turned to him and grinned. 'That was so much fun.'

He shook his head from side to side, not quite believing what he was hearing. 'Jesus Christ, Jenny.'

'Where to?' she asked.

'There's only one place we can go,' he replied. 'We've pretty much outstayed our welcome in Lyon. We need to get off these roads before we come across any patrols.'

An hour later they found a wooded area near Champier and hid the car in undergrowth away from the roadway, covering it with branches. Taking the radio from the back, they set off on foot for the sanctuary of the Vercors plateau, to find Sacha's maquisards.

Many hours later, as night was once more beginning to fall, they staggered into the maquis camp, hungry, dishevelled and completely exhausted.

Part Four

1944 - 1945

Chapter Twenty-three

16th April 1944

Magdalene Agnew had lived in Vassieux-en-Vercors all her life. She loved her home; a small modest cottage on a hill overlooking the town. She had never felt any inclination to move away, the lure of the big city having no appeal to her as it had many of her friends over the years. Her earliest memory included this place, sitting on her grandfather's knee as a youngster, on the very step where she herself played with her own grandchildren. Her husband, Marcel, had died many years ago, long before the Great War, and so was spared the suffering of losing both of their boys at Verdun. Had it not been for her daughter, Gabrielle, then she may also have joined them in the afterlife, her grief so overpowering she had at one time considered ending it all.

Over time she had come to live with her grief and had gradually started to appreciate her quiet life in Vassieux. The war that raged to the north of the country had not affected her too much, the Vercors Massif being remote from the main cities. Even though there had been many hardships, they were no worse than she had experienced during peacetime.

Magdalene was by no means a political woman. Affairs of state held no interest for her. As long as those in power left her alone, she saw no reason to concern herself with them. To her, it was all quite simple. She kept herself busy with other matters, deliberately avoiding any need to form opinions on things she had no control over.

But there was one thing that she did have an opinion on and that was all things German. She hated them. Pure and simple. She despised them with a passion. They had taken her boys and in doing so, they had stolen her happiness. She could never forgive them for that.

Then the STO order had been passed in Vichy, and suddenly all the young men of the town had disappeared, along with those from many other towns and villages nearby. They defied the order and took to the hills, forming bands of partisans, maquis groups that sought to fight back against the Nazis and those collaborating with them.

Whenever she could, she would help them. They often visited her cottage, seeking a bed for the night, a cup of coffee or a hot meal which she would willingly provide. She had formed many friendships with these young men, for she saw in them the spirit of her own two sons, lost so many years ago on the battlefield fighting the very same foe.

It was a bright Sunday morning. As Magdalene stood on the porch looking out towards the town, she heard movement behind her. It was Troy, one of the two maquisards that had knocked on her door the previous evening seeking shelter for the night. Along with Hugo, Troy had been sent by their group leader, Sacha, to ask for bread and milk, and any other supplies that could be gathered from the townspeople. Of course, Magdalene had let them in, fussing over them as though they were her own children, laughing at their jokes and listening to their elaborate tales of how they would one day rid France of the Boche for good. She loved their bravado and hoped it was not misplaced. Troy and Hugo reminded her so much of her two lost boys. Both so young, so brave. She would do anything for them.

'Good morning, Mother,' smiled Troy stretching his arms. She smiled back at him maternally. She took no offence at this familiarity, as she knew it came from a deep respect they held for her. In fact, she was proud they thought to address her in such a way.

'Bonjour, Troy,' she replied. 'How did you sleep?'

'Very well, thank you.'

'And what of Hugo?'

'I presume the same,' he laughed. 'He's still snoring.'

Magdalene wiped her hands on her apron. 'Would you boys like some breakfast?'

Troy stepped out onto the porch. 'That would be perfect. We'll have that then we'll get out of your way. And thank you again for your generosity and for what you've done for us. Sacha should be here soon with the others to help carry it all. I know he appreciates it as much as we all do and I thank you on his behalf.'

She nodded and walked past him, back into the cottage to prepare the food.

Troy took a cigarette case from his pocket. He looked at the pathetic homemade cigarillos and sighed. Getting good tobacco was proving more difficult these days. The stuff that came with the air-drops from England just wasn't to the same standard as he was used to. But then, he could hardly complain. It would have to do. Maybe after the war was won, he would again be able to purchase a higher grade of cigarette.

He put it to his lips and was about to follow Magdalene into the cottage when something caught his eye and made him stop.

It was activity in the town below.

A convoy of trucks appeared from the north road and began to park up in the town square. Armed men jumped from the tailgates and began to form up in rows.

Although some distance away, Troy could clearly make out their blue trousers and jackets and the wide blue berets they wore so arrogantly, upon their heads.

The uniform of the Milice.

'Hugo,' he called through the doorway. He heard a faint grunt and so shouted louder, more urgently. 'Hugo, get your arse out of bed right now.'

***

A bearded Sacha Marchand took the carbine from his back and crouched behind a tree. He could see the village of Vassieux-en-Vercors a mile or so ahead. Columns of smoke rose into the mid-morning air and he could hear the occasional crack of a rifle shot. He raised his hand and the group of six maquisards with him all took to the ground, or found cover behind trees and bushes.

He pulled a pair of binoculars from his pocket and put them to his eyes. He surveyed the area for a few moments and then pulled them away.

'Milice,' he said, handing them to Alain, his second in command, who was crouching beside him. 'What brings those bastards here, I wonder?'

Alain took the binoculars and followed where Sacha indicated. 'Probably us,' he replied. 'After all, we've become a pain in their behinds recently. Hugo and Troy are down there. What shall we do?'

They had agreed to meet their friends that morning, after Sacha had sent them ahead the previous day to gather the provisions the villagers had donated to them. They had been instructed to take them to Madame Agnew's cottage on the outskirts of the town where they would be collected by their group the following morning.

The sound of further gunfire reached them.

Sacha shrugged. 'There's not a lot we can do. There's too many of them. We're heavily outnumbered. If we go down there then we'll be slaughtered. I'm afraid Hugo and Troy are on their own now.'

He stood up and turned around. 'Come on. Let's get back to camp. There's nothing we can do here.'

Nobody moved. 'Come on,' he insisted. 'Right now.'

Unenthusiastically, the men got to their feet, slinging their rifles and carbines over their shoulders. Following Sacha they turned their backs on the village and slowly trudged away. Alain stopped and looked back. He was not comfortable with this. But, as Sacha had said, there were simply too many Milice for them to handle. Any attempts to fight them would only lead to disaster for them all.

He sighed, then turned to follow Sacha and the rest of the group as they walked up the path, reluctantly abandoning their friends to their fate.

***

Troy and Hugo hid behind the cottage, out of sight of the Milice who were starting to drag residents from their homes, forcing them into the square. They had set fire to three properties when the occupants had not moved fast enough when ordered to get out. Their cries of terror could be heard, even from so far away.

They had both been about to head into the village, guns at the ready, when Magdalene stopped them.

'Don't be fools. You don't stand a chance against them. Go. Hide. Get away from here.'

Coming to their senses they stopped. They looked around and knew it was clear there was nowhere to run. The cottage stood alone on the hillside. Fleeing would take them across open ground that could clearly be seen by those in the town. The only thing they could do was to hide and wait it out. Hopefully, they would be left alone and the collaborators would soon move on.

After a few minutes they heard a vehicle approaching. Troy risked looking around the side of the wall and was horrified to see a small truck stop at the front of the cottage. It contained six Milice who got out and stood before it. He watched as Magdalene stepped down from the porch and approached them.

'Can I help you?' she asked, rubbing her hands against her apron.

A short, arrogant looking man, who was clearly their commander, stepped forward. He held a clipboard in his hand and looked down at it.

'Your name?' he asked curtly.

'It's polite to look at someone when you're addressing them, young man,' said Magdalene softly.

He looked up and snarled. 'Just answer the question, woman.'

Magdalene let out a sigh. 'Magdalene Agnew. And to whom am I speaking?'

'How long have you lived here?' he said, not looking up.

'All of my life, which, as you will appreciate, is a very long time.'

He looked up at her but did not respond.

'Madame Agnew,' he said after a while. 'Have you ever come into contact with the maquis? We know they operate in this area and we also know they're being aided by people from this town.'

Magdalene did not answer straight away. 'Why are you doing this?' she asked after a while.

'Excuse me?'

'Why are you doing this?' she repeated. 'You're all Frenchmen. Yet you work for the Germans. Do you not love your country?'

The Milice commander looked her up and down and then turned to his men.

'Okay, boys. Turn this place upside down.'

He placed the clipboard on the bonnet of the truck and pulled a revolver from a holster at his hip. He stood silently watching as the five Milice barged past Magdalene and entered the cottage.

Magdalene stepped forward. 'You have no right to do this.'

'I have every right,' he replied. 'There are terrorists operating in this area being aided by people like you and we're here to put a stop to it.'

Magdalene looked beyond him as the sound of gunfire suddenly erupted from the town. She also spied two buildings just off the main square starting to burn.

'What are you doing?' she yelled. 'Stop this at once. There is nothing here for you.'

The Milice officer raised the revolver and pointed it at her head.

As Magdalene looked on in horror the side of the man's skull suddenly exploded, throwing blood and brains across the ground in front of her and ripping the blue beret from his head. His body fell to the side, hitting the dirt with a thud. It spasmed once and then lay still.

The Milice who had entered the cottage came rushing out to see what had happened. Troy and Hugo emerged from their hiding place, their weapons at the ready, smoke issuing from the barrel of Troy's Sten gun. There were two in the doorway, the others behind them. Without warning both maquisards opened fire, their bullets knocking the two at the front back into the cottage. Those still inside could be heard diving for cover.

Troy looked over his shoulder, back towards the village. He could see the Milice reacting to the gunfire, a large group of them racing towards one of the trucks.

Hugo slung his rifle over his shoulder and grabbed Magdalene. 'Come on. We need to get out of here right now.'

Troy fired short bursts towards the cottage, shattering the windows as Hugo dragged a wailing Magdalene to the truck. They were about to get into the cab when gunfire broke out from one of the windows. Troy felt his legs give way and fell to the ground. It took a short while for him to realise he had been hit. He raised the Sten and fired another burst but the bullets flew harmlessly into the wall.

Hugo was having difficulty with Magdalene who had by now fainted. He picked her up and threw her unceremoniously into the rear of the truck before returning to the front where Troy lay, blood pouring from his shattered legs.

'Get out of here!' yelled Troy. 'Save yourself.'

'I'm not leaving you,' replied Hugo, grabbing him under the armpits, his back now to the cottage as he dragged him around. Troy let out a scream, the pain of his broken legs intense.

Troy tried to raise his weapon once more, but the strength had left him completely and he dropped it back to the ground. Hugo could hear the sound of the second truck getting ever closer. When he saw the desperate gaze from his friend, he realised it was over. The three surviving Milice who had been in the cottage were now outside.

Slowly lowering his friend back to the ground he turned around.

The three men stood in a semi-circle around him, their pistols pointed at his chest. A few seconds later, the truck arrived.

'On your knees, scum,' shouted the Milice in the middle, who now assumed command.

Hugo considered going for his gun, but as he thought this, he was surrounded by a larger group of Milice. He looked down at his comrade and saw Troy had lost consciousness. From the way the blood was pumping from the wound in his leg, he knew there was no hope for him and he would bleed out very soon.

He got to his knees, unslinging his rifle from his back, throwing it to the side.

A red-faced Milice officer approached and grabbed his hair, pulling his head back. He forced the barrel of a revolver into the side of his head.

'Get that bitch out of the truck,' yelled the officer. 'Bring her here.'

Moments later, Magdalene was dragged from the rear of the truck and forced to kneel beside Hugo. She was shaking with fear. Tears streamed down her face.

'How many more are there?' shouted the Milice officer. 'How many more terrorists are you hiding?'

Magdalene looked at him blankly.

'Maybe this will jog your memory.' The officer pointed his revolver at Troy's unconscious body and fired. The bullet hit the young maquisard in the temple. As blood shot out of his head like a miniature red fountain, his body jerked in spasm before going still.

Magdalene screamed. Hugo went to stand but was hit from behind and fell forward into the dirt.

'I only need one of you,' stated the officer, who seemed to have calmed himself. 'You'll tell me what I need to know.'

Hugo was forced back to his knees.

'You… You murdering terrorist. Where is your base of operations?'

Hugo spat at the man, the spittle hitting his boot. The officer raised his hand and hit him on the side of the head with the revolver, once again knocking him to the ground.

'Put this piece of shit in the truck,' he ordered. 'We'll speak to him later.'

Then he turned to Magdalene. He stepped towards her, put the pistol to her head and fired a single shot. She fell to the ground next to the body of Troy, the blood from the hole in her skull mingling with his.

He turned to his men, who watched on indifferently.

'Burn this shit hole down.'

***

On their return to base camp, Sacha was met by a group of excitable maquisards, all eager to talk to him. Animatedly, they spoke over each other. He was not able to understand what they were trying to tell him. He raised his hands.

'Okay, okay. Quieten down. Stop this… Arnold, what's going on?'

They stopped gabbling and Arnold Jeunier stepped forward. 'We're getting word that the Milice are attacking villages and towns all over the area. They're slaughtering villagers and taking some away for questioning. What shall we do?'

Sacha thought for a moment, before speaking. 'I know. They're in Vassieux right now. I was afraid of this. We need to get everything packed and get to somewhere safer. We can join forces with Descour's group and take if from there.'

Arnold looked beyond him. 'Where's Troy? And Hugo?'

'I'm afraid they're gone,' replied Sacha awkwardly. 'They're both either dead or captured by now. There was nothing we could do for them.'

The band started chattering again, unhappy at the news they were receiving.

Again Sacha raised his hands. When they ignored him, he took the carbine from his shoulder and fired a shot into the air. A hush descended on the group once more.

Sacha raised his voice. 'Now listen to me. All of you. Trust me when I tell you there was nothing we could do for them. They're gone. We can assume this place is now compromised and if we don't move from here then a large force of Milice or Boche will very soon be upon us. If you want to fight, then that's fine, we'll fight. But we need to do it in a more organised way. Remember what our friend Francois taught us last year. You may not like it but what he said was true. We need to pick our fights. We've got to be clever if we want to get through this and kick the fascists out of France. Now, do as I say. Pack up everything and get ready to move out. We'll mourn our friends later. But right now, we must take care of ourselves.'

There was a subdued murmuring as they gathered together their things.

'Leave anything you can't carry. Take only essentials,' shouted Alain.

Twenty minutes later, they moved out.

***

Frank stepped into the office and saluted.

'Away with all that nonsense, young man,' said Colonel Harding irritably. 'You know I can't be bothered with that sort of thing. Now sit down and listen to me.'

Frank had arrived in London the day before, after being summoned to Baker Street from the training centre in Scotland where he had spent the last few months as an instructor, training potential SOE agents.

Upon their return from France, almost nine months ago, both he and Jenny had been thoroughly debriefed before being sent on to other duties. Frank had wanted to return to France without delay, but Buckmaster had decided his skills would be more useful training new recruits. Instead he had been ordered to Arisaig to assist with this. Although he had enjoyed his time there, he always maintained his skills were best suited in the field, particularly when an Allied invasion of France was clearly getting nearer. He felt this posting had been something of a punishment for what had taken place in Lyon and his failure to prevent the CNR meeting from being discovered by the Germans. Although he knew it was something he had had no control over, nevertheless he still felt partly responsible.

Jenny, on the other hand, had been sent back overseas. Frank had no idea where whe was. He had not seen or spoken to her since they had arrived back in England.

So it was something of a surprise to him that three days ago he had been ordered to London to report to Baker Street, particularly when he was only half way through a training course. He presumed that whatever it was he was being summoned for, it must be urgent.

Frank sat down and faced Harding. He did not speak.

He knew Harding was aware of him being upset at his imposed sabbatical. He was therefore not going to give his superior the satisfaction by asking why he had been summoned to London.

Harding looked at him for a few moments before taking a cigarette from a pack on the desk and lighting one. He did not offer one to Frank.

Finally Harding broke the silence. 'So how was Scotland?'

'Blustery,' replied Frank.

'Quite.' Harding took a couple of puffs from the cigarette. He turned and looked out of the window. 'Have you noticed the difference, Graham?'

'The differencc?'

'Yes,' replied Harding, his eyes fixed on something outside the window. 'The difference in the place since you were first here. London. Rarely do we hear the air-raid sirens anymore, thankfully. The city's starting to get back to some sort of normality and there's a huge sense that the final victory is almost upon us. You can feel it in the streets. There seems a positivity about the place now, that was lost for a very long time. I've sat here in this chair almost every day for the last few years, looking out of this bloody window. I've seen the changes happen, right before my eyes.'

'I don't think I've been here long enough to notice,' replied Frank. He had no idea why Harding was rambling on like this.

'You know, Graham, sometimes, when I look back on it all, I still feel an immense sense of loss. What has it all been for, eh? The first war was bad enough. I saw so many killed. So many young lives wasted. I genuinely thought something like that could never happen again. That the politicians simply wouldn't let things get that bad. Yet here we are, eh? The same thing all over again. History repeating itself.'

'I suppose you're right, sir,' replied Frank.

'And who's to say that once this one's over it won't all flare up again. The human race has a self-destructive nature, my boy. It has the propensity for perpetual self-harm. It never ceases to amaze me how cruel we can be to each other.' Harding pushed the pack of cigarettes over to him. 'Here, take one.'

Frank took a cigarette from the pack and placed it into his mouth. Harding leaned over the desk, a lighter in his hand and touched the flame to the end.

'I often think of your brother,' went on Harding, sitting back. 'I remember the bravery and tenacity he showed in getting to the beach when we all thought he was lost. I see a lot of him in you too. What you set up over in Lyon was highly commendable. It's a pity it went awry in the end, but I don't think you could have done anything about that. You did well to last as long as you did. Anyway, the reason we've asked you down here is because of what you did in Lyon. The connections you made and all that. Particularly on the Vercors Massif. We could use you back there now.'

Frank smiled. He had waited months for this. He sat quietly smoking his cigarette while Colonel Harding filled him in.

'As you'll probably be aware, the invasion of Europe isn't too far away. Where and when that will happen, well, I couldn't tell you even if I knew. Which I don't, by the way… The time has come to make use of the Resistance and, in particular, the maquis. There are groups all over France and the powers that be want to use them to cause as much mayhem as they can when the invasion takes place.

They could be very useful in tying up German units to give our regular forces the chance to advance into the country and end this bloody war once and for all.

'We need to use people like yourself, Francis. You know the Vercors. You know the area, its people and how they think and operate. You can supply them from the bases in Algiers and you can help them in keeping the Jerries occupied. Take the fight to them. They've been doing bits and bobs while you've been away, but we want that activity to increase.

'You'll form part of a Jedburgh team. You'll be SOE's representative. Our officer, who'll liaise with and advise the maquis in the sector of the Vercors you're familiar with. You'll liaise with their hierarchy. From all accounts they've a decent set up there and are itching to get at the Germans. How does that sound?'

Frank had heard of Operation Jedburgh whilst in Scotland. Small bands of Allied special forces operatives created for this type of guerrilla warfare. Usually made up of an SOE man or an American OSS officer, a liaison officer from the country where they were to be deployed and a radio operator. He was aware there were many of them already operating in Europe and other theatres of war, some of them working with the Special Air Service.

'Will I be in charge?'

'Yes, you will. You know the Vercors and you its people. It makes sense for you to lead the group. What you don't get to choose is who'll be in your team. That's already been decided.'

Frank raised an eyebrow but said nothing. He knew that after such a long time out of the field he could not make any demands. He was just content to be going back to France. That was enough for him.

He blew out the last of the smoke and stubbed the cigarette butt into an ashtray on the desk. 'I've a couple of questions for you, sir if I may. Firstly, do you know who I'm going in with?'

Harding picked up a document from a wire tray in front of him and studied it.

'You've a Free French officer, Gerard Basson, who's seen service in Africa. He's to act as liaison officer. Your radio operator will be, let me see, a Sergeant James Davies. He's Royal Signals but has been working special forces for a good while. Both come highly recommended. I'm trying to get a few SAS to accompany you, but I'm struggling, to be honest. It will probably just be the three of you initially.'

'Thank you, sir,' replied Frank. 'Secondly, when do we leave?'

Harding replaced the document and sat back. 'As soon as we can arrange it. First you're to go back to Scotland for some further training and then you'll be dropped into theatre as soon after that as we can arrange. The sooner you're on the ground the better. Make contact with your old friends and then take it from there. There'll be other Jedburgh teams operating in the area, some of which will be led by those OSS types from America. Try to get on with them if you come across them. Work with them. But more importantly make as much trouble for the Germans as possible.'

Frank smiled. 'Gladly.'

'I'll sort out all the necessary paperwork,' said Harding. 'I'll get the travel warrants sent to you and then you can head off when you're ready. That's it, young man. Unless you've anything else to add.'

'No, sir,' replied Frank standing up.

He was about to salute when he saw a snarl start to appear on Harding's face and so put his arm down. Instead he offered his hand and Harding took it, shaking it enthusiastically.

'Good luck, Graham,' he said. 'Do yourself and your brother proud. Give those Boche a bloody good kicking.'

'Thank you, sir,' said Frank turning away. 'I'll do my best.'

He had his hand on the door handle when Harding spoke again.

'Oh, I almost forgot. Congratulations. You've been promoted to major. With the possibility that you'll come across other teams, including Americans, I thought it best to avoid any unnecessary conflict or confusion on the ground. To make sure they know who's in charge.'

'Very good, sir,' said Frank, nodding at him.

'Okay,' said Harding dismissively taking another document from his tray, his attention now moving to other matters. 'Off with you.'

***

Four weeks had passed since the Milice had attacked the villages around Vassieux-en-Vercors. They sustained a presence there until the 24th April, burning and destroying farms, taking away anybody they suspected of being in the maquis or those who had helped them in any way. They returned many times, each visit more ruthless and cruel than the last. Families had been torn apart, people taken away, none of them heard of since.

But it had no effect in dissuading the population from assisting the young men of the maquis. Their ranks had swelled, as more young Frenchmen made their way to the plateau in order to join the partisans fighting the Nazis. As the numbers grew, organising them became a necessity, recognised by the Free French and the Allies. How they could be utilised following an invasion was not yet decided. This caused some confusion between London and Algiers, which filtered onto the plateau itself.

Shortly after escaping the Germans in Lyon, Francois and Jenny had been ordered back to London. They left the radio with Sacha who had made use of it, asking for the occasional supply drop from England, which on occasion was complied with, but more often than not went ignored.

Each time Sacha saw Arnold Jeunier use the radio he had to smile to himself. The boy had taken to Morse code like a duck to water having been given a crash course by Jenny Crane before she had to leave. He was by no means perfect, sometimes having to send a signal more than once and it took him a long time just to send the simplest of messages. But at least the lad tried. What he lacked in experience and training he made up for in enthusiasm. They had initially used Francois' codename, 'GREYMAN', during transmissions but had, in time, changed it to 'SACHA' once England had verified who they were. He presumed Francois had sorted this out upon his return home.

Rumour had it there was still a price on the "Grey Man's" head, him having upset the Gestapo in Lyon, and in particular Klaus Barbie, when he was operating there.

After the Milice attack on Vassieux-en-Vercors Sacha had taken his men to join with other groups deeper inside the plateau. Together they presented a formidable fighting force. The leader of this larger group, Marcel Descour, had the intention of at some point declaring the Vercors Massif a separate state, independent of Vichy and German rule. It was to be controlled and administered by the maquis themselves. The Germans had few troops in the area, other than the garrison at Grenoble, and the local population were still very much pro-maquis, offering food, shelter and any other assistance as and when it was needed, despite the recent attempts by the Milice to stop them. It would be a slap in the face for Pétain and would show the French people that the Nazis and collaborators could never win.

From information coming in from England, Sacha felt certain the Allied invasion of France was just a question of time, possibly just weeks away. His initial urge to fight the Nazis in open warfare had given way to a more cautious approach following the April assault on Vassieux. Hitting the enemy with small attacks and then retreating to the hills was surely the best option when the fighting started. His superiors thought differently. The time for "petite guerre", the little war, was over, they argued. It would shortly be time for the Germans to feel the full rage of the French people.

There was no doubt the Vercors Maquis were becoming a capable force and could be put to great use once the invasion took place. But the Allies had not yet landed and the Germans still held France. Word was coming from London that the Nazis were suffering defeat after defeat on the Eastern Front. The Russians were advancing further westwards, towards Germany, and at a great pace. Sacha was convinced once the Allied landings happened, then the Greater German Empire and Third Reich would crumble before them.

Late one Friday night, in early June, whilst Sacha was resting near the campfire, he was approached by Arnold Jeunier. He was carrying a rifle over his shoulder, which he never seemed to be without, and the battered radio Francois Aubuchon had given him months ago.

'Any news?' asked Sacha on seeing him.

'Yes,' he replied, sitting down cross-legged next to his commander. 'I've just had word we're to expect a package in two nights time.'

Sacha raised himself onto his elbows. 'What package?'

'I'm not sure. They've given me the co-ordinates for the drop. They say there'll be a supply drop with it too.'

'That's good news,' replied Sacha, lying back down.

He closed his eyes. What could this "package" be, he wondered? He had a good idea but decided not to think too much about it. If London were sending supplies and reinforcements then something big was about to happen. Something momentous was about to take place and he had to make sure he and his men were ready for it when it did.

Chapter Twenty-four

4th June 1944

Frank struggled to hear through the drone of the B-24 Liberator's four engines. Basson was trying to tell him something. He pointed to his right ear and shouted as loud as he could that he could hear nothing. Basson nodded and sat back against the fuselage, closing his eyes.

Frank thought maybe it would be a good time to get some sleep too, but knew he would not be able to. It had been a very long few days. Now they were on their way, days were only going to get longer. They had travelled down to RAF Harrington in Northamptonshire the previous day, after first stopping off at Ringway for a couple of practice jumps. It had been a long while since Frank had jumped from a plane, his journeys from France to England mainly being by Lysander during his years operating out of Lyon.

He looked at Basson. He was not sure what to make of the man. He was of average height with a long nose and large lips. He had lost his hair so had taken to shaving his head completely giving him a rather odd look, making it difficult for Frank to guess his age. Although his English was perfect, he was a quiet man, not indulging in idle chit-chat, which some people found rude. But it did not offend Frank in any way, as he quite liked the fellow. Basson had seen action in North Africa, as he himself had whilst in the Royal Artillery. Because of that there was a mutual respect between them both.

Turning to his left he observed his radio operator. Sergeant James Davies was a short, stocky man about the same age as Frank, with a mop of black hair that was far too long for King's Regulations, and a longish fringe he occasionally flicked back with his hand when it fell into his eyes. He had been on active service since 1941 and had taken part in many special forces operations in Africa and Greece. He had volunteered for the Jedburghs after hearing that a good friend of his had been killed over France whilst returning from a bombing mission in Germany. The rumour was that his friend had been machine-gunned after baling out of his Stirling bomber after it had been hit by flak. If Davies did not hate the Nazis already, this action had rubber-stamped his determination to defeat them.

Whereas Basson had a quiet nature, Davies was quite the opposite. If he had a view on something then he would voice it, having no consideration for the etiquette of rank. Frank found this quite refreshing. The stuffiness of some officers he had met during his career was more to be irritated by, rather than getting upset by a lower rank daring to have an opinion on something. Major Lowndes came to mind when he thought of this, his immediate superior during his time in the artillery.

All in all, he was more than happy with the team that had been put together. Team "GREYMAN" they had been named. It was a codename he had used before. Although he was in no way superstitious, he felt it had been lucky for him so far.

Further along the plane he saw more teams, each of them looking both eager and nervous in equal measure. He wondered if his own countenance appeared the same. He smiled to himself. Probably, he thought.

Although he knew the area he was going into, and had spent many months in the region, this time the return was very different. Now he travelled without any forged documents and in the uniform of a British army officer. And this time he would not be working alone. These other Jedburgh teams would fly on to other areas, further to the north, with orders exactly the same as his. To liaise with the Resistance and cause as many problems for the Germans as they possibly could.

Operation Jedburgh was a military operation. As such, the participants were to wear the uniforms of their respective countries. They were all soldiers and this wasn't a spying mission. It was a legitimate act of open warfare and should any of them be captured then they should be treated in accordance to the Geneva Convention.

But they were all well aware that capture for them, despite the Geneva Convention, could mean certain death. Each of them was under no illusion of that. It had been explained to them all that Hitler's Commando Order of 1942, something the Allies had only recently found out about, would come into play if they were unfortunate enough to fall into the hands of the Nazis. Their uniforms would not help them. Hitler, they had been told, had been incensed by the tactics and success of British commando and special forces operations. He had personally ordered that anyone carrying out such missions, whether in uniform or not, should be shot out of hand, or handed over to the Gestapo and treated as spies.

This, thought Frank, only made him more determined that their mission should be a success.

He was tapped on his knee by a United States Air Force airman and looked up. The man held up his hand, his fingers splayed.

'Five minutes, Joe. Rebecca's calling,' shouted the airman.

Frank smiled. 'Thanks, pal.'

"Rebecca" was the name of the transponder the maquis would be using on the ground, to guide the plane in. The Liberator's "Eureka" receiver would have picked up the signal in the form of an audible "ping". As the plane got closer to the target area, the "pings" would become more frequent, making it easier for the aircraft to locate the drop zone. The system had proved a success and was being used on virtually all flying missions such as this.

Frank nudged his two colleagues. 'Come on. Time to make a move.'

The three of them stood up and checked their packs. They assisted each other, tightening buckles and ensuring all clips were secure. Each of them had been supplied with an American M1 carbine and a Colt automatic pistol. They also carried ammunition, medical supplies, K rations and pieces of silk with maps and radio codes printed on them. Davies carried a box containing the "Jed Set", a Type B Mark II, or B2, radio, a set Frank was also very familiar with. Frank had also ensured an extra Thompson sub-machine-gun had been packed in one of the supply canisters, his own preferred weapon of choice.

When all three were happy, they hooked their static lines onto the hawser, that stretched across the aircraft's ceiling, and waited near the door, where the airman now stood. After a few moments, he pulled it open.

An immediate rush of cold air blew into their faces and the already deafening sound of the Liberator's engines seemed to treble. Frank again felt the strap of his helmet, ensuring it was fastened securely. He took one last glance inside the aircraft and noticed most of the other Jedburgh teams were looking at them. Frank raised a hand in farewell as the green light came on above the door.

'Go, go,' shouted the American airman, slapping Frank on the shoulder.

Without hesitation, he stepped into the darkness.

Almost instantly he felt the canopy snap open above him. He looked up and was relieved to see both Basson and Davies had also jumped successfully. In the darkness, he could just make out canisters of supplies being thrown from the open door of the Liberator as it gradually moved away and out of sight. The roar of its engines faded away until he was left with the peaceful silence he found so relaxing at this stage of all the parachute jumps he had made before.

He glanced down at the leg bag swaying beneath him, dangling just past his boots. Below, beams of flashlights and torches swept through the darkness, signals from the reception party awaiting their arrival. They were descending into a clearing. Unable to gauge his falling speed in the darkness, he locked his gaze on the pack below, using it as his point of reference.

With a dull thud it hit the ground. He braced himself. Then he too was down, the canopy of the parachute billowing around him. He looked to his left and saw the others landing not too far away.

He stood up and unstrapped the helmet, throwing it to the side. He started to gather his parachute in and became aware of people running towards him. A young boy appeared at his side and said to him in French, 'Here, Monsieur, let me help you with that.'

Frank recognised the voice immediately.

'Bonjour, Charles,' he said, smiling at the young Parisian. 'It's very nice to see you again.'

Charles Mercier grinned back at him. 'Bonjour, Francois. It's very nice to see you too. Welcome home.'

***

Sacha was equally pleased to see him and shook him roughly by the hand before holding him by the shoulders.

'Good to see you again, Francois. And in uniform too!'

Frank smiled and turned to his two companions. 'May I take the pleasure of introducing you to Captain Gerard Basson of the Free French forces and Sergeant James Davies of the British army.'

'Welcome, welcome,' he said to the two men. 'It's good to have you with us.'

'Thank you,' replied Basson, shaking his hand. Davies looked on, bewildered, not understanding a word that had passed between them.

'I have much to tell you, Francois,' said Sacha. 'But first we must eat.'

After the canisters had been collected, Charles led the way to their new hideout, a cave deep inside the plateau. Had he not been following the young Frenchman, Frank had little doubt he would have had trouble finding it. Inside, around twenty more maquisards sat or stood around, cleaning weapons, talking quietly or eating. One or two lay asleep, not waking despite the activity the visitors had created. Nobody seemed particularly excited about their arrival.

Sacha led them to a corner, where an old, battered oil lamp sat on a wooden crate providing a dim light around them. He sat down on a rock with his back to the wall. The three men joined him, sitting on the ground.

Davies took off his beret and ran his finger through his hair, flicking the fringe out of his eyes.

'If it's all the same with you, boss, I'd like to get some shut eye. Let's face it, I'm hardly going to be able to understand what this bloke says.'

'Fine,' replied Frank. 'I'll fill you in, in the morning.'

Davies stood up and walked back through the cave where he gathered the sleeping bag from his pack and placed it just inside the entrance, near to a small campfire.

As they watched him, Sacha told Frank and Basson of what had happened in the intervening months. Frank expressed his sadness at the loss of Troy and Hugo.

'Things have changed a little since you were last here, my friend,' went on Sacha. 'We're more organised now. We're still lacking in numbers but have caused one or two problems for the Germans over the past few months. We take our guidance from Huet and Descour…'

'We're not here to undermine anyone,' cut in Frank. 'We're here solely to assist you in any way we can. You know what we can do for you. Gerard is here to liaise between you and Algiers. London has very little say in how things are handled here. The maquis are French and so the Free French are the ones who ultimately decide how best to use you. That makes sense to us. But the thing is, Sacha, the invasion is imminent. It must be. That's why we're here. Our orders are very simple. To help you cause as much trouble as possible. The top brass want us to tie up as many Nazi troops in the interior as possible, throughout France, when the invasion takes place. To prevent them being sent to fight the Allied advance. The end is coming Sacha. It really is.'

'I hope so, my friend.'

'I'm the same as you,' said Basson calmly. 'I've been away from France for far too long now. This is the first time I've set foot in my home country for four years. I've no idea how my wife is, or even if she's still alive. We're here to get you what you need and to kick the Nazis out once and for all.'

Sacha stood up. He was smiling. 'I've a bottle of cognac somewhere. Let's drink to that.'

***

The following day Frank was reunited with others he had befriended the last time he was in the region, including Alain, and Arnold Jeunier, who now sported a short beard. "Double H" had been right. These men respected him and would follow him into battle with the same loyalty they showed Sacha.

The team spent the day patrolling the nearby countryside with a small group of maquisards, including Alain. It was intended to show Basson and Davies the terrain they would be operating in. The Vercors Massif covered over five hundred square miles. The cliffs to the east faced the city of Grenoble and the area was dotted with hamlets and towns, the largest being Vassieux-en-Vercors, the main base for the maquis in the area. The hills were full of cave systems where they could plan their operations.

Frank was aware that due to its remote location, the plateau could be well defended with the right amount of equipped and trained troops. The problem was that they were short in numbers, and so a guerrilla war was currently the only real option open to them. But their leaders were of a different opinion, partly because the majority of them were ex-army officers.

In the evening, upon their return, Davies settled down with the Jed Set and started to receive messages from London.

'Boss,' Davies shouted to Frank, beckoning him over. 'You've got to hear this.'

Frank approached him. 'Go on.'

'We need to tune into the BBC,' replied Davies. 'There's to be some kind of announcement tonight.'

Quickly they gathered around an old radio receiver Sacha brought up and waited patiently as he tuned in to Radio Londres. As night began to fall, they listened patiently as one news programme after another finished. And then they heard it. The last three lines of the first stanza of Paul Verlaine's poem, Chanson d'Automne. The first part had been broadcast four days ago, signalling Resistance groups to be on the alert, and ready to act.

'Blessent mon cœur
'D'une langueur
'Monotone.'

Sacha looked up. He caught Frank's eyes, who nodded.

Noticing the exchange, Davies asked, 'What's going on?'

'The invasion,' replied Frank. 'It's the coded message telling us it's happening tomorrow.'

There then followed a series of abstract sentences, each seemingly nonsense. Frank knew they would be specific coded instructions to various Resistance cells throughout France. He could not help smiling.

He turned to the group. 'Prepare yourselves, my friends. France is about to be liberated.'

There was a huge cheer as each of them realised what this meant. After four years of Nazi tyranny, the Allies were finally coming. They would be striking back at the Germans. This was the beginning of the end.

Sacha held up his hands. 'Do not celebrate just yet, my friends. There will be plenty of hardship to endure before the final victory. We must be prepared for it. We must make sure we do what we can.'

'Where will it take place?' asked Alain.

Frank shook his head. 'I've no idea. But it'll be many miles from here, on the west coast somewhere. It'll be many weeks, if not months before they arrive here. We still need to remain patient. But the time to make your mark is upon us, gentlemen.'

***

The following morning it was confirmed that a massive Allied force had landed in Normandy, where intense fighting was taking place to establish a bridgehead. As Frank cleaned his Thompson sub-machine-gun he was approached by Charles Mercier.

'Bonjour, Charles,' he said. 'What can I do for you?'

'I'm leaving,' he said.

Frank raised his eyebrows. 'Leaving? Why's that?'

'I need to get back home,' he replied. 'To Paris. If the Allies are coming, I want to be there to meet them. And I need to make sure my family is all right.'

'Okay,' he replied. 'Have you spoken to Sacha and your cousin?'

'Yes. He's fine with it. He won't let me join in with any fighting here anyway, so I'm not much use.'

'I wouldn't say that, Charles,' replied Frank, putting down the gun. 'You've been very helpful.'

'First I'll return to my uncle's farm,' he went on. 'I'll collect Charlotte and take her with me. She needs to find out what happened to her mother and father.'

'Be very careful,' said Frank. 'Getting back to Paris won't be easy. It's very far and the Germans will have heightened security right now. Be discreet and take your time.'

Early that same afternoon, after Charles had left, Frank, Davies and Basson set off north with a group of fifteen maquisards. Alain and Arnold Jeunier were in their number. Sacha had been summoned to the Villa Bellon in nearby Saint-Martin to attend a leader's meeting with François Huet, the overall maquis commander on the plateau. From intelligence gathered, the Germans looked to be building up a force to the west of Grenoble and may be looking at making a move at the northern tip of the Vercors.

Frank did not want to get involved in any meeting, preferring to stay out of French politics. Instead he was content to lead a team out on patrol. Sacha had given instructions that should they come across any enemy activity and an opportunity arose then they could engage. He left it to Frank's discretion.

By the evening they arrived at a small hamlet not far from Saint-Nizier-du-Moucherotte.

Saint-Nizier would be the first town the Germans would come to should they attack the Vercors from the north. From the hamlet, they had a good view off the plateau where the occasional light at Grenoble flickered in the near distance. Frank set up his headquarters in a barn where the farmer, an old man by the name of Obier was pleased to accommodate them. The man was very enthusiastic in helping the war effort, taking a particular shine to Sergeant Davies, forcing a bottle of wine upon him.

'Bloody hell, this fella's a bit keen, boss,' he said uncorking it with his teeth.

'Don't drink too much of that, Jimmy,' said Frank. 'Clear heads, please.'

'One mouthful can't harm,' he said taking a large swig from the bottle. He wiped his mouth on the sleeve of his tunic before re-corking it. From the look on his face, it was not exactly a vintage that he had just forced down. 'Bloody hell, boss. I wouldn't put this piss on my chips. Tastes like bloody vinegar.'

He handed the bottle back to Obier who grinned and then held it out to Basson.

Basson shook his head, laughing. 'Non, Merci.'

Obier informed them that the Germans patrolled the area regularly and a force of around the same as their own would visit each of the local hamlets every couple of days. Frank positioned guards on the road leading from Grenoble with orders to report any enemy movements.

After only an hour, as dusk was beginning to descend upon them, a young maquisard entered the barn.

'Two trucks headed this way,' he shouted.

Frank grabbed his Thompson. 'How long?'

'Ten minutes at most,' he replied. 'We can see the lights coming up the hill.'

'Okay, everyone. Into position.'

***

From the cover of a low wall, Frank observed the trucks through his field glasses. Just as the maquisard had reported, there were two of them. There was also a motorcycle and sidecar combination at the front of the small convoy which the lookout must have missed. An MG42 machine-gun pointed menacingly forward from the sidecar, and the familiar steel helmets used by the SS and Wehrmacht could be seen on the riders' heads. To the rear of the trucks were two further motorcycle outriders.

He had half of the patrol spread out along the wall, all lying low with their weapons and grenades ready. The other half were behind the wall opposite, led by Alain and Captain Basson. Sergeant Davies crouched beside Frank, his M1 carbine cocked and ready to go.

As the patrol got closer Frank whispered down the line. 'Steady… Steady… On my command.'

The German patrol looked to be struggling up the hill. The road was in a bad state of repair, the heavy vehicles hitting almost every rut and pothole as it trundled forward. Frank had selected an area where the road bent slightly, knowing the Germans would have to slow to a virtual crawl.

When they were fifty yards away, he cocked the Thompson and flicked off the safety catch.

Beside him, Davies took two Mills bombs from his tunic pocket and placed them on the ground at the foot of the wall.

Slowly the patrol drew closer. Frank could hear a grinding noise as the driver of the lead truck struggled with the gears. They could not have been doing more than ten miles per hour as they passed the two groups waiting in ambush.

'Now!' shouted Frank and stood up. He fired a blast of the Thompson into the motorcycle combination, knocking the driver from his seat, causing it to veer to the side of the road. The gunner in the sidecar had no chance as a further hail of bullets hit him in the chest and head, killing him instantly, his corpse slumping down into his seat.

All around there was pandemonium as the maquisards jumped from their hiding places and peppered both trucks with rifle and machine-gun fire.

Davies pulled the pin from the first grenade and lobbed it to the rear of the patrol and then did the same with the second. As the two motorcycle riders frantically attempted to turn their machines around in a futile bid to escape the carnage, the grenades exploded. Both of them were caught in the blast, throwing them to the side of the road where they lay, unmoving. Davies vaulted the wall, firing his rifle into the cab of the second truck.

As the German soldiers tried to get out of the rear of the vehicles, they were hit with a hail of gunfire, many of them falling dead into the road. One or two managed to get off a blast of their MP40s before they too were silenced by the crossfire.

After only a minute it was all over.

Alain and Basson approached Frank, breathing heavily. Both trucks were starting to burn.

'Any wounded?' asked Frank.

'It doesn't appear so,' replied Basson, slinging the carbine over his shoulder.

Frank sat back on the low wall and took out a pack of cigarettes. He took one before offering the pack to the two men. Each of them took a cigarette and Basson lit them from a lighter he took from his trouser pocket. Davies stood on the opposite side of the road, observing them quietly.

They watched as the maquisards moved from body to body, collecting weapons and ammunition and anything else that may be of use to them.

Suddenly there was a disturbance at the rear of the second truck. Two maquisards appeared, holding a young German soldier roughly by the arms. They dragged the terrified man towards them. As he got to Frank, the prisoner dropped to his knees, his hands together as if in prayer. He was babbling in German, clearly asking to be spared.

The man wore the insignia of the SS on his lapel.

Alain looked at Frank. 'Well, what shall we do with him?' he asked.

One of the maquisards pulled a pistol from his pocket and jammed it into the man's neck. 'Do you want me to end him?' he asked.

Frank blew out smoke and shook his head from side to side. He looked closely at the German. He was blond and had blue eyes. The typical Aryan. The so-called master race. And here he was, on his knees pleading for his life.

Frank's thoughts turned to his brother, Jack, who had died at Dunkirk four years ago almost to the day. According to Colonel Harding, Jack had witnessed the massacre of British POWs by the SS, led by an old childhood acquaintance, who himself had blond hair and blue eyes. Otto Finkel. A nice young lad, as Frank remembered. A boy who had grown up to be a murdering Nazi. A member of the Waffen-SS, just like this person kneeling before him, desperately begging for mercy.

'Well?' asked Alain. 'Shall we execute him?'

Frank took a last drag from the cigarette and threw it to the ground, grinding it into the dirt with his boot.

'As I see it, we have three choices here,' he announced, more to himself than to anyonc else. 'We can execute him. Put a bullet in his brain right now, walk away and forget about it. Or we could take him with us as our prisoner. But let's face it, we don't really have the capacity to take prisoners, do we? The third choice is to disarm him and let him go.'

He paused before continuing. 'Now, I know the easiest thing to do is to simply shoot him and move on. But, gentlemen, that's not who we are. That's not what the British Army does. It's not what anyone on the right side of all of this should do. We're better than that. We're above that kind of thing. If we behaved the same way as the Nazis then we're no better than they are. If we're as bad as them, then what on earth are we fighting them for? It wouldn't make any sense. In a war such as this, we need to maintain our humanity, we have to keep our dignity and we've got to have the moral right to be fighting it. I know there's been many atrocities carried out by the Nazis, and I'm sure even on the Allied side there have probably been some instances where we could have conducted ourselves better. But, like I say, we're better than them. We're not murderers.'

'So what are your orders?' asked Basson.

'I should leave this up to Alain. We're here to assist and to advise. We're not here to lead and control. My advice on this one is to strip the bastard down to his underwear, take off his boots and let him go.'

There was a murmuring among the group as they contemplated Frank's words.

Then Alain spoke. 'Strip him. Let him go.'

The two holding the SS soldier looked up. 'Surely not,' said one of them. 'He'll come back. He'll fight and murder again.'

'Strip him,' repeated Alain. 'Not another word. The rest of you. Get ready to move out.'

Quickly, the German took off his clothes. Once his uniform had been taken, he was thrown to Alain's feet. He grabbed the man by the elbows and hoisted him up. The German stood before him, shaking with fear and cold.

'I can't believe you're letting him go,' said one the maquisards defiantly.

Alain took a revolver from his pocket and lifted the soldier's right hand. Placing it against his palm he pulled the trigger, shattering the hand. The man screamed in pain, blood pouring from the wound. Frank watched on but said nothing.

Grabbing a field dressing from his webbing belt, Alain threw it at the German where it unravelled at his feet. 'Here. Now piss off.'

He spun the man around and kicked him hard in his backside. By now the German was weeping. He stooped down and picked up the bandage with his good hand before half running and half stumbling back down the roadway.

Alain turned to the group. 'Like Francois has just said, we're not murderers. That man's war is over. He won't be back. I'll hear no more on the matter. Now come on, let's move out.'

Alain turned to Frank. 'You were wrong, my friend. There was a fourth option.'

***

Three weeks passed.

Two days following the Allied invasion, the maquis leadership ordered the Vercors to be locked down. As expected the Germans had moved in on Saint-Nizier and taken the town on 15 June. They had stopped there, not advancing into the plateau any further, instead using it as a base for future operations. The other three main roads into the plateau were to be blocked by the maquis, and the area made secure.

Still low in numbers, and poorly equipped for the size of area they were to cover, the maquisards did what they could. Any enemy patrols attempting to enter the area were swiftly dealt with. The terrain of the Vercors Massif made it easy to defend the approaches with limited numbers. There were many narrow roads and passes, flanked by steep cliffs from which the maquisards could repel any German advances, as long as they remained small in number. Each day, the Germans sent out patrols, probing the area for weaknesses. Every time they were repelled. Frank was under no illusion that these probing attacks were merely reconnaissance missions for a much larger battle that was yet to come. He worried just how only three thousand poorly equipped men, mainly amateurs, could take on thousands of hardened German troops, should they be sent to quash them. In Frank's view, the only way to fight them was to use guerrilla tactics, striking the Germans in small hit and run operations, rather than take them on in open battle.

He was also aware the maquis leaders were urging their superiors in Algiers to send trained reinforcements and heavy weaponry, but their requests so far seemed to be falling on deaf ears. After the announcement of the invasion, more and more men were heading to the Vercors to join the maquis. Descour and Huet were finding it increasingly difficult to equip them. It was becoming a problem.

Frank had contacted Baker Street with the issue, but was told this was a French matter and he was to continue to do what he could. London's main focus was to support the invasion force and, as such, their hands were tied. Frank found this very hard to stomach. He felt the same as many maquisards: that they were being abandoned.

After much harassing and cajoling the Allies finally sent in a small force of American commandos. Frank and his team travelled to Vassieux to meet them. There he found a team of only thirteen men. They had been sent specifically to train the new recruits who were arriving daily. Frank found that, although they were committed and highly professional soldiers, without the necessary equipment they would have limited effect should there be a strong German attack, which he was sure would happen very soon. After spending two days with them, he decided to leave, to get back to the front line where his group could be more effective. He had argued that it was trained men they were short of. If the Vercors Massif was to be held then they needed to arrive in larger numbers. When this was transmitted to Algiers and London, once again it went unanswered.

Colonel Descour managed to get hold of some uniforms and many of the maquisards who received them now gave the appearance of an effective fighting force, even if they were not. At least, thought Frank, it lifted their morale and everyone he came into contact with was optimistic that they could hold the plateau until the arrival of Allied forces.

'There's no more you can do,' said Basson one afternoon when they were assisting at a road block in the east of the plateau. 'You can only do what you can do.'

'It shouldn't be this way,' he replied. 'They ask these men to rise up and harass the Germans yet do nothing to support them. It stinks, Gerard. It's not right.'

The sound of gunfire could be heard up ahead and when Frank looked down the slope he saw several of trucks about a mile away. A large group of SS jumped from the tailgates and spread out across the roadway.

'They're not letting up,' said Frank as he watched them through his binoculars. 'They come in bigger numbers each day. We need more men. Or to take to the hills. It's that simple.'

As Frank watched on he saw the Germans dive for cover. A couple of seconds later, he heard the noise of the Bren guns as they opened up on them from the cliff-face to his right. He knew there were other groups of maquisards on the roadway ahead of the Germans. Seconds later, their weapons opened up too. The Germans returned fire from their covered positions and an exchange of gunfire took place for a few minutes before the enemy soldiers retreated back to their trucks and drove away.

'See,' said Frank. 'They're merely testing us. They'll be back soon, with much larger numbers and much heavier firepower. Mark my words.'

***

That evening, after they had been relieved, they returned to the small village they been using as base of operations. Frank noticed a tricolour flying from the steeple of the chapel they had been using as their headquarters. A Cross of Lorraine had been drawn in the middle of the flag. He did not give it much thought until he entered the building and went to the corner where he had left his gear.

Sergeant Davies approached him. 'Hello, sir,' he said, handing him a leaflet. 'I don't know what any of this means but they've been putting them up all over the place. The natives seem quite happy about it. What's it say.'

Frank took the paper from him and read it. 'Apparently the Vercors has been liberated.'

Davies was puzzled. 'Eh? Who by?'

'Us, apparently,' replied Frank. 'The maquis.' He then translated for him. 'On the third of July 1944 the French Republic was officially restored in the Vercors. Our region is in a state of siege. The National Committee of Liberation requests that the population do the impossible, as it will itself do, and put all available means at the disposal of the military commanders, who have the weighty task of protecting us from an increasingly barbarous enemy. Inhabitants of the Vercors, the great Republic has been born in your land. You should be proud. We are sure that you will know how to defend it. We hope that for the Vercors, the fourteenth of July will be yet another occasion to show your republican convictions and your attachment to the great fatherland. Long live the French Republic. Long live France. Long live General de Gaulle.'

'Bloody hell,' responded Davies, running his fingers through his hair.

'Bloody hell indeed,' replied Frank. 'When the Germans get hold of this, we're in for some fun, believe me.'

'When you say "fun", do you mean "shit"?' said Davies.

Frank looked at him and handed back the leaflet.

'Shit indeed, Jimmy. Shit indeed.'

Chapter Twenty-five

The Vercors Massif was effectively under siege. The Germans were being repelled at each road route onto the plateau but, at the same time, the maquis were also being contained within. Supplies could not get in, the population relying on their own stores and produce for survival.

Frank saw this as something of a stalemate that could only be broken by one side. And that side was the Germans.

The enemy had the firepower and the manpower to put down any insurgency should they wish. With the occasional fly over by the Luftwaffe, he sensed the Germans were gathering themselves for an offensive. The skirmishes that had taken place so far had merely been probing attacks by the Nazis, testing the strength of the maquis and searching for the best areas to concentrate their attacks. Without proper supplies and reinforcements, the near four thousand maquisards now on the plateau would be in serious trouble should they decide to go for an all-out assault.

All over the region, tricolours and the Cross of Lorraine flew from every church spire and flag pole. Over the last few weeks, in preparation to receive reinforcements, a makeshift landing strip had been constructed near to Vassieux-en-Vercors. Frank felt this could only have a provocative effect on the Nazi leaders.

It was with a sense of relief that Algiers finally agreed to a supply drop. They chose the fourteenth of July, Bastille Day, on which to do it. That morning, over a hundred B-17 Flying Fortress aircraft of the United States Air Force filled the sky, the roar of their engines reverberating like thunder as they flew over the plateau.

Frank and his group witnessed the drop from the tree line of a nearby hill. Wave after wave of B-17s, their bomb doors opening to release hundreds of parachutes with silver-grey canisters slung beneath, containing weapons, ammunition, food and medicines - vital supplies for the fighting that was surely to come. They watched on as these containers floated slowly to the ground below. Frank noticed a lot of them had missed the target area and drifted away into deep ravines, out of reach of the maquisards and villagers who were out in their scores to retrieve them.

'Come on,' he said. 'Let's go and help.'

With Basson and Davies at his side, he stepped out of the tree line, and, together with the other fifteen men of his group, walked down the hill towards the drop zone.

They got half way when the Luftwaffe arrived.

They heard them first. The unmistakeable sound of Junkers 87B Stuka dive-bombers. The sirens fitted onto the spats of their wheels screeched out like demons from hell. Frank looked to the sky. Some of the B17s were turning away, as their fighter escorts headed to intercept the dive-bombers. They were joined by a small group of Messerschmitt Bf109E fighters. As the pilots from both sides engaged in deadly air combat, those on the ground stopped what they were doing, mesmerised by the spectacle taking place in the skies above them.

But this did not stop the Stukas from their deathly dives. Seconds later, the bombs started to fall.

Explosions rocked the ground ahead of them as the bombs hit their targets. Frank could hear the screams of the wounded as the shrapnel and concussive effects of the ordnance hit them. The ground seemed to erupt all around, throwing earth and human beings high into the air. As the Stukas pulled up from their dives, the rear gunners fired their machine-guns at anyone within range. Then two Bf109s broke away from the dogfight, flying low over the drop zone, strafing anyone in their path.

'Take cover!' shouted Frank and dived to the ground. He pulled the Thompson from his back and readied it. Although he knew it was pointless, the planes going way too fast, he fired a burst nevertheless. If nothing else it made him feel better.

He looked back to the sky and could see the B17s heading away from the area, closely followed by the USAF fighter escort as they abandoned the fight and headed to join them. Frank knew their orders would be to protect the bombers. With limited fuel they could not stay in the area long before returning to their bases in Africa. This left the people below at the mercy of the Germans.

The hamlet nearby was targeted next. Another wave of dive-bombers screamed down, releasing their bombs from from only a couple of hundred feet before pulling away. They could hardly miss. With no anti-aircraft weapons to concern themselves with, and small arms fire from the maquisards below being their only hazard, the Luftwaffe pilots could pick their targets with impunity. Frank watched as building after building crumbled to the ground, their walls and roofs ripped apart by the Nazi bombs. He could feel the air move around him and covered his ears with his hands, burying his face into the ground.

Frank looked up to see the Messerschmitts sweeping in for another strafing run, raking the already-ruined hamlet with gunfire, determined to kill anything that moved. A hundred yards away, a maquisard stood exposed, a Bren gun braced at his hip as he unleashed round after round at the diving aircraft. He was squarely in the plane's path, yet made no move for cover. Then, with sickening suddenness, a 20mm round struck him full in the face and his head vanished in a burst of red mist. For a heartbeat, his body remained upright, then collapsed lifeless to the ground.

To Frank's side, Davies was firing his carbine into the sky. He was joined by others in the group, some standing and shouting abuse at the Nazi aircraft. Their bullets had no effect, flying harmlessly short of the speeding aircraft.

After what seemed an age, the planes turned away and headed back to their base, leaving a scene of death and destruction in their wake.

Quickly Frank got to his feet and raced down the hillside to join those who had survived. Many of the maquis leaders had been there to meet the air drop. Frank saw Sacha among them.

'What's the situation?' asked Frank, wiping sweat from his forehead.

'In regards to the supplies it could have been better,' he replied. 'We've lost a few but at least it's something. What we need is men and heavy artillery.'

Frank winced. 'I can't see that happening any time soon. This is probably as good as it's going to get, Sacha. What's needed is another invasion on the Mediterranean coast. Those fighting in the west are still way too far away.'

'We can't expect to win here if we don't get the support we need.'

'I agree. It may have been better to keep up the "petite guerre" for a little longer. Give the Allies time to reach us.'

They spent the rest of the day retrieving as many canisters as they could and assisting with the wounded. The dead were gathered into a large pile for burial. It was much later when Frank's team left to go on another patrol.

Frank looked back down the hill. He could see fires still burning in the hamlet, the survivors desperately trying to save whatever they could from the flames. He felt bad about leaving them. His instincts were to go back down and help, but he knew he and his team were of more use elsewhere. They had to man the roadblocks and stop the German infantry from coming into the region.

He had a bad feeling this would not to be the last time he would witness such death and barbarity. He prayed the Allied advance would progress swiftly, or those in Algiers and London would see sense and send them the men and equipment they needed.

These people did not deserve what was happening to them. If reinforcements did not arrive soon, things would only get worse.

***

Over the next few days, the Germans continued with their probing attacks on the three main routes into the Vercors. The feeling of an imminent full scale attack by a much larger force began to grow among the maquis leaders. Again requests for more supplies and reinforcements were radioed to Algiers and London. Either they went ignored, or the responses were mere messages of support. There were no promises of practical help. The feeling of desperation was starting to spread amongst them.

'We have men here without weapons,' said François Huet one evening in Saint-Martin. Frank had travelled to the town to meet with the other leaders to form a plan of defence. 'They ask us to keep the Germans occupied, to rise up, yet they don't send us help when we need it.'

They were standing in the Villa Bellon, a large house that Huet was using as his headquarters. A large map of the area was on a table in front of them.

'So what's the plan?' asked Sacha who was standing to Frank's left.

Huet leaned over the map. 'There are three main routes onto the plateau,' he explained. 'Here, south of Grenoble; here, on the road to Crest; and here on the road to Romans-sur-Isère. We need to defend them all. If the Germans break through any one of them they can get onto the plateau in force and then we're in trouble.'

'Their attacks are getting stronger by the day,' put in Frank. 'Each time they come, it's with more troops. It's as though they're testing us. Seeing how strong we can defend. They'll soon realise that with one huge effort, they can break through. We won't be able to stop them if they hit us with significant numbers.'

Huet sighed. 'We can only do what we can do. Should they get onto the plateau then we'll make a stand in Vassieux. If it looks like we can't hold them then we'll retreat south and hide in the forests until the Allies get here.'

One of the other maquis leaders spoke. 'That could be some time yet, François. From what we can gather they've been held up. We have no idea when they'll reach us.'

'Like I said,' returned Huet. 'We can only do what we can do. We've around four thousand maquisards. They're eager to fight. But let's face facts. They're poorly equipped, haven't had time to be sufficiently trained and most have never been in combat before.'

'Can I make a suggestion?' cut in Frank.

'Go ahead.'

'Disperse them now,' he replied. 'Break them up and spread them throughout the plateau. Carry on the guerrilla war as you've been doing for months. We can never beat the Germans in a full on battle. They'll destroy us. Take to the forests and hills and hit them in small attacks…'

'Out of the question,' interrupted Huet. 'We've declared the Vercors a free state. The Vercors is France. We fly the tricolour from every town and hamlet. That can't change, my friend. If we get the support we've asked for, we can make a huge difference here. The rest of the country is counting on us. What we do here will spark other insurgencies. In the Massif Central and throughout France.'

'The rest of the country probably knows nothing of what's happening here,' argued Frank. 'They're not looking for us to take a stand. Their concentration is on the Allied advance, not on four thousand maquisards defending a few hills and mountains in the south.'

Huet's face reddened. 'I've told you the plan. That's it. We stand and fight and await the support that will come. They will not abandon us.'

Frank saw no point in carrying on with the conversation, as Huet was clearly not for turning.

The talk then moved to practical matters, including the deployment of resources to the three main arterial routes onto the plateau. An hour later the meeting broke up. Frank left the building, followed closely by Sacha.

Once outside, Sacha handed Frank a cigarillo and lit it for him. They stood in silence for a short while, blowing smoke into the early evening air.

'You do know we'll be defeated, don't you?' said Frank.

Sacha shrugged. 'Probably,' he replied. 'But what can we do? We've asked and asked for assistance and we're getting ignored. Okay, so we've had a few supply drops, but nothing on the scale of the fourteenth. And then we couldn't recover everything.'

'What can we do?' replied Frank, exasperated. 'We can disperse these lads now, Sacha, that's what we can do. We can't win. There'll be a massacre. The SS are not the ones to take prisoners, my friend. And if they do they'll all be shot, including us. These uniforms won't protect us. Look around you. Look at all these boys. They're keen and they're proud and they're brave. But they're also naive and untrained. They won't stand a chance otherwise.'

He finished his smoke and left Sacha, to join his team which was camped on the outskirts of the town. He filled them in on what had just taken place.

'Get on the Jed Set,' said Frank to Sergeant Davies. 'Get another message to London. We need them to speak to those who matter and get weapons and men without delay. These people need our support.'

'Right away, boss,' replied Davies. He walked away to carry out the order.

Frank turned to Basson. 'Is there anything you can do, Gerard?' he asked. 'They're your countrymen. Can't you talk to them? They won't listen to me.'

'I can try,' he replied solemnly. 'But I don't think I'll get very far. If their minds are made up then I doubt an outsider like me will have any influence.'

'Give it a go anyway,' said Frank.

He sat down amongst the group. They had been with him since he had landed on the plateau, Sacha having given them to him to command. He looked at each one of them. All brave Frenchmen, he thought. All willing to fight for what they believed in. To die if necessary, to free their country from Nazi oppression.

They deserved much better than this.

Chapter Twenty-six

21st July 1944

The convoy was much larger than anything that had come before.

Trucks full of troops, and half-tracks and motorcycle combinations led by Panzers, snaked along the road, heading towards the plateau. As they neared the cliffs that rose high on either side, the tank turrets turned, pointing their long barrels upwards. Soon they began to fire. With no anti-tank weapons with which to defend themselves, the best the maquisards could do was take cover from the flying shrapnel and rocks. Trees were smashed and uprooted, sending splinters flying in all directions before crashing to the ground around them. The maquisards returned small arms fire where they could, but this had little effect as the convoy proceeded up the hill and beyond them.

Frank looked to the sky and saw numerous German planes in the air. Heinkels towing small gliders. They no doubt contained battle-hardened troops, bypassing the roadblocks as they started the main attack. The assault they'd expected had finally arrived.

'This is it, boys,' he shouted above the din. 'They're breaking through. We can't stop them. It's pointless staying here. Fall back to Vassieux. Jimmy, get on the radio. Let them know the Germans have broken through.'

Frank was aware the main part of the German attack would take place at the largest town on the Vercors as this was where the main body of the maquis was located. Once that was crushed, then the German victory would be swift and merciless, giving them free reign throughout the whole of the massif to seek out and destroy any smaller pockets of resistance. If they were to put up any kind of a stand then that was where they needed to be.

On the clifftop opposite, Frank could see the defenders start to move out, their leader clearly of the same opinion as he. One or two hung back, firing Bren guns onto the trucks below, and throwing grenades which exploded harmlessly to the side of the road. The Panzers turned their attention to them, but before they could fire, the maquisards pulled away and ran for the safety of the trees behind.

They moved as purposefully as they could. They had to get back to the main force before the Germans were able to set themselves up. Frank knew that due to the terrain it would take the best part of the day before that happened. Ahead, he could see the gliders circling, their pilots looking for the best areas to land safely, before dropping out of sight to deliver their human cargo. Ironically, they would use the airstrip built for the reinforcements that were not forthcoming.

For the remainder of the morning they raced through the forest, pushing as hard as they could to get to Vassieux until, around mid afternoon, they saw the town ahead of them. A group of German soldiers had set up a position just outside of the town, blocking off any escape route to the north. As Frank had suspected, small gliders were scattered across the airstrip, having deposited the German troops who now looked to control entry to the town.

As Frank watched, he saw two trucks arrive as an advance group from the forces that had broken through the access roads converged with the glider borne troops that had set up this bridgehead.

Frank guided his team around the Germans. An hour later, he met with Sacha and other leaders in the main square. They were busily organising detachments to go to defensive positions around the northern area.

'We've taken a lot of casualties,' said Sacha. 'We're on to Algiers now. They'll have to send in reinforcements now the Germans are here.'

Frank could not hide his frustration. 'It'll make no difference, Sacha. They're not coming. We're here on our own. We need to start thinking of an evacuation plan right now. There are thousands of them gathering. They've much better equipment and are much better trained than we are. And they've been preparing for this since the day Huet and Descour declared the Vercors independent.'

As he spoke, an explosion rocked a nearby building, blowing a huge hole in the roof, sending tiles raining to the ground. Inside, the upper floor began to burn.

'Mortars,' shouted a nearby maquisard. 'Take cover.'

Frank watched as the group he was with dived for cover. He did not move. Instead he pulled the magazine from his Thompson, checked the ammunition inside and pushed it back into the weapon. He suspected he would be using it very soon.

More explosions burst in and around buildings near them as mortar bombs rained down upon the town. The sound of small arms fire could be heard amongst the cries of the wounded as the defending forces returned fire.

Finding shelter in a nearby house, Sacha began to brief Frank.

'We're consolidating the first aid stations,' he said. 'Any wounded need to be transferred to the cave at Luire. There's a Red Cross hospital being set up there. If you have any wounded then that's where they'll need to go. It's safe and well hidden.'

'Fine,' replied Frank.

'We've squads at all the main points we think they'll attack and more in the hills engaging with their main force. They'll hold them off…'

'We've not enough men…' interrupted Frank.

'We just need to hang on until reinforcements arrive,' said Sacha. 'They've a large group of glider troops just outside of town and it looks like an advance group has arrived from their main force to support them. They've probably been sent here to hold us down whilst the main force push through.'

'I've seen some of them,' explained Frank. 'If they're breaking through at all the access roads and mountain passes then we won't be able to hold them. We need to think about dispersing now, before it's too late.'

'Huet's calling the shots,' said Sacha. 'I hear what you're saying, my friend, but he's the man in charge.'

Frank left the building and went to find his men. They were setting up a defensive position on the north-eastern side of the town. In the distance he could see a squad of Germans gathering, digging themselves in.

'Okay,' he shouted. 'Three of you, come with me. The rest, concentrate your fire on that group over there.'

He was joined by Basson, Alain, and a young maquisard named Jean-Paul. They checked their weapons and set off, following Frank as he led them back into town, circling to the far right of the assembling German squad. He vaulted over a low wall and, keeping low, ran along a shallow ditch, staying out of sight. At last, they reached a slope just below the German left flank and took up position.

Cautiously, Frank crawled up the incline, Basson and Jean-Paul either side of him. Alain brought up the rear. He peered over the ridge and looked across at the Germans who were as yet unaware of their presence. There were eight of them. The covering fire from the town was falling short. None of them seemed in any way unsettled by it, as they checked their rifles, machine-pistols and stick grenades. Further along, he could see other groups digging themselves in and setting up mortar positions.

Frank slid back down the ridge and whispered to his comrades. 'On my command. We hit them hard and fast and then get straight back to the town. As fast as we can.'

He cocked the Thompson and pulled a grenade from his tunic pocket, pulling the pin with his teeth. Beside him, Basson and Jean-Paul readied their weapons, Basson also pulling a grenade from his pocket.

Slowly they crawled back up the incline. Frank looked at Basson. Silently he mouthed 'one, two, three,' then stood up, throwing the grenade into the group of Germans that stood only yards away from them, still unaware of their presence. Quickly they dropped to the ground as the grenades exploded amongst the German soldiers, killing three instantly and leaving others lying wounded on the ground. As Frank and Basson got to their feet again, they were joined by Alain and Jean-Paul. All four fired into the soldiers in front of them, moving their weapons from side to side, creating an effective kill zone.

Frank saw their bullets were hitting their targets. Seconds later, all eight of the Germans lay dead, their twisted corpses lying in a heap of blood and gore.

Further along the line, more enemy soldiers dived for cover whilst others made their weapons ready to return fire. Before they had chance to shoot back, Frank shouted. 'That's it, let's go… Now!'

Basson and Alain reacted instantly, ducking out of the Germans' line of sight and scrambling down the slope. Jean-Paul hesitated, holding his position and continuing to fire his Sten gun at the advancing Germans.

"Come on, Jean-Paul!" Frank shouted. "Get moving!"

The young Frenchman turned his head to look at Frank and lowered his weapon. As he started to carry out the instruction, Frank saw his beret fly from his head and his legs buckle under him. At first he thought the lad had simply lost his footing as the young man tumbled down the incline, coming to a stop at his feet. Frank bent down to help him up but then saw that the top half of his skull had been ripped off, blood and brain matter spilling out onto the grass.

'For Christ's sake,' he muttered.

He could hear shouts from behind. The pursuing Germans were very close. Ahead of him, Basson and Alain were running for the cover of the low wall which led to the sanctuary of Vassieux. He pulled another grenade from his pocket, primed it and threw it in the direction of the German voices before turning and sprinting after his colleagues.

He heard more screams as the grenade exploded, but did not look back to see what damage he had caused. He ran as fast as he possibly could, fully expecting a bullet to hit him. As he jumped over the wall, bullets pinged and ricocheted around him. Luckily none of them found their target. He lay in a heap on the ground, gasping for breath.

'Come on, Frank,' he heard Basson's voice beside him. 'Let's get out of here. We can't hold them here.'

Basson lifted his carbine above the wall and blindly fired an extended burst at the advancing Germans. He pulled the weapon back down, put in a fresh clip of ammunition, then did the same again.

Frank risked a look over the wall and saw that the group of following Germans had retreated back to where they had come from. 'Come on,' he said. 'Let's get back.'

The mortar attack on the town had not abated and buildings were continuing to be hit by the bombs. Fighters carrying boxes of ammunition ran from group to group, dropping off vital supplies to the town's defenders. Frank noticed some badly injured maquisards being treated by civilians who were doing all they could to help, applying bandages and fixing slings to broken arms.

He found Sergeant Davies, who had a cut across his forehead.

'You okay, Jimmy?' he asked upon seeing it.

'I'm fine, boss,' he replied. 'Just a flesh wound. A small bit of masonry hit me, that's all. Nothing to worry about.'

'Nevertheless, get it seen to. There's a group of women back there with bandages and things. Go and get it cleaned and taken care of. When you've done that, get on the Jed Set and let London know we're under heavy attack here. We need them to pull some weight with the French. They could have troops here by the morning if they get their arses into gear. Or at least organise a bombing run.'

Word was getting through that the Germans were attacking hamlets and villages across the plateau as the main body of their forces advanced towards Vassieux. They were taking no mercy with any maquisards they found or any civilians they suspected of harbouring or assisting them in any way. The population of whole villages were being slaughtered by SS troops, it was being reported.

That evening, as Frank sat with Basson and Davies, trying to get some rest, he could hear fighting in the hills to the north and southwest as small groups engaged with the Germans, the occasional flash of light indicating where the action was taking place. The Germans outside of town had stopped their barrage and Frank realised they would probably not engage in a full on assault until they had more troops at their disposal. Huet had considered organising an attack on them from the town but the enemy had better weaponry and were dug in. Any attack would probably prove futile. Instead, he had decided to increase the pressure on the Free French in Algiers to send help, and wait it out.

'What chance have we got?' asked Davies. His wound had been taken care of, the bandage pushing his hair higher up his forehead causing the fringe to stick up slightly. Had they not been in the situation they now found themselves in, Frank would have thought it comical.

'Christ alone knows,' he replied. He could feel tears of frustration start to form in his eyes but forced them back. 'I've known some of these men for a long time,' he went on, looking over at Alain and Arnold Jeunier, both of whom sat with their backs against a wall, trying to get some sleep. 'All they want is peace. To go about their lives without having to deal with this kind of shit. They don't deserve this.'

'So what's your plan?' asked Basson. 'For us. If it all goes wrong.'

Frank raised his eyebrows. 'If? It already has, my friend. We can't abandon them. All we can do is stay and fight and hope Algiers or London hears our calls and does the right thing. You never know, if we hold out long enough, the Allies might get here.'

'Sounds like wishful thinking, boss,' said Davies.

Frank smiled wryly. 'Yeah, Jimmy. I suppose it does. Ever the optimist, eh? If it comes to it and we have to make a break for it, then we simply go to the forests and hide. Hit the Germans with the same tactics we used before. Wait it out until the advance gets here. We've got to assume now that they're not going to send anyone to help us. They'd be here by now if that was the case. Let's see how the next few hours play out and then take it from there.'

For the first time in his life, Frank realised he did not have a real plan. He really did not know what to do. And he did not like it one bit.

***

The following morning, Frank was asked to attend a meeting with Huet, Sacha and other officers of the maquis.

'We need experienced groups to go out and hold them up,' explained Huet. 'Cause them problems, be a pain in their backsides. Find them and engage them wherever they can be found.'

'I don't think it'll be too hard locating them,' interjected Frank. 'I'll go. My lads are all experienced and good at what they do.'

'Fine,' said Huet. 'Take as much ammo as you can carry. Whatever we can spare, then move out. Head to the north-east. I'll send other groups to the south. We need to hold them off for as long as we can.'

An hour later, they were ready to move out. Basson and Alain had made sure every man had enough rations for three days, with each one responsible for carrying and managing his own supplies. Frank had no intention of babysitting anyone.

The mortar barrage had started again and buildings continued to burn around them. The crack of rifles added to the noise. The shouting of the officers could be heard as they tried to organise the defence.

Davies approached them, his carbine slung over his shoulder and the Jed Set in a rucksack on his back. He had sent a message to London giving a situation report on the activities of team GREYMAN. As he got nearer, there was a distinct crack of a rifle. He fell over, landing heavily.

'Sniper!' Frank heard someone yell. They all dropped to the ground or took cover behind walls.

Nervously Frank looked over to where Davies lay. He was thankful to see he was moving, his right hand gripping his left shoulder where blood seeped between his fingers. As long as he was out of the sniper's sights, he would live. He was contemplating what to do when he saw movement to his left. It was Basson.

Without thought to his own safety, he ran to Davies and grabbed him from behind by the armpits. Frank saw the dirt a foot to his left side lift up, as a poorly aimed bullet hit the ground.

Frank took the Thompson from his shoulder and turned to where he thought the sniper may be. He fired a short burst, followed by another and then dropped back into cover. He looked over and saw Basson had managed to get Davies to safety behind a brick outbuilding.

'Watch yourselves!' he shouted, turning again to where he thought the firing was coming from. He saw someone running, around a hundred yards ahead and brought his field glasses up to his eyes.

It was a German carrying a scoped rifle. He fired a burst from the Thompson in his direction, but the soldier was soon out of sight.

'He's gone,' shouted Frank. Taking the binoculars from around his neck he threw them to Arnold. 'Keep a look out, Arnie. If he comes back, let me know. Or better still, kill him.'

Frank ran to the rear of the outbuilding and found Basson frantically removing the radio pack from Davies's back. He tore open his tunic to reveal a jagged hole in the man's shoulder, blood oozing from it.

'Bloody hell, boss,' said Davies, smiling. 'That hurt.'

His bravado was short-lived as he let out a soft moan. Basson turned to Frank. 'He's done, Frank. He'll need to get this looked at by a doctor. The bullet's still in there.'

Basson took a field dressing from his tunic breast pocket and pressed the pad against the wound. 'Here, Jimmy. Hold this tight against it. Press hard. You need to stop the blood.'

Frank thought for a moment. 'Okay. Get him on his feet and over to that dressing station. He'll need to go to the Red Cross set-up at Grotte de la Luire. It's over for you, Jimmy.'

With the assistance of Basson, Davies gingerly got to his feet. 'Sorry, boss,' he winced.

'Not your fault, you daft sod,' replied Frank. 'You'll need to get someone to look at that properly. Two wounds in as many days. Not your week is it?'

With the help of one of the men, Davies slowly walked away.

Frank sighed turned to Basson. 'Is the Jed Set all right?'

The Frenchman bent down and took it from the rucksack. 'Looks fine,' he replied after giving it a quick examination. He replaced it and put the pack on his back.

'Right,' said Frank. 'Let's move out. Keep low and follow me. We've work to do.'

They set off, heading in a north-easterly direction, skirting the German forces. Once they crossed the tree line and were in the forest, Frank felt he could relax a little. The sound of gunfire and mortar bombs grew quieter as they walked away. Soon, the only sound that could be heard was their own footsteps as they trudged through the forest and away from Vassieux.

Frank felt as though he was deserting the town. He knew that was where the main battle would take place, but his orders to create problems at the rear of the German forces seemed sound enough. It was as though he was abandoning them to an unknown horror that was yet to come. His advice had fallen on deaf ears and the frustration that had grown over the last couple of days was likely to spill over into full blown conflict with the maquis leadership. Leaving them to it was probably the best thing right now.

The loss of a good soldier like James Davies irritated him. The man was more than a radio operator. His performance in action was as good as he had seen from anyone. He had been a great character to have around the group, despite his lack of French. The man had often cheered him up when he felt low, which had been many times over the last few weeks. He hoped the wound was not too serious and he would heal quickly.

Late that afternoon they came across a small farm. Two buildings burned furiously as they approached. Frank had the men fan out as they cautiously approached it. When they got closer it was easy to see that whoever had set the buildings ablaze were now long gone. On the ground between the two buildings the bodies of a woman and two men, one no more than a boy, lay dead, their corpses crumpled and twisted. Frank approached them and bent down to examine them. All three had their hands tied behind their backs. They had been shot in the back of the head.

'Dear God,' whispered Basson under his breath. 'Was there any need for this?'

Frank shook his head. 'None whatsoever. But this is what we're dealing with, Gerard. The SS. They don't care about human life. It's meaningless to them. Look at these people. Farmers. That's all they are. No threat at all to them or anyone else. Yet still they execute them.'

'We shall bury them,' stated Alain.

Frank was about to tell him to leave them, as they didn't have the time, but thought better of it.

He took out his cigarettes and lit one as Alain, Arnie and two others searched for spades to dig the graves. He sat on the wall in front of the burning buildings and quietly smoked as he watched them cut away the binds from the wrists of the corpses and straighten them, giving them the dignity denied them by their killers.

One day, he thought, this will all be over. One day this will all stop and people will be able to live normal, peaceful lives once more. One day, he may understand just why some people would want to do something like this to other people.

But he doubted it. For as long as he lived, he would never understand the evil in some men.

When he thought about it, he realised he did not want to understand it. He wanted to be a better man than that.

Chapter Twenty-seven

For the next two days Frank's band of maquisards carried out surprise attacks on small groups of Germans, hitting them hard before escaping back into the forests and hills. He knew to engage a larger force would be tantamount to suicide so picked smaller squads to attack. He had no idea if it made any difference, but assumed if the Germans were employed in trying to catch him and his team then it prevented those same troops from harassing innocent villagers.

It was extremely dangerous work. Two of his group had been killed by German gunfire and another two had been left wounded on the battlefield, shot as the others escaped through the trees. They had heard the crack of a pistol as their comrades were executed by the SS soldiers pursuing them.

Whichever direction they looked they could see palls of smoke rising from hamlets and villages across the plateau. It was becoming apparent that the reinforcements they had begged for were nowhere to be seen. The Germans had free reign over the region. With only small pockets of maquisards roaming the forests and hills, and the main force at Vassieux poorly equipped and insufficiently trained, they were not able to prevent them from taking control.

It was now the 24th of July. From the information Frank gained from London, when he had made contact with them the previous night, the Allied invasion was going well. The armies had a firm foothold in France and were advancing purposefully inland. In the east the Russians were also pushing the Germans back. Between them, the Nazis were being squeezed and it surely would not be long before they choked. Frank was sure the end could not be far away.

Frank had wondered why the Germans were bothering with them at all. The maquis could quite easily be contained on the plateau. Why the Nazis had not just allowed them to stay there, cut off from the rest of France where they could do no harm, seemed odd to him. Surely the German forces currently being poured onto the massif could be better served fighting the armies that were advancing upon them. It made no military sense to him whatsoever.

He supposed this was a "saving face" thing. The maquis had declared the Vercors a liberated area, had raised the French flag, and blown a raspberry in the face of the Nazis. Their pride would not let them allow that. Consequently, they were showing no mercy wherever they went.

It was a warm morning. The group, now consisting of only eleven men, including himself, Basson, Alain and Arnie, had spent the night sheltering in a secluded cave. It was a place Alain, being a native of the area, was very familiar with. Apparently he used to play there as a small child and they were easily able to avoid the German patrols. After eating a small breakfast of dry bread and apples, they collected their weapons and prepared to move out.

They became aware of the familiar droning of a German aircraft and looked to the sky. A large number of planes were heading in the direction of Vassieux, Dorniers and Heinkels towing gliders full of combat troops.

'It looks like they're about to start a major assault,' said Basson to Frank. 'What do you want to do?'

Frank thought for a moment. He had to make a decision. He looked to Alain, Arnie and the others and could see the desperation in their faces. Alain had relatives in Vassieux.

'Let's head back,' he said. 'We're doing no good out here anymore and we've lost four good men. They'll need us there.'

They checked their weapons, making sure they were all fully loaded. Cautiously they set off in single file down the hill, each of them on heightened alert. The last thing they needed was to be ambushed by a German patrol.

After an hour they came to a roadway that split the forest in two. Frank halted the group and told them to take cover. He stepped out onto the road and looked in both directions. In the distance he could hear the rumble of motorised vehicles coming from the west. As he took cover behind a tree, he observed a German convoy proceeding towards them.

Quickly Frank moved back to where his men were waiting. He spoke to Alain and Basson.

'There's a convoy coming. We need to wait here until they pass.'

Alain turned to the others and passed on the information. Slowly they moved further back into the forest, concealing themselves behind trees and bushes. Frank could not risk any of them being spotted for it would mean death for them all.

Soon enough, the convoy rolled past their position. A staff car, followed by half tracks and trucks full of troops, including two that towed artillery pieces; short stubby weapons each with six rocket-firing tubes.

Watching them go by, Frank was filled with a dread stronger than he had felt since the uprising began.

'They don't stand a chance,' whispered Alain, his face ashen. 'If this is only a small section of what they're going to throw at them.'

'My thoughts exactly,' replied Frank. 'Those are Nebelwerfers. Once they get started it'll be a slaughter. It might be difficult for us to get back to Vassieux. The Germans will be everywhere now. I can't believe how much hardware and personnel they're throwing at this thing.'

Once the convoy had passed, they continued with their journey. After a while, Frank stopped and leaned against a tree. He watched each of them as they walked by. Over the past week he had seen the wave of optimism that had arisen when independence was declared quickly flip to one of anxiety, pessimism and, in some cases, downright fear.

He was not sure of his own feelings about what was happening. Like the maquis, he too felt abandoned by Allied command. He had been sent back to France to cause as much trouble as he could and liaise with local insurgents. But the promise of assistance had not been forthcoming. Without it, they stood no chance of any kind of success. It made him feel sick to the stomach.

As the afternoon progressed, the sound of gunfire grew stronger and the stench of burning constantly filled their nostrils. Between explosions and bursts of gunfire, they could hear shouting and screaming.

Shortly they came to a clearing. Frank guessed they were approximately four miles outside of Vassieux. As they reached the tree line, they could see activity ahead. They took cover behind a group of trees to observe what was taking place.

Approximately forty yards ahead of them stood a large group of soldiers. Frank counted around twenty-five, dressed in the battle fatigues of the Fallschirmjäger, German paratroopers. From where he was positioned, he could see the SS insignia on their collars, patches on their upper arms denoting the flags of countries other than Germany. He could not be sure specifically which nations they belonged to, but was aware some thugs from Russia, the Ukraine and other eastern European states had joined forces with the SS. They had a reputation for extreme brutality.

They were standing next to a half-track and two Opel troop trucks, casually smoking cigarettes and eating from mess tins. In front of them, a small group of maquisards knelt on the ground, their heads bowed and their hands tied behind their backs. Frank counted seven of them.

An SS officer marched up and down in front of them, offering them insults in a language that Frank had never heard before. Occasionally he would stop in front of one of the young Frenchmen and slap him across the head, or deliver a kick to another's body.

There was no doubt in Frank's mind they were preparing for an execution.

Alain tapped him on his shoulder. 'What do you want to do?'

Frank turned his head. He could see the desperation in his friend's eyes. These were his countrymen, his friends. They were fellow maquisards. But for God's grace, it could be them out there waiting for a bullet to the back of the head.

'Prepare the men,' he said. 'We're not leaving them there to be murdered.'

He had to think fast. The SS could start the killing at any time. 'Take Arnie and three others and head over there, to the right flank. We'll go to the left, near that fallen tree. Set up the Bren and wait for my signal. We'll try and get as many as we can in the crossfire and then attack them with grenades. We'll advance on them in groups. We'll go first and then cover you. You do the same for us. Concentrate your fire on the half-track, we can't let them get into it and man that thirty-four.'

'This is very dangerous,' said Basson. 'We could hit some of our own. Or we could all be killed or captured.'

Frank tried to stop an ironic snigger, but failed. 'You don't say, Gerard. This is war. All of it's dangerous. This is how I see it. We've a choice here. We can walk away and leave those poor bastards to be murdered, or we can try and save some of them. If we do nothing then they're all certainly going to die today. If we stop and fight, then maybe we can save a few…Look, I don't know if this is tactically the right thing to do, my friend, but I sure to God know it's the moral one.'

Alain and his group set off to the position he had indicated and Frank moved out with Basson and the other four maquisards. A little later they were all in position.

The terrain ahead was flat, giving no advantage to Frank and his team for firing directly into the rear of the half-track. Complicating matters further, the SS could easily take cover behind the trucks and regroup. Frank knew that after the initial assault, he would need to lead his team in a flanking manoeuvre to cut off any soldiers who managed to find cover.

'Make sure your aim is true,' he whispered to those nearest him. 'Make every bullet count.'

Ahead of him, the Nazi officer walked behind the prisoner to the extreme left of the line and took his pistol from the holster at his waist. Frank watched as the man raised the weapon and cocked it.

Frank turned to the young maquisard to his right. 'Simon, can you take him?'

Simon had proved himself a very good shot with the .303 Lee Enfield rifle. He held it firmly and confidently. He nodded, 'Just say when, Francois.'

'Okay, boys,' said Frank. 'This is it.' He paused for a moment. 'Simon… when you're ready, lad.'

No sooner had Frank issued the order than the young man fired the rifle.

The officer, who was lowering the weapon to the base of the first man's neck suddenly flew forward onto the prisoner, knocking him to a heap on the ground. Simon's bullet had hit him square in the back, killing him instantly, his body now lying on top of the man he was about to execute.

Firing broke out to Frank's left as the Bren gun opened up hitting a group of SS soldiers before they had chance to react. Frank raised the Thompson and fired a sustained burst at a small group standing to the rear of the half-track, knocking two off their feet. A third man, managed to make it to the other side of the vehicle, out of the line of fire.

Most of the prisoners, realising what was happening, had thrown themselves to the ground. Then two of them stood up and broke for the trees to Frank's left, running as fast as they could, their progress hindered slightly due to their hands being tied.

With horror he watched as another SS soldier, who had managed to make it to the cover of one of the trucks, cut them both down with a burst from his machine-pistol, their bodies falling lifelessly to the ground.

'Come on,' shouted Frank, breaking from the cover of the trees, firing the Thompson with his right hand whilst taking a grenade from a pocket with his left. He had only two left and wanted to make sure he used them effectively.

He could sense Basson and the others following him, crouching as they ran, some firing their weapons whilst the others rushed forward, eager to get to a position of cover, no matter how slight. He could hear bullets pinging off the half-track as the Bren gunner concentrated his fire upon it, and saw more SS soldiers fall to the ground.

Although the initial surprise of the attack had caught them off guard, it was clear to Frank that well over half the Germans had made it to safety and were getting organised.

He dropped to the ground beside Simon, who was reloading the . 303. 'Good shot,' he said, patting him on the back. 'Cover me.'

Frank stood up, pulling the pins from the grenades. Quickly he lobbed one towards the half-track. He could see it was a poor throw, the grenade flying high over the vehicle. The second was more successful, landing inside, where an SS soldier was desperately trying to gain access to the MG34 machine-gun. Frank knew that should he make it then the weapon would cause havoc with the maquisards and the attack would be repelled easily.

And then he saw something flying over the vehicle towards them. It was the first grenade he had thrown being returned by the Nazis on the far side of the half-track. It landed ten yards from him. Instinctively he threw his body over Simon's, protecting him from the blast.

He closed his eyes and waited. He felt the air shift around him as the grenade exploded. He was suddenly hit by a flash of heat. He took a breath and looked up as the second grenade went off inside the half-track, blowing the SS paratrooper into the air, his body landing with a thud a few yards away. Instantly, the vehicle began to burn.

To his right Alain's group advanced, moving forward a few yards before dropping to the ground, just as he had ordered.

He got to his knees. 'Come on, lads,' he shouted, reloading the Thompson. It was then that he noticed the blood on his arm. The sleeve had been ripped and blood trickled down to his hand. He flexed the arm once and was happy to see there were no broken bones. The wound was superficial.

The surviving four prisoners had by now got to their feet and were sprinting towards the safety of the trees, passing Frank and his fighters as they did so.

He was about to advance further when something in the air suddenly caught his eyes. At first he thought it was a flock of birds, but soon realised he was badly mistaken.

'Grenades!' he shouted at the top of his voice, diving back to the ground.

One landed in front of him. For a split second he hesitated, before grabbing it and throwing it as hard as he could in the direction it had come from, where it exploded harmlessly. He looked up as many of the grenades went off, throwing shrapnel in all directions. He watched in horror as two of Alain's group were hit, throwing them into the air. One was clearly dead but the other screamed in agony, both of his lower legs separated from his body.

The SS paratroopers were getting organised. They were now firing back at them from the cover of the vehicles.

Frank knew realised their situation was hopeless. They could not win this.

'Retreat!' he screamed at the top of his voice. 'Alain! Back to the trees. We'll cover you!'

Through gritted teeth he fired at the paratroopers taking cover behind the vehicles. Those around him did the same and once Alain's group had reached the tree line, they set up their weapons and returned fire, giving Frank and his small group the cover they needed to effect a retreat.

Stooping, Frank fired from the hip as he walked backwards to the trees. In his peripheral vision, he noticed the bodies of a further three French fighters lying prone, unmoving on the battleground. One of them was another of the prisoners they had tried to rescue.

After what seemed an age, but was only a matter of seconds, he reached the trees and jumped behind a fallen trunk. He took a breath before raising his head to survey the damage. The clearing was littered with corpses. To his right, the Bren gun was still firing. He knew it must be running low on ammunition.

Basson, blood pouring from a gash in his head approached him from the right.

'We need to get out of here,' he yelled above the din. 'We've lost five men and three of the prisoners have been killed. We need to get out of here now.'

Frank nodded. Once the three prisoners had been released from their bonds, and they had collected the "Jed Set" from where they had hidden it, he led the small group back to Alain and the Bren gunner, who now fired sporadically at the Nazis near the trucks, keeping them at bay. The half-track burned furiously to the side, thick black smoke billowing into the air.

'We've got them pinned down,' said Alain. 'But we're very close to running out of ammunition for the Bren. They'll be able to outflank us if we don't move soon. We need to go.'

'And they'll be calling for reinforcements,' cut in Basson.

Frank thought briefly before speaking. 'Okay, boys,' he said. 'This is our situation. We have minimal ammunition and the Jerries will be out for revenge for what we've just done. We need to break up and try to get to the main group at Vassieux. There's nothing else for it. Our band of merry men has come to an end for now, I'm afraid.

'Alain, you take the three prisoners, Arnie and two more with you. Head north, away from Vassieux and then double back round. When you get deeper into the plateau, split again. Let's make it as difficult as possible for these bastards to find us. Keep to the forests and ravines and clear of open spaces. The rest of us'll head south and come up from the south-west. They won't follow us until they've more men. Hopefully it'll be a little while before they arrive. We need to use the time to get as far away as we possibly can before that happens.'

Keeping the SS paratroopers pinned down with rifle fire and the occasional burst from the Bren gun, they slowly began to move out. Frank and Basson hung back, the last to leave. Basson took over the Bren until the other group was well into the forest. They waited five more minutes before Frank gave the order to pull out.

There were now only three in the group, Frank, Basson and the young maquisard, Simon, who had killed the SS officer. Their ammunition was low and the rations they had would not last more than another day.

As they trudged away, deep into the forest, a new sound hit them, coming from the south-east. From Vassieux. Heavy gunfire, rockets and thunderous explosions carried to them, despite the trees having a slight muffling effect.

Frank looked at his two companions and winced, shaking his head from side to side. Maybe heading back to Vassieux was not such a good idea after all.

***

Over the next twenty-four hours the three men cautiously made their way to the south of the plateau, keeping to the woods and evading German patrols. If the group they attacked had attempted to pursue them, then they saw no sign of this as they were able to move swiftly away from the battleground now they were a much smaller number. Frank hoped the other group, led by Alain, had also been able to get to safety, but he had no way of knowing.

Basson had cleaned and bandaged Frank's wounded arm as best he could with a field dressing. Although he could use it without much trouble, and the bleeding had stopped, the Frenchman was no medic. He knew it needed to be treated properly to prevent it getting infected.

They had managed to fill their water bottles from a stream but the food had run out. If they did not eat anything substantial soon then the fatigue they were already feeling would only get worse.

The relentless sound of gunfire and fighting coming from every direction and the smell of smoke hung in the air. Nobody spoke about it but it was clear to them all that things were not going well.

By late afternoon they found themselves on a wooded hill to the south of Vassieux. Frank used his field glasses to survey the town. Plumes of smoke rose high from destroyed buildings. Frantic activity was taking place around the outskirts, where groups of maquisards tried to find cover from the German mortars, rockets and small arms fire. Further to the east, he could see fires burning as the Nazis carried out reprisals on other hamlets and towns. The whole plateau seemed to be on fire.

'What do you want to do?' asked Basson.

'Get the radio set out,' he instructed. 'I'm going to send another message to London. They need to send reinforcements before they're all massacred.'

The message he sent was short and to the point. 'FROM GREYMAN. URGENT. IMMEDIATE REINFORCEMENTS NEEDED ON VERCORS PLATEAU. SITUATION CRITICAL. ADVISE.'

It was half an hour before a response came back. It was equally succinct. 'TO GREYMAN. UNABLE TO COMPLY WITH REQUEST. GOOD LUCK. HH.'

Frank yanked the earphones from his head and let out a frustrated bellow. He stood, kicked the "Jed Set" before picking it up and hurling it against a tree. It shattered on impact and dropped to the ground in pieces. He kicked the wreckage repeatedly until it was completely destroyed. Simon and Basson watched in silence. There was no need to ask what the reply had been.

He leaned against a tree and took a few deep breaths.

'Come on,' he said, once he had calmed down. 'Let's get down there and see what we can do. That's if there is anything we can do.'

They approached the town from the south, out of the line of sight of any German positions. An hour later, inside the bomb damaged building being used as field headquarters, he found Sacha, his head bandaged and left arm in a sling. He was with the other surviving maquis commanders. All of them carried an injury of one form or another.

Sacha looked genuinely pleased to see him. 'Bonjour, Francois. What's the situation with your group?'

Frank shook his hand. 'We took a few casualties and had to split up,' he explained. 'There's just myself, Gerard and young Simon. Alain took the rest north. I don't know where or how he is, or even if he's still alive. The Germans are all over the plateau, Sacha. They're burning every village and hamlet they come across, killing civilians and executing any maquis prisoners they take. I've been on to London. There aren't any reinforcements coming. We're on our own, my friend.'

François Huet approached them. He looked harassed and dejected. 'I hear what you say, Francois. We can't hold out for much longer. This needs to end.'

As if to emphasise his point, an artillery shell landed outside, causing the whole building to shake. 'We're running short of ammunition and we know the enemy are preparing for an all out assault on Vassieux. If we don't evacuate then we'll all be slaughtered.'

Frank felt relieved. At last, someone was starting to see sense. The situation was now beyond hopeless.

They left the building, in search of food and water, and to see if they could get more ammunition for their weapons. He was aware the three of them had not slept for nearly forty-eight hours. If they did not get rest soon, then they were in danger of being unable to function.

Passing many battle-weary partisans, they found a house at the rear of the town. Remarkably it was undamaged. The elderly occupants provided them with a thin broth and some stale bread, before the three of them collapsed exhausted, all falling into a very deep sleep.

***

Frank managed around four hours sleep before he woke up, fully alert. Basson and Simon snored loudly to his side. Outside, the sound of gunfire could be heard and the occasional shell landed nearby with a resounding crash, throwing debris from the already battered town high into the air. The cries of injured fighters and civilians filled the night around him making him wince. It was clear the end was close.

He stood up and collected his weapon before stepping outside. He took a pack of cigarettes from his pocket and, seeing it was the last one, threw the empty carton onto the ground. Lighting the cigarette, he took a deep drag. He ran his hand through his hair which was long and dirty and then felt the stubble at his chin.

Frank was a mess and he felt it. He had not had a proper wash or shave in days. He was under no illusion that he stank. But then so did all of them. Personal hygiene was the last thing on anyone's mind right now. It was all about survival, nothing more.

He was joined by Basson, Simon following, bleary-eyed, behind him. The three stood against the wall in silence. They watched the dark, starry sky, illuminated in parts by the fires that burned in the villages and the flashes of explosions. Up there it looked so peaceful, a stark contrast to what was taking place on the earth below.

Frank turned his head to see Sacha walking towards him. He drew the last from his cigarette and threw the stub to the ground, crushing it with the heel of his boot.

'Huet's giving the order to scatter,' he said matter-of-factly. 'The situation's hopeless here. It's every man for himself, I'm afraid.'

Frank did not know whether to laugh or cry. It was the right decision. But it should have been made days ago, as soon as the Germans attacked the plateau in force.

'We need to get to the hills and forests,' went on Sacha. 'Hit them as and when we can. In small groups like before.'

'There'll be reprisals,' stated Frank. 'They're already happening.'

'We can only hope the Allies hurry up and get here,' said Sacha bitterly. 'We don't have the resources or manpower to do anything more. They abandoned us, Francois. They asked us to rise up and then they left us to it. How many times did we ask for help? How many? Yet they ignored us. I will never forgive them for this. You need to make preparations and get out of here, my friend. Head south. Get off the plateau if you can. Stay safe.'

He walked away, dejected, leaving them feeling just the same as he did.

No one spoke for a while. There was nothing to say.

'Come on,' said Frank after a while. 'Let's move out. There's no point in waiting.'

They collected their gear and set off, retracing the route they had taken when they entered Vassieux only hours before.

As they crossed into the forest Frank stopped and looked back at the town. He had never felt so despondent in all his life. Just as the Allies in London and Algiers had abandoned them, they in turn were now deserting the people of Vassieux.

And God only knew what fate awaited them now.

***

They found shelter that night in a shallow ravine and slept another deep sleep. When they awoke, Simon was gone. Frank assumed the lad had set off to find his family. He did not blame him one bit. The fight for the Vercors Massif was over. The insurrection had been crushed mercilessly. He could understand Simon's need to find out if his family were okay.

In the distance, they could hear sporadic gunfire and twice that morning, a German aircraft passed overhead, the Nazis on the lookout for any escaping maquisards. They decided the best course of action was to get off the plateau altogether, but knew it would not be easy to do so without being caught. The roads in would all be blocked and the perimeters would no doubt be being patrolled by the Germans.

Frank knew that should he and Basson be captured, then they would be executed, despite them wearing the uniforms of legitimate combatants. Harding had told him as much before he set off from

London. From what he had witnessed on the plateau, he was sure they both would be shot out of hand.

In the afternoon they reached a clearing that gave them a view of the valley below. Frank took out his binoculars. He scanned the town they had left the previous evening. He could clearly see buildings burning and the movement of German soldiers walking through the rubble. Even from so far away, he could hear the sound of gunfire as the Nazis systematically went through the streets, gunning down anyone they came across, no matter if they were innocent civilians or maquis combatants. Mixed amongst them he saw the blue uniforms of the hated Milice.

He could watch no more, turning his head away. 'Come on, Gerard,' he said. 'Let's get away from this place.'

They spent the rest of the day heading south. Three times they managed to avoid SS patrols; groups of around a dozen men. They hid in ditches and covered themselves with branches and foliage as the soldiers walked by, once within only a few yards of them.

As darkness fell, they reached a cliff at the edge of the plateau. Below they could see numerous farmhouses in the distance, their lights burning, their occupants unaware of what had just taken place on the high ground so near to them. They watched as German motorised vehicles patrolled the roads, on the lookout for anyone trying to escape.

Frank waited for a patrol to pass.

'What do you say, Gerard? Do you want to chance it? There looks a way down over there on the left. It could be a bit tricky, but I'm sure we could make it if we're careful.'

Basson looked to where he indicated. 'Do we really have an alternative? Maybe we could do it. Yes, let's give it a try.'

They discarded everything they did not need including their larger weapons, keeping only a pistol each and an extra clip of ammunition. Hanging onto branches and moving slowly from rock to rock, they made it to the roadway, both of them sweating hard, despite the cold of the night. They were about to cross the road when they heard vehicles approaching. Jumping behind a boulder they watched as the lights of a half-track passed them, the soldiers inside looking up to the cliff face. It carried on down the road until, finally, it was out of sight.

'Quickly,' said Basson. 'That farm over there. Let's go.'

Keeping to the shadows the two men ran across a furrowed field towards a group of buildings five hundred yards away. Nervously, Basson looked behind for any sign of German activity. After what seemed an age, they made it to the side of a large barn. Across a small yard stood a farmhouse, the lights burning in the kitchen where Frank could see two people inside, a man and a woman. Thankfully, neither of them had seen them approach.

The door to the barn was unlocked and they quietly let themselves in. It was dark but they could just make out a ladder leading to a hayloft. Carefully they climbed up the ladder and into the loft where they both collapsed, exhausted into a pile of hay.

***

Frank was awoken by the sound of a vehicle outside. At first he had no idea where he was and it took him a few seconds to come round. He looked around but there was no sign of Gerard Basson. An uncharacteristic panic started to set in. For the first time since his return to France, he was alone and he did not like it. He had grown accustomed to the company of others and had come to rely on that comradeship to see him through the past couple of months.

He was about to get up, to go in search of his friend, when suddenly the door to the barn opened and four gendarmes entered. They all carried pistols and began an immediate search, looking behind bales of hay and inside the cab of a tractor he had not noticed the night before.

He took the pistol from his pocket and cocked it. He stood up and moved to the edge of the hayloft. He was about to raise the weapon when he caught his foot on a loose plank of wood and stumbled, dropping the gun, where it landed with a thud on the ground below. Frantically he looked around for a method of escape but there was none. The only way out of the building was by the way he had entered.

He sighed and sat down, his legs dangling over the edge of the hayloft. He looked down at the four gendarmes, all of whom stared up at him, their weapons pointed in his direction.

'Come down,' said the tallest of them, a sergeant with a bushy moustache. Another gendarme went to retrieve Frank's Colt from the floor and handed it to his superior. The sergeant looked at it, made sure the safety catch was on and then put it in his pocket.

Frank did as he was told and climbed down the ladder. Two of the gendarmes grabbed his arms and forced them behind his back, fastening handcuffs to his wrists.

'I'm a British officer,' he said boldly. 'And as such should be treated in line with the Geneva Convention.'

The sergeant glared at him. 'I don't care, Monsieur. You and your like have caused nothing but misery around here. You'll come with us to the police station. Where's your friend?'

'What friend?' replied Frank. 'I'm alone.'

'Two of you were seen entering the barn. Where is he?'

'I really have no idea what you're talking about.'

As they led him out of the building to where a police car was parked, the sergeant ordered two of his officers to check the area. After five minutes they returned, shaking their heads.

Frank caught the eye of the farmer and his wife who stood nearby, watching. They turned their heads away, not willing to look at the man they had betrayed. He glared at them until he was past them, daring them to look at him. Neither of them did.

'Very well,' said the sergeant. 'Let's get him back to the station.'

They placed him in the rear of the car, between two policemen, then drove out of the farmyard.

Frank had no idea where they were taking him. For a fleeting moment, he did not really care. He had no idea what had happened to Basson. He just hoped his friend had managed to get away. He must have had a very good reason for leaving and not telling him what his plans were.

He was extremely fatigued. All he wanted to do was sleep. Then he wanted to wake up and find out that all this had been a dream and none of it had actually happened.

But in his heart of hearts he knew the nightmare he was living was far from over.

Chapter Twenty-eight

Davies's arm hurt like hell. Each time he tried to move it, a sharp pain shot up and around his neck, occasionally causing him to cry out. He tried his best to keep quiet, but it was difficult. He felt such a fool. There were many inside the cave with much worse injuries than he, and some of them never made a sound.

The Red Cross dressing station was well hidden. The cave was one of those places that if you did not know of its existence, you would be hard pressed to find it. A narrow path around the side of a hill led to a large opening in the rocks, partly covered by hanging branches and foliage. Inside, it stretched back for around a hundred yards, offering shelter from the elements and refuge from the fighting taking place nearby. Stretchers littered the floor, a badly wounded freedom fighter on each. Some had injuries that clearly needed to be dealt with in a proper hospital. Others, the walking wounded, sat around in blood stained bandages, nursing broken limbs and other less serious injuries.

Not all the patients in this rudimentary hospital were maquisards. Some civilians and a couple of German soldiers were also being cared for. An American with a bad injury to his shoulder and head, sat alone in the corner sleeping peacefully. Being the only other English speaker in the cave, Davies had tried to engage with the man, but so far they had managed to exchange only a few polite words.

They were being looked after by two doctors and a group of French nurses. They worked tirelessly to give what aid they could, carrying out basic operations, sometimes with little or no anaesthetic. They had limited medical supplies; bandages, anti-septic creams and a small amount of morphine.

A Jesuit priest, a middle-aged man by the name of Yves, assisted them, giving comfort to the wounded wherever he could. Davies had never been a religious man. In fact, he did not believe in God at all but he was grateful for this unassuming priest's attempts to keep up morale. Davies could speak little French and had no idea what the man was saying, but he could see the respect everyone had for him. Yves had tried to engage him in conversation, and he was grateful for the attempts the man had made, but it was pointless. Instead he had simply said a prayer over him and given him a blessing. Davies did not have the heart to tell him he was an atheist.

Although away from the front line, Davies could still hear the sound of fighting. It was clear to him the insurrection was not going well. It was only a question of time before it was put down. Being holed up in the cave was frustrating him. He needed to be out there, to be a part of what was happening. He promised himself that when the pain subsided and he got some movement back into his arm, then he would leave and seek out Major Graham and Captain Basson.

But he was not to get the chance.

It was mid morning when they came.

At first he thought the sound of German voices was just a dream. He had been dozing, trying to catch up with some sleep, when he was violently shaken awake by one of the nurses. He looked to the sunlight at the cave entrance. There was movement outside. And then, with horror, he saw the familiar shape of German army helmets and realised it was all over.

There was no escape for him, or for any of them. There was only one way in and one way out and the Germans had it blocked off.

He watched as Wehrmacht troops entered the cave, roughly grabbing the nurses by their collars, or hair, and dragging them outside. More of them entered, thrusting their rifles and machine-pistols into the faces of the wounded, forcing those who could walk to stand up and go with them.

Davies got to his feet, pulling his tunic over his shoulders with his good hand. He could see Yves ahead, bending over one of the stretcher cases, attempting to get the man to his feet. As Davies passed him, he noticed tears in the priest's eyes. The man he was trying to help did not have the strength to get up.

A fierce looking soldier thrust his MP40 into Davies's side, forcing him to join the others who were now lining up on the path a few yards away. It seemed as though he was still dreaming. He could not understand how they were going to get the rest of them out, those without the ability to walk. Nothing seemed to be registering properly in his brain.

He was pushed into the line with a group of wounded maquisards and ordered to move further up the path, away from the cave.

Behind him, a young French nurse stepped forward and spat squarely into an officer's face. He calmly wiped the spittle away with a gloved hand, then raised his other, clutching a Luger. Without hesitation, he pressed the muzzle into her face just above her nose and pulled the trigger. The shot cracked through the air, the force of the bullet hurling her backward. She crumpled into the dirt at his feet. A fountain of blood shot up from between her eyes briefly, before her heart stopped beating and she lay still, the blood caking her face in a grotesque red mask.

The other nurses screamed, one collapsing to the ground. A doctor picked her up and spoke to her, imploring her to regain her composure. She remained stooped over, unable to stand straight, the man's arms around her shoulders.

Then the shooting inside the cave started.

Davies found it hard to stop himself from running back in, to try and put a stop to the massacre that was taking place. The rattle of MP40 machine-pistols and the crack of rifle fire filled his ears, the noise rising to a crescendo inside his head, so much so that he could not stand it. The screams of those about to die could be heard clearly, cutting deep into his brain, until they stopped, they too cut off by German bullets.

Outside, the doctors were gathered, along with Yves, the friendly priest who had done so much to comfort the wounded maquisards. Those same young men who now lay dead on the stretchers inside the cave. With horror, Davies watched on as they too were cut down in a hail of bullets, the Germans mercilessly firing their weapons at them, not stopping until their bodies stopped jerking in their deathly spasms. After a few seconds, they all lay still, a heap of corpses at the front of the cave entrance.

The officer who had murdered the nurse walked over to them, shooting in the head those who still showed any sign of life, including the priest, Yves.

The surviving nurses were led away by the Germans, past Davies and the small group he was standing with. They were all clearly distraught at what had just happened. As they were led away, Davies knew they would not be treated respectfully. He had witnessed what the Germans had been doing out on the Vercors to anyone caught assisting the maquis. The fact that these people had also been looking after wounded German prisoners would have no bearing on how they would be dealt with.

With the prisoners in the cave now executed, the Germans turned their attention to those that had left the hospital on foot.

The officer barked orders to his men. They acted at once, roughly pushing and shoving Davies and the rest of the walking wounded, indicating for them to walk along the path and away from the cave.

It was only now they were heading away from the carnage that Davies realised the pain in his arm had subsided somewhat. He was completely fatigued and his mind was starting to play tricks on him. He wondered just what he was doing there. He was a British soldier and there was not another British soldier in sight. There were people all around him, speaking languages he did not understand. He simply did not belong there. None of this was any of his business.

After five minutes, they were ordered to stop. They were not moving fast enough for their captors, whose aggression and lack of patience was beginning to tell. Their bloodlust had been raised and it seemed it needed to be satisfied once more. Murdering defenceless wounded partisans and shooting unarmed women in the face was simply not enough for them.

Davies considered making a run for it. Perhaps he could jump from the path into the bushes below and get away that way. Or maybe he could disarm one of the guards and fight the rest off with a captured weapon. He shuffled his feet as he contemplated these options. He just needed to wait for the right moment to strike.

They stood in single file, their backs to the rocky hill. The guards that had forced them to march what was, in reality, just a few hundred yards, stepped away from them, their weapons pointing at their chests and heads.

Davies was instantly brought back to the reality of the situation. Yet still he found it hard to comprehend. He was about to shout out to them, to tell them that one day they would feel the wrath of God upon them for doing this, before he remembered he was an atheist and did not believe it. So he said nothing. God did not exist. Of that he was convinced. If he did, then things like this simply would not happen.

As the bullets hit him, he realised that in the next few seconds he would find out one way or the other if he had been right to believe that. Or, maybe he had been wrong all along.

***

'You will tell me exactly what you were doing in that barn.'

It wasn't a question. It was a statement. Frank smirked to himself. Who in the hell did this guy think he was?

He had been brought directly to the police station. It was a single storey building on the edge of what looked like a small town. He was taken into a windowless room at the rear, and made to sit in a chair which was fixed to the floor. They had handcuffed his wrists to the chair arms and then left the room, closing the door behind them. He had no option but to sit and wait until the gendarmes returned, which they did, a quarter of an hour later.

There was a wooden table in front of him. The sergeant with the bushy moustache sat opposite. Another gendarme stood guard by the door. He had no idea which town he was in but knew from the direction they had travelled that it was south west of the Vercors plateau. He had no idea if the Germans were in the area but presumed they could not be too far away. He also understood that if they got hold of him, then if the rumours about Hitler's commando order were correct, it would mean he would be executed, no doubt after a period of torture first.

One thing was for sure, he was not going to give these gendarmes any satisfaction. None whatsoever.

'I went there to sleep,' he replied. He put no expression into his voice and tried to keep his face as straight as he could.

The sergeant raised his eyebrows. 'How did you end up there?'

'I was tired. I saw the barn. I thought, hey, that's a good place to have a kip.'

'Do you think you're being funny? Where's your friend?'

'What friend?'

'The farmer told us he saw two of you. Where's your colleague?'

It was Frank's turn to frown. 'I've absolutely no idea what you're talking about. Maybe the farmer had drunk too much wine.'

The sergeant took another tack. 'You're wearing British army uniform. What are the British doing here?'

Frank laughed. 'I don't know if you're aware, but the British are currently at war with Germany. The Germans are currently occupying France. So therefore I have a legitimate reason to be here. What's more, you, as a Frenchman, have a legitimate reason to let me go.'

'It's a bit late for that,' replied the sergeant. 'We've already called the area commander. The Germans will be here for you shortly. They're in charge here, not us. We've to comply with what they ask.'

Frank was enraged. He could not believe what the man had told him. 'They don't even know of my existence. They only know I'm here because you told them about me. You're a bloody idiot!'

The sergeant slammed his hand on the table. 'I will not be spoken to in this manner.'

'Get out of my sight,' said Frank. 'Go on. Just piss off out of here.'

The sergeant stood up. 'Come on, Harold,' he said to the gendarme standing at the door. 'He's the Germans' problem now.'

They both left the room. So this was how it ended, he thought. Betrayed twice in the matter of an hour. Once by the farmer and the second by the gendarmerie. Both of them French. The very people he was fighting for.

He sighed to himself. This was out of his hands now.

***

Gerard Basson watched as the police car arrived. He had left the barn to urinate, going outside, to the rear of the building to do it. From where he was standing he could not be seen from the farmhouse. He knew to go back into the barn would mean discovery. All he could do was watch, unable to alert Frank.

There were four policemen. As they got out of the car, the farmer and his wife approached them. They spoke for a short while before the farmer pointed to the barn. Immediately the gendarmes pulled out their sidearms and cautiously approached the building, led by a sergeant with a large bushy moustache.

As they entered the building, Basson crept around to the other side and sprinted to the farmhouse. The farmer and his wife waited in the yard, their focus completely on what was happening at the barn, unaware Basson was now at the building behind them. He crouched behind a barrel and watched, holding his breath.

After only a couple of minutes they came out. Frank was with them, his hands manacled behind his back. Two of the gendarmes put him into the rear of the police car whilst the sergeant spoke to the couple. Basson could not make out what was being said, but it was clear the farmer was being thanked. The sergeant clapped the man on the shoulder and got into the passenger seat. A few moments later, they pulled away, taking Frank with them.

He waited until the farmer and his wife had gone back into the house before walking around to the front door. He took the automatic pistol from his waistband and knocked.

A few moments later it opened. The farmer, a middle-aged man with a balding head and bulbous nose stood before him.

'Ah, Georges, what have you…'.

The smile left his face when he saw it was not the police sergeant returning.

Basson raised the pistol and pointed it at his face. 'You and I need to talk, Monsieur… Inside. Now.'

The man stepped back, his face white. Behind him his wife let out a scream.

'And you need to be quiet, Madame. Otherwise I'll kill the both of you, believe me.'

'Please, M… Monsieur,' stammered the farmer. 'My wife…'.

'Shut up and sit down,' ordered Basson, waving the pistol in the direction of the kitchen, where he could see a wooden table and four chairs.

Basson indicated for the two to sit down, then stood in front of them.

'Where have they taken my friend?' he asked. 'Don't lie to me.'

'I don't know, Monsieur,' replied the farmer.

Basson raised the pistol and fired into the ceiling, bringing plaster and dust down onto the pair. The woman let out a scream and began to cry. The farmer started to shake.

'Have either of you any idea of what's been happening on the plateau?' asked Basson. 'Are either of you aware that as we speak right now, our fellow countrymen are being murdered by the Nazis, villages being razed to the ground? Just a few miles from here. Yet you betray those of us who've put up a fight. If you saw us go into the barn last night then why didn't you come and see us. We could've done with some food and water. But you didn't do that, did you? Instead you called the police who'll probably hand over my friend to the Nazis to be executed. I should shoot the both of you right now.'

'Please, Monsieur, I beg you…'

'Unfortunately I'm not able to do that,' went on Basson, ignoring him. 'Do you have a car?'

'I have a truck out back,' replied the farmer. 'The keys are over there. Please take them. Take it. Please don't shoot us.'

'You're going to come with me,' replied Basson. 'You'll drive me to where they're holding him. And what's more, you're going to take me right now.'

He found some rope under the sink, and after the wife had been tied to the chair and a gag placed into her mouth, Basson forced the farmer outside to where an old battered truck was parked behind the farmhouse. Roughly, he forced the man into the driver's seat and climbed into the passenger seat beside him. All the time he kept the pistol pointed at his stomach.

Shortly, they pulled up across from a police station. Basson recognised the patrol car parked outside. He knew it was the place where they had taken Frank.

He leaned over and took the keys from the ignition and dropped them into his tunic pocket.

'If you leave this truck or try to warn anybody at all about me, then I'll go back to your hovel and shoot you and your wife. Remember, I know where you live.'

He got out of the truck before the man had chance to reply. A few people passing by looked over. On seeing Basson's uniform they crossed the road and hurriedly walked away.

He put the pistol into his waistband and casually walked into the police station.

Three gendarmes were sitting in the corner, drinking coffee. The sergeant he had witnessed taking Frank from the barn stood behind a desk, a pen in his hand writing onto a pad in front of him. He looked up as Basson walked in. The gendarmes nervously rose from the table.

'Hello,' said Basson, casually. 'Which of you gentlemen is in charge here?'

'Erm, I am,' said the sergeant.

Basson held out his hand. 'Good morning, Sergeant?…'

'Dupont, Georges Dupont.'

Dupont put the pen down and took his hand, shaking it limply.

'Ah, Sergeant Dupont, let me introduce myself. I'm Captain Gerard Basson of the Free French forces. I understand you're holding a British army officer here. Would you be so kind as to go and get him for me?'

Dupont looked at him blankly. 'And why on earth should I do that?'

'Because, my good man,' replied Basson calmly. 'The army of the Free French and her American allies are only a matter of a couple hours away from here… Yes, Dupont, you heard me correctly. Today is a wonderful day for this town. Today is the day of its liberation from Nazi oppression. We were sent ahead as part of a reconnaissance patrol. I've a platoon of soldiers only a mile from here.'

Dupont hesitated, his hand hovering over the pistol in his holster. He looked to the three gendarmes who stared back at him equally bemused.

'You see,' went on Basson. 'Should you hand over any of our friends to the Nazis, then I'm afraid that some may see that as a collaborative act. As such, those actions would be open to certain criticisms. By criticisms I mean arrest and probable execution. So, you see, if you don't want to find yourself hanging by your fat neck from those streetlights out there, by this evening, then I suggest you go and get that British soldier right now.'

Dupont still looked uncertain at what to do.

'Now!' shouted Basson fiercely. 'Or suffer the consequences.'

Dupont now looked very worried. 'Quickly,' he said to the gendarmes. 'Go and get him. Release him now.'

The three gendarmes sprung into action and rushed to the door leading to where they were holding Frank. A minute later, he walked out with them, rubbing his wrists.

'Good afternoon, sir,' said Basson in English, as Dupont handed Frank his pistol and beret. 'Would you like to follow me… Thank you, Dupont, your patriotism will not go unnoticed.'

Confidently both men walked out of the building, watched all the time by the four gendarmes. As they passed the police car, Basson pulled the pistol from his waistband and fired two shots, one into each front tyre. Grabbing Frank by the arm he ran to the truck where the farmer still waited.

'Out,' shouted Basson pointing the pistol at him. 'Get out, now.'

The farmer opened the door and jumped out, clearly petrified. He ran to the opposite side of the road, just as Dupont and the three gendarmes came running from the building. Only Dupont had his pistol in his hand.

Basson gunned the engine and put the truck into gear. With a roar he performed a U-turn and sped away. A minute later, they were speeding down the roadway and out of the town. They had not gone more than half a mile before a German staff car approached on the opposite side of the road, heading fast to the town they had just escaped. Basson assumed they were on their way to collect a British commando from the local gendarmerie.

As the staff car drew closer, Basson swerved the truck into its path, forcing it off the road, where it crashed into a ditch. He looked in the rearview mirror and saw one of the men in the back had been thrown from the vehicle and now lay still at the side of the road. He did not stop to see how any of the others were.

'Dear God,' said Frank, laughing. 'That was bloody close. Thank you, my friend. You just saved my life.'

Basson glanced at him. 'You'd have done the same for me, I'm sure.'

'Where were you?' asked Frank. 'This morning. What happened?'

'When you need a piss, you need a piss,' laughed Basson.

Frank grinned. This was the closest he had ever come to being captured. He had almost accepted the inevitable. But this close shave had somehow given him a new zest, a new determination to survive this war.

And for the first time in a very long while, he believed he actually would.

Chapter Twenty-nine

Lyon - 3rd September 1944

Frank jumped off the jeep before it had come to a complete halt, causing him to stumble forward slightly before righting himself. A group of young women looked on from a pavement café. One or two laughed at him. He smiled back at them. It was a long time since he had seen happy faces in Lyon. The streets were full of people, singing, dancing and waving tricolours at every military vehicle that passed. Anyone in a uniform was showered with gifts, kisses and flowers, from people of all ages. It was a true celebration. A party that would go on long into the night, and probably way beyond.

The news of the Germans pulling out of the city had not come as a surprise. The only thing that did shock him was that they had done so without torching it.

After Operation Dragoon, the invasion of southern France on the 15th August, it became clear that it would not be much longer before the Nazis fled the whole region. They had left Grenoble almost two weeks ago, which saw them abandoning their hunt for the maquis on the Vercors Massif once and for all. Their troops needed to fight the advancing armies on all fronts and could not be tied up chasing a few partisans in the hills.

Frank felt sad knowing the uprising had happened too soon. He had believed at the time that they should have waited for Dragoon to start first. The insurrection may have been more successful had they done this. It was clear now that the focus of the top brass in London and Algiers had been on organising the invasion. A small uprising, as they saw it, would have been very low on their list of priorities. Frank had mixed feelings about the whole thing. They knew the desperate state the maquis had been in and should have at least sent something, if only to boost their morale.

He entered the building where he was told he would find the man he was looking for. He had not seen Gerard since the liberation of

Grenoble. They spent the few weeks preceding, hiding out at various locations, including a return to the Vercors plateau where they witnessed the aftermath of the Nazi reprisal on the town of Vassieux. There they found hundreds of corpses left to rot in the sunshine, murdered by the Nazis. When they had gone in search of the Red Cross hospital at Grotte de la Luire, they found the bodies of many more people, all murdered where they had lain, or taken out of the cave to be shot. It was with a heavy heart that they found the body of their friend and Jedburgh comrade, Jimmy Davies.

With the liberation of Grenoble, Basson had been ordered back to the Free French forces. Frank had managed to make contact with "Double H" Harding who had ordered him back to London to be debriefed.

Frank had refused.

He had unfinished business in France and he was not prepared to leave until it was done. He told Harding as much, arguing that his senior officer owed it to him to give him a little unrestricted independence, if only for a short while. After all, he had sent him into the inferno and been unable to support him once he was there. No matter how much Harding's hands had been tied, Frank felt he was owed a certain amount of freedom. He then spent some time resting and recuperating until he heard Lyon was about to be liberated. Hitching rides off various Allied vehicles, he made his way back to the city he knew so well.

He found Gerard Basson on the first floor, poring over a map of the city. As Frank walked in, he looked up, a huge grin on his face.

'Frank. It's so good to see you.'

'You too, my friend,' he replied, shaking his hand firmly. 'How's the situation?'

'They've gone,' said Basson. 'They're falling back quicker than we can keep up with them. Running away like the dogs they are.'

'Have you been to Gestapo Headquarters yet?' asked Frank. 'Has there been any sign of Barbie or his henchmen?'

'None,' replied Basson. 'They've run away with the rest of them. We've men going through their offices at the École du Service de Santé Militaire to see if there's anything we can use to locate them, and at the Hotel Terminus too. If they're in the area then we'll find them. They'll answer for their crimes.'

Frank spent a couple of hours with his friend before heading out once more. There was another person he needed to see before he was prepared to head back to the British. He hoped that he would be able to find him.

As he walked the familiar streets, Frank was able to look at them with fresh eyes. Whereas before they seemed dull and sombre, filled with unsmiling, dejected people, now the opposite was true. He saw happy faces wherever he looked, the mood of the population upbeat, a new confidence for the future spreading throughout the city. How long this would last, he had no idea, but it needed to be enjoyed while it did. The people of Lyon had suffered more than most over the last few years. They deserved it.

Finally he came to a very familiar building. He approached the front door and knocked. The last time he had been here was over a year ago. He remembered how it had been raining, the streets deserted, and how he had hid in the shadows before approaching Monique's apartment, watching the roads for any signs he had been followed. Today was markedly different. The sun was shining, the streets were full of people and he brazenly wore the uniform of a British army officer, no longer needing to hide his true identity.

There was no reply so he tried the handle. Remarkably, the door was unlocked. Cautiously he entered. He was initially met with an odour of mustiness, as though it had not been lived in for quite some time.

Inside, it was much as it had been left when he had taken Monique away on the night she killed Keller. The telephone on the stand in the hallway was still there and when he opened the drawer, the notebook with his old number was there too. A jacket belonging to either Monique, or her sister Catherine, still hung on the coat stand and a pair of black shoes lay on the floor underneath.

He walked to the living room and saw that, again, everything was as it had been left all those months ago. A thin layer of dust covered the tables and mantelpiece and a ray of light cut through the gloom. He could see dust particles moving around, dancing chaotically in the light. The threadbare rug contained a large red stain, where

Keller had bled after Monique had stabbed him. The ball of wool and half-knitted sweater sat on the seat by the side of the fireplace. A reminder that this place had once been inhabited by someone who enjoyed the simple things in life, wishing only for a peace she was ultimately unable to find.

And there was no denying he was partly to blame for that.

The bathroom contained her toiletries, those she had not had time to pack. The bedroom was equally unkempt, the unmade bed covered with the clothes she had been forced to abandon when they would not fit in her bag.

He did not know what he was expecting to find. He half hoped he would find her, sitting there, knitting by the fireplace, much as she had done before he involved her in an enterprise she had no heart for. But he knew that could never be the case. She had been forced to move, torn between two sides, both of which she hated. He was overcome by an enormous sense of guilt. He had no idea what had become of her. Now that it was all over, he just wanted to return her to her old life and apologise for his own part in her misery.

He suddenly felt an intense feeling of claustrophobia and so left the building. Out on the street, he took a packet of cigarettes from his pocket and lit one. An old man passed him, and on seeing his uniform, patted him on the shoulder as he walked by, thanking him for freeing him from the Nazis. Frank smiled at him in response before throwing the half-smoked cigarette to the ground and walking away.

There was someone else he wanted to see. Someone else who could maybe provide a few answers for him.

***

Finding Clement Vallin was easier than expected.

He had feared his old friend may have been caught by the Gestapo during the period after Jean Moulin and the others of the CNR had been captured at Caluire-et-Cuire. As he approached the office building where he worked, he saw him standing outside, his arms folded, smiling at the people cheering and dancing in front of him.

At first he did not recognise Frank. He was used to seeing him in civilian clothing and not in the uniform of a British army officer. When he realised it was him, he raised his eyebrows in surprise, before smiling broadly. He walked over to Frank, his hand extended.

'Aubuchon,' he said. 'What a wonderful surprise. I thought you were dead, my friend.'

'Not just yet, Clement,' replied Frank, smiling back at him. 'And my name's Frank Graham, not Francois Aubuchon.'

'Ah, and the infamous "Grey Man", I presume.'

'Guilty,' Frank laughed.

'You caused such a furore with the Gestapo, you know. Barbie wanted your head on a plate.'

'He came close to getting it a couple of times,' replied Frank.

'I'm so glad he didn't,' said Vallin. Then his expression darkened. 'The stories about him and what he did are horrendous.'

'Does anyone know where he is?' asked Frank.

'He vanished with the rest of them,' explained Vallin. 'Good riddance I say. But then these monsters need to answer for their crimes. They need to be captured and put on trial for the things they've done.'

They went inside to his office. After Vallin had made a coffee for them both, they sat down at his desk, the place where not so long ago they would sit and talk about how they could frustrate the Nazis as part of the Resistance.

After a few more pleasantries, Frank became serious.

'So what happened to Monique?' he asked.

Vallin raised his eyebrows and sat back in his chair. He sighed loudly.

'Monique... Monique...' he said thoughtfully. 'I passed her on to my contacts who promised to get her over the Alps into Switzerland.' Then he paused. 'I hear things did not go well.'

'What do you mean?' asked Frank sitting forward.

'I'm led to believe she proved to be a bit of a handful. Hard to control.'

'What happened to her, Clement?'

Vallin sat forward and drummed his fingers on the desk nervously. 'Apparently she had an argument with those assisting her and abandoned them out in the mountains. They tell me she ran away. They looked for her for hours and then gave up. I've no idea if she made it or not, to be honest with you. But the likelihood is that she perished out there. Without a guide, it's very dangerous. I've heard nothing more about her since.'

Frank could not be sure if his friend was being truthful with him. After all, Monique had attempted to betray them at Pariset, passing on the information of the false airdrop to Keller and the Gestapo. Whether the group that took her over the mountains knew this he did not know. But if they did… well, Frank had seen how collaborators and traitors were treated by the Resistance.

He assumed in all probability the woman was dead. What's more, he had made a personal contribution to the poor girl's fate. It was something he would have to live with.

The conversation turned to other things.

'What are your plans now, Francois?'

'In the long term? I'll return to London, I suppose. See what they want with me. Now that France is almost fully liberated I can't see my skills being required for espionage here anymore. They may even send me back to my unit in the artillery.'

'And the short term?'

'I'm going to find a bar and get very, very drunk, my friend,' replied Frank.

Frank left the office a few minutes later after first arranging with Vallin to meet him and Gerard Basson at a bar just off the Place Bellecour in a couple of hours time.

As he strolled through the city, he somehow felt detached from it all. It seemed an anti-climax. He had seen too many killed. He had been responsible for the deaths of many, whether at his own hand or through decisions he made. He was unsure how to feel about it.

When he saw a group of young women being paraded through the streets, their heads shaved, bruises to their faces and wearing signs stating how they had slept with German soldiers, he wondered if they were, in fact, just exchanging one tyranny for another. He watched on indifferently as they sobbed, the maquisards who were their captors laughing and swearing at them as they pushed them along. What would become of them he didn't know. But the one thing for certain he did know was that it would not be pleasant. He had seen the corpses of some accused of collaborating hanging from trees and street lamps. He wondered what made these acts different to those the Nazis had carried out.

He pulled a pack of cigarettes from his pocket. Taking one out he tapped it on the packet before putting it in his mouth. He was about to light it but decided he did not really want it and threw it to the ground instead.

He thought of his friends in the Resistance; Claude Benoit who had taken his own life rather than be taken by the Nazis; he thought of the cousins Michel and Pierre, killed on a botched mission and he thought of his childhood acquaintance, Jean-Luc Descartes who he presumed to be dead along with them. He thought of the sisters, Monique and Catherine, and was filled with an overwhelming sense of guilt at what had happened to them. He thought also of Jean Moulin and the others involved in the meeting he could not protect. All taken by the Gestapo to be tortured and murdered. He thought of the boys in the Vercors, fighting and dying to protect their homeland, and he thought of his Jedburgh colleague and friend, Jimmy Davies, gunned down in a massacre that had taken many more innocent lives.

He thought of them all and knew their faces would never leave his memory. He would remember them all for as long as he lived.

As he walked through the streets, to find the bar on the Place Bellecour, he felt there was nothing to actually celebrate. It was over, at least for Lyon, that was true, but there was still a lot of heartache and pain to come.

And his part in this war was far from over.

Chapter Thirty

Bremen, Germany - Late May 1945

Frank had not heard the name Otto Finkel for a very long time. He had to read the report twice before it sunk in. The description of the prisoner was compelling. It had to be him. Blond hair, blue eyes and a rather large scar running down the left side of his face.

There was even a photograph to accompany the report. A grainy, slightly out of focus picture showing a tank commander, sitting on the hull of a Panzer. He was wearing a jet black uniform with SS insignia at the collar; his features sharp, cold and focused. In his hand he held a Mauser C96 automatic pistol. From the terrain in the background, it looked like to have been taken in Russia.

Frank's heart skipped a beat. He had a good feeling about this.

He picked up the photograph and squinted his eyes. He could see the resemblance to the child he had once known, so long ago now. Almost in another life. A young unassuming boy who had been involved in a terrible accident Frank had borne witness to, the scar from that day clearly evident in the photograph he held in his hand.

The stories he had read about this man were truly shocking. His brother, who had perished in the sea off Dunkirk five years ago, had witnessed him commanding a group of SS as they murdered a group of British prisoners of war on the retreat to the beaches. There were more reports of him being involved in the round up of Jews in France and Italy. He had also taken part in the Einsatzgruppen death squads in Russia in the early years of the war. He was responsible for all those crimes. His name was on a list of many SS members the British wanted to speak to.

And now the Americans were reporting they may have him in their custody.

US Rangers had caught a man in Bavaria that fit his description. They were holding him in an administration centre just outside Munich and had enquired if the British wanted to interview him.

Frank had not been in post for long. On his return from France he had been recruited into a small, elite unit tasked with ensuring that fleeing Nazis would not escape justice. The Allies were circulating lists of officers and officials, compiling detailed files on the most wanted among them. Frank had a particular interest in the fate of Klaus Barbie, the infamous "Butcher of Lyon", having crossed paths with him during the war. But that morning, when the file for Otto Finkel landed on his desk his focus had shifted to that. Everything else was put to one side

The war in Europe was over. Berlin had fallen to the Soviets and Hitler was reported as being dead. The discovery of death camps in Germany and Poland had shocked the world. Those responsible were either in custody, dead or on the run.

The whole of Europe was in a mess. Millions of displaced people roamed the continent and hundreds of cities lay in ruins. Now the fighting was over, a massive task faced the Allies in putting some sort of order to it all. It was in this confusion that those in power feared any perpetrators of the worst crimes the world had ever seen may escape justice. Those who had suffered at their hands deserved to see them stand trial for what they had done.

Frank and his team had been given a list of contacts in the American sector, counterparts with the same reference as them. He saw the name of one man, stationed just outside Munich He picked up the telephone in front of him.

He dialled the number on the sheet and was surprised that it connected straight away as they had been having trouble over the last few days with establishing lines of communication. The phone rang for over a minute. He was about to hang up when it was suddenly picked up.

An American voice greeted him. 'Hi, Major John Redford speaking, how may I help you?'

'Hello,' said Frank. 'Major Frank Graham here. British Army intelligence. I was wondering if you could do us a favour.'

'Hello, Frank,' said Redford. He sounded tired and harassed. 'What can I do for you?'

'Sorry to bother you with this, I appreciate you're probably busy…'

'Ain't that the truth,' cut in Redford. 'It's a madhouse down here. I'm guessing it's the same for you guys too. What a mess.'

'I couldn't agree more,' said Frank. He wanted to get to the point. He still held the picture of Finkel in his hand, not able to take his eyes from it. 'Your boys are holding a fellow we may be interested in. It's possible you've got Otto Finkel, a Haupsturmführer of the SS. If it's him, we believe him to be responsible for the murder of unarmed POWs near Dunkirk in '40. We'd really love to speak to this man about that, and other matters.'

'Ah, yes. I haven't met the guy myself, but I understand Colonel Walker has someone in his cells that seems very dubious. This guy has a terrible scar down his face and a really shit attitude, I'm told. The Rangers found him hiding in a barn in an ill-fitting Wehrmacht uniform. They got suspicious so handed him over to military intelligence. They suspect he may be someone we all could be interested in, although the guy's denying he's anyone of any importance.'

'It's the scar,' explained Frank. 'That's what's got my attention. We've a report on the man. In fact I'm looking at it right now. Is there any chance that if I courier it to you, you could interview him and maybe confirm it's him or not. If it is, we want him.'

Redford paused for a moment. 'Okay, no problem. Do you want to come down here and speak to him yourself?'

Frank thought for a moment. 'No. I've loads to do here and can't spare the time, unfortunately. Particularly if it's not him. It's over four hundred miles. If you could be so kind to pop over and speak to him. Confirm it for us?'

Redford let out an audible sigh. 'Okay. That's probably a good idea.'

'I'll courier the report down to you overnight. You'll have it tomorrow. There's a photo of him in it that you can compare. I'm guessing if it's him, you'll know pretty much straight away… And there's another thing.'

'Yes.'

'There's a personal reason I'm interested in this particular chap. I knew him briefly as a kid. I was with him when he got the scar. It was a boating accident in St Malo, Brittany, in the summer of '28 I think. My brother saw him again in France in '40. It's actually his account of the shooting of the British POWs that's in the report.'

Redford whistled. 'Jeez. In that case I'll make it a priority. Give me your number and I'll get back to you tomorrow after I've seen him.'

Frank passed on the telephone number and put the receiver back in the cradle.

He sat back in the chair and looked again at the photograph. He closed his eyes, the memories now flooding back.

He was back in that rowing boat, out on the cove in St Malo. His brother, Jack, being a total pain, dragging them all out onto the water to hunt for fish the boy simply did not have the skills to catch. None of the others had been interested. Frank himself just wanted to read his book; the quiet Italian, Marco, just going along with the rest of them; and the French boy, Jean-Luc Descartes, seemingly indifferent to the whole thing. Frank remembered how Otto Finkel had argued with Jack, trying to get him to be reasonable and take the boat back to shore. If anything, Finkel had been the only sensible one among them.

He remembered how the weather had taken a turn for the worse and how they had started to drift out to sea. How the janitor from the hotel, the simple-minded Claude, swam out to help them and how they had stopped him from getting into the boat with them for fear of it capsizing. He remembered how Finkel had fallen, striking his face on the side of the boat before disappearing beneath the water and Jack diving in to save him.

Frank opened his eyes. He did not want to think about it any longer. He did not wish to remember the trauma they had gone through when they found out Claude had drowned and Otto had been disfigured. All for the sake of Jack's determination to catch a bloody fish and for each of them to save face in front of one another. A childish misadventure that had shaped the lives of many of those involved.

But it was Frank's belief that whatever happened that day on the cove had no bearing on how they all behaved afterwards. Why should it? His late brother Jack and himself had grown up to be good men. At least that's what he hoped he was. Jean-Luc Descartes had fought for his country and probably died in one of the camps they were discovering. Frank had no idea what had happened to the Italian boy, Marco Roncalli. He made a mental note to try and find out one day.

Otto Finkel, probably the only sensible one among them that week, had turned into a murdering SS officer. Frank had no explanation for it.

***

The following evening, after a busy day interviewing German prisoners of war, Frank returned to his desk to find a handwritten note had been placed upon it. It simply said 'Major Graham, please ring Major Redford, US Army, on the following number ASAP'. There was a number written underneath.

Frank felt his heart rate start to rise and sat down. He picked up the receiver, dialled the number and waited. After a while a young woman's voice spoke.

'Good evening, how may I be of assistance?'

'Hello,' said Frank. 'Major Redford, please. It's Major Graham of British Intelligence.'

A moment later Redford was on the line.

'Hi Frank. It's him,' he stated simply.

'You sure?'

'One hundred percent.'

'What was he like?'

'One arrogant son of a bitch,' replied Redford. 'At first he tried to deny he was Finkel. It didn't take much to get him riled. You should've seen his face when I mentioned St Malo. He went white. Ugly bastard too. That scar really is something.'

Frank was elated. This was a major breakthrough. 'That's great news, John. Fantastic job. Can you thank your boys for me.'

'Hey, no problem,' replied Redford. 'I'll have him transported to the British sector as soon as I can arrange it. He's all yours, Frank. And you're quite welcome to him, believe me.'

Frank hung up the phone and stood up. He raised his fist in the air and shouted, 'Yes!'

Everyone in the office stopped what they were doing and looked at him blankly.

'Sorry,' he said and sat back down. This was the best news he had heard in a very long time. He checked his watch and saw it was probably too late to start the reports he needed to write relating to the interviews he had done that day. What was more, he did not have the will to start them after hearing the news that Otto Finkel had indeed been captured.

Instead he put on his hat, said goodbye to those at the desks near to him and left the building. He would go in search of a drink. For the first time in a very long while, he felt like celebrating.

***

Frank's elation was short-lived.

Four days after the conversation with Redford confirming Finkel's capture, the American called again.

'Hey, Frank,' he said quietly. 'Are you sitting down? I've some bad news for you.'

Frank felt a growing irritation in the pit of his stomach. He half expected what Redford was about to tell him. 'Go on.'

'It's Finkel. He's escaped.'

Frank could tell by the man's apologetic tone that he was finding it hard to tell him this news. He took a breath. He did not want to get annoyed.

'How the hell did that happen?' he asked with a sigh.

'He killed one of his escort and shot a couple of other guys. He then stole a jeep. We've men out looking for him now, but don't expect good news any time soon. He could be anywhere by now.'

'I'm sorry to hear about your men,' replied Frank. He could think of nothing more to say.

'If I hear anything, I'll call you straight away.'

They were about to hang up when Frank had another thought. 'Barbie,' he said. 'Klaus Barbie.'

'The Butcher of Lyon? What about him?'

'Have your guys got any leads as to his whereabouts?'

Redford paused. 'None that I've been made aware of. You meet him on holiday too?'

Frank laughed. 'No, nothing like that. I do have a kind of personal association with the evil bastard though. If you get hold of him, I'd like to speak to him.'

'If I hear anything, I'll let you know.'

Frank thanked him and hung up.

He had known this had all been too good to be true. From what he knew of Finkel, he was not the type of man to take being captured lightly. He would have always been looking for a way to escape.

Frank did not know how to feel about the whole episode. He knew he should have been angry at the Americans for letting him go, but they were the ones who had caught him in the first place. He was sick of being angry. Sick of feeling negative thoughts all the time.

He realised what he needed was a break. He had been operating for nearly five years in continual stress. He had lost his brother to the war, and done many things he was not proud of. He had seen good men and women perish and killed more than his fair share of people himself. He was just so tired of the whole thing.

Yes, he needed a break. He needed to get home and spend some time with his father and maybe seek out Jenny Crane again. For old times' sake. He was desperate for some laughter in his life.

He stood up and picked up his cap. He would go straight to his Commanding Officer and ask for some leave. If it was denied then he would demand a transfer away from all this shit.

If anyone deserved that, then he was sure it was he.

Epilogue

London, September 1964

Frank ran his fingers through his greying hair and looked at the picture on his desk of the two most important people in his life. He was going to miss Jack and Monica so much, but he knew this new posting was probably the best thing for everyone right now. His divorce from Jenny had not gone well, if those things ever could. He still loved her and knew he always would, but they had simply grown apart. It was the war that had brought them together and it had been the peace that had pulled them apart. The truth of it was they had been hanging on for years hoping things would go back to how it had been in the early days. But ultimately it was not to be; he was as much to blame for that as she was.

The children were at the age now where they kind of understood what their parents had been through during the war. Jack was in the last year of school and Monica the year below. They were old enough to travel together to America to visit their father during the school holidays. He knew there would be many happy times to come and looked forward to exploring Washington and the east coast with them both.

He had already decided this would be his last posting. Once it was over, he would take early retirement. God knew he had earned it, he thought. He had served his country as much as anyone ever could. Nobody could deny him a break from it all.

He had joined MI6 after being demobilised from the army in early 1946. Due to his command of French and his experiences during the war, he had initially been assigned to the Paris office. From there he had returned home and spent the early part of his career in various European capitals before settling in London. When the chance of a posting to America had come up, he thought it a good idea to take it, to get out of everyone's hair for a while. He bought a small property on the south coast, not too far from where his father lived, and planned to move there once his time in Washington was done. He currently rented it out but would move in once home for good.

He still had many things to organise. He had found tenants for his apartment in the city. It had to be handed over to them in the next few days. With having sold his car the previous week, getting about the city was becoming a bit of a pain, but he supposed he could endure the inconvenience of public transport for a little longer.

It was mid-afternoon when the phone call came.

It was a familiar voice, someone he had known for a very long time. Someone he both trusted and respected.

'Bonjour, Francois,' said Sacha Marchand. 'How are you, my old friend? All set for the United States?'

Frank smiled. Since the war had ended, he and Sacha had become firm friends. Sacha was now an officer at Interpol and had enjoyed a very successful career.

'Oh, you know, a thousand things to do and no time to do it in.'

'I hope all goes well for you… Does the name Heinrich Vogel mean anything to you?'

'Should it?'

'I don't know. Maybe,' replied Sacha. 'You see, a man with that name entered France through Charles de Gaulle airport this morning. On an Argentinian passport. His details have been passed to us by the airport authorities. He came in on a flight from Buenos Aires. There was something about him that didn't quite sit right with them so they took a copy of his passport and his details. He told them he was there on business.'

'I'm still not sure why this has anything to do with me,' replied Frank, bewildered.

'Let me continue. You see, we're interested in anyone coming over from South America with German sounding names. The man was very nervous, apparently, sweating and shaking when he handed over his documents. He has a strong German accent, is around fifty years old, blondish hair, blue eyes. And he has a very large scar running down the left side of his face.'

Frank stood up, almost dropping the receiver. 'What?… Say that again.'

'A deep, ugly looking scar down the left side of his face.'

Frank could not find the words. He simply could not speak.

'We ran his details through our systems and think this could be Otto Finkel. I can get a copy of the picture over to you, if you wish.'

'Yes… Yes. I wish.'

'The funny thing is he didn't seem too bothered about them taking a picture of his passport. He just accepted it when they told him it was routine procedure. He's a return ticket for next week. Flying back from Paris. I'll get the picture over to you as quickly as I can.'

Frank hung up the telephone.

That night he could not sleep. For years Otto Finkel had not been far from his mind. Although he had not killed Jack personally, he has had his brother's men killed. It was only by the grace of God Jack had been spared.

He remembered his frustration at having very nearly caught him back in 1945 and how he had seemingly vanished off the face of the earth following his escape from the Americans. Nobody had heard a thing about him since. The man had remained on wanted lists throughout Europe and also in Israel, where Wiesenthal's Documentation Centre had a particular interest in the man.

He had to be sure it was him before he made any kind of decision. He did not want to build up his hopes again. He needed to know for definite this man was indeed Finkel before he flew out to France to confront him.

The following day, he could not function properly, anxiously waiting for the courier to arrive with the photograph.

It was delivered to his desk just before noon. Nervously, he opened the envelope.

He only needed to look at it once. There was no doubt in his mind. This was Otto Finkel all right. He looked much older than he did on the pictures he had seen of him since the war. But it was clearly him.

He rose from the desk and walked to David Morris's office. Morris was his head of section and would need to sanction any request for leave. Frank did not want to take this through the official channels just yet.

'Dave, I need a few days off,' he stated simply.

Morris looked up from the report he was reading. 'Any particular reason why?'

'Yes,' he replied. 'There's some things I need to sort out before next week.'

'I thought you'd everything boxed off.'

'Something's come up. Something personal,' replied Frank.

Morris paused for a while. 'Fine. If it can't be helped, it can't be helped.'

Morris focused his attention back to the paperwork on his desk, the matter closed.

Frank knew there was a flight leaving from Heathrow that afternoon. If he was quick he could probably make it. He would get a taxi back to his flat and collect some things first. He did not need to pack much, just a change of clothes, his passport and the Colt automatic he had kept since the war.

He tidied his desk, shovelling everything into the drawer before locking it and pocketing the key. Taking the jacket to his black suit from behind his chair he put it on and picked up his briefcase.

He said goodbye to the others in the office. As he walked to the exit he collected his grey overcoat from the stand near the door and put it over his arm. He had a feeling he would be needing it, for it looked like it was about to rain.

Author's Note

René Hardy's involvement in the capture of Jean Moulin remains unclear.

On 7th June 1943 he was arrested by the Gestapo but later released. He was in attendance at the Conseil National de la Résistance (CNR) meeting at Dr. Dugoujon's residence in Caluire, Lyon, but escaped. He was the only prisoner not to be handcuffed. After the war, he stood trial on two separate occasions for collaboration, but was found not guilty both times. He denied any involvement in the raid, claiming innocence right up to his death in 1987.

Jean Moulin was tortured whilst in Gestapo custody, Klaus Barbie personally conducting his interrogation. He revealed nothing. He died from his injuries when being transported to Germany, on 8th July 1943.

Klaus Barbie evaded capture until he was extradited to France from Bolivia in 1983. He stood trial for crimes against humanity in Lyon in 1987, was found guilty and sentenced to life imprisonment. He died of cancer in prison four years later.

On 5th June 1944, the night before the D-Day landings, Charles de Gaulle encouraged the maquis in the Vercors Massif, along with other groups throughout France, to rise up and tie down the Germans in their areas, in order to prevent them sending troops to assist in halting the Allied advance. Bands of maquisards had already been organised by former officers of the French army and were awaiting this call to arms. Opinions on how they were to be used post invasion differed between commanders in Algiers and the Free French in London, which caused a lot of confusion when the time actually came. Expecting full support, an airstrip was constructed near to Vassieux-en-Vercors to allow for reinforcements and heavy weaponry to be flown in.

The Germans made two preliminary attacks in the north of the plateau, and on 15th June 1944, took and occupied the town of Saint-Nizier. There were many requests for support throughout this period, and for clear instructions on just what those in Algiers and

London expected of them. The maquis cut off all passes and roads onto the plateau and on 3rd July 1944, the Vercors was declared an independent state. Tricolours and the Cross of Lorraine were flown in many towns and hamlets throughout the massif.

On 14th July, Bastille Day, the United States Air Force carried out a huge airdrop. Unfortunately, many of the canisters fell off target into ravines and were unable to be retrieved.

On 21st July, led by Generalleutnant Karl Pflaum, the Germans attacked in force, centring their activity around the town of Vassieux-en-Vercors. Desperate requests from the maquis for assistance, in the form of troops and heavier weaponry, went ignored, and the insurgency was crushed a few days later. In the aftermath, the SS systematically searched the Vercors for any fleeing maquisards and executed those they found. They massacred the civilian population of Vassieux and murdered wounded maquisards along with doctors and the Jesuit priest, Yves de Montcheuil, at the Red Cross hospital in the cave at Luire, as depicted in the novel. The nurses were sent to concentration camps. The survivors of the insurgency took to the hills, occasionally attacking German units, until the Germans pulled out of the area following Operation Dragoon, the invasion of southern France on 15th August 1944.

The insurgency on the Vercors Massif in July 1944 was doomed to failure. After its declaration of independence, the maquis leadership on the plateau incorrectly assumed they would be supported in full by the Free French in Algiers.

Four thousand ill-equipped and poorly trained résistants were simply no match for the ten to twelve thousand experienced and well-equipped German battle troops. The tactics of the maquis leadership in fighting from fixed positions against a much superior enemy force has been criticised by historians. The often contradictory orders and instructions coming from Algiers and London only added to the confusion amongst the leaders on the plateau. Continuing with guerrilla warfare may well have been more effective. Pleas to Algiers for reinforcements proved fruitless. The reason for the lack of support has been debated by historians, and vary from military incompetence (the messages were not getting to the right people), to simple forgetfulness. The probable truth is that resources were needed for the upcoming invasion of southern France (Operation Dragoon), the success of which saw the Germans abandoning the plateau some weeks later.

Acknowledgements

There are many people I would like to thank for their contribution to the writing of this novel.
Codename Greyman was first published in 2019, and this newly edited and refined edition has been made possible through the encouragement and support of many people.
Firstly, I would like to thank all at Jelso Publications for their support, encouragement and advice during the editing and writing process.
Many thanks goes to my ex-colleague Sharon Harris, for taking a look at the new edited manuscript and offering words of advice and encouragement, and also to Sabrina Cass for her kind words on the completed book. I must also extend a big thank to another ex-colleague, Heather Farmer, for giving me the idea for one of the book's early scenes.
Many thanks to WW2 France historian and author, Genevieve Montcombroux, whose support and advice in regards to this second edition has been invaluable.
Thanks to all at Aspects of History magazine for their support and encouragement. This magazine is a must read for any history buff, and is run by some wonderful people with a passion for history. They are very supportive of all the authors on their platform. I can highly recommend it.
A huge thank you must go to my good friend Damien Lewis, bestselling author and historian, for all his support, mentorship and more importantly, friendship. It is your encouragement and advice that keeps me motivated in all my writing endeavours.
Another huge thank you goes to my daughters, Jessica and Sophie, for all your love and encouragement - it's for you that I do this and I love you both dearly.
Finally, my biggest thank you has to go to the love of my life - my wife, Dawn. Your support, loyalty and love have enabled me to do this thing full time, without which I would still be working twelve hour shifts with the fire service - something for which I will be eternally grateful.

Selected Bibliography

The following books have helped immensely with the research for this novel:

The Resistance - The French Fight Against The Nazis by Matthew Cobb, (Simon & Schuster, 2009)

They Fought Alone by Maurice Buckmaster, (Panther, 1960)

Resistance, Memoirs of Occupied France by Agnes Humbert, (Bloomsbury Publishing, 2009)

Forgotten Voices of the Secret War by Roderick Bailey, (Ebury Press, 2008)

The Secret War by Max Hastings, (William Collins, 2016)

Secret Agent: The True Story Of The Special Operations Executive by David Stafford, (BBC Books, 2000)

The White Rabbit: The Secret Agent the Gestapo Could Not Crack by Bruce Marshall, (Pan Books, 1967)

The Secret Agent's Handbook: The WWII Spy Manual of Devices, Disguises, Gadgets, and Concealed Weapons by Mark Seaman, (Public Record Office, 2000)

Special Operations Executive Manual: How to be an Agent in Occupied Europe, (William Collins, 2014)

The Cruel Victory: The French Resistance, D-Day and the Battle for the Vercors, 1944 by Paddy Ashdown, (William Collins, 2014)

Vercors 1944: Resistance in the French Alps by Peter Lieb & Peter Dennis, (Osprey Publishing, 2012)

WWII France: A Writer's Guide by Genevieve Montcombroux (Whippoorwill Solitude Publishing, 2004)

Printed in Dunstable, United Kingdom

81371069R00178